Just Rose

Just Rose

L.T. Marshall

Published 2017 by Creativia
ISBN: 978-1976372117
Cover art by Designs by Jessica Meeks
This book is a work of fiction. Names, characters, places, and incidents are the product of the author's imagination or are used fictitiously. Any resemblance to actual events, locales, or persons, living or dead, is purely coincidental.

Chapter 1

Rose pushed the damp tendrils of hair from her eyes; sweat running down her forehead and dripping along her nose every time she looked downwards. She was physically fatigued, her denim shorts leaving her legs exposed and burning on the hot paving stones, but her determination wouldn't let her give up on the torturous task at hand. The weeds and paving stones had ruined her manicure and her hands felt like sandpaper. She had made a huge start on the mammoth chore and wasn't about to give up now. If anything, Rose was a stubborn woman when her mind was on a task.

Looking up, she could feel the sun burning her already tender face and naked shoulders, exposed by the flimsy white vest top she was wearing. The sun had climbed to the highest point of the day and was mercilessly trying to cook her. Trying was an understatement! Her hot red shoulders were a sure sign it was succeeding. Arching her back, she stopped for a moment, looking at the fluffy cloud in the clear blue sky and contemplated a little break until the heat started to cool down. That way she could get some relief from its beating rays.

Leaning back on her haunches, she looked around the wild overgrown jungle she now called her garden with a heavy sigh; she had managed to clear about four feet of the path from her chipped and faded once bright red door. It was a start, a major improvement at least; She would now be able to come and go through the door without fighting with the plants around her ankles. She only had another two feet until the rickety little gate was clear, and that meant a leisurely walk from the gate to the door; unlike the day she arrived. That day had almost been like an Indiana Jones manoeuvre to get through the wilds and into the cottage.

Her mobile phone began to ring in her back pocket, reaching back she slid it out to answer, her mother smiling back at her from the screen photo, staring up at her in all her beautiful glory. A feeling of warm affection spreading through her stomach.

'Hi Mum.' She smiled and got up on her knees to stretch out lazily, leaning back and sliding to lay flat on the scorching stone path. An impromptu break had been decided for her.

'Hi honey, I hope you don't mind me calling darling? Just checking up to see how you're settling in. We haven't heard from you since your first day there.' Her mother's warm tone made her feel happy and a little bit guilty.

'Sorry Mum, I've been so busy; this cottage had such a lot of cleaning and organising, it was a bit of a mess.' She admitted, straining her back to get the kinks out and tipping her head back to feel the sun on her neck and exposed cleavage, both had been neglected when hunched over.

'That bad? It was left all boarded up and packed... Did she not have a caretaker keeping it habitable?' Her mum sounded confused about the state in which Rose had found the cottage.

'Yes; someone had been doing repairs and such but the grounds are wild, the interior a sea of canvas sheets and the place just smelled of damp and had about three inches of dust.' Rose glanced up at the window from her crazy angle, seeing Muffin, her fluffy white Chihuahua watching her quizzically from his perch on the wooden ledge. He was dying to get out, but she knew he would just run off into the unfamiliar surroundings if she let him loose.

'Olivia would've been upset to know it had become so unloved.' Her mother whispered tearfully; Rose felt the same tug of emotion at her aunt's name. A sunken ball of heaviness stopped her thoughts and forced her to push her aunt from her mind's eye, bringing her back to the present. She was getting good at dismissing her grief whenever Olivia's name arose.

'I know Mum... It wasn't exactly the cottage of my childhood memories... Colourful and homely it was not; so many memories of being here with her, only to be faced with an almost derelict shell.' Rose picked at her nail with her thumb in distraction. She always found it hard talking to her mother about Olivia, in any way.

'I guess not living there for the last eight years took its toll... She was happy in Shropshire though, with George. I think she missed the cottage, but she had found a new home.' Her mother's wistful tone carried a melancholy through Rose's stomach, she shook it off with a sigh and tried to refocus on the sunny surroundings instead.

'She always loved this place as much as I did; I guess it's why she left it to me in her will.' Rose smiled to herself at the touching legacy her Aunt had left her. What that had meant to her.

'So, what are you doing today, Darling?' Her mother changed the subject quickly, feeling that same pang of loss and heartbreak and eager to brighten the mood. It was still too soon; even after eighteen months of life without her, both women getting so good at pushing it down and misdirecting when it got too painful.

'Gardening... With a spoon.' Rose laughed and her mother followed, she had never been the one with green fingers in the family, and this only proved it. 'I'm almost done. The house is habitable, she left almost all the furniture behind. I have my studio set up ready to work and well, Muffin, seems to love taking walks in the surrounding rural emptiness.' She sounded more positive than she felt today. She didn't want to admit that she still had so much more to do and hadn't left the cottage in the two weeks here, due to endless cleaning of the two-bed, one-story thatched roof cottage.

So much for a fresh start and new friends!

So far it had been a new life as a recluse, in a stinky musty cottage with endless manual labour.

'So, you're settling in well then? Do you regret leaving London to go back to the highlands?' Her mum sounded wary, concerned almost.

Rose had always followed her own heart impulsively, ever since she was a child, and now coming here and leaving everything behind her. All her life she had been fiercely independent.

'Not even a little bit.' She assured her, and it was true, she hadn't even thought of her six years in the big city since her arrival. She had always felt there was something more out there for her in the world that London hadn't given her. It was as though she was holding her breath, waiting for that moment of clarity as to where her next steps were to be taken. Holding on, treading water, rather than just living and moving forward until the elusive something better came along. The cottage had been that chance for her.

'I'm glad you decided not to sell it Rose, Olivia would be so happy to know you've decided to make it your home... Much like she did at your age and she was really happy there, Darling.' The uplifted tone in her mother's voice made Rose feel better. Confirmation that she had made the right choice coming here, although she had never needed it, she knew it in herself that this place was the key to a her own happy ever after.

'I always had really good times here too Mum, with her... Painting and drawing and just enjoying this crazy, small town, and its quirky inhabitants. I needed a fresh start; my life was becoming so stale.' Rose flipped onto her stomach, her fingers working into the edge of the overgrown lawn and twisting stems distractedly.

'Rose, you've always been my baby, but, out of the three of you, you were the one who was most self-sufficient, who followed the beat of her own drum... Olivia washed off on you so much in your young life. I guess because you were her only niece and she couldn't have a child of her own. You were like a daughter to her too and you make me so proud, I love you Darling.' The emotion in her mother's voice was raw, her mother obviously just wanted to get it out there, between them. An acknowledgement that dismissing her aunts name in conversation was not because they didn't miss or love her. It was because it was still so hard to accept she was gone.

'I love you too Mum. Look I really should go, I'm starting to burn and I think Muffin is crossing his legs, he needs out.' Rose didn't really want to end the call but her heart ache was becoming a little too prominent, she didn't want to upset her mother more by asking her to stop talking about Olivia.

They said their goodbyes and she hung up the phone quickly, sighing to herself before turning, rolling to her knees to get up from the ground. She was about to head into the cottage when the sound of tyres on the gravel behind her alerted her to a visitor and halted her in her tracks.

Turning to see the small red post van approaching she pasted on her friendly smile, although he came daily they had never actually met as he usually posted letters through the slot while she was still inside cleaning and fixing up her new abode. Today she had been up and outside early to get some much-needed sun and it was about time she met her mailman.

As soon as the van pulled near, it parked by her rickety gate and she was faced with a little, old, red-cheeked man, with white receding hair and a smart royal mail uniform in navy blue. As he rounded his van with a handful of letters he smiled her way with a devilish twinkle in his merry face.

'Hello my dear. How are you? So nice to see what you look like at last.' He almost gushed at her when she straightened herself and tried to smooth down her dishevelled, grubby clothes. Rose extended her hand to meet his outstretched palm as he pushed mail under his armpit to shake it.

'Hi there, I'm fine, thanks. Yes, all moved in and settling well, now I have the place cleaned up a bit more.' Rose beamed at the friendly face, she had walked halfway down the path to meet the small man, who was now retrieving her post and taking the letters he was holding to her, she noted he had another in his right hand that he seemed to be holding back.

'Well my dear, there's been a lot of talk, you know... At the church! All about our new inhabitant and the lack of your presence in town;

will be nice to tell them all it's a very pretty young lady.' He continued smiling her way.

'Be away with you now… ' She giggled at his obvious charm. 'Young maybe, not sure about the very pretty!' She gushed and decided she liked this man, there was something familiar about him in a very genteel way.

'Oh, weesht now lassie, take a compliment! Here, I have something extra for you… Mr Munro has asked me to deliver this here personally.' He held out the long golden envelope in his other hand towards her briskly, extending it to Rose, who took it politely with a smile.

'Thank you.' She took the long, smooth envelope, still frowning and still confused; the look all over her face.

'It's an invitation to the annual charity dance.' he said as if in answer to her look. 'It's time they all met our newest community member.' His smile was genuine and bright and Rose felt herself smiling back.

'Well, thank you, Mr…?' Rose lifted eyebrows towards him, to encourage a name at least, if she was going to see him frequently then a name would be nice.

'Oh Hen, it's Tommy. Call me Tommy. I'm the caretaker for the big house as well as the village postie… Well, the misses and I, we take care of the repairs like… And I'm the one who was patching up this place in Miss Olivia's absence.' He patted the gate frame affectionately. The mention of her name caused a saddened look on both of their faces and he bowed his head. Rose couldn't help but notice the genuine reaction, guessing right that he'd known her aunt well and it explained the familiarness to her.

'Well, thank you so much! It means a lot to me that you cared for this place… She was my aunt… I used to come here a lot in the summers. Did you know her well?' Rose said gently, curious as to whether she had previously known this fellow in her childhood, even though her gut told her so.

'Oh, my goodness!!! Miss Rose? Little Miss Rose Turner? You know I thought you looked a lot like Miss Olivia when you opened the door, and now you say it! Damn, I see it!' He was almost jumping on the spot, pumping her hand enthusiastically again, his little red cheeks now overtaking his whole face. 'Same exotic beauty she had, and those dark brown eyes!'

'I am yes, I'm sorry I don't... ' She was trying to get a word in edgeways, pulling her hand free from his hot embrace but his renewed energetic state had him cutting in over her.

'Of course, you won't remember me! You were such a wee thing, I never really saw much of you; just the odd glimpse in passing. The wife though, she used to bring you her jam tarts, because you had a sweet tooth and always gave her such a warm welcome.' As soon as he said it, the memory in Rose's head was jarred to the forefront. A pleasant round lady who always brought her tissue paper wrapped confectioneries, whenever she had been here for holiday.

'Oh yes, I do remember her. And those tarts! Of course, I remember her! ... Alice was her name, I'm sure, right? ... It's such a small world, isn't it?' Rose could see his smile widening to a grin, obvious devotion to his wife and confirming her memory was accurate.

'Yes! It's Alice and it really is, I can't tell you how made up I am that Olivia's niece is our new member. We were all worried that some American had moved in as there's been talk, you know? Of a Yank around here.' He leaned in with a whispered frown as though spies could possibly here him insulting an American.

Rose laughed, knowing only too well the small-town mentality on newcomers, especially those they classed as foreign. Like children whispering in fear of a strange intruder to their lands. She shook her head and beamed at him a little more.

'Well can you tell her that I said hello. And, I remember her tarts, and cakes, so fondly.' Rose was feeling more relaxed in the presence of this man. Somehow, she knew this is what she had wanted, a reminder of the people she would soon get to know. Olivia's people and the reason she had always felt so at home here.

'I shall my lovely girl; now you promise me you will get yourself into town and start mingling. There's an awfy lot of people eager to meet you and today is the church book sale. Prime sunny day for a bit of introducing, if you know what I mean.' He winked at her knowingly and gave her shoulder an affectionate pat.

'I suppose you're right, I've been cooped up here long enough. A drive into town might be a good idea.' She gratefully smiled back at him, the sudden longing for more human companionship, now she had a taste of it.

'I'm guessing you're here on your own, seeing as there's no man sorting this mess out for you Hen?' He was now frowning at her with a lot of fatherly concern, a lot like her own dad used to display. Rose sighed down the giggle once more.

'I have my little dog with me, but no man. Completely single I'm afraid.' She couldn't help but smile at this, knowing how old fashioned this place was and it's view on unmarried young girls living alone. Soon she would have half the town trying to mother her.

'Well, that's a shame, but I guess it may be a good thing too.' He winked cheekily. 'I hear Rob's available nowadays and quite a catch according to all the town women.' Winking her way, looking at the watch on his wrist and sighing. Rose was trying to ignore his imminent matchmaking, as really, love was not on her agenda anytime soon and for all she knew the guy Rob could be horrendous.

'I'm sure he is really nice; I will definitely check out the book sale in town.' She was now walking him back to his parked van via her open gate, dismissing his suggestion as easily as she could. No matchmaking for her.

Hell no!

'Yes, make sure you do Lassie, will be nice to get some of the fellows up here to sort this out for you. This is a man's work, not for someone as dainty as you. I'll talk to Rob and see if the gardeners will come over for you and sort it out.' He had now left the garden and paused to think about his offer but Rose was quick to refuse.

'It's fine, really, I'm sure your friend Rob has other things on his plate, I'll just look into hiring a gardener from town if it gets too much for me. I am more than capable of manual labour honestly.' Rose had always been someone capable of doing things herself and even though she was ultimately turning down his offer, she didn't relish doing much more of this on her own.

'Rob is the laird, he oversees wee things like this, to keep the town happy and beautiful; he has a crew of full time gardeners for the grounds and would take a half day to do this. Let me talk to him.' He gave her another affectionate beaming smile and all she could do was smile back.

Setting me up with an old man Tommy? Tut Tut!

Rose had no intention of being harpooned into a date with some aging land owner, she had met the Laird in visits as a child and was pretty sure even then he had been married with children. Not her cup of tea at all. But then tastes among church going older women we're bound to be completely out of whack with the tastes of a twenty-eight-year-old girl from Edinburgh.

'Well thank you anyway, don't go out of your way.' She was trying to thank him but he was already waving her off with a shaking head, which meant he was ignoring her refusals. He slid into his little van and with a beep of the horn pulled out to U-turn and left with another wave out of his side window.

Rose waved back, a feeling of complete deflation running over her now she had returned to rural silence. She hadn't minded the quiet and peace the last couple of weeks, but now she was craving people after that interaction. She was intrigued about this dance too and she was not about to go to a ball, in however many weeks, knowing not a soul of her new community.

Rose turned back to the cottage and pushed open the door, walking inside just as Muffin peaked out to check all was clear, before snorting with a nose in the air as though he had personally chased off the visitor. He turned his little white bushy butt and trotted back off to her room, lately he'd been hoarding bones under her bed and loved nothing more than to lay in the dark underneath and chew on his prized possessions.

Moving further inside, after she closed the door, she pulled open the long envelope, dumping her other mail on the table in the hall and revealing a cream, elegant invitation with gold and brown scroll. It was announcing the event at Munro manor and was very classy. She frowned at the name Robert Munro under the Laird title and sighed, hoping to god the matchmaking wouldn't continue at a public event as she really had no desire to date an older man at all, and judging by memory this one had to be in his late sixties by now.

The event was to raise funds for a local charity, they wanted to help build a new wing on the hospital and extend the children's ward to include long term care rooms for children with more serious illnesses.

How could Rose refuse that?

She put it on the top of the fridge, lightly running her fingers over the luxurious paper and already mentally going through the dresses in her wardrobe. She had never been to a dance that was so formal sounding before; she wondered if she would have anything at all to wear that wouldn't look out of place in that big house.

She picked up a mirror and looked over her appearance almost automatically, while still mulling it over and shook her head. Sweaty and mucky, dirty fingernails and hair piled on top of her head in a haphazard mess.

This wouldn't do for a town trip.

She turned, dropping the mirror and headed to the bathroom to run a bubble bath in a bid to remove the sweaty smell of desperation. A little spruce up and a trip to town to meet her new neighbours would help. If she played it cool and mingled, then they might not even notice that she was trying to find herself some new friends before it became glaringly obvious that she had none.

You know, make the first move, meet the locals. No longer be the stranger at the dance, but someone familiar. Less likely to get stared at.

Her internal pep talk was helping to quell the tight knot of apprehension at putting herself out there for the first time in years, hopefully by the time she came home it would have no need to even exist.

Chapter 2

After her long soak in the tub she opened her wardrobe to put on a dress. It was proving to be a gloriously sunny day and she felt like a town book sale demanded she made a little more effort with her appearance, after all, her community were getting the first glimpses of the 'outsider'. She had been here a couple weeks, cooped up in this cottage, surrounded by the mess and eating microwave food and oven meals. A trip to suss out the local shops was not a bad idea, she could pick up something fresh, maybe even some cakes and take Muffin for a stroll beyond the gravel road that led out onto the main road from her own tree covered nook.

Pulling out a fitted baby pink sundress which flared out from the waist and brushed her knees, she slid her feet into matching flat pumps and brushed out her long dark hair, pinning it up the back of her head loosely, so tendrils fell around her face. Her skin had tanned to a lovely shade from all the garden work the last couple of days and she applied minimum make up. A spritz of her favourite perfume, a quick glance in the mirror to approve how she looked with a satisfied nod.

She grabbed a cream coloured canvas shoulder bag to throw her purse in and girly essentials, like strawberry lip balm and sun screen spray. She picked up her baby pink framed sunglasses, Audrey Hepburn style, and picked up Muffin and his leash.

Ready to rumble!

Rose was singing to herself tunelessly when she swept out to her car, with dog in tow.

Her little pink mini shone in the sunlight in front of the cottage, relieved to be free of both boxes and roof rack and crying out to be driven. Lovely and clean from her morning washing and polishing it days before. Rose had always had a pink obsession, since childhood, always obsessed with all things pink, girly and sparkly. Her car had been her one indulgence in London, going for a baby pink, tiny, car that suited her girly - All things cute! Obsession. She had hated that every male she had dated criticised it and it was partially why none of them made it beyond two weeks with her.

Blaring the summer hits CD, she pulled out with Muffin in the passenger seat and headed along the road; pulling out into the main road and reaching speed quickly, she was singing and smiling at how free she felt, energised by this impromptu outing and the glorious sunshine which was not typical for Scotland this early in the summer. It was truly shaping up to be a wonderful day.

Out of nowhere, the nose of a black car poked out in front of her from the tree edged hedge way, causing her to swerve and scream as she tried to hit the brakes in alarm. Her car skidded halfway across the road with an almighty screech before slamming to a halt and Rose fell forward on her steering wheel, trying to catch her breath; sure, she had just suffered a major heart attack.

Grabbing at Muffin to feel he was still in one piece, her hands began shaking violently and her heart pounded through her chest; trying to keep her head on the wheel to steady her breathing and calm her nerves, she could feel her rage rising.

Who in the actual hell???? What the actual f...?

Her car door was ripped open from beside her, causing her to snap up and around and glare angrily into the steel coloured eyes facing her, which had suddenly appeared a little too closely.

'Are you o...' A smooth and deep voice that sounded genuinely concerned tried to infiltrate her red haze but she had already hit maximum rage.

'What in the actual hell are you doing???' She screeched at the face before her, not really taking in the jet-black hair, tanned skin or intense grey eyes belonging to the tall stranger. Ordinarily this kind of sexy would have put Rose in a slump of panting hormones but Rose just saw red!

'You could have killed me!!! Are you aware that road is a sixty? You pulled out into traffic on a god damn sixty!' She pulled herself out of her seat, releasing her belt to square her small five feet four to the huge six-foot frame before her. Anger searing her every nerve at the sheer stupidity of the man. He quickly stood back, looking almost shocked as she continued to yell at him about his idiotic driving manoeuvre with hands firmly on her hips and letting fiery Rose loose.

'Whoa there Penelope!' Splaying his hands in defence as he tried to calm her rant. 'Look, I'm sorry! I'm sure I got as much of a shock as you! Most folks know how bad the view is for me coming out and cross to the other side to pass the manor opening!' He was defensively moving away from Rose as she continued to wave her hands about, cursing at him about recklessness and moronic men with stupidly fast and flashy cars, Rose was on a roll. She stopped suddenly, realising something he had said.

'Who the hell is Penelope?' She blinked in confused fury, but he only laughed at her sudden change in persona, then tried to smother it with a cough.

Smooth move mister! Asshole. God, You're Hot!

Rose had only just seemed to notice this little fact, now that she was inches from him.

His whole shocked manner seemed to do a sudden flip into smiling, good humoured, if not a little embarrassed, but Rose was beyond oblivious in her mental state.

'You!... Sorry, it's just... Pink car... Pink dress... Fiery little lady who comes out like a bat out of hell, like she's about to rip my head off...' The handsome stranger stood with hands up defensively, smiling at her like it was the most obvious thing in the world to everyone except her. Rose stood motionless. Cluelessness and confusion all over her face, which only added to her internal irritation at his far too good-looking smugness.

'Penelope Pitstop from wacky races?' He tried again to get her brain to connect to whatever the hell he was talking about. 'Look never mind. It's just, that's what I thought when I opened your door.' He was laughing now, in a rather deep and husky way which only enraged her more and brought out another bought of fury.

'Screw you and your stupid wacky whatever's! Next time watch where you're going, asshole! Or next time I won't swerve!' She turned and threw herself back into her car in the most unladylike manner, attempting to grab her door, so she could dramatically slam it. All previous ounces of rage reconnected with her inner diva, but he grabbed it first.

'Allow me.' He slammed it shut with the force of a guy who had reconnected with anger. The humour absent from his face and replaced with 'I'm pissed off, lady.' Their eyes glinted at one another angrily, fire meeting fire. Sparks igniting in the air around them and almost crackling with the collision.

Rose didn't wait for any further conversation, putting metal to the floor she sped off without any hesitation, almost taking him out with her wing mirror in the process and giving zero cares about it.

Rose wasn't sure why this guy had invoked such a furious response, but all she wanted was to put a huge sea of distance between her and that smug laugh and get rid of the ball of internal anger writhing inside of her. She could see the arrogant sod in her mirror, shaking his head after her, watching her drive off before walking back to his flashy black car and sliding back in with the grace of a cougar.

'Asshole!' She screeched loudly, angered at the sheer effortless grace the idiot was displaying.

Muffin was looking at her with his wide, wise eyes, almost telling her she had simply lost the plot.

'Well, he is! Mr, I'm so good looking with my big muscles and sports car and expensive clothes. So Mr smooth that I think I can give you a cute pet name and you forget I almost killed you!' She slapped her wheel, eyes darting from the road to rear view mirror manically as she tried not to cause further accident with stupid driving.

'Fuck you! ...Ow, that actually hurt.' She lifted her fingers to her mouth and blew them gently in a bid to soothe the burning self-inflicted pain, releasing some of her tension as she did so. That 'almost' crash had given her a massive fright and her reactions since had been some sort of delayed mental breakdown, brought on by a near death experience. Being confronted by a guy who was far too handsome for an early morning rural drive had just added to her extreme reaction.

I mean who the hell was he? Wearing designer clothes and a flashy car and looking a little too suave for the highlands. Men like him were normally arrogant Londoners, and she had met enough of them to last a lifetime.

Pushing that irritatingly flawless face out of her mind's eye, she suddenly felt remorseful for swearing angrily in front of Muffin and sat back in her chair, trying to release the tightness of her muscles. Flexing her shoulders and tilting her head from side to side to flex her neck. Slow steady and calming breaths and internal chanting to cool her jets.

The black sports car appeared in her rear-view mirror, coming up behind her fast and she instantly tensed back up, teeth gritting and eyes narrowing angrily. Putting the foot down, she sped away from him before reaching the sign for the town and slowing back down again as she passed it. Completely pointless, but satisfying to say the least, riled by the way this man made her feel. Throwing daggers from her eyes in the mirror, she slowed to thirty and meandered through town looking for a car park as the car behind her turned off at the huge museum; she sighed with relief at his departure.

Hot or not, I don't need you behind me today!

'Asshole.' She muttered to no one in particular and hit the indicator to turn into a big half empty car park. Within minutes Rose found a space easily and expertly deposited her car, latching Muffins lead on and exiting gracefully with a much sunnier disposition.

Although the town was bustling with pedestrians, it seemed most came via a little free bus from surrounding areas and not many drove. The streets were quiet from traffic and felt peaceful, despite the people milling around. Wandering about, she soon managed to navigate her surroundings, quaint little shops ranging from the normal grocery stores to little cute boutiques, home decor, crafts and tourist shops. Several cafes and a huge bakery shop that sat very close to the car park she had used.

It was a pretty and picturesque little town, lots of barrels filled with flowers and park benches to pretty it up and lots of potted trees and quaint old-fashioned street lamps. It was more beautiful than even her memories and she could see the appeal for tourists. This was proper highland charm right here.

She decided to browse the shops first, before going in pursuit of the church she had yet to see, buying the odd necessity and really getting a feel for the place. Rose was happy to find, that although it wasn't exactly the small town of her childhood memories, it was enough unchanged that she got a familiar tug of emotion deep in the pit of her stomach; just the same. This had been Olivia's favourite place, she would have loved to see that it was thriving but still held all the same charm as before, as though caught in a time warp.

After successfully not finding the church in the small town and seeing a lack of mulling locals Rose decided to head to the coffee shop, situated in the bakery to rest her weary feet. It wasn't sign posted and there were no obvious roofs rising above the rest to indicate where the church would be. She had put Muffin back in the car with a bowl of water, a new bone, the windows opened and the radio on, before coming to get something to eat and ask for directions.

She was sure that in this little place, her car and the dog, would be safe from a break in. Besides, her alarm was loud and immobilised her car easily and although Muffin wasn't much of a guard dog, he did have this incredibly scary toothy face he pulled when he was frightened and tried his version of a broken growl. If nothing more it would scare away any lingerers; It did make him look a little rabid and possibly mentally unhinged.

As soon as she opened the door, the smell of newly baked bread and fancies hit her like a warm hug. She wanted to fall into that smell, it was so heavenly and had memories flooding back and filling her up with so much warmth, chasing away the last ounces of anger. She could almost feel herself transported back to her childhood and eagerly swept in to see if they still stocked her favourite cakes.

The tables were almost all empty with the odd couple or group, sitting far apart, quietly chatting and oblivious to her entrance. There was a relaxed, friendly atmosphere, despite being a complete stranger here and she felt better that no one was openly staring and pointing as she had feared.

The girl behind the counter, dressed in a green uniform reminiscent of school dinner ladies smiled at Rose as she approached, with no expression other than friendly.

'Hi there, what can ah get for yeh today?' The girl asked in a polite, yet very heavily accented brogue that suggested she had grown up in the farms surrounding the town.

'Hi, can I have a jam tart and a hot chocolate please. Thank you.' Rose smiled back and pulled her purse from her shoulder bag, breathing in the fresh ground coffee bean smell wafting her way.

'Sure thing, will just be two ticks for yeh.' The girl turned on her heel and moved off to arrange Rose's order on a tray, allowing her a moment to properly look around the clean surroundings.

Glancing around she took in the bright, simple decor, the mint coloured walls and dark wood floor which all seemed new. The cases of fancy patisseries and treats and the huge display case, showcasing elaborately decorated cakes for seasons and celebrations. It didn't have small town oozing from it and it saddened Rose a little. This bakery had been one of her favourite places to come on a weekend with her aunt, back when it had been a small corner shop and not the huge one she now stood within.

The bakery her aunt had loved had been small and quaint and had obviously grown into the neighbouring shops over time, to accommodate more seating and bigger kitchens. The woman who used to run it had been an Italian woman called Bella. A large round warm lady who had enveloped little Rose in cuddles and always satisfied her sweet tooth with a cream cake when they had come. Rose guessed this is what success looked like when a small-town bakery managed to keep going for decades. As she looked around at the modern art, and clean, simple window dressings, Rose was suddenly aware of the young woman at the window table, smiling at her openly.

Rose glanced away awkwardly, assuming she was smiling to someone behind Rose, but a quick look showed no one had come in behind her and she was the only one standing there. Rose looked back again, catching the girl's eye and gained another bright smile. This time Rose smiled back and returned her gaze to the counter as her hot chocolate and strawberry tart was placed on the tray in front of her. Rose took the little round wooden tray with its paper lace doily and moved off, looking to choose a seat. The girl beckoned to her with a waving hand, catching her eye and tapped the table, showing she was offering her a seat. Rose hesitated, then followed the gesture and approached shyly

'Hi.' She got close and slid her tray on the table opposite the dark-haired stranger.

'Hi, there.' The girl smiled the most dazzling smile Rose had ever seen, all perfect straight white teeth and pretty, pouted lips, although there was something vaguely familiar about it. She had long black hair, the colour of raven feathers, pale flawless skin with peachy blushed cheeks and dazzling green eyes that sparkled out at you mischievously. She was dressed casually and it made her appear very young. She was young, maybe in her early twenties or late teens and stunningly beautiful in a casual, naïve, sort of way.

She extended her hand announcing her name was Abby, Abigail but everyone called her Abby. That she was killing time and could do with the company.

'I'm Rose Turner, I just moved into the little cottage at the main road as you enter the village.' She smiled back at the pretty face and saw her nod, hinting she knew exactly which cottage.

'It's really nice to see a new young face, especially a girl. We don't get many new comers.' Abby beamed her way, lifting her mug and sipping down some coffee; Rose felt an instant ease with this girl, a genuine friendliness.

Conversation soon began to flow and Abby told Rose she was studying art history, held up textbooks from the seat beside her as if to prove her story was legit. There was a book face down on the table in front of her, and a plate with a half-eaten chocolate doughnut and now empty coffee mug. She was waiting for her brother, collecting her after four and loved to spend her free time in Bella's bakery. Rose absolutely loved this girls down to earth, straight shooting attitude and genuine openness, she had always found the people in this village to be like this.

Rose was thrilled to hear Bella was still around and still owned this place. She learned that Abby was nineteen and incredibly easy to talk too, sweet and genuine. That despite looking very young, she was very mature and well spoken, her accent although typical for around here, had a slight upper-class clearness to it, much like the male strangers this morning.

The girls found conversation flowed effortlessly and had an immediate connection, both were artists and loved to paint! Both obsessed with the Sunflower painting by Van Gogh and both didn't like abstract art in the slightest. Abby 'oohed' and 'ahhed' over Roses dress and almost died of envy when she told her that her car was pink too.

'Rob told me he'd never let me have a pink car.' She laughed 'He said it would embarrass his manly self to take it for maintenance. Of course, because I would be completely incapable of doing such things; being a woman!' She joked with a slow shake of her head, and a sigh. An obvious look of sibling love in her eyes when she said his name.

'So, Rob is your brother?' Rose enquired, trying to imagine her own older brothers being that way so many years before. It had been a long time since her two brothers and she shared the same time zone, let alone home.

Why did that name ring a bell? Rob?

'Yes. Older, pain in the ass brother, who sometimes thinks he's my dad!' She smiled, moving her book aside and leaning her elbows on the table. 'I mean my dad's still around, but Rob takes care of all of us. My mum passed away when I was fourteen and he just sort of took over. Dad was a mess and well, he's in his seventies now, so it made sense.' She looked far away for a moment, then returned to reality, returned from a moment of sadness that Rose knew only too well; missing a loved one was something you never got over. 'Dad married a younger woman you see.' She winked cheekily. 'Rob was born when dad was already in his late forties, and well, I came in his late fifties.' She shrugged. 'I guess they wanted more kids in between but it never happened. So just the two of us, in that big house, and then dad of course. The rest of the family lives further away.'

'It's nice though, that he's so protective and you're obviously close, both my brothers live abroad. One in the RAF, he's currently in America and one emigrated to Australia to become a marine biologist. My parents live in Edinburgh, so I'm here all on my lonesome.' Rose couldn't help but notice the effortless way the two women had just slipped into sharing life stories. It really felt as if she had always known Abby.

'I couldn't imagine not having family around me all the time. Don't you get lonely or scared?' Abby scrutinised Roses face seriously. Trying to figure out the girl.

'I'm used to it; I lived in London for six years to further my career and I didn't really make many friends. The life was too fast paced and everyone just wanted to succeed or party. I missed normal slow living and genuine people.' Rose took a mouthful of her drink and watched Abby toy with her empty mug.

'You sound like Rob. He lived in Glasgow for a couple years when he went to Uni to study business, he said he couldn't wait to come home and just get back to home life, the town and the Manor.'

It suddenly hit Rose sitting there, that one tiny word within a sentence. Manor! This was Abigail Munro! She was the Laird's sister!

Running through the scene earlier in her head and piecing the fragments together in a split second, she felt her stomach lurching as it clicked into place. That familiar smile. That black hair, and although the eyes were not grey, she had his eyes. That same cheeky look when he smiled. The hint of dimples when she smiled. Just like his. That flawless skin and attractive bone structure. The easy confidence and the upper-class dialect which was not common around here.

Surely, he couldn't be? Could he?

He'd been leaving the Munro estate and he did say 'Most people know I have a bad view of the road.' Or something along those lines. Rose felt the colour drain from her face as it sunk in that her first encounter of the day with the asshole, had not been just any asshole, but this lovely girl's brother and the Laird of her new home town. The Laird, who had invited her to his ball!!

'Are you okay?' The look of concern on Abby's face only struck it home, so alarmingly like his.

Damn!

Even the same question as he had yanked open her car door. They were so alike it was traumatising; Rose feigned a smile and then let her head drop into her palms groaning aloud. She felt like a moron, prize 'A' idiot, and this sudden dawning of events had her reeling with regret. She felt Abby's hand touch her arm, concerned her new friend was having some sort of mental breakdown.

'I met him!' She mumbled, covering her face and trying to rub away the realisation. The urge to pour her own hot chocolate over her head swiftly coming over her.

'Rob?' She could almost hear the surprise in Abby's tone.

'Yes! He almost killed me with his car this morning and then…'

'Penelope?!?!?!' The sound of his deep familiar voice moved her to jump up, right off the table. Snapping her head up to meet his tall figure coming towards her from the open door. Shocked into momentary silence by the sight of him towering at the side of the table right next to her, larger than life, so close she caught her breath. His sudden presence making her feel hot and bothered, flustered with no real reason, except that maybe he was a little bit hot in a sculpted white shirt, rolled up at the sleeves and some super snug on the ass jeans. Both Abby and his eyes glued to her face with a look of concern, strikingly similar! Yet not! One was extremely feminine and one extremely masculine, in the disturbingly male way that made women like Rose lose all compos mentis.

'Are you okay?' Both of them, almost in unison.

Oh god, it was undeniable that they were related.

She slid her chair out quickly, mumbling some incoherent reason for getting going and avoiding looking him in the face as she tried to slide by. Caught between embarrassment, awkwardness, and just sheer cringe factor. Now she could fully see him without the red veil of rage she had to admit, he was romance hero worthy.

He caught her by the waist as she made for a lame exit attempt, stopping her and towering over her fragile frame like some kind of Neanderthal. No hesitation in laying his hands on her tiny figure, which only enraged her almost compulsively. His hot male hands encircling her body, burning through the thin fabric of her dress with an almost searing heat, causing immediate anger and uneasiness at his touch. Unsure at why she was reacting this way, and it was only bringing the fury back to the forefront. She shoved him off defiantly, hands meeting with hard chest beneath his thin shirt.

'I'm absolutely fine! … No thanks to you and your dangerous driving. Where did you get your license? … A lucky bag!!' She surprised herself with her venomous reaction, as she saw the storm move into his eyes again. Clearing away the concern to be replaced with a matched annoyance, fury to challenge her own. Burning between them like a beast about to erupt; self-combusting fire.

'So I see. Not lying there dying or passing out from a concussion, as I feared; but alive and spitting just like earlier. And I could ask you the same thing, Penelope. I'm sure driving eighty on the road to town was highly responsible.' His angry glare sent prickles up her spine, that smug face only inches from hers. Her breathing hitched.

'Just trying to get away from you. In case once again your idiot driving caused me to crash!' She thrust her hands on her hips in a show of bravado and pulled her small height up to meet him head on.

'Getting away from me is becoming a habit today!' Rob crossed his arms across that massive expanse of male muscle and leaned back on his heel, somehow it only angered her more.

'Yup. Absolutely!' She spat.

'Great! Don't let me stop you.' He stepped back, giving her some much-needed breathing space. Sparks sizzling in the air between them with no real sense at all to the anger fuelling the scene. No real argument in the petty comments, just rage, heat and sparks.

She had no idea why this guy made her so angry. Every nerve in her body reacting like hot piercing needles and the urge to smash a mug on his head. His overly good-looking face absolutely screamed for her to throw her drink in it; it seemed they both evoked that reaction in each other. He moved out of the way, gesturing her exit dramatically, almost bowing as he nodded and murmured some incoherent insult. To which she spat one back before marching off with a bag in hand, twisting the handle like it was his neck.

Oh, my god! He was a complete jerk! Arrogant sod with his sultry cold eyes piercing like daggers!!

Poor Abby sat watching this whole scene in absolute disbelief; Rob, her normally laid-back, gentle and well-mannered brother. This seemingly nice girl, who had just spent a half hour acting like old friends. They had turned to instant fire and brimstone in each other's presence. She had no clue what to say to defuse the situation, but just sat there agog. The tension between them sending off an electric atmosphere like she had never experienced; Abby raised a knowing eyebrow at Rob and a tiny smirk. Rob frowned a 'What?' at her in aggravation.

Rose stalked out in a very dramatic fashion in a flurry of ruffled petticoats, leaving half of her drink and cake sitting and almost taking out seats with her swinging handbag. Abby just sat staring at Rob in bewilderment. He told her he would wait for her in the car, then stormed off in an equally bad mood, taking the opposite direction to Rose. Walking out the door only seconds behind the pink-clad woman and glaring at her walking away as he stalked to his own car.

Chapter 3

Rose drove home gripping her steering wheel and cursing under her breath like a demented maniac. Trying to remove the feeling of his hands on her body, hating the way it still felt as though she could feel him touching her. Ignoring the rosy blush which had spread up her chest and cheeks and the warmth low down in her pelvis. The feelings she couldn't explain happening inside of her, common sense batting the observations away.

Rose was still spitting nails at home an hour later. She had come home almost ripping her dress off, trying to remove the feeling of him on her skin and was systematically scrubbing every inch of her living room like a fevered crazy person on a mission. No one had ever ignited this kind of response in her and she was damned if she was going to dissect it in any way at all. Instead, she was trying to power shift it out of her very core with exertion.

She had hauled the covers and plastic from the old leather couch finally, and pulled it into place by the fire. Had dragged the mismatched armchair to the other side and started ripping into random boxes in a mad rage, determined to put all the pent of energy into something productive.

Three hours later she was still slamming around, dragging tables around, moving footstools from the closet and dragging out an array of thick woollen throws, all heaped on the floor. She really had no method to her madness. Just a need to pull things, rip things and use a box cutter to stab at cardboard aggressively.

Muffin had sensed the psychotic rage and had been hiding under the bed since their return, he was happy with a huge bone the butcher had gifted him. He knew a crazy woman on a cleaning mission when he saw one and knew best to keep a distance.

It was the sharp knock at her door which brought her back to reality with a swift slap. It was pitch black outside, she had seen no headlights appear on the gravel road in front of the house and it was getting late. This sudden realisation of her own vulnerability was sobering, a lone woman in a remote and dark area with no one to call for help. Cooling her hot temper and making her simmer back down to an almost submissive state; she tried to peer out the window, pushing the curtains aside, but could only make out a dark figure.

Damn, she needed lights out there!

Going to the door, she called out bravely, aware that it could be anyone. Praying that wandering psychopaths were few and far between in the highlands, keeping her hand on the lock and asking who was there. She was relieved at Abby's response and opened the door to the girl whose arms were laden with a brown bag filled to bursting. The most welcome sight she had ever seen, an instant surge of genuine happiness and joy.

'Can I come in for a few minutes?' Abby looked nervous and awkward, but Rose smiled and pulled her in from the dark and cool night air enthusiastically. Her smile wide and encouraging; she was actually so happy to see her again and the anger and pent up need to massacre boxes dispersed at the sight of her. Like a calming breeze. She had wondered how she would get in touch with the girl again after the way she had left things.

Abby looked around the hall as she came in, noticing the art and canvases on the wall, all painted by Olivia Grey. Her aunt had been an amazing fine artist in oil paints. That had been Roses first mission, her first week here. Her inspiration and joy; a gallery of her most treasured paintings to warm her heart when coming and going. A reminder of that amazing figure in her life and a way to keep her with her.

Motioning for Abby to follow and relieving her from the burden of the brown bag, they moved through to the living room, Rose apologising for the mess and clearing some cushions from the couch so they could sit. Abby complimented the efforts at getting it cosy and admired some of Roses new purchases, cushions, candles and trinkets. She had only ever been at this cottage as a small child many years ago, Olivia had given her some tuition in drawing at her father's expense, but she still remembered it vaguely.

Abby dipped into the bag full of cakes and doughnuts from a nameless shop and explained she would have been around earlier, she had gone away with Rob for a bit, while he sorted some business in the next town and was only just back. He had dropped her at the opening of Rose's road, knowing she was coming here. It seemed the whole town knew who Rose was now. Strangers didn't stay that way for long in a town like this, everyone knew everyone, and everyone knew their business before long.

'And he was okay with that?' Rose was surprised.

'Why not? I like you. Even if he doesn't!' Abby smiled, throwing a wink at her, the hint of cheekiness behind those sparkling eyes. Rose bashed her with a soft cushion and they both laughed, there was something so familiar about Abby, an old friend returned and it had made for an instant ease between them. Rose tried to ignore the bitter knot in her stomach that Rob Munro didn't like her. She tried to convince herself it was because the feeling was mutual and he simply left a bad taste in her mouth.

'I'm sorry about acting like such a crazy weirdo at the bakery Abby, he just seems to bring it out of me.' Rose felt her cheeks redden, fidgeting with the glazed doughnut she was turning in her fingers.

'Rob seems to do that to women. Don't worry about it, you said he almost wiped your car out. I would have been pissed too.' Abby gave her a reassuring smile and patted her knee in a very mature manner. 'Rob's my brother, so I know better than most that he can be an asshole! You don't need to apologise at all Rose.' Both girls regarded each other for a second and broke into wide smiles.

'Coffee?' Rose offered brightly, relieved that Abby was understanding and Abby nodded.

'If it's not a bother, I mean if you're busy I can head off.' Abby smiled politely.

'Don't be daft, I really could use the company.' Rose smiled and beckoned the girl after her as she made her way to the small kitchen. Abby, lifting the bag and following her, seemed relieved. There was an immediate sense of calm and companionship. No awkward silence or uneasiness.

'You know though?' Abby butted into Roses thoughts as she hauled out cups and coffee granules to fill them. 'Rob isn't really one to spark quite so quickly, you two certainly have a fire.' Abby watched Rose carefully, every movement of the teaspoon as though waiting for a reaction. A strange look and a twinkle in Abby's eye; Rose could almost swear it was a look of mischief.

'I think what we have is mutual dislike. Instant disagree-ability. I'm very partial to my car and not being run off the road.' Rose threw her an airy look and tried to steer the topic away from the man who was currently making her heart beat up a gear. 'So tell me, this ball… Are you attending? Do you want a date?'

Abby broke into a wide grin.

'Don't I ever! That would be so much better than being a third wheel with Rob and whomever he drags along. I'm currently man-less and it pretty much sucks.' Abby slid into one of the kitchen chairs and began laying out the pastries on the platter Rose had put out. Rose finished up with the mugs of coffee and brought them over, sliding into the chair opposite and mirroring Abby's casual slump.

'You're kidding, right? How can a girl, looking like you, not have a date?' Rose raised eyebrows with genuine surprise; Abby was stunning.

'Aww are you calling me pwetty?' Abby jested with kissing noises and lots of dramatic eye fluttering. 'Seriously though, people in this town tend to give me a wide berth. When my mum died, I became a bit of a loner and people are just used to leaving me alone. I think boys think I'm weird.' She gulped down some hot liquid and messed with the handle of her mug.

'That's understandable, maybe people didn't know how to approach you. People aren't good with grief. They never know what to say, especially younger folks.' Rose lifted her mug and turned it in her palms, enjoying the heat it gave off and remembering the awkwardness of her flat mates when she had news of Olivia's car accident.

'You sound like a granny saying things like that.' Abby jested. 'What, are you like fifty?' She poked with a twinkle in her eye and a cheeky wink.

'Twenty-eight actually. Cheeky!' Rose dipped her fingers in her hot coffee and flicked them at Abby childishly, smiling as she did so.

'Old then. Not as old as Rob, but almost. You two are totally ready for slippers by the fire and matching bathrobes.' Abby flicked some sugar from her doughnut back at Rose and received a pout in response.

'Shut up weirdo. I guess it's a date, we can be sad and single together. Maybe it'll be you and I buying matching bathrobes soon enough.' Rose giggled at that and Abby only cheered.

'I actually like the sound of that, it's about time I had a real decent girlfriend. Most of the chicks my age suck. They either moon over my brother or just want to know how much money he's worth.' She pouted and blew a strand of hair off her forehead in the most childish manner.

'I promise to do neither of those things; if you're lucky I may even be persuaded to go to second base at the party.' Abby laughed at Rose's Joke.

'Then I am most definitely taking you.' Abby jested with a wink and a smile and both girls laughed.

Somehow, the conversation seemed to flow even more fluidly after that, lost with a cup in hand and cakes on a plate. The subjects they covered were vast and random. Two minds alike in so many ways, both with a quick sense of humour.

They went through two pots of tea and more than half of the confectionery, giggling like school girls and finding the most insane things to talk about as the time drew on and they chatted and laughed, finding more in common than they ever thought possible.

Abby had a quick wit about her, a cheeky tongue and almost verging on the crude when it came to her jokes. She was refreshing and honest and said exactly what she meant. There was no second guessing. She was upfront and didn't mince her words which Rose absolutely loved; she was the kind of friend that Rose missed having, the kind she had left behind in Edinburgh to embark on a career so many years ago as a freelance illustrator.

When Abby's phone lit up and beeped, she made her apologies about leaving. Explaining her brother was here to collect her so she didn't attempt to walk home; it was getting late. He had obviously returned home, from wherever, and discovered she was still here. Rose felt her heart quicken at the thought of him coming here, sitting outside in his purring black car only feet away and pushed down the blush she felt rising.

How the hell could that ass have such an effect on her?

She walked Abby to the door and stood in the open frame, feeling the cool night air on her skin and getting hugged goodbye. She was relieved when she saw he had waited for Abby part way down her road, far enough to keep his distance, but close enough she could make out his profile in the car when Abby illuminated the interior by opening it. Looking at his sister and saying something that made her smile, she saw him smile too, an easy happy natural smile as his eyes ran over his sister's face. He pinched her cheek and received a bat in the arm from Abby before they were drawing away and heading into the darkness.

For an asshole, he really was incredibly handsome! It did crazy things to Roses stomach, in a way that was not entirely bad. But then enraged her for the ability to do it.

Jerk!

Chapter 4

The next few days went by incredibly quickly, Rose was so busy getting into the swing of sorting out the rooms in the cottage in the last sweep of effort; She had made a huge dent. She could now easily use the rooms without tripping over boxes or stray pieces of furniture and even Muffin had his designated cosy corner full of toys and a snuggly bed. All of her personal things had found homes and most of the packaging was sitting in the hall ready to go away.

She had spent time on her laptop and phone sorting out her next illustration project and had the dates in hand. She was awaiting the manuscript for the story along with the author's notes on how she wanted the character's scenes to lay out. All was set and her fee had been signed off on. Her first payment in the bank and it was making everything feel more final. She had celebrated the new commission by buying herself a dress online for the dance and then felt incredibly stupid when her first thought was what he would think of it. This really bad habit he had of creeping into her mind unexpectedly and then she would slap it away again, feeling irritation rise. She had pushed the thought down the back of the sofa with all the ooze and dust of previous years to fester.

Thanks to Tommy the gardens had been brought into order by a local man Malcolm, and his teen son Liam, with the taming of the gardens they had even added chicken wire to the back fence for her, making it Muffin safe. She knew Rob must have okayed them being here and felt slightly miffed at the fact she owed him some thanks. There was not a single escape route for that fiery little fur ball and he was now enjoying running around like a mad hound in the garden, rolling in the newly shorn lawn and exploring the now tame flower beds, which had surprisingly been full of gorgeous wild flowers.

She had worked out a regular deal with them to keep the place trim and fabulous. An inexpensive necessity that didn't infringe on their manor working hours. So, she didn't need to be any more thankful to that arrogant sod up in his mansion for anything more. The garden was looking beautiful. She had been overwhelmed with emotion when she had seen the neat long garden with its stepping stone path to the outhouse's blue door. Trim flower beds and a washing line leading down the side of the garden. A small metal patio set purchased locally was laid out on the now cleared paving stones to the right of the door and It brought back so many memories of back garden picnics on days like this. Summer tents made from bed sheets and rolling around playfully with her aunt, lost in some youthful game.

As the week progressed, Abby came by most mornings for a quick cup of tea as she headed to the bus stop a good ten minutes' walk out of town. That was the upside to both the cottage and manor entry roads being only a mile apart on the same road. Abby loved walking and just loved walking right in here for tea and Muffin cuddles. Rose could almost set her watch by her visits and really looked forward to the young girl's arrival every day. She had helped move the remainder of the furniture in place in each room, carted boxes to the garden and helped take a lot of packaging and trash to the local dump in the back of Rose's car. She had been a godsend in helping with the finishing touches and a dab hand at D.I.Y. Showing up one morning with a wheelbarrow full of power tools to hang up heavy mirrors and pictures and tighten some loose hinges. She had taught Rose what a rawl plug was and the joy of a power drill.

Rose had finally taken delivery of her new kitchen appliances, and the very helpful men even put them in place for her. Probably sensing she was pretty useless at any sort of manual labour that involved moving appliances and had no idea how to plumb a washing machine or attach a gas cooker. They had even removed her old appliances free of charge. She guessed her coffee and cakes, delivered with a smile had swung that. The kitchen overall was not too bad. It was made from real wood units in need of a sand and varnish, but there was something so quaint and shabby chic about them that Rose intended to whitewash them instead of replacing them.

Most of the jobs in the house were easy cosmetics, elbow grease and just a lot of time spent doing tedious manual labour. All in all, she was finally getting the place to resemble the cosy home of her memories. It had not taken much painting either. Her aunt had only ever lived alone and had the paint touched up every year until she left. There was nothing that a wipe down and clean couldn't remove and the majority of the walls were cream with stained dark wood beams and dark wood floor. She had found old sealed cans of paint in the shed and had managed to use the name to purchase a new tin for touch ups. Nothing Rose wanted to change. She was in love with the mash up of old vintage furniture and new modern things in her cosy little home and had finally found the refuge she had been seeking.

In week two, Rose and Abby had taken a four-hour round trip to Ikea a few towns south and managed to pick up so many bargains that she had the whole place looking modern yet quaint. Vintage meets Ikea. Somehow it worked and was pretty much the home she had always dreamed of.

Trips to town had resulted in meeting a handful of locals, full of character and charm. The old women who organised jumble sales, the old men who stood around waiting for the women to scour the second-hand shops on a Wednesday morning and then on to the church weekly coffee morning. Young mothers, with toddlers and babies, who frequented the parent groups. Kids going to and from the local schools who loved to hang out in town on lunch hour. The general locals who worked in every shop and stall and always greeted her with a huge smile and chit chat. Rose had done more socialising in under two weeks here than her six years in London and Abby was fast becoming the friend she had longed for since leaving home.

It was on a morning trip to town that Rose stopped into the bakery to pick up cakes for Abby coming over. Lost in thought after placing her order at the counter, she was rummaging in her bag for her purse; head down and humming to herself on another gloriously sunny day, full of summer joys.

'What's got you so happy Penelope?' Robs voice infiltrated her thoughts and the sudden haze of sexy aftershave over swept her as his body heat came dangerously close behind her.

'I'm in my favourite bakery, buying cakes! Do I need any other reason?' She answered immediately, half smiling before reminding herself how much she didn't actually like this guy. She glanced back to see he was adorned in a white shirt and jeans and looking his usual dapper self; which only made her annoyed with the way it made her feel like sighing.

'Sweet tooth, much like Abby. I can see why you two get on and spend so much time together.' He smiled with a dazzling almost sexy grin, but Rose just frowned and turned back to the counter to try and ignore his presence.

Easier said than done.

'It's partly for Abby, we're meeting later.' Rose answered tonelessly then smiled graciously when the counter girl appeared with a large white paper bag, fit to bursting.

'How the hell you two stay so thin, with an order that size, is beyond me.' He observed with another smiley tone, Rose just sighed.

'Lucky I guess. Good genes.' She paid for her purchase and turned to leave but he didn't move to let her pass. She frowned up at him towering over her, a little impatiently and sighed when he still didn't move.

'Look Penny. Maybe we could have a do-over? You and my sister are practically inseparable and I think we got off on the wrong foot. Would be nice if we could just put it in the past.' He pushed his hands casually into his back pockets, emphasizing his muscular frame, making it clear he wasn't moving and Rose had to avert her eyes, pretending to check her cake bag contents.

'Mmmmm hmmmm.' She said distractedly, trying so hard not to let her eyes wander back up or betray the sudden hot flush he was causing.

Okay, so maybe he was a little too attractive.

'You could sound a little more enthusiastic about it.' He jested, a hint of that Abby mischief tone that caught her a little off guard.

'Sure whatever.' She sighed and straightened up, meeting that intense grey gaze which was very firmly locked on her face in a rather disturbing way. Knowing that this was the mature and sensible way to behave, she thrust her hand towards him reluctantly. 'Rose... Not Penny! Rose Turner and I guess, your new neighbour.' She smiled with all the effort of warmth and friendliness she could muster.

'Rob; as you know. Rob Munro, and yeah, kinda figured you were in Olivia's old place; seeing as you're her niece.' He smiled knowingly. 'Town grapevine was talking about you for weeks before you showed face.' He smiled again, having a little bit of an effect on Rose's heart rate and making her suddenly feel awkward.

'I guess that's the curse of a small town. Everyone knows everything.' She moved to try and get around him, but he turned as she did so.

'I guess I'll be seeing you around a lot more with Abby, the dance too?' He wasn't smiling anymore but his tone was still friendly and Rose felt herself soften a little. He was really trying to be the gentleman, trying to be nice and she guessed she could cut him a little slack. For Abby's sake, it would be a lot easier if she tried to get on with him.

'I guess you will; Ab's keeps trying to talk me into coming up to yours for a tea and cake fest.' She softened her tone and gave a genuine soft smile his way, catching his eye which still seemed locked on her a little too intensely.

'You should; our housekeeper makes some of the best. You're welcome anytime Penny. Would be nice to see Abby with someone; she spends too much time alone for a girl her age.' That maternal tone in his voice pretty much killed the last traces of hostility in her, she was a sucker for some genuine affection between siblings and he seemed like a protective brother. She loved Abby dearly, so he was only cementing a slight like for him now.

'She's amazing, I'm lucky to have met her and we have so much in common.' Rose beamed, smiling at the mention of her new best friend. Rob smiled too, obviously pleased.

'She had a rough time when our mother passed, I like seeing her smile again, it's been a long time since she was this happy. I guess I have you to thank for that.' Rob's distracted by the counter assistant bringing him a large box, smiling his way with doe eyes.

'There you go Mr Munro, sorry it took a while. Aggy had'nae set up the regular orders yet.' The girl blushed his way and fumbled with the box a little as he took it in one hand. Nodding down with a casual gesture, oblivious of the girls blushing and obvious crush on him; he smiled back at Rose.

'Better get these up to the church, the old biddies will eat me alive if their book club meeting is biscuit less.' He waved at the girl behind the counter, causing another wave of furious blushing and placed a hand on the small of Roses back unexpectedly. 'I'll walk you out Penny.'

Rose was too stunned to resist and too homed in on just how many tingles his touch caused, to refuse, he guided her forward out the already open door into the blinding sun before he removed his hand as he went into his pocket for car keys; it was then that Rose spotted the familiar black car parked across from them.

'Where are you parked?' He asked absentmindedly as he pressed his key, the car beeped and flashed before making a tell-tale unlocking noise. Rose looked around for a moment, mind blanked and taking a second to actually think of the response.

'I'm not... I walked here for some exercise and a change of scenery after a morning of sketching over my desk.' She moved to walk off and leave him to get to his car, but that hot firm hand came straight back to the small of her back immediately.

'I'll drop you home if you want? It's hardly out of my way, seeing as the church is practically in the manor drive.' He smiled her way, giving her no choice as he was manhandling her effectively and as much as she wanted to refuse she found her feet following him to his car and standing politely back while he deposited the box in the boot. He ushered her around to the other side and opened her door for her, guiding her in effortlessly before closing it after she slid in.

Rose suddenly felt awkward, confined in the small space as he got in and realised she would rather have walked, had stupidly allowed him to coerce her without any resistance. She had no clue how to behave around him and up until ten minutes ago, had only felt hostility towards him. Now she was somewhere between shyness and well, nervousness. It was too late to refuse a lift now, she was sitting in his overly priced man machine and already scared to touch any of the array of buttons and levers littering the dash.

'That's a really pretty dress.' He cut into her thoughts, making her blush unexpectedly as she skimmed her hands over her lap nervously, to smooth out the floral summer dress; it was knee length and a little floaty. He was putting on his seat belt and she followed suit, aware that his eyes did a small skim over her legs.

'Umm thanks, I like vintage looking clothes I guess, girly clothes.' She couldn't look at him as he started the car, a hand coming to behind her seat as he turned to look out the back window and reverse out of the parking space; he felt a little too close for comfort and her heart rate was elevated.

'It suits you. I wish Abs would dress less like a homeless kid and dress a bit more like you, she has a severe weakness for ripped jeans and t-shirts with offensive logos. Maybe you will rub off on her in time.' He winked at Rose and this time she knew for sure she blushed, annoyingly so. She couldn't help but smile though, he was right about Abby, she did have a weakness for t-shirts with tongue in cheek prints and a tad rude. She was a student and she definitely dressed the part.

'Abby is a rebel, give her time to find her own style and she will eventually outgrow all her cannabis leaf tops.' She watched the road go by, the passing scenery as he got them out of town and knew this trip would be brief. It was only 2 miles to the manor opening and hers was less than 50 yards further.

'Yeah, I guess. She's a lot like my mum was. Feisty and stubborn and loves to get a reaction from people.' He smiled again, only it didn't reach his eyes and Rose felt a little tug of sadness for him, she couldn't imagine what losing your mother would be like; the thought didn't bear thinking about as her own sweet mother's face flitted across her mind's eye.

'She is that.' Rose giggled softly, trying to avoid the topic of death, which was still a sensitive area for her too. 'I have yet to see her dressed up for the dance though, I have no idea what to expect.' Rose tried to relax back in her seat but it was proving difficult when a muscular arm was stretched beside her as he tensed it on his steering wheel and rolled up his sleeve, exposing tanned skin and well-defined forearms. He obviously worked out and Rose's instant reaction was to inhale quickly and look away.

'Knowing her, something revealing or outrageous.' He frowned and looked in his rear-view mirror, a serious look on his face.' Like I said... Abby likes a reaction.'

'In general, or does she just like winding you up?' Rose laughed, looking back at the perfect profile and square jaw. He was clean shaven but there was a hint of five o'clock shadow that gave him a rugged look.

'Oh, it's definitely to wind me up. She loves nothing more than sending me into heart failure. Payback for being a shitty brother when she was tiny.' He smiled Rose's way and then nodded as the opening to her cottage loomed before them too quickly. 'Home sweet home.'

Rose smiled and felt a tad disappointed that it was over already, from disliking him she was warming to him and wouldn't have minded a longer car ride to continue this chit chat. He pulled up in front of the cottage and jumped out as she was unclipping her belt. Coming around to open her door and give her a helping hand to get out of the low car. She felt another blush creeping up when her hand hit his and was enveloped by it as he pulled her up and out. He took the bag of confectionaries from her and walked her to her door.

Rose almost grinned with the sheer old-fashioned chivalry that was completely unexpected. Surprised with his gentlemanly manners. He waited on her unlocking her door before handing her back her bag and stooping to scoop up a suddenly appearing Muffin, who came running like a bat out of hell at the door opening.

'Whoa there tiny.' He smiled and ruffled Muffins fur. 'Cute and somehow you.' He smiled lazily back at Rose and then held Muffin out to her, accepting her little bundle of fur, who immediately went into licking overdrive, she smiled back.

'Yes, I guess he is. Thank you. For the lift.' She hesitated, unsure why this felt awkward and then held her smile frozen on her face as he made to leave.

'My pleasure Penny. Guess I will see you around.' He turned on his heel and walked off casually towards his car, the confident stride of a man with a lot of sex appeal. He turned when he got to his side of the car and waved, standing as she moved inside with a small wave of her own as she cuddled in her wriggly fluffball and shut the door to block him out, stretching at the spy hole to watch him slide into his car and expertly pull away smoothly.

Rose turned and sunk back against the door, only too aware of how her face was flushed and her breathing shallow. Her body a little too on high alert for her liking.

Okay, so he had an effect on her! She would have to be dead from the waist down not to appreciate his gorgeousness.

Chapter 5

Before long it was the day of the dance and despite being in town a lot beforehand, she never ran into Rob Munro again. Seeing him again, dressed in Black tie and in his own opulent setting made Rose shiver in anticipation; a dread overtaking her already stretched nerves. He would be on his home turf surrounded by his own friends and belongings and she would be like a fish out of water. Facing him again was not really something she was looking forward to. He had a knack for making her feel awkward and out of her depth and she wasn't entirely sure if she even liked him.

Abby had promised to wait on her out at the front entrance so she would walk her in and they had agreed on eight pm to meet. At least that way she did not have to look around nervously, trying to find a friendly face. She could walk confidently with her friend's arm and smile and look radiant instead.

Rose had woken that morning with a very strange churning feeling that followed her through the hours. Excitement and dread at the same time. She was looking forward to a proper night of wine and dancing, good music. But her heart was thumping every time she thought about that handsome face and his cold steel grey glare that did crazy things to her insides.

Now she had made more friends in the town and had Abby, she felt more confident about going, but that feeling of nervous anticipation in the back of her mind followed her. She was so restless, she could barely concentrate on anything.

She tried to sketch some ideas in her art room, tried walking Muffin to town and back to get rid of some of the pent-up energy and only felt more restless. She took a bath at lunch and slathered herself in every expensive product she owned. Shaving and moisturising, pruning and preening and throwing on a light sundress to go sit in the garden. She felt like her nerves were on edge and kept checking her watch every five minutes. Listlessly aware that she was counting the minutes until the ball began.

She had cooked a full breakfast and lunch, trying to kill time through the morning, but only picked at both, her appetite had deserted her. She had the cottage looking spotless and neat and nothing on TV held any interest for her.

Abby was helping with the big house today, so no morning visits from her either.

Maybe that's why she felt so agitated?

Maybe she needed some company that was not furry with four legs. Maybe she just needed human interaction to distract her and jumped in her car for the second trip to town that day. Poor Muffin was exhausted from their walk, so she left him asleep on the rug in the living room, snoring and dreaming of chasing some poor cat. His little legs twitching as he lay stretched on his side and small whimpers and growls as he snorted through a closed mouth.

The short car journey was pleasant as the sun still shone brightly in the sky, the weather had been glorious these past few weeks and had given her such a deep tan and healthy colour in her face.

She spent half an hour in Bella's bakery and finally reunited with the woman after all these years when she popped in to check on things. Lots of laughs and cuddles and reminiscing. The large round woman was exactly as she remembered, only with a few greyer hairs and laughter lines. The conversation pulled towards Olivia and Bella gave her many condolences and a bag of cream confectionaries.

From there she found the church was having an outdoor stall in the town centre and selling jumble and books. That killed a lot of time and lots of small talk with the knitting club who loved nothing more than to shower Rose in affection. They called her their 'adopted grandchild.' They gave her a free crochet mug mat for her desk and a bag of dog cookies for the now famous Muffin.

Everyone in town loved Muffin, her small furry friend. Always happy to see him and shower him with smooches and hugs, treats under the table. They liked to think Rose couldn't see, but she chose to turn a blind eye. Although of late his little pot belly was starting to become obvious and she would soon have to kerb all these extra day time treats.

Rose wandered around for a bit, window shopping and killing time. Lost in her own thoughts. Not really paying attention, but trying to stretch out her day a little longer rather than going back to clock watching at home and pacing her rugs until they were threadbare.

She was carrying a large beach bag with a rainbow stripe print, which held all her purchases and gifts; her long lemon sundress touched the ground as she walked, flowing loosely around her legs. It had a fitted strappy bodice showing off her tanned shoulders and arms and her slim figure well. It was doing a great job of making her feel cool in the baking heat too. Her long brown hair hung around her shoulders in soft gentle waves, thanks to her new curling iron and her face, as usual, with minimal makeup and her favourite cherry lip balm which stained her full pout to a slight rosy tint.

She looked at her reflection in a boutique mirror and admired the change in her since coming here. It wasn't just the tan. It was her whole being. She looked happier, healthier, more relaxed; she fitted with this country living more than she ever fitted with the busy city streets and clogged air. Her mood had generally been lighter and more carefree. The smog free air, making her feel like she could really breathe living here.

She was unaware of how carefree and elegant she looked as she wandered about, unaware that eyes had been watching her from afar and as she drew ever closer to them, they did not dare to interrupt her. She looked so lost in thought and stunningly beautiful.

She became aware of the museum looming above her as she wandered aimlessly about. Raising her eyes up, she took in the large ancient building with its grey stone walls and gothic arched entranceway. The way it stretched above her like a massive foreboding castle, so dark against the bright surroundings.

Huge banners gently flapped in the breeze, announcing the current exhibition and she felt inclined to go in. Something pulling her towards the dark, shadowy entrance. The museum mainly held a lot of Scottish artefacts and history, but the side hall changed every few months to bring in new visitors. Today the banner displayed a modern art-themed exhibition from some aspiring artist who had been a local once. The artwork hinted at abstract, but she still felt the intrigue enough to venture on. She hesitated about going in, then took the plunge and walked forward.

'Penelope.' the warm tones in his voice had an instant impact and she stopped. That familiar lurch in her breastbone. Swinging round to see where it came from. He was perched on a stone planter by the door in the shade. She had not seen him sitting there.

God knows how long he had been watching her?

He had on another white shirt, unbuttoned at the collar and sleeves pushed up, exposing those rather hunky arms, a pair of faded jeans and white trainers. Practically every time she saw him, he was in varying degrees of formal meets casual, which somehow only added to his charm and he had on sunglasses shielding those stormy grey eyes from sight. She felt a nudge of disappointment that his best feature was shielded from view. His short black hair was ruffled on top carelessly, casually styled. Unlike those London men with their shiny puffed hair do's and manicured hands. He looked relaxed and smiled. Thousand-watt voltage sprang from that smile and all Rose could do was dive into her bag to fake look for something so very important she instantly needed it. She was aware that it had become instantly difficult to breathe normally.

'Rob.' She kept her tone even and eyes down, intent on her hands and there rummaging. Trying to keep herself calm and sane with such a mundane task as sorting through, looking for a plausible item to drag out. 'And my name is Rose!' She was keeping the irritation out of her voice. Trying to sound, light and nonchalant. Of course, she did not want him to know how much he annoyed her using that stupid pet name, hadn't she already made it clear that it was not her name. Her heart was pounding through her chest, which annoyed her immensely.

Stupid reactions to this man!

'I know!' a voice deep and smooth, sexy. She heard him slide off the planter and her heart beat upped a gear, her fingers began trembling as she sensed him moving closer. Aware that she was fumbling.

'I just think Penelope suits you.'

She ignored him. Well tried to. Cursing inwardly as she still fumbled in her bag. Finally locating her sunglasses, she pulled them out and pushed them on, shielding her eyes and sweeping her hair back from her face in a bid to look relaxed and unaffected. Throwing on a sarcastic smile, she marched away from him into the museum, annoyed with how juvenile he made her feel.

'Well have a wonderful day, Mr Munro. Would love to stay and chat but I want to see this exhibit before I need to head home.' She smiled and made for the Museum doors quickly. Unaware that he was grinning at her sudden need for eyewear when entering a building away from the sun. Or the way he was looking her up and down . She heard him call out a goodbye as she practically hoofed away from him and in return threw up a hand in a wave that implied indifference; she would be damned if she let him see how much he got to her. Her heart rate was competing in the Olympics and she felt slightly faint.

Oh my god, why did this guy invoke such trauma to her just by being near?

She immediately dashed behind a pillar at the open wooden door and turned to peek out. He was walking away. That manly walk that real guys have when it's not really a swagger but not really a weak girly trot. Just a typical guy walk, all wide shoulders and strong legs and going about his day, unaware of the crazy woman peeking out at him from the darkness of the building.

What was he doing here anyway? Did he not have a dance to organise? to oversee? To lord over?

She pulled herself away as he turned out of sight, leaning back against the wall behind her to gather herself and take some deep breaths. Sighing as she tried to push the picture of his tight, jean clad butt, out of her mind's eye. Cursing herself at the lack of ability to do so. The coldness of the stone in this dark corner, tucked behind the pillar, made her feel instantly calmer. Hidden from his view. Somehow sobering and grounding her. She really hated the way he caused her to self-implode like this at every meeting. If he knew how much he affected her he would probably enjoy it. He seemed like the kind of guy who would get a kick out of it. She pulled her glasses back off her face and threw them in her bag.

Excellent choice Rose! Sunglasses in a dark building! Could you be any more obvious?

She smoothed down her dress and bravely walked back into the light of the room. Acting as though nothing had happened. Hiding in the shadows was completely normal. She looked around the vast hall, deserted on such a sweltering day and tried to find some poster or sign with information or at least directions to the art exhibit.

While in Rome!

There were large wooden doors to the left and right, but both firmly shut with No entry signs screwed in place. She figured she would kill some time surrounded by art, which always had such a soothing effect, and try and forget what that smooth voice and dazzling smile had done to her. Not that it had been an effect in a good way. Hell no! It rattled her in a really, really bad way. In a 'he's so annoying and irritating' way. Such a jerk.

A jerk with a nice ass in a pair of jeans, though.

Damn him!

Her heart beat was finally trying to regain its previous calm rhythm, but her hands were still trembling. She pushed it away and focused ahead. The large hall echoed as her sandals clip-clopped across to a wall mounted glass case at the far end with huge welcome signs hanging from the ceiling. Inside all the information she had been seeking and an array of small artefacts surrounded the posters and brass etched signs on glass floating shelves. There was a door off to her left with an 'Office' plaque above and a red rope stretched across, preventing her from venturing further. There was a glass sliding window beside the glass case, with a large etched sign reading 'Admissions' above it and a clearly placed bell to ring for assistance. The entry fees were printed on a laminated A4 card, propped up in the sliding window and a cheery old lady with curly grey hair was sitting inside with her nose stuck in some trashy novel. Rather than ring the bell Rose instead gently knocked on the glass smiling.

Once She had purchased her entry ticket the lady came out and moved the rope for her to pass and pointed her in the direction she had been seeking. The museum was much like most she had been in. Large, old world, airy buildings with polished floors, old wood stairs and beams, glass cabinets and that distinct musty smell of old things. Large gothic windows kept the place bright and were draped with heavy red curtains with gold tassels. The windows, however, were frosted so she could not see out into the surroundings. That familiar echoed noise that caused people to whisper as she moved around the polished floors slowly.

The halls she passed through had the odd browsing tourist, peering into the lines of cases and displays. She could hear some sort of documentary film playing somewhere in another room, the noise faintly echoing throughout and the sounds of a battle thrashing to some bagpipe music. Overall the place was deserted.

The art exhibit was in one of the rear halls, at the furthest part of the museum, a huge white walled room with soft floaty music gently pouring over you as you entered. There was a table set up with pictures and information about the artist, and a pile of brochures. She browsed the pamphlet quickly, taking in the man's mature face and grey hair, his background history and the basis behind his work before turning and strolling eagerly into the room. There were huge abstract paintings on the walls and large sculptures stood on plinths dotted around. Nothing she could identify as a real object just more abstract design made from various mediums in a flowing graduation of colour. It was almost as though someone had melted a wax rainbow and frozen it mid-pour. He seemed to like working through colour graduations, sometimes sticking to one colour and working through tones and sometimes the entire spectrum running from one blended colour to another. She found herself captivated by all the colours and fluidity in his work, like being pulled into a colourful dream in a magical wonderland made of melted things. She could see why a lot of his words related to flowing and freedom in the descriptive plaques. Standing to ponder a large, almost sunset like pieces on a stand in the corner and lost in thought when a voice interrupted her.

'Afternoon Ma'am, you like that one?' It was an easy American drawl, southern sounding and male. She was slightly startled, but smiled, covering her reactions and keeping her focus on the art piece.

'Yes, there's something about it, like you're standing on a tropical beach watching the sun come up.' She kept her gaze on the painting as the voice came closer and moved to her side.

He was a very tall, a very muscular blonde American. Classically handsome in that chiselled American way, with piercing blue eyes. His hair was tied back in a ponytail and immediately made her think of the movie Thor. She had to admit, he was pretty hot. All women loved a bit of hunky eye candy and this one was appreciated.

'The artist is my uncle' He smiled, showing some overly pearly whites and a dazzling cheeky smile. She smiled back, blushing slightly. Aware that all good-looking men had the ability to make her feel awkward. Maybe it was the ugly duckling syndrome from being a none too attractive child in puberty.

'So, is that why you're here? Are you the muscle to make sure people admire his work?' she laughed and turned more towards this handsome stranger, feeling truly geeky in mentioning his muscles in such a lame line.

'Something like that.' He was standing with his hands behind his back, his chest straining behind a grey t-shirt with a designer logo and a pair of jeans straining at his footballer's thighs. 'I came with him for the trip when they asked him to show his work here'

'He stays in the USA now then?'

'Yeah, he moved out there a few years ago, he married my aunt when she came over for a little Scottish holiday and they spent a long time living here before heading back to the states' He smiled Rose's way, his eyes skimming her appreciatively and Rose ignored the slight feeling of uneasiness.

'I guess you're close then, seeing as you came with him?' She tried to ignore the way he was fixated on the tight bodice of her dress and crossed her arms over her waist in a bid to cover up a little.

'Yeah, we are. He's a good guy and I needed a break. I have an injury that's healing. ' He pointed down to his knee in a manner which suggested he probably was someone who played football, the build on him suggested American football.

'I couldn't resist a trip to Scotland to see some castles and haggis.' his winning smile again had her smiling too, putting her back at ease and forgiving the way he had been ogling her; there was something about his easy manner and a quick smile that made Rose feel a little at ease. Maybe it was just a pretty face had the ability to make you relax, although that seemed to be the opposite for Rob Munro, that handsome face most certainly didn't make her feel at ease.

He walked with her to the next painting, explaining his injury more and his sabbatical. He was from Arizona, hence the southern drawl and was a career sportsman. He seemed to have a celebrity status back home and was enjoying the peace and quiet of being a no one in this country. He also seemed to enjoy talking about himself without coaxing, somehow Rose found it a little arrogant.

They admired the next work of art briefly, pointing out the colours and flow of the piece before moving on quickly, Rose was starting to feel listless again and wanted him to let her browse alone again.

He seemed like a decent guy, if not a little bit too self-absorbed. He made all the right noises and acted like an adult anyway. His name was Matt... Very American! and he was twenty-nine, single and owned his own ranch. Rose could not help but think of a tonne of Mills and Boon romance books that reeked of romantic heroes like him, and the very thought made her blush a little more. It was so stupid.

He was hanging out at the museum while his uncle was upstairs in one of the curator's offices, discussing some minute details over a painting that had been offered for sale. He was his driver and bodyguard, not that he needed it, but the pretence of his needing his nephew stopped Matt feeling like a third wheel.

Rose was trying to wander off and put space between them unsuccessfully when Matt's uncle appeared with a tall woman at the door. Rose was immediately captivated by the woman's tailored perfection, cream and black Chanel suit on her tall supermodel body, her dark red curls falling like a tumbling brook from the top of her head and her glittering green almond eyes. Black expertly applied winged eyeliner set in a pale flawless skin with peachy tones and a spattering of freckles. Her pouty mouth was stained with dark red lipstick giving her a seductive yet dominating appeal. She was stunning in a very magical fairy-like way meets American vogue, business woman of the year. How you would imagine a wood nymph or a naughty sexy pixie to look if she was from New York.

She had on black high stiletto heels, peeking under her cream slacks and killer French manicured nails in deadly points, tipped with black. She oozed class and sophistication and immediately drew you under a spell at her presence. She gushed over Matt in an insincere tone, exposing ample cleavage under her suit jacket and a hint of black lace and a satin camisole as she spread her arms to kiss his cheeks in a very French debutante manner; almost enveloping them all in her expensive perfume. Her accent was only subtly Scottish, with an air of upper class and silky smooth like honey. She screamed sex and allure with every word, breath and movement. It was almost impossible not to be drawn in by her.

Matt did not seem overly susceptible to her charms, wary almost, and kept his distance once she released him from her embrace. He almost seemed hostile towards her.

She introduced herself to Rose as Morag Spencer, the curator of the museum, then dismissed her with a smile before turning her attentions to the men. It was obvious Rose was in the way and the patron was sending her every female signal that it was time to go.

Maybe not so alluring after all.

Rose excused herself, feeling a wave of unwelcome warmth as Matt placed his large hand on her arm, pulling her over to kiss her cheek rather surprisingly before saying goodbye. It felt strange to have a stranger's touch on her skin. She was not sure she liked it. She figured back home that was a normal action to part ways, but it had knocked her for six. His aftershave still lingered around her face, slightly catching in her throat as she left the building in a weird mood. Unsure why the handsome man's brief kiss had unsettled her. It seemed an innocent enough gesture. Common maybe where he was from.

She could not remember finding her car or driving home that afternoon, lost somewhere in daydreams and thoughts of large American men running around the football field, except it was not Matts' face she was envisioning. Instead someone with decidedly darker looks and greyer eyes.

* * *

Muffin was thrilled to see her, acting as though they had been separated for months and throwing his tiny furry self all over her like a hyper-rodent on heat. His small pink tongue attacking her hands and face ferociously when she tried to sit down on her bed. She barely had time to rustle up something to eat before she needed to start getting ready and realised her answer machine was flashing with a tonne of messages.

Every single one of them was from Abby. Checking in. Sharing excitement. Confirming eight pm at the front car park. Describing her final choice of dress and finally wishing her luck. Every call ended with 'Don't need to call me back. I'll see you there'. Rose laughed.

She figured Abby was as restless as her and lack of physical contact today was turning her into a phone stalker. Rose pulled out her mobile, realising it was switched off with a dead battery and threw it on her bed.

Ok, so she had to get herself together.

She had plenty of time to relax and do her hair and makeup, pull out her new dress which had arrived a few days ago. Locals had told her that the dance was very formal, evening gowns and black bow tie. It was all rather exciting.

She had chosen a long, pale dress, in ivory with layers of puffy chiffon in an over the knee length skirt, giving it an almost fairy-tale princess feel. It puffed out just enough to look beautiful, but not so much she looked like a cloud. The bodice was fitted and studded with pearls, crystals and embroidery, rather subtly along the sweetheart neckline in matching ivory. Its straps were wide forming little cap sleeves, but leaving her shoulders bare. When she had tried it on for the very first time, Abby had gasped in awe. She had worried it was a little too bride to be, but Abby assured her that her tanned skin and dark hair tumbling down from a romantic up style would make it look perfect. She had pale shoes in a darker shade with high heels and peep toes, made from a similar satin to the bodice on her feet that made her long legs look amazing. Matching clutch bag and her newly polished pearl coloured toenails and manicure finished the look.

Abby had helped her practice a few simple up do's on her hair and her makeup was pure nineteen fifties glam tonight. Black-winged eyeliner, subtle blush and rose coloured almost nude lips, pouting at full capacity. Her hair, although mostly loose curls, was pinned up at the nape of her neck with a small vintage crystal clasp and had let small tendrils fall and hang prettily around her face and ears. She looked every bit the princess from a romantic fairy-tale. She suited romantic vintage clothes, somehow, they made her look even more beautiful.

Pulling on a cream cashmere coat her mother had given her for her last birthday in London, she looked every bit Audrey Hepburn.

She took a few deep breaths, checking the time and putting both her purse and invitation into her bag. She had decided to drive to the dance, but Abby had promised her a taxi to return; leaving her free tonight to get merry and dance the night into drunken oblivion. Her stomach was doing a crazy Rhumba and churning with nerves by the time she pulled into the long manor road. Other cars were coming and going, lots of hustle and bustle both on the road and the huge wide car park at the doors. Ushers were signalling for cars to park and deposit guests and others were driving cars off the wide space onto a sectioned off lawn as a makeshift car park.

Fairy lights were hung in all the surrounding trees and the fountain in the centre had floating candles and magical lights draped all over. A small orchestra was set up at the entrance, welcoming people with soothing music. It was so opulent and classy that it was breath-taking and she had not even ventured inside. Rose parked off to the side of the house in the area, Abby had described to her, that way her car would be out of the way for an overnight stay and close enough to the house to leave her coat for later.

As soon as she exited her car, Abby was by her side screaming with delight and twirling her around, swarming her with compliments on how beautiful she looked. When she slid her coat off and dropped it into her car seat Abby began wolf whistling and again the spinning and turning while she admired her dress. She was caught up in her enthusiasm and started giggling with excitement.

'You my beauty, are going to knock men's eyes out tonight.' Abby giggled and once again twirled Rose under her arm.

Abby was dressed in a long satin gown in a gorgeous emerald green. It was slinky and clingy in all the right places and swept the floor as she walked, opening a slit from floor to thigh on her left leg. It had a draped neckline revealing her modest cleavage and thin straps on her dainty shoulders. It made the girls pale skin and raven hair even more stunning. And she complimented her friend with the same enthusiasm she had received. It made her look so much older than her nineteen years and it tugged at Rose's heart a little to see the woman before her. Rob had been accurate with his 'revealing or outrageous' prediction; this was certainly revealing, but still classy and Abby looked stunning.

'Talk about me...Look at you Ab's. You are the belle of the ball.' Rose beamed, looping arms and excitedly toddling on heels towards the bustling entranceway.

'Aww shucks, you make me blush' Abby jested and squeezed Rose's arm a little tighter. 'All ready for a night of schmoozing and boozing Miss Turner?' Abby's eyes twinkled merrily.

'Definitely, I need a good night more than anything.' Rose was swept up in the excitement now and her nerves were tingling.

As they entered the grand stone stairs past the orchestra Rose could see even the green of Abby's eyes seemed to have darkened to the colour of the dress, and her peachy, almost natural lipstick, made her seem so much more seductive. She could not tell her enough how beautiful she looked and how every young man's head turned as they walked through the hall into the main ballroom. Unaware the glances were not just for Abby.

The air was buzzing with excitement and chatter. Groups of over excited happy people at every turn, a huge turnout already. Grand chandeliers hung low, illuminating the room with a magical glow, tables set up with crisp linens at one end and extravagant lily and rose centrepieces. A vast dance floor with glittery lights and floral arrangements dotted all over on stands and a wide sweeping buffet table full of delicious looking hors d'oeuvres. It was the most elegant room she had ever seen and she mentally tried to work out how much money could they surely raise for the charity when spending so much on the decor, music and food.

There was another orchestra set up in one corner on a stand, playing vaguely familiar songs with a classical twist. The entire atmosphere brought goose bumps of excitement to Rose as she explored the food table with Abby, admiring all the delicious morsels on offer. There was everything from seafood, delicious meats and cold pasta, to bowls of salads with dressing and chicken wings. There were rolled pastries and things on sticks she could not even identify and of course a huge mountain of champagne glasses beside an array of miniature desserts.

Abby nudged her as handsome men in black bow ties and crisp suits walked by, winking at the girls; giggling girls in puffy dresses and tightly pinned hair do's followed with friendly grins. There were more people here than Rose knew even lived in this area and half of them were completely new to her. Rose's eyes wandered around the room, taking in the people, the beautiful clothes, sparkly accessories and the elegant setting. She was aware of the way her eyes were searching every dark-haired males face as they jumped from one to the other. No matter how much she told herself to stop it, it was like she had little control and the urge to seek him out carried on regardless.

When her eyes met with a tall straight back of a tailored black jacket over wide shoulders, a male with cropped black hair and a tanned strong neck, her stomach fluttered and her heart skipped a beat. She would recognise him even from the back and at a distance and that only disturbed her more. Abby was chatting at hyper-speed in her ear and handing her a champagne glass filled with slightly pink bubbly liquid, unaware of her friend's sudden silence. Rose kept glancing towards his back, unsure how to react.

To avoid? To go over? To pretend she had not seen him?

As she was contemplating what to do he turned away from the group of people he was with and Rose got to see his face properly. A slight change in her heartbeat. Unable to look away. He was looking out onto the sea of people with a smile on his face, someone was still talking to him and his attention was wherever they were pointing. His handsome face looked even more chiselled in the dim lights and his white shirt, black bow tie and jacket, made him more like James bond than Laird of the manor. He looked so effortlessly at ease. He suited the whole bow tie, dinner jacket, set up and Rose could barely feel her knees anymore. Her breath had caught in her chest and suddenly made her feel lightheaded.

God dammit.

How could she be so stupid? How could she not realise that every time she reacted to this man in this way her body was trying to tell her something apparently obvious.

She had a stinking huge crush on him!

Like a hormonal teenager who followed around the high school heartthrob. Suddenly aware of this resounding fact made her feel immediately vulnerable, confused and emotional all at the same time. Like a light being switched on in a dark room, only to find you're naked on a stage in front of strangers! Completely shocked at her own discovery and then an inward groan at how incredibly dumb she was. She winced, turning herself to the buffet and trying to reel in the crazy thoughts that were spilling all over her dress and table like a severed artery.

Jesus!... What the hell?... How could she be so blind?

Abby was lost in conversation with an elderly woman to her side over crab sticks and was oblivious to her friend's sudden life altering realisation, or the sheer crumpling effect it had had on her posture and state of mind. She glanced back, trying to catch sight of Rob again, just to be sure he did in fact cause these fluttering's, lack of breath and insane light-headedness. This insane need to beat him round the head anytime he appeared charming and stopped her in her tracks.

That was her mind's way of highlighting how irresistible he was to her, surely?

Rob was still in the same spot as he had been seconds ago, looking like he was bathed in angelic light. If it was possible to have rainbows indoors, she would have seen one arcing over him. She was pretty sure she was seeing stars already. Maybe that was just the lack of oxygen as breathing was near impossible at that moment.

He turned slightly and revealed that, latched most purposely to his arm, was a tall, curly haired redhead, with a supermodel body poured into a figure hugging cream dress. Slit in all the right places, leaving nothing to the imagination. Morag Spencer; overly sexed museum curator was possessively spilling over Rob in an obvious way!

Rose felt the last of her breath escape her. A sudden thud to the chest and prickling tingles ran the length of her body. Deer in the headlights sprang to mind. Rose dropped her glass of champagne, seemingly removed from the actions of her own limbs and it snapped her back to reality.

Abby cursed and jumped away from the shattering glass, as both girls then swept down to start mopping the mess with napkins in a rather frantic manner. Rose felt her bottom lip start to tremble as her eyes welled up, but they were ushered aside by two waiting staff in uniforms and handed a new glass of champagne. She had lost control of her faculties in the most juvenile way, aware she was literally losing her calm facade and turning into a bowl of melting jelly.

'I need to go to the bathroom and clean this.' she couldn't look Abby in the eye, afraid the tears would start tumbling, so kept her gaze fixed on the dampness on her floaty skirt and tried so hard to behave normally. Abby took her hand and dragged her off in the direction of the bathroom

'Come on babe I'll help!'. Abby smiled warmly and Rose could do nothing but allow herself to be pulled along. She felt numb and distraught, all at the same time.

Rose began panicking as she realised their route took them directly into Rob's path and as his eyes met hers, his expression changed, from a cheery guy at a party to sudden recognition and something else. Something she couldn't fathom. An instant moment passing between them as eyes locked. She was fighting back every single emotion any hormonal woman had ever met, trying to keep a straight face while being dragged by an overzealous slightly tipsy teen. Trying to keep her face blank in an effort to get past a guy she had only just discovered she had a massive almighty longing for.

For the love of god!

Rob reached out and caught hold of her by the waist in a lightning flash move, halting her abruptly. Something he seemed to just love doing was putting hands on her. His halting them stopped Abby in her tracks, who almost ripped Rose's arm off.

'What happened?' Rob's eyes flitted across Roses dress, alarmingly close and still holding onto her. She could barely formulate a response.

'We had a little spill, that's all.' Rose tried to sound, light and upbeat, but she could not bring her gaze to meet his. Her whole focus was on the hot hand placed across her abdomen through the thin satin material at her waist. No longer bringing fury to her body, but instead making her melt into a puddle and causing an inability to function. She liked it better when she thought his touch irritated her. He had moved close enough that she could feel his breath on her hair and his aftershave surrounded her senses. It was as if the whole room had ceased to exist and they were alone in a little-cocooned bubble.

'Abby use one of the en-suites upstairs. You know how busy the ladies room will be right now.' his voice was sliding over her like toffee sauce on hot apple pie, she did not want to move, speak. or even look up. She heard Abby reply in agreement before his voice turned back to her above her head.

'You look really beautiful Rose...Really... Just amazing.' He almost whispered those words in her ear as her brain manically realised it was the first time he had said her actual name.

'Not Penelope?' Were the only words she could formulate with him this close to her face. Almost brave enough to meet his gaze, she instead lifted her chin high enough to focus on his bow tie. Aware that now her forehead was almost touching his chin, the closeness sending goosebumps in every direction. It was almost impossible to breathe normally, her hands trembling once again. He really did turn her into a nervous wreck with very minimum effort.

'Not tonight.' There was something softer in his tone, he sounded breathy and he was seriously affecting her ability to breathe 'Tonight, just Rose.'

As though sensing something unjust going on, the tall, slender Morag, appeared, pulling at his arm, thus releasing his hand on Rose and pulling him away from her.

'Rooooobb baby, come dance with me. I want to be wrapped up in these beefy arms already.' She crooned in a sickly-sweet baby voice and for a moment Rose thought she saw Rob grimace. It was so fleeting that she almost missed it and couldn't be sure she even saw it at all.

Sudden chill where warmth had once been, Rose looked away and then back, catching his eye as he turned her way for a brief glimpse. Something translated between them instantly, in that mere second. His normally light grey eyes were dark and loaded, but she could not fathom the message or the look. Then he was turning and gone and Abby was pulling her towards the hall; her emotion caught in her throat, threatening to choke her. Looking back at him as she was dragged away by Abby and he was dragged away by Morag, she watched him disappear into the crowd. Taking her heart with him.

Chapter 6

Upstairs in the house was a lot less grandeur and old fashioned. It was more modern and tasteful, like Hollywood celebrity homes. Unexpected and airy above the noise and chaos below; Abby dragged her along a long row of doors to her own and unlocked it.

'Rob made us all get locks on the doors to our personal rooms last year.' She smiled, shaking her key so that it jingled, that dazzling beautiful smile aimed at Rose.' When people get a bit drunk they tend to go wandering, and although nothing has ever been taken from here, it's the thought of old drunk people having nookie in my room that bothered him.' she laughed and led the way into a pink and cream decorated boudoir. Rose smiled in response, but she was far from feeling like it.

The cool, calm exterior was quick at having a soothing effect on her, providing her with a much-needed breathing space. Abby's room was everything Rose had imagined it would be. Frilly, girly, almost princess-like in a childish way. Yet surprisingly, a bookcase full of trashy novels and Jackie Collins books. In a way showcased the innocent, naïve side of Abby perfectly, while hinting at the naughty unseen side too. A girl stuck somewhere between childhood and womanhood, with a foot firmly planted on both sides.

The huge four poster bed layered with fluffy throws, pink sheets and satin cushions was draped in white voiles, dotted with fairy lights and the floor was scattered with the contents of her makeup drawer on a plush white fluffy rug.

Her bathroom was white and modern with the odd hints of pinks in towels and accessories, matching the room and Rose immediately fell in love again, with this girl, and her layers of personality. They were more alike than she could ever imagine.

The girls sponged off Rose's dress, easily removing the champagne and patting it dry with thick fluffy towels in the large bathroom. Rose was beginning to regain her control and smooth away the craziness of being in his presence, rationalising internally that she was being stupid and it was nothing more than a silly school girl crush. She had no reason to feel upset about Morag, it was obvious that someone like him would be with someone like that. Rose was no competition at all, not that he had implied she could be.

It did not take long with the help of a hair dryer to remove all evidence of the mishap and Abby teased Rose for her clumsiness. Something inside held her back from telling Abby exactly what had caused her clumsiness, and although she was longing to ask about Morag, something stopped her. The quietness up here was a welcome break and gave Rose enough time to pull herself back together again.

She was being so stupid. She barely knew him at all, and what did she know? They couldn't stand each other's company for more than forty seconds without arguing! Five Seconds of him whispering compliments and she was suddenly a bowl of goo!

She did not need this drama or craziness in her first month of her new home and he was the Laird for goodness sakes. If anything, it could make living here impossible, not to mention drive away her new best friend and that would break Rose's heart. It would be a disaster and such a mess if she couldn't stop fixating on him in such a childish manner.

Giving herself an internal talking too, while the girls touched up their hair and makeup, she pulled on the normal Rose persona and straightened her back. A new resolve to get a bloody grip on herself and have an enjoyable time. No Rob drama for her tonight, she would just have to wear blinkers and close her eyes, anytime he passed with his overly sexual date!

* * *

Back down in the hall, the room was alive with dancing and laughter. The sounds competing with the orchestra and everything was in full swing. There was to be an auction soon, selling donated items from local businesses and then afterwards, there was to be a human raffle! Rose found this hilarious; many men and women in the community had put their names forward, offering to be slaves for a day and everyone had bought tickets at the door. Rose herself, caught by the women with the tickets, bought a few strips in the name of raising money then tucked them into her bag for safe keeping. She had scrawled her name quickly across the book, telling herself it was pointless. She never won anything in raffles or tombola's.

Abby dragged her up a few times to dance. Sometimes young men intervened, pulling them off to dance beside each other and Rose soon brushed off her school Scottish dancing skills and joined in screaming with laughter. Rose soon forgot about her earlier mental breakdown and was so lost in having a great time, dancing, eating and sipping bubbly that she really got lost in the atmosphere.

When a familiar blonde haired hotty pulled her over to dance, she almost didn't recognise him. At first, the tailored suit and cut hair, threw her, but that southern drawl immediately brought her back to reality. Matt looked so different with his newly spiked hair.

'What do you think Miss Rose?' He bent and ran a hand across his hair, Rose felt obliged to do the same, considering he was leaning in her face, running her fingers across the jaggy surface as he bent down like a school kid, showing off his new toy.

'Very nice. A little bit of a makeover?' She smiled and pulled back, feeling a little too claustrophobic with how close he was to her. It was obvious he had been on the whisky already, he was very merry and seemed to have a lot less inhibitions than there meeting at the museum.

'Fancied a change; all you Scots seem to prefer short hair over here.' He winked at her and moved a little closer, sliding arms around her waist rather forwardly. Rose squirmed and tried for a smile, giggle and wriggle to get loose but he only pulled her against him.

'Dance with me Miss Rose.' His mouth came a little too near her face and she leaned back to gain some space.

'Doesn't look like you're giving me any choice in the matter.' She smiled through gritted teeth, trying again to loosen his hold but he seemed oblivious to her discomfort.

'I can't pass up having the prettiest girl in the room in my arms, can I?' He again pulled her hard against him and Rose realised this was futile. She didn't want to be rude and cause a scene, despite not really wanting to be stuck in this American Thor's overly muscular arms, she knew a dance was harmless.

He swung her around the floor to a fast-paced jig as soon as the music started, despite her protests to dance, and dragged her heaving and panting back up to him when she tried to escape. Abby was wrapped in the arms of a hefty younger lad with strawberry blonde hair and farmer's rosy cheeks, and offered no salvation for poor Rose. Abby was practically nose to nose with him as he was telling her something so obviously interesting, her eyes were locked with his. A sizzle of chemistry between them that signalled Abby would be no help for a while and Rose felt completely out of her depth.

Rose felt uneasy as Matt pulled her into him for the slow smooch song, not that she had managed to evade his grip even for a minute, but at least a fast-paced song had offered her some body space, this song however seemed to give him an excuse to haul her against him hard. It felt weird and awkward being held against his torso. When he locked her fingers in his huge bear hand and pulled them to his mouth to nibble, she couldn't resist the urge to glance around wondering where Rob was. Almost praying for anyone to save her, she squirmed her hand free and tried again to wiggle some room between them with no avail.

Like casting out a safety net and looking to see dry land, she looked out across the room again, praying for a glimpse of Rob to distract her from her fate worse than death. She caught his eye across the room momentarily, unable to read the expression on his face, but he was facing this way, watching the dancers, watching her. His overly slutty, serpent lady, practically humping his leg. She was whispering something in his ear and stroking his cheek with her long red fingernails as he stared practically blankly at the dancers. He seemed oblivious to the sweet nothings being whispered at him. His eyes focused intently on her.

Rose felt a shiver run up inside her and turned back to concentrate on what Matt was saying loudly into the side of her face. It was so hard to concentrate, aware of eyes burning into her from across the room, aware that he was watching her and that she had no idea of a single thing Matt had said for the last three minutes. She had been so lost in her own brain and he was now staring at her in a really odd way.

'What now?... Sorry, the music...I didn't hear?' She focused back in his face apologetically.

'I said... What about you let me walk you home after this? I heard you live close by?' He had a smarmy kind of smile on his face, and his eyes were narrowed lustily. His focus was on her mouth and making it blatantly obvious where his mind was heading. Rose immediately felt her stomach drop from its happy nesting place to the floor and her face went cold as the blood escaped from the closest orifice.

Panic! Cringe!

He wanted to take her home. She knew only too well in grown up terms what that meant!

Shit, shit, shit.

Rose wasn't one to have random one night stands, even with hot muscular American romance heroes. Especially not with ones who had a look of a predator about to devour some innocent prey. She was physically beginning to recoil. Even without a stinking crush on another hot man, she still wouldn't have been inclined to do so.

She began making fumbling excuses about staying with Abby tonight and maybe another time.

Like never!

Rose's eternal need to be polite was sometimes a curse and wished she had Abby's blunt ability to tell people to get lost.

She was almost willing the song to end, to give her an excuse to bolt from his overzealous grip to the lady's room. He was not buying any of it and holding her a little too close for comfort, his mouth descending, no matter how much she turned and tried to dodge it. The song was incredibly long and he was taking no form of NO as an answer.

Oh my god, how the heck was she going to get out of this one?

His grip was like a vice and he had no intention of letting her flee.

'Can I cut in?' like a warm sunrise over a chilly morning. That familiar voice coming over her, bringing with it the effect it always seemed to have on her. Melting her bones. Rob's voice stayed her crazy manic panic. He expertly manoeuvred the pair apart, effortlessly shielding Rose behind his body in one swift move. His height and build equalling that of Matt. 'Sorry mate, we just have something to discuss that can't wait!...Business!' He said smoothly to the other man with a cheeky tone to his voice, a tone that also carried a hint of authority.

Matt shrugged and dived forward, planting a kiss on Roses' cheek before informing her he would be at the bar when she was done. It was obvious he wasn't going to argue with Rob, but he was still trying to make a claim on Rose. She resisted the urge to wipe her face in revolt. Instead faking a smile and shuddering inwardly.

Rose almost melted into Rob's arms with relief as he turned her, pulling her into dance against him, a lot softer than the yank had been, a lot more welcoming too. Even though she barely knew him there was something about being in his arms that felt familiar, that his presence made her feel safe and at home. No awkwardness or uneasiness. Just a sense of belonging. And of course, a rising heat deep down inside her that came from being hot for his body. A complete contrast to how she had felt with Matt wrapped around her.

Panic dispersed, nerves calmed; the noise drowning into the background with her tipsy mood returned. He was watching Matt walk away across the crowded floor and not meeting her gaze just yet. Giving her time to revel in the closeness; to gaze at his perfect profile and the way his eyes changed tone almost every time his mood did. The smooth curve of his neck down to his wide strong shoulders and the perfect cut of his tailored suit.

As soon as he was satisfied, he turned his attention back to her. Locking her eyes with his and lowering his face towards her so they were close enough to talk over the music; manoeuvring her expertly, slow and steady. It was obvious this was not his first dance as he took control and made her feel like a 'Strictly come dancing' contestant. She had to reel her eyes back in, aware that she should stop looking at him like prize meat before he noticed.

'Business?' her voice sounded so childlike and pathetic, she wanted to slap herself for being so transparent. She needed to reel her faculties back in and not make it so god damn obvious. The steel grey eyes locked with her own chocolate brown ones intensely and a smile appeared

'You don't miss a trick do you Pen…? Rose!' He spun her in time with other dancers and pulled her back, taking her breath away and letting her feel the strength straining under his clothed body. He could pull her around effortlessly, with a grace and ease that made her feel like she was floating on air. His hands, causing a delicious heat where he laid them and the sheer graze of brushing against him had her stomach fluttering. Her lower body warming up with a little too much longing. She had never met a man who could physically turn her on with the briefest of touches or looks, without even meaning too. He smelled strongly of a delicious designer aftershave and just the closeness to him was like a drug, making her feel giddy and giggly, breathless and carefree.

'You looked like you needed rescuing from him. Figured I would be your hero.' He smiled down at her, sliding her closer as the tempo slowed and he changed the speed of the waltz he was leading her in.

'Rescuing?… Hmmm… I think you were imagining it.' Rose tried for a playful tone, relaxing into the mood that he was putting her into and not quite ready to admit just how relieved she was to be rescued from an over amorous footballer.

'I don't think so. You looked like a kitten trapped down a well. If I had left you any longer I reckon you were going to form the foetal position at his feet.' He smiled, that devastating smile which floored her every time and pushed her away, turning her under his arm and pulling her back in, so that she gently collided with his torso, his arm came up around her back, pulling her in tighter for a second. Her body responded, letting the hard-carved muscles of his chest meet her soft curved ones. She could have sworn his heart beat was as fast as hers, his breathing equally shallow before he released her a little again. Their eyes locked as his darkened and changed again.

'Is that something you do often? Save damsels in distress.' Rose smiled up at him, catching his gaze on her face and being mesmerised into locking eyes with him.

'Only the beautiful ones.' He winked; his expression somewhere between humour and seriousness and Rose felt her breath hitch a little more.

'That's a little unfair. I'm sure plenty of moderately pretty girls could do with a hero intervention at times.' Rose jibed, trying to cover the way her chest was heaving up and down at a faster rate and her body was beginning to tingle at his proximity.

'Possibly. Maybe I should reform my ways and stop being so shallow.' Rob broke into a smile this time, complete humour and Rose couldn't help the childish giggle that broke loose from her.

'I'm not complaining; you pretty much just told me I was beautiful.' Rose grinned, her face heating and her blood almost certainly pumping faster in her veins.

'There's no denying that Miss Turner, have to say I think you could easily be the belle of the ball tonight.' His eyes darkened and his tone took on a huskier sexier tone that made Rose unable to formulate a reply, his gaze moved to her mouth, which caused her to part her lips involuntarily. The urge to be kissed by him suddenly springing on her from nowhere and with such an intense force. Her own eyes moved to his perfectly formed mouth longingly. He had the kind of mouth that looked made for kissing. Sensual and perfectly formed.

'I don't think your date would like to hear you say that.' Rose breathed, almost losing her voice completely as he moved alarmingly close to her mouth, her mind obviously disliking his advances and hitting her with reality. He seemed to regain control of his senses at her remark, loosening his hold enough to let her relax on her heels and again meeting her eyes, although a little less intensely this time.

'I daresay she wouldn't be pleased, but you can't deny the obvious.' He winked again and this time when he turned her under his arm, in time to the music and pulled her back, he didn't bring her as close.

'You're such a flirt.' Rose smiled, although it didn't reach her eyes; the awareness that his whole demeanour had changed with the mention of his date had her wondering if she was more than just a casual escort. Possibly his girlfriend.

'You effortlessly bring it out in us simple men, with your sweet vulnerable, damsel in distress signals.' He was back to light humour and a wink and Rose couldn't help feeling a tinge of emotion that didn't feel entirely good in the pit of her stomach.

'Maybe that's part of my method to reel in unsuspecting men.' She sounded breathy and was fighting hard to control her voice, she could not break the gaze between them, despite her growing melancholy and her humour was starting to wane.

'I thought that trying to drive your car into them was a better method' his voice was husky and equally quiet and this time he pulled her a little closer with a step, bringing her back in line with his mouth. It was as though the music around them had drifted far away, along with all the people and the rest of the room. Neither said anything more. Just silence as they stared at one another and continued to dance. Rose was trying to extract the meaning in his eyes and Rob seemed happy to just watch her there, moving slowly to the music. Transfixed on one another. So much translating between them without any actual uttered words.

The applause started around them as the song ended. Breaking the moment and bringing them back to reality. Rob reluctantly stepped away from her to join in; releasing her and smoothing down his jacket.

She felt instantly disappointed and realised that the heat had risen to her face as she caught sight of herself in one of the long floor to ceiling mirrors on the wall. She looked rosy-cheeked, flushed and wild-eyed, like a lust fuelled animal. Rob was looking a little shaken himself and small glances towards her did not go unnoticed by Rose.

Abby appeared beside them as equally rosy-cheeked and announced she was in love before Rob caught her under his arm and warned her of the dangers of telling a big brother that. Rose watched them, feeling amused, out of breath and strangely affectionate towards the brotherly protectiveness. It was warming her in ways she had never experienced. Abby's intrusion giving both of them a chance to cool off and return to the previous mood and give her a moment to wonder what it had even meant.

Was there an attraction on both sides?

When he released his sister, he caught Roses eye again, an unreadable look and a smile, just for her. Something in his expression, as he moved towards her, made her think he had something more to say, but that was brought to an abrupt halt when Morag slunk into view and draped herself across his shoulders

'I was so lonesome waiting on you Robbie baby!' She slurred huskily; he tried to disentangle her arms from around his neck. It was obvious she had been hitting the champagne a little too hard and was rather worse for the wear. He didn't look amused and looked at Rose with an almost pained expression; Rose wondered what it was meant to translate.

'I'm sure there were plenty people keeping you company. I've been less than five minutes Morag.' His tone was dry, expression deadpan as he was trying to unwrap her and place her arms around her own torso before turning her around to free himself, but she was persistent. Like an eight-armed beast desperate to capture her prey.

'Take me upstairs Rob! Please, baby. I need you to take me to bed.' her speech slurring incoherently and her eyes were drooping. She was not so attractive now in this state; all the sexual appeal and classy control, sizzling into a hot mess on the floor. He grimaced, casting

Rose an apologetic smile and once again tried to untangle her long, slender arms from wrapping around his waist under his jacket. She had a snakelike way of moving her hands into his clothes, trying to get under them. Any longer and she would be undressing him right there on the floor. Rose felt the jealousy rearing up inside her stomach, causing her to look away and down at the glass she had been handed by a passing waiter.

'Sorry girls, I need to deal with this.' He threw her and Abby an apologetic soft smile before he turned and scooped up Morag over his shoulder; she let out an excited squeal and he walked her off in the direction of the doorway without another backwards glance. Both Abby and Rose watched them leave, Abby rolling her eyes and returning to her drink and Rose feeling less than merry.

Caveman style exit, right there. Dragging off his woman for some drunken fun, no doubt. He did not even flinch at the woman's weight; just up and off, walking like he was carrying nothing more than a piece of clothing.

Rose felt her insides instantly crumble into a million pieces and her throat restrict at the sight of him dragging off his girlfriend. Confused by what had taken place between them even more now that he was literally dragging off his woman to bed!

Why did it have to be her? of all people! A born seductress that Rose had no chance of competing with. Why did he have to have a woman at all? One that was not Rose!

* * *

His departure clouded her enjoyment of the evening. His obvious intentions with that woman making her feel emotional; she returned to Abby and tried to ignore the horrid sick feeling in her stomach, tried to stop herself watching the door like a stalker, hoping he would return minus that wench and trying not to imagine what they were doing upstairs.'

Matt came and swooped her into another couple of dances and she managed to convince him she was sleeping in Abby's room tonight, giving herself a respite from his verbal advances. Another couple of men in varying ages got her up to dance and always gentlemanly they kept their hands to themselves. The life had gone out of her party mood though; she drank more champagne and began to feel a little worse for wear as the night went on.

Abby dragged her to the bathroom an insane number of times to check her makeup and confess her undying love to her new dance mate. Rose played the part of an excited friend well, but her heart was now somewhere in the gutter along with her enthusiasm.

His name was Duncan. He was a local boy who helped run his family's farm. Abby had known him for years at school and always had a little crush on the rugged, quiet boy, but never had the guts to talk to him without others around. He was very homely in a handsome, capable way; tall, muscular like a typical farm boy and something gentle about his face. He didn't seem overly shy to Rose when she talked to him briefly, just quiet and mature. He could not take his eyes from Abby for one second though, and Rose had a gut feeling that tonight was not a one off. She would be seeing a lot more of this one around. Rob might not be too pleased to see him as often as Rose suspected was coming.

Somewhere through the chaos of the night and the ever-increasing crowds of rowdy drunken townsfolk, Rose lost Abby, and could not find her way to the ladies' room. She had been meandering and trying to lift her spirits again, wandering tables and drinking way more alcohol than she had intended. She ended up leaving by another door from the hall and crammed into a smaller hall, surrounded by unfamiliar faces. Pushing past them and realising just how drunk she actually was, she managed to find her way to a quiet empty side room. Tripping, cursing her drunkenness and staggering around aimlessly. The door was open and chairs had been placed around as a makeshift time out room for people straying out of the ballroom; there was a side door to the garden outside, allowing air to keep it cool and clear from people having a cigarette and Rose headed straight towards the darkness.

The cold air hit her immediately, making her head swim and her legs begin to give way. She had not realised just how much she had drunk and suddenly it did not feel so good. Surrounded by the darkness, she felt alone and a tad vulnerable. Like she was trying to walk on top of a fairground ride, tipping from side to side and spinning.

A drunk man made some lewd comments as he passed her and walked into the house via the door she had exited. Her eyes followed him with suspicion and pushed forward further into the garden and quiet to put distance between them. She could see a garden bench under a willow tree off to the side in the darker part, away from the lights and fairy lights and attempted to head that way. Longing for the seat and solitude. Noise from somewhere behind nearby bushes floated her way, making her feel more in need of a quiet secluded place; somewhere to calm her spinning head and lurching stomach. So, she ventured beyond the bench, further into the cool night air, passing the tree and losing a shoe or two in the process, she stumbled further on. Oblivious to the fact she was now barefoot.

Hopelessly drunk and throwing caution to the wind, losing all care about what it would do to her dress, she climbed a small fence into a rose garden. Catching the hem on the fence it tugged her back and caused her to fall over the other side, a magnificent ripping noise, she rolled onto a damp lawn and burst into fits of giggles followed by insane sobs and the need to cry hopelessly. She was not having fun anymore. She did not want to be here.

Rose had never been a good drunk, she sucked at it hugely and now here she was like a little lost puppy, crying in thorny bushes. She did not even know why she was crying.

Well, partly she did; visions of Rob and his lady friend swimming into her mind's eye. She was not enjoying the dizzy spinning that overtook her and made the world start moving around her. She did not like the seasick nausea coming up from her feet through her body.

Close your eyes, Rose, make it stop.

She started chanting to herself, unaware that anyone could or would hear her and tried to calm the spinning around her. Allowing the darkness to seep in and calm the turmoil of her body.

* * *

'Rose? Rose? Wake up honey… Rose, can you hear me?' Warmth was touching her face, stroking her like a puppy and pulling her out of the peaceful darkness. The silky smooth, deep voice was so familiar, so soothing and safe. Rose did not want to open her eyes, but she did want that voice to envelope her. To make her feel safe. She was a little cold and it sounded so warm and cosy. Reaching out towards the voice and wrapping her arms around it, feeling its strength, so close and so real. Revelling in the heat coming around her.

'I'm going to lift you. Can you open your eyes for me? or say something?'

'Hmmmmm…That would be lovely… Only Rob can…' She was lost somewhere between drunken darkness, dreams and attempts at lucid consciousness.

'It is Rob! Rose hold on.' That sexy voice was like liquid honey over her, she could feel a warm breath on her cheek and smell a familiar desirable scent.

She felt warmth take her arms and wrap them around something equally hot and firm, enjoying the feeling, but immediately opening her eyes in fear as she was hoisted up.

No. Nope, not a good feeling!

A spinning out of control, the world flipping sideways kind of feeling. Stomach flipping and lurching kind of horrible upside-down reality. Her face was inches from Rob and he was holding her in his arms, her skirts piled in front of her and her feet poking out, pointing at the air; her toes feeling the breeze as they were completely free from shoes.

'Where am I?… What the..? … Oooowww I feel… I'm going to be sick!' She panicked and gripped him tighter with wide eyes and a lot of disorientation. Rob immediately returned her to her feet, supporting her upper body and aiming her towards the nearby rose bushes as she was violently sick. A lot of alcohol gladly exiting her small frame.

'Jesus Rose, I thought you were dead when I found you.' He was still holding her as she fell back against him, resting her spinning head against his chest. His hand coming up to support her skull and one around her waist that was doing a wonderful job of holding her up. His voice was strange; not his normal soothing deep tones, but higher, full of panic or emotion. She did not know. Right now, all she wanted to do was lay back down. Leaning heavily against him, aware that she had little control of her limbs anymore.

He was wearing only his shirt and trousers. No bow tie or jacket.

Had he been undressed by his serpent? Bitch!

Rose tried not to break into fresh tears with that little thought and pushed it out of her head.

The darkness around her when she had come here had lifted a little. The sky was beginning to lighten as dawn approached.

How long had she been out here?

Her head began to ache as the spinning returned and now the shivering had begun as she realised she was icy cold.

'How did you...? Where am...? I don't feel good' She was still very drunk, confusion and foggy headedness still raining supreme and now she just wanted to go back to sleep. Nausea was rising again.

'I have been looking for you for hours. Abby found your bag in the hall; your mobile phone going straight to answer machine. I checked your cottage and even all the rooms of this god damn house.' He sounded husky and alarmed, his tone betraying genuine emotion. 'I only found you by following your shoes and part of your dress stuck to the fence out here, passed out in the flowers and literally looked so pale and cold.... I thought...Well, I'm here now and you're okay...Well, you will be when I get you inside and warm and dry, the damp grass has your dress sodden.' He was turning her towards him, a protective arm encircling her shoulders as she laid her face against the smooth white shirt; his heartbeat strong as she allowed herself to slide back into disorientated semi consciousness. He really was like a safe harbour that had a pretty firm hold around her. She sighed against him.

'Rob! I was having a little break… I needed some peace and…' She slurred.

'Shhh now.' He scooped her back up into his arms, lifting her bare feet from the dewy grass and nestled her in against him. Pulling her in tight and high enough so that she rested her face against his neck. She automatically reached an arm up around him, savouring the security of being held and feeding her cold bones from his body heat, prime spot to inhale that yummy smell of his without it being obvious.

'You gave me such a fright, I've never been so scared to touch someone in my life!' Once again with the strange tone in his voice that sounded a lot like genuine anxiety. 'When I saw your chest move and knew you were breathing… Jesus Rose!' He trailed off as though the memory was upsetting and just tucked her head under his chin a little more firmly. She could feel movement through his body as he obviously had begun walking them back to the house.

Her eyes had drifted closed again, still too drunk to function as she felt the motion and movement around her. Pulling her into sleep like a gentle rocking of a crib and trying to keep the nausea down. It was best if she let the darkness move back in, keep the nausea and spinning at bay.

'Penelope… That's my name!' she laughed softly to no one in particular, back in the midst of lucid dreaming. Drunkenness finding amusement at random.

'Only when you piss me off sweetheart. Rose the rest of the time.' That deep familiar voice.

'That's what Rob calls me, you know? … I was looking for Rob but I never found him… Probably with his sexy fairy…' The lure of sleep was making her incoherent once again.

Rose passed out, not hearing the confused response or the journey back to the house into Rob's ground floor bedroom, past his office.

Chapter 7

Rose woke with the banging head from hell, her mouth was dry and fuzzy and the merest hint of light, when she attempted to open her eyes, was agony. She tried to turn over, feeling unfamiliar cotton sheets around her and the unfamiliar smell of laundry detergent she did not use. Confusion breaking through the fog.

Slowly opening one eye, she took in a masculine room around her, wooden slatted blinds letting a little light peep through from outside. Just enough to make her retract under the covers until she adjusted. Her stomach was mimicking a washing machine and when she resurfaced to try again, the first thing she saw was a glass of iced water on a little wooden table. Reaching out, she took it gratefully and slowly sipped some until at least her fuzzy mouth improved. She sat up slowly, blinking and adjusting to the semi-gloom of the room, her head not spinning too much if she moved carefully and she regretted getting so crazily drunk last night.

It was obviously a male's room. Dark wood, navy, cream, and blue bed sheets. The leather armchair, by a big stone fireplace opposite the bed, had a rumpled blanket and cushions still in place as though someone had slept there. There were large dark bookcases lining one wall, filled with various books, trophies and picture frames. Her eyesight too blurry to focus on the pictures and try and figure out where she was.

Her dress was hanging up on a wooden hanger on the front of a huge mirrored wood wardrobe door, looking tatty, ripped and stained with grass and muck. She groaned inwardly, trying not to think of how much that dress had cost. Trying not to take in the fact that repair was unlikely. Pulling back the covers, she looked down to see she was wearing a pink oversized t-shirt nightdress, printed with kittens, and sighed with relief. She had no bra on under that dress and the scantiest underwear, which could have been embarrassing. She hoped whoever dressed her had been as female as the nightie covering her fragile body.

The room smelled strongly of a very familiar male scent and as her memory came back from parts of last night she realised with a warm fuzzy feeling where she was. Followed by a suddenly dreadful thought that she had no memory of how she got here or exactly what happened. Her last memory had been dancing wildly with a group of women to a favourite popular song about Scotland, and then nothing but blackness. Her achy head and cloudy memories evading her the more she tried.

Looking around the room there were three doors. One left open wide, led to an en-suite bathroom and she made her way slowly, like a fawn trying out new legs. Her head was thumping so badly it was making her feel nauseous, so was relieved to see the pack of aspirin placed thoughtfully on the sink with a clean glass. Whoever had left her here, obviously knew what a hangover felt like.

After using the bathroom, washing the mess off her face from tear stained smeared makeup and unpinning what was left of her hair, she ventured back out. Swallowing the aspirin with her iced water and trying not to gag with the effort. She picked up her dress, noting the huge tear and chunk of missing fabric and the absolute sodden state of it; trying desperately to remember what the heck she had done.

Surely, she had not gone rolling in the garden with him, had she?

Her dress suggested she had done something unspeakable and well it did look as though someone had chewed her dress up. Ripped it open to reveal a leg or more. She rubbed her head, torn between shame and confusion. Remembering the pictures on the shelves, she turned, walking towards them just to make sure she was guessing rightly at which 'Him' it was. Relief flooded through her as pictures of Rob, Abby and various other Munro looking people splayed before her on the shelves. She would have cried if pictures of Matt had stood before her instead. That was some compensation at least. The confirmation gave her a warm glow inside, knowing that this was his room, his bed and he had most likely brought her here. If she had done something slutty and unthinkable, then at least it was with the right guy.

Oh my God...Abby!

Abby would never speak to her again if she had done unspeakable things in her garden with her brother!!!

Falling back to sit on the bed, she balled up her fists and rubbed her closed eyes rather aggressively. Trying to get a handle on her memories. It did not help and opening them again did not change the scene before her. Sighing and feeling utterly deflated her eyes again fell on the armchair facing her.

Wait a second.

The armchair had pillows and a blanket left crumpled and tossed aside. Someone had slept there or at least had tried too. She spun around looking at the bed, realising only the side she had woken up on was dishevelled. The other side was still flat and neat and untouched on the massive king-sized bed. Falling back with relief she started to try and think over the events in a sensible manner.

If She had gone randy rolling in the garden with Rob, then he would have had no qualms sleeping in a bed with her surely?

He did not strike her as the shy type or the refrain before marriage type either. He certainly wouldn't have had need to dress her in a kitten covered nightdress that looked more like Abby's style than...Jesus. Morag!

Snapping upright and causing an immediate stomach lurching reaction that had her running to the bathroom to throw up, she tried to calm her racing thoughts.

He had a girlfriend!

Morag!

Where the hell was she last night? Where was she now?

As she clearly asked him to go to bed with her and he clearly scooped her in a fireman's lift and left.

Did he have more than one bedroom? Is that where he was?

Was he that kind of guy that had a woman waiting at every turn?

Then who the hell slept in here, watching her?

Tossing and turning on the bathroom floor, with her head propped against the toilet bowl she could feel the pressure from her sore head threatening another onslaught of sickness. The stress was not exactly helping and when someone knocked lightly on the bedroom door out to the right, she almost did not want to answer.

'Bathroom...being sick!' She called out weakly and managed to use her foot to reach out and swing the bathroom door a little shut. Concealing her from prying eyes. Whoever had knocked, entered the room and she heard the clinking of dishes as they slid something onto the bed. She stayed curled up, listening by the toilet, wishing she had lifted her glass of water to cradle in here, she needed to remove the burning awful taste in her mouth.

Almost reading her mind, the door slowly moved open, revealing bare male feet, sweat pant clad legs, a muscular torso that was clothed in a grey t-shirt and manly hands holding her glass of water. Rob smiled down at her, bending to hand her the cold glass. He looked bright and cheerful with no hint of a hangover at all and far too attractive for Rose's liking, she felt completely dishevelled.

'How are you feeling? Besides the needing to throw up that is.' He smiled her way, having the good grace to not recoil at what must have been an awful sight.

She took the glass gratefully, shyly and a little reluctant to look him in the eye, suddenly aware how her seating position was making the short nightie ride up even more, exposing her lace thong. Pulling it down over her legs to create a cocoon only widened the neck, revealing her cleavage and lack of bra. There was no winning with this one and struggling with it only made her stomach lurch some more.

'Like there's a herd of horses stamping on my skull and my insides have been replaced by a spin dryer.' She grimaced and took a much-needed sip of water in a bid to avoid eye contact. Mortification creeping over her slowly.

'Hangover from hell, then? Not that I'm surprised considering the state you were in.' He walked out of the bathroom, returning seconds later and handed her a white fluffy bathrobe, obviously realising how uncomfortable she must have been feeling. Gratefully, she pulled herself up and shrugged into it with help from him. Aware of how close and just how good he looked this morning. There was no hint in his manner that anything sexual had happened between them. He stood back, leant against the bathroom door and watched her silently.

'I didn't do anything stupid last night, did I?' she couldn't meet his gaze.

You know, like let you ravage me in the bushes.

Turning her back to him as she tied the robe, needing a moment to gain control of her body and its usual crazy routine of falling to bits at his arrival, she caught sight of them both in the mirror and the amused smile playing on his face as his eyes wandered down over her back.

'Besides crawling through the garden, scaling fences and sleeping in rose bushes? Nah you were the picture of sophistication. I do now realise why your name is Rose though; flower baby.' He smirked her way and caught her eye in the mirror, making her blush instantly.

'Oh, my god! I did what??' She spun round, eyes large with disbelief and then laughter. Embarrassment tinging her cheeks.

'I found you snoozing in the garden, rather damp and grass stained but completely out cold.' Still lazily leaning on the door frame his eyes looking over her unashamedly.

'Oh God!' Rose groaned, cringing at that statement.

'Next time you want to drink yourself into a coma and go rambling in the wildlife, give me a heads up so I can at least escort you!' He extended a hand towards her, beckoning with his head to follow.

Like an obedient pup but awash with shame, she reached out, placing her hand into his and revelling at the touch that was becoming familiar. Inwardly scolding herself for being pathetic and acting like a prepubescent teen.

He turned slowly, enveloping her hand in his securely, before he led her to the bedroom in a very authorative manner, sending shivers running the length of her body at both her hangover and his close proximity. On the bed was a tray of food, scrambled eggs, toast and coffee.

'Eat! I'll come back with some clothes for you from Abby and you can use the shower, or the bathtub if you prefer. I need to nip out for a bit but I'll take you home when I get back. I'll drive your car over later before I go for my run.' He let go of her, sliding past her, their bodies briefly touching and sending a hundred tingles through her already alert self. He stopped catching her eye as they touched and seemed to shake himself mentally too. Moving off to give her space and grabbing a hooded top from a nearby coat rack. She felt the coldness wave over her as he moved off, disappointment at the loss of his touch.

'Rob?' she stopped him as he was walking out of the room. 'Who stood guard?' she motioned to the armchair where the blankets were strewn across the arm.

'Me!... Had to make sure you didn't choke in your sleep ...Abby dressed you with the help of Alice McKay, if you're worried I took advantage.' He winked and smiled oddly at her, pausing a moment to look down briefly where the robe had moved open, revealing a hint of cleavage, before turning to head back out. Rose felt her cheeks colour and pulled the robe tighter. Sparks flying off inside her like the fourth of July.

'Thank you... Thank them.' She wavered a little breathlessly.

Not that I would mind you taking advantage.

She would just like to have a memory of it if he had.

She had to drag away her eyes from his departing form, a little too aware of how much his shirt and sweat pants clung in very muscular places and showcased his perfect physique a little too well. Aware of how little oxygen was left in this room as she struggled to take a breath and steady her jelly legs.

'You will probably see them before I do.' He yelled back from the hall before heading off, opening another door and disappearing.

* * *

Rob was right. Before long Abby had burst into the room full of life and energy, despite the fact she should be as hung over as Rose, she bounced on the bed sending the tray of leftover breakfast sliding about and hugged her friend. It was obvious by her attire that she had probably not even been to bed yet and her alcohol stench was strong.

'You crazy girl! Imagine going for a crawl in the garden, you drunken whore.' She laughed wholeheartedly before slumping down beside Rose.

'Excuse me! I'm not a whore… Drunken idiot, but never whore!'

'Well, true, but the way you were wrapped around my brother when he brought you in here last night. I'm not so sure. I reckon he would have only had to ask!' Again, with the hysterical laughter as she batted at Rose, making seductive motions and pouting kisses in the air.

'No?… Oh God!… Abby tell me I wasn't being a wanton slapper?' Rose almost barked in shame, trying desperately to drag back any ounce of memory from Rob bringing her back in here. If only she had even the tiniest memory of how she had behaved, of anything that had happened.

'Was I that bad?' She cringed, furrowing her brow and waiting to hear the embarrassing tale.

'Yes, but No…You were pretty out of it really. You were the typical damsel in distress with arms looped around his neck and face pressed against him, but asleep. You never woke up really at all. We had to take your dress off and put on something to cover your modesty, seeing as you were hell bent on throwing off the covers every two seconds. Poor Rob would have had an eyeful. Not that I think he would have minded, being a hot-blooded male and all. He hung about out there till we dressed you and then sent me off to bed.' She winked cheekily.

'Oh, my god. I'm mortified. I can't believe I caused so much drama.' Rose winced at the thought but felt a little relieved that nothing had really happened.

'Shut up. It's hilarious. Sadly, your story was topped by the two fat wives having an outright scrap on the lawn at three am and one of them getting her knockers out.' She laughed so hard she held her ribs. 'All over some gangly little weasel who was having it away with both and neither are married to it!' She mock vomited on the bed. Rose covered her mouth in minor shock, taking delight in someone else's drama and rendering her own little episode un-newsworthy. Abby briefly described the scene and finer details before returning to the topic.

'Seriously though Rose. You did scare us. Rob was frantic when we couldn't find you. He even dragged that poor yank out of his taxi and demanded to know where you were.' Abby had moved up the bed and was rearranging the sheets to get comfy. 'Hot as he is; and those muscles! Phew...Move over Thor! Well, he had sauntered into the taxi and Rob, I don't know what he was thinking; literally dragged him out. Was quite heated between them. I don't know what Rob said, but they exchanged some serious looking words before he dropped him back down into the taxi and he left.' She shrugged. 'I have rarely seen my brother like that you know... He's not normally aggressive and scary like that!' She eyed Rose seriously, make up residue around her eyes making her look tired this morning.

'Ughhh.' Rose groaned at the thought that she had caused all this and covered her face with her palm shamefully. She tried not to picture that little scene, but it flew effortlessly into her mind's eye. Thor meets Bruce Wayne! That had a pretty seductive ring to it.

'He was running about like a madman with my phone, trying to call you. We found your bag under one of the seats in the main hall when the raffle was drawn. Oh, by the way, your name came up, you won a man for the day.' She laughed with that but continued. 'He even went to your cottage to see if you were there as we had your keys and your car. I have never seen him that way, he's normally so cool headed and in control of everything.'

'I'm sorry Abby. I really am. I'm such an arse.' She leant forward, pulling the girl into a hug and stroked her hair. Genuine remorse at causing everyone so much stress. A tinge of happiness at knowing Rob seemed to care about her in a way that she may care about him, girlfriend or not.

'What do you mean, I won a man for the day¿ Her brain snapped back to focus at the ridiculous insert of information.

'The raffle! Rob came back down after a bit, he had been depositing Morag in the guest room as he had donated himself as a slave for a day and well, your name was pulled. Rob's your man! Morag followed him back down and took an absolute bitch fit too, that was pretty awesome and he told her to go F off too; she was proper going off on one at him.' Abby grinned, lifting her head to face Rose. 'I hate that woman with a passion. Stuck up cow!'

'What?...I won Rob?... Ok, I'm lost... What am I meant to do with a slave for the day?... About Morag... You never told me that before, why don't you like her? And why did she pitch a fit?' Rose was trying to grapple with the surge of information, her mind still too slow and foggy to keep up. The little tit bit that Rob put her in a guest room was niggling at her too. Men didn't put girlfriends in guest rooms.

'You know they have to come spend a day with you at home, do whatever you ask within reason. No naked naughtiness or sexually abusing your slave. Not that he would mind, judging by the man eyes he was casting your way last night.' She winked and Rose felt her cheeks colour instantly. Unable to formulate any sort of denial. 'Make him cook or clean or do some crappy manual labour. You get him for eight hours on the day of your choosing'

Roses head went into a spin, trying not to let her over active imagination fly away with her and focus on what Abby was still saying. Eight Hours of Rob Munro alone with her in the cottage! She would need a pacemaker at this rate.

'Slow down Ab's.... I thought Rob and Morag were a couple?' Rose nudged her leg softly, her brain going into overdrive on the only subject she wanted to discuss right now.

'Morag is what I would call a leech! Stuck on, sucking the life out of him eternally, yet he seems oblivious to how bad she is They're friends, ex couple and as far as I am aware, occasionally date, but nothing oober serious.' Abby flopped back on the bed to stare at the ceiling and sighed. 'Morag hates Rob being Laird and having responsibilities, mingling with the community and dealing with mundane issues that take him away from her. She's clingy and needy and it's obvious she suffocates him; she treats me like a fucking leper too.'

'I'm sure Rob sees something in her Abby, I mean he's with her after all, right?' Rose frowned, her stomach back to washing machine mimicking, only this time it wasn't entirely alcohol related. Talking about Rob and that woman was decidedly bad for Rose's constitution.

'I think he feels responsible for her. They used to be an item, back years ago, but she ruined it all with a pregnancy tale. They got engaged and then he found out she was lying and that pretty much put an end to anything really serious between them again.' Abby sighed loudly as Rose regarded her silently, gnawing ache in her chest making her wonder why she was even wanting to know any of this.

'That's horrible.' Rose blanched.

'Morag tried to commit suicide soon after, I guess that's what sealed Rob's fate. Since then he has taken her under his wing, stayed friends and whatever else they are; God knows. He looked after her because he felt guilty, he felt like he pushed her that far and now, I guess, it's gone on so long that they are something, maybe not serious but she is always with him.'

'Maybe he does still love her?' Rose interjected with a very lead heavy chest.

'I don't know what he feels for her; I don't know why he puts up with her to be honest!' she climbed off her brother's bed and rummaged in a nearby drawer. Pulling out a black ring box she hopped back on the bed and revealed a beautiful vintage engagement ring. A diamond shaped setting, filled with delicate diamond stones surrounding an intricate design with a central deep pink crystal. 'This belonged to my mum and a million Munro wives before! It's been a tradition in this family that the sons give it to the next Munro wife and it gets passed down from mother to son, to be given to the girl they want to marry. It's ancient! Rob never once gave it to Morag, not even when they got engaged. He bought her some fabulous, expensive ring but never this!' She gave the box to Rose allowing her to pick it out and examine the precious beautiful piece. Up close it was far more intricate and stunning, her breath caught in its delicate beauty.

'If he really gave two shifts about her then she would be wearing that ring. Rob may not be a traditionalist or anything, but I know for a fact he would use that ring on the woman he loves.' Handing it back in the box carefully, aware of its value, Rose nodded, feeling a little lifted inside, but hoping it did not show. 'If Rob falls in love and that ring makes an appearance then I'll know it's for real. Morag has never ever laid eyes on it, as far as I know, and they have dated for fifteen years on and off; she probably doesn't even know it exists. Rob had it cleaned a couple years ago, so I know he's well aware of it being here, he's not forgotten!' She got up and put the box back in the drawer with a sigh. Turning and leaning against the unit, she looked sad and frustrated

'He isn't happy Rose. He's stuck! He has always had this profound sense of duty. With her! With us! With this house and his stupid title! He takes it all very seriously and I think it will make for a shitty, unhappy future, if he doesn't get his head out of his ass.' The girl sagged against the drawers, a faraway look of hopelessness son her face.

'Abby, you need to let him make his own choices; as hard as it may be to watch him. You can't make someone do what you want. Even if you think you know best.' Rose drew up off the bed and walked towards her friend, placing a hand on her shoulder gently and leaning in to meet her down turned eyes. 'Rob doesn't strike me as the kind of guy who would just settle for mediocre. He seems like the kind of guy who goes after what he wants! Maybe he does love her, maybe he doesn't. But I am pretty sure that either way, he will do what he wants, what's best for him. Even if you don't agree.' Rose hoped so anyway.

'Why could he not just fall in love with someone like you?' It wasn't really a question, more of a desperate statement without meeting

Rose's eyes. Rose laughed in amusement masking the inner somersault and her mental -

Yes why, can't he?

Chapter 8

Later that day, Rose finally had been deposited back at the cottage. Rob had never returned from whatever business he was dealing with, so sweet Tommy had brought her home; appearing at the bedroom door to inform her Rob had called to make him act as chauffeur. She had felt the instant disappointment weigh down in her stomach at that revelation.

With her torn dress in hand and dressed in some of Abby's jeans and designer ripped t-shirt emblazoned with a punked out puppy, her hair was tied up in a girly ponytail and she had some pink trainers on, he drove her home. A perk of being a comparable size to Abby.

Soiled high heels in hand and her clutch bag under one armpit, she thanked the elderly gent at her gate and he told her Rob would return her car later when he came back. He had not wanted her to chance driving with the amount of alcohol she had consumed last night, even if it was only a short trip and had made it clear he wanted to return the mini himself. She had agreed, feeling warm and fluttery in her stomach at his protectiveness and knowing she would get to see him again soon. Silly school girl flutters that she scolded back down.

Rose sighed with relief as she watched the little green metro bump away down the gravel road, glad to finally be home and alone after such an eventful few hours. She needed some breathing space and a long nap in her own house. Her hangover still plaguing her, despite the power shower she had taken in Rob's room. She had spent way too long looking at his toiletries and smelling his aftershave while getting ready.

The cottage, much like Muffin, welcomed her like a beautiful familiar friend and for the first time, almost with new eyes Rose really did feel like she was home. Muffin ecstatically jumped around her ankles, whining for affection, so she showered him with cuddles and kisses and a brief walk to relieve his bladder.

Rose took in the rooms before her, blinking; being away all night was almost like refreshing her sight and the realisation as she walked in the door at how cosy and welcoming and homely the cottage finally looked. Her living room with its overstuffed leather couches and plush rugs, small wooden tables, strategically placed with lamps and trinkets. The huge fireplace and mantle lined with pillar candles and modern photo frames of her family. The neutral tones ranging from creams, to caramel, browns and chocolates in her furniture, throws, cushions and rugs, just made her want to roll onto the couch and sleep forever surrounded by her safe haven.

Without opening her curtains, she pulled one of the thick fluffy throws she kept folded in a huge blanket box against the wall. She laid down on the couch discarding her dress and accessories, kicking off Abby's trainers and swiping all her cushions to one side to make a cosy day bed. She pulled up her throw and slid the Tv remote from the wooden chest, which served as a coffee table. Muffin cried to get up beside her and she lifted him gently, letting him snuggle in the hollow of her stomach as she curled on her side, revelling in the little hot water bottle. Clicking on some old western movie for atmosphere and drifted off to sleep, wrapped up in quiet cosiness.

* * *

The fright with which Rose woke sent a horrible beating pulse through her stomach, causing internal shakes at the loud hammering in her head. Momentarily disorientated, it took a few seconds to come back to her surroundings and realise the noise was someone at the door. Sitting up in a hurry and startling Muffin from his sleep with a yelp, he angrily leapt from the couch and went to lay down under a side table to return to the land of slumber. Muffin, as far as dogs went was one lazy little beast at the best of times. Disturbing a nap was a fate worse than death.

It was darker than when she had laid down and there was some modern horror movie on the Tv, strangling screams echoing from it. She shrugged off the throw weakly, yelling out to whoever was about to get throttled

'I'm coming!' before stretching and stifling a yawn. Catching a quick glimpse of her dishevelled appearance and messy ponytail, she walked to the door and pulled it open while running fingers through her hair and rubbing her sleepy eyes. She was surprised at the darkness outside and the person standing there.

Matt stood towering in her doorway, all bright teeth, smarmy grins and blonde hair, shining at her. She felt that thud of disappointment again. Overkill of aftershave choking her, he was clad in a leather motorbike jacket, and matching trousers. Catching a glimpse of behind him into the dark, revealed a shiny motorbike gleaming in the moonlight with a helmet propped on the seat.

Figures that the flashy yank would have a flashy ride.

Muffin, appearing from the lounge, walked between her legs to sniff at his shoe protectively, snorted in disgust and glared at the stranger with a low feeble growl. Matt frowned at her little fur ball and attempted to lean down to pet him, which only sent Muffin scurrying back for cover in the main room with a bark, he was not fond of strangers generally and this was a customary Muffin reaction when on his home turf, except when he met Rob. Matt straightened back up to face her, looking a little bemused.

'Cinderella, I see you found your way home then?' He leaned heavily into her door frame taking up her entrance way in a rather imposing fashion. Rose moved back slightly, aware of the lack of space in the small hall and suddenly feeling claustrophobic. She just wanted him to turn around and go away again. His leather jacket smell and designer scent made her queasiness return full force; hangover still lingering.

'Um, yeah, how did you know where I live?' Irritation barely concealed in her voice, she was in no mood for this type of visitor.

'Small town baby… I tried this morning but there was no sign of you. Wanted to make sure you got back okay.' He was trailing his eyes up and down Rose, like a dog eyeing up a juicy bone and it made her suddenly uncomfortable. He did not seem to care that it was fairly obvious that he was undressing her in his mind's eye.

'Well, here I am. I would invite you in but…' Without warning, he suddenly came forward, pushing past her in the hall without waiting for her to finish. She was rendered speechless by the fast motion which left her standing in an empty open doorway.

'Sure, thanks!' He moved down the hall, taking up way more space than necessary and eyeing up the paintings as he shrugged off his tight leather jacket.

Rose felt irritated but she did not have the energy for drama; swinging the door shut a tad rather aggressively, she figured a cup of coffee, then send him on his way when she found out what he wanted. Her hangover still had her feeling rough, her senses telling her he had some sort of pre-planned motive for showing up like this.

She managed to slide past him and make her way into the kitchen, ignoring his facial gestures as their bodies collided in the small space, the dirty wink. The grin suggestively aimed at her face that made her want to throat punch him. She had to duck past his hand that seemed to gravitate way too close to her rear as she moved past him.

Creep!

She was not someone who enjoyed invasion when abruptly woken from a hangover nap; and was not someone who liked overly hormonal men trying to get a quick grope in passing.

He rambled on about the dance and minor details and people while she got the cups ready and the kettle began to boil, her mind blocking him out as she made empty noises as though she was listening. Empty small talk as he followed her a little too closely. Nodding and humming in the right places, she just wanted him to leave.

Passing him the mug across her kitchen table that he was hovering besides, she did not wait to invite him to sit but just plonked down at the nearest seat and began sipping. He realised they were not heading back to her cosy lounge to snuggle on the couch and reluctantly sat down; watching her face, a little too closely; she figured he was probably trying to work out his chances of getting her to her bedroom.

'So, to what do I owe this flying visit?' She said brightly, faking a smile. No point beating around the bush when she felt like she was on the verge of a physical breakdown, her headache still painfully hanging around her head.

'Like I said baby, just checking you got home and the such. Your mate Lord Big Shot sure as hell made a heck of a scene outside the party. Thought I had tucked you away somewhere in my taxi, trying to kidnap you.' He laughed easily, showing that dazzling smile and bringing the handsomeness back to his face. Rose relaxed a little.

Was she being prickly due to a hangover? Was her mind overreacting? He was concerned. Not here to try and molest her.

Maybe.

'I'm sorry about Rob. He was worried about me. I stupidly wandered off and got lost in the gardens.' There was no point in going into the embarrassing details.

'What's the story there? You two?' He pushed his mug aside and leant his forearms on the table, hunching lower so he could gaze right into her face. It made her uncomfortable again. Something in his eyes that made her want to pour her hot drink over his head. She sat back, taking away the temptation.

'No story. We hardly know each other. I'm his sister's best friend, that's all.' She avoided his eyes, feeling discomfort and hoping he didn't pry more. She did not like the way he was interrogating her over Rob Munro.

'So you're not screwing him, then?'

She choked on her coffee at his bluntness.

'Heck No! I don't...Screw...People. I'm not a slapper!' Although in the back of her mind, the thought of doing it with Rob brought a very warm sensation to the pit of her body in a rather shameful way. She hoped it also made it very clear to him that he was not going to get any time between her sheets. 'Look Matt. I know being Mr all America you're all very forward and like to bed hop casually, but I'm a small-town girl and this place is very old fashioned. People don't just screw around here like it's nothing. Sex is a big deal!' She knew that was not entirely true, but taking the moral high ground was better than a straight-out refusal. She did not want to be overly cruel. He raised his eyebrows laughing. Thick skinned.

'You watch too many movies.' He finished his coffee with a large glug. 'And sex is fun and doesn't need to mean anything. Just two attractive people who get turned on by one another and like how it feels.' He winked at her and extended a hand confidently. 'Come on, I'll show you just how good I can make you feel. I am really good at making women squeal.'

'Em, no thanks!... Really!' Her voice flat, recoiling to the kitchen sink quickly and making it clear he was not going to get any rolling on the bed with Rose. He shrugged, only mildly disappointed and got out of his seat.

'Well, sweets, as much as I love your company and would love to bend you over this table right now, I am a man with needs. Plenty little horny women in this place that won't say no.' He covered his manhood in a vulgar gesture which caused Rose to grimace in distaste. He walked towards her, planting a kiss on her cheek and lingered close a little too long for her liking. His aftershave almost choking her.

'If you ever change your mind and need a horny male to meet your needs. I'm your man!' He ran a hand down over her butt and tried to cup underneath. Rose physically recoiled, suddenly feeling like she needed a bath and a Dettol scrub, pushing his hand away hard.

'I'm sure I won't! But thanks anyway.' She managed to slide out, away from the sink and head towards the front door anticipating he was leaving. Gesturing that he was being made to leave.

'One thing!' his voice was behind her, following her down the hall as he hauled on his jacket again. Grabbing the door and pulling it open she only half replied

'What's that?' She snapped, moderately annoyed.

Without warning, he spun her around in the open doorway, slamming her body against the peeling wood so hard it momentarily winded her. Crushing her with his own weight and planting a hard, forceful kiss, on her mouth; her arms had been caught mid-swing in his strong hands and he had pinned them at each side of her head. Forcing her into submission. Pushing her lips apart he tried to deepen the kiss but she clamped them back shut, trying to bite him in the process but he was too quick. He moved back to tilt his head and laugh

'Fiery! I like that in a girl... Well, I'll leave you with that and maybe next time you will want more.' He released her quickly, almost dropping her.

Rose did not even have time to react in the violent way she wanted too; a surge of rage bubbling up within, just waiting for the release of her hands so she could beat him around his smug head. Barely time to catch her breath and start yelling at him when her face paled as her eyes caught sight of the figure coming towards them and her entire being dropped to the floor metaphorically. Rob was standing on her garden path like a steel cold statue, glaring at the pair in the doorway. Her pink car parked at her gate behind his strong tall form. Her keys swinging from his finger mid-air and mid-step.

Oh shit!

Words failed her. Her breath caught and rendered her mute. Rob stood motionless with no expression and it was obvious he had witnessed that little scene. Matt looking smug, sauntered past him, throwing back a huge smile and wave, a moment passing between the two men that did not bode well for Rose.

'Laters, beautiful!' He jumped on his bike, pulling on his helmet and took off in an alarmingly fast fashion, engine rumbling and kicking up stoor. Rob and Rose just stood looking at each other, neither breaking the silence for what seemed like an eternity. He held up her keys, shaking them and threw them in her direction. Rose fumbled to catch them, but missed and had to swoop down to retrieve them as she caught sight of Rob's trainers turning away, walking down her path.

'Rob??' Panic flooding through her, she called out impulsively. Her voice returning. He stopped by her gate; no response. Just pausing. His white t-shirt glowing in the dark, showing his sculpted shoulders and wide frame. That longing inside her to reach out and touch him.

'He just sort of jumped me just then. I was trying to get him to leave.' She fumbled with her keys in her hand and cursed how weak she sounded.

He shrugged without turning to meet her gaze.

'Nothing to do with me who you kiss Penelope.' There was something icy in his tone that made Rose want to weep. The body language stiff and cool and obviously determined to walk off. The use of her pet name brought back a faint memory of him telling her he used it when he was pissed.

'ROB!' She was losing her control, out of frustration. 'Look at me!'

His shoulders dipped slightly, indicating a sigh and he turned his head to look at her. Still, his body remaining in poise, ready to walk away. His expression gave her nothing but his eyes in their steel beauty looked like a rolling storm. He looked pissed off, truly!

'What?' His calm even voice, again giving nothing away.

'Thank you for my car. For last night. This morning!' She was trying to defuse the situation, bring back some of the charming Rob from this morning. Trying to initiate conversation and a return to the interactions of the morning. He was doing a good job of being completely cold and closed off and didn't look set to budge

'No problem. I need to go!' He said it coolly and his expression matched, without another word he moved off.

Rose wanted to cry. All she could do was fake a smile and watch him walk off. Breaking into a jog when he hit her gravel road, leading away. A smooth, effortless run from a seasoned jogger. Not one single look back at her. Rose closed the door after watching him fade into the darkness and slumped down into the hall, pulling her knees into her stomach. Feeling that familiar wrenching surge in her stomach and the way her heart plummeted.

Bugger!

Chapter 9

The week passed with little to no drama. Life slid back into the norm for Rose and she pushed the encounter from her mind, trying to focus on just getting on as before. She began work on her new commission, which took most of her days lost in her imagination. Paint flowing onto paper and locked away from everyone. Abby came by and never mentioned anything about Rob or the dance again. Not that she needed too and Rose quelled every urge to do so herself, in a bid to get her childish crush under control.

Rob had kept his distance and even in passing, a small polite smile, which never looked genuine and never any conversation. He was keeping his distance, being a gentleman and his usual attempts at humour with her were gone. Rose felt deflated and tried to push it all down deep inside. Tried to ignore the ball of anxiety building up inside her and push the heaviness away. Disappointment becoming her constant companion where Rob Munro was concerned.

Matt thankfully never re-appeared. Anytime she heard any sounds resembling a motorbike roar, she would hide in her cottage adamant she wouldn't answer the door, but luckily, he never came knocking again.

Life settled back into pre-dance days and when Rose finally got around to cleaning out her clutch bag she found a folded sheet of paper pushed neatly inside. She didn't recognise the light cream paper and pulled it out to unfold its silky smoothness. It was the prize certificate of a slave for the day with Rob Munro's name on it. Obviously put there by Abby when they had found her bag under a chair that night. Her stomach flipped. Not sure what she should do, she pushed it back into her bag, but then pulled it slowly back out.

There was a mobile phone number under his name on the printed card. Directions to contact your 'slave' to finalise details. She stood motionless, pondering it for a moment, silently gazing at the number. A thought began to form in her head, slowly and surely and building into a very stupid idea.

Had it been almost a week? Surely, he wouldn't still be mad, right?

Despite Muffins large knowing eyes. watching her in dry speculation, she knew if she hesitated that she would lose courage, so immediately grabbed her phone. Punching in the message and number and hitting send as soon as earthly possible, in case she changed her mind. Once she did her common sense kicked in fully and forcefully and regret washed over her. She looked at the sent text

'I believe I have slave services to recoup!'

It was so desperate and corny.

Fuck, Fuck, Fuck!

What the heck did she do that for? Was she really so desperate to see him that she had lowered herself to this? Forcing him to come to her?

The agony of waiting for a reply that you really regretted even sending was far worse than she could imagine. Her hands began to shake, her stomach flipped and her nerves went into overdrive. No guy had ever made her feel this crazy scared over a stupid text.

What was she doing?

'I believe you do!'

Beeped onto her phone seconds later, making her stomach flip and butterflies take hold.

Argh, what the heck kind of response was that?

She could read nothing in that message. Short, blunt and emotionless. No hint of whether it was a calm response, an angry one or an amused one. She felt even more uptight now. Taking a moment to steady her nerves, trying to not overreact to so little information and think out a response.

'So, when are you free?'

Aloof. Yes, that was a good reply.

It gave nothing away, no hint at how much of a hot mess she was right now. It took a few minutes for the response this time and each second was agonisingly long.

Rose felt like an idiot standing with the phone in her hand, motionless in the middle of her room. Unable to lay it down and staring pensively at it.

'I can do four hours this afternoon, and four hours tomorrow. If that doesn't suit, then will have to be next week when I get back from London.'

Rose's heart rate elevated, her hands trembling. Stopping herself from the immediate reply of YES, YES, YES, she held back waiting to seem less eager. She had no idea why she was having such a meltdown in reaction to his responses. It was not like they were going on a date; she was simply forcing him to come be in her company for two half days. Hardly something to be proud of.

Looking up at the mirror, taking in her appearance, she suddenly had the urge to bath, fix her hair and put on a dress.

Oh my god, what was she doing? This guy had a girlfriend! Sort of... Well, possibly.

Even Abby did not know and he was mad at her for sure. Maybe? Not that he said he was, but well, he seemed really pissed that night. Maybe she was reading into that too much but he sure had been distant and cool at every meeting in the last few days.

Was it hatred for Matt or was it that he liked her?

Surely, she was wrong about that. Did she care? This was more about her wanting him to come over.

'See you this afternoon then. xx'

She folded, sending him a text without the premeditated review of what she was writing.

Fuck, why did she add kisses?

Too late the text was sent.

'**Sure. Be up at 2pm then x**'

This time his response was immediate.

He responded with a kiss!

Rose almost gushed with stupid giddy teenage delight. She needed to stop over reacting to every tiny detail when it came to this guy, she really was losing her marbles. People added kisses to texts all the time, it meant nothing. Abby always added three. Her mum five. Rose was the queen of kisses on texts.

It was more of a nice sign off than anything, right?

Saving his number properly in her phone, she caught herself looking at his final message a few more times in a really stalkerish fashion and gave herself a shake. Even for her, it was being obsessively weird and she had to snap out of this. Anyone would think she had never fancied a man before in her life. She had to admit though, no one man had ever gotten under her skin the way he did.

It was noon and she really needed to pick up some of her mess.

No! She needed a bath!

Torn between cleaning up and grooming, she opted for the latter, and headed to dig out her scented bath products with nervous excitement. Nothing at all to do with his impending arrival of course. She just wanted to be fresh and lovely and made up for herself.

* * *

True to his text, she heard his car pull up at 2pm on the dot. After much preening and pacing and clock watching and ignoring Muffin staring at her knowingly.

Peeking out of the small work room curtains, she could see the sleek sporty black car park neatly beside her own pink car. Watched him slide effortlessly out, wearing a printed t-shirt with a faded vintage logo on front, jeans and trainers. Somehow the casual attire made him seem so much more youthful and carefree than his normal white shirts and tailored pants and a lot more sexually devastating. Her heart quickened as she smoothed down her floral dress and checked her loose hair and makeup. She looked pretty. Not overdone, just natural and feminine. Her nerves already jangling.

'You stay here.' She commanded, watching no protest as Muffin curled up under her desk to take a nap, she closed him in the room out of the way.

The chap at the door sent her nerves into a spin and she hurried to let him in. He seemed larger today, towering above her, more in the absence of her heeled shoes. His frame taking over the doorway. His hands were shoved into his pockets as he smiled and followed her into the hallway; both seemed unsure as to what to say and stood for a moment awkwardly, looking at one another. He broke the silence first.

'You look really pretty today, Rose.' His gaze was focused on her face after his eyes had swept over her dress. Each moment had given her goosebumps as though he was physically touching her and she high-fived herself inwardly for choosing the strappy one with extra cleavage moulding abilities. She smiled a thank you and physically had to stop herself from reaching out to run a hand over that close hard stomach, inches in front of her. It just cried out to be uncovered and nibbled. She scolded herself inwardly.

Calm your blood down missy!

'So, have you figured out what you want me to do for you?

Well that was a question with numerous responses.

His eyes were taking in her bodice as he spoke, it was obvious he was trying not to look at her ample cleavage and failing. Typical male move, but somehow it was not offensive in the way it had been with Matt when his eyes devoured her, instead it upped her heart rate and started a little volcano low in her pelvis. He returned his gaze to her eyes, regaining that cool control and giving nothing away. The only clue to any change was the lightening of the grey colour to a smooth pale hue. She had never known someone whose eye colour could change like a mood ring.

'Umm yeah. Well, I could do with some help in the kitchen. Need some doors sanded to white wash later and have kept putting it off.'

She was unbelievably nervous and finding his gaze hard to stand. It had taken her the entire time in the bath to figure out what she would ask him to do while here. Aware that she had got him over without any other intention than to see him again.

'In that dress?' He frowned with a hint of a smile and again the eyes ran over her figure.

'Yeah, maybe I should change, I guess.' She felt incredibly dumb. She must have looked like a horny desperate housewife, waiting for the labourers to arrive.

'No, it's okay. I can do whatever needs to be done. You stay like that... You can supervise; I'll need to take the doors out back for the dust.' He avoided her eyes with his response, instead looking down at her skirt. He seemed for the first time in all the encounters between them, unsure too. She didn't know what to make from what he had said; maybe he just liked her dress and there was nothing in this at all.

His bulky frame in the hall made standing apart almost impossible, suddenly aware of how close they actually were and how shallow her breathing had become, Rose moved off, leading the way to the kitchen. She needed to get some distance so she could at least act like a normal person in front of him. She felt the heat from behind her as he followed closely and it was still causing havoc with her own body temperature, the silence almost deafening.

It did not take long for the atmosphere to begin to settle between them. First, hot flushes of being in his company again began to simmer down, although she was finding it impossible to keep her eyes from devouring him anytime he wasn't looking. The distance between them and initial awkwardness at seeing him again smoothing away.

Coffee was poured and half-drunk while he expertly removed her cupboard doors with the power drill left behind by Abby. He moved the drawer and door fronts to the garden and set up a makeshift trellis from chairs and old wooden planks found in the outhouse; making a call to a friend and twenty minutes later a vaguely familiar local boy deposited a bag of tools and sandpaper at the front door. Rose smiled her thanks and helped Rob move it all to the garden. Making sure she kept her distance as it was the only way she could really function normally around him.

Pulling out an electric sander and extension cable he set up, mask on and began to remove years of antique pine wax and grime from the wooden doors. Rose could not help but watch him with baited breath, every tensed muscle and male movement had her light headed.

Mesmerised by the sheer turn on of a gorgeous male, tanned muscles straining under semi-fitted work clothes, doing some manly manual task. She suddenly saw the appeal of men's calendars depicting sweaty mechanics and tree surgeons and had to keep chastising herself. Dragging her gaze elsewhere and finding small tasks to occupy her in the kitchen and garden. She took a couple of strolls inside to cool her burning cheeks and calm her overly hormonal self by sticking her head in the freezer. Several pep talks about keeping control of her raging lust were doing nothing to make her insides behave. She really was hopelessly smitten with this one.

Keeping him supplied with cool drinks, sandwiches and occasional light conversation was all a bit much for her. Rose really did have the worst kind of lust for this man. The kind that robbed you of appetite and sleep and made you behave like a prepubescent teen, discovering hormones for the first time. Given half the chance she would be humping his leg and licking his face.

* * *

The time passed quickly and Rose felt more and more saddened as she saw the hands on the clock click closer to six. He would be leaving soon. He had worked through all of her wooden doors and drawers and was expertly wiping them down with special cleaning cloths his friend had dropped off. They had not really talked much due to the noise of the tools he was using and it suddenly felt like she had wasted her time with him. She wanted to claw back the hours and give him a task that involved being topless in her room, like maybe painting a wall or possibly testing out her bed springs.

'I will leave them in the outhouse tonight and be back tomorrow to finish them however you want. Just figure out what you want and text me. I'll pick it all up in the morning before I come over at ten.' He was dusting himself down, wiping his hands and pulling the mask up off his head, using his forearm to wipe his brow. It was these tiny extremely male actions that made Rose want to throw herself at him in a wanton manner. Effortlessly masculine.

Did he not know how devastating that was to a single little woman like her whose last date had been five years ago? Did he not know how seriously hot and sexy he was when he was just acting like himself?

'Uh huh.' She was barely listening, watching as he lifted his t-shirt slightly to flap it and remove the dust some more. His tanned six pack peeking out below in dark contrast to the soft light coloured t-shirt.

'You said whitewashed, right?' He was focusing on the task of removing the dust from his clothes and not really looking at her.

'Right!' Still not listening, still mesmerised by that torso, biting her bottom lip and trying to control crazy urges going insane inside of her.

'Rose?' His voice almost sounded like he was laughing, definite amusement as he had brought his gaze to her face. This caused her to snap focus to his face 'Are you daydreaming?' That beautiful grin only helped to send her into a blushing mess.

'Um uhh…what? …No!' Her cheeks flushed.

Damn, had she been drooling? Had he caught her staring at him?

'I was…um… Thinking… About. You know… White wash!' She lied terribly. Pasting on a smile to cover the flush running up her face and averting her eyes to focus on the glint of his eyes in the sun. He flexed his jaw subtly and Rose almost groaned.

For goodness sakes man! Don't do things like that!

That square, chiselled, lightly stubbled jawline, moving in such male ways after watching tanned six packs flexing, it was enough to give her a stroke. He seemed oblivious to what he was doing to her.

'I'll swing by in the morning. We can go to the hardware shop together and you can see what you like!' He smiled easily and went back to finishing the patting down of his jeans.

Rose felt the elation flutter inside, knowing it meant more time alone with him and the sexiest body known to mankind.

'Um sure. I'll be ready.'

Of course, she would!

'Great. I get up early, but I have to pick up Morag from the airport before I come for you.'

And there it was like a slap in the face, a sobering bucket of ice thrown over a moderately drunk person. A kick off a ledge. Heart plummet, face tightening and brain crashing back to reality in a very undignified manner.

'Right.' Her voice now lacklustre, she scooped herself up from her patio seat and led the way inside. No longer ultra-sensitive to his heat behind her in the small hall. Closed up and prickly. That sinking thud of heaviness returned. Nothing killed an overzealous libido like a man mentioning his girlfriend.

He briefly outlined the plan tomorrow seemingly oblivious to the change in her mood or the loss of sparkle in her eyes. She made all the right noises and agreements and even his closeness to her was doing nothing to lift that heavy pit in her stomach. She felt like hitting him with his stupid sander and bag of tools now.

'Right…Tomorrow.' She sounded tired and deflated, although he didn't seem to notice.

Why would he?

He moved to walk out the door she was holding open for him with a sexy smile and then something extraordinary, something that seemed to shock them both by the look on his face and hers. Almost without a moment's thought, he scooped down, planting a light kiss on her mouth. The way you would kiss a loved one goodbye, a long-term lover, or maybe a child. A nothing, grazing of the lips kind of parting that seemed so natural and unmeaningful in a normal situation.

Rose's stomach flipped over. Sizzling sparks as their lips met so randomly and so spontaneous, that tiny affectionate peck had them both stop and look shocked.

What the..?

He said nothing at first, just broke into an apologetic smile and laughed. Both taken aback by the sensation and the act.

'Sorry Rose, it just seemed to be automatic there. I wasn't thinking about what I was doing.' He brushed a stray tendril of hair away from her face, an automatic affectionate response to defuse the awkwardness then realised that even that was inappropriate and dropped his hand quickly. 'Guess it just felt like normal to kiss you goodbye.' He shrugged but the hesitant look in his eyes gave her, for the first time, some sort of insight that he was not as cool and controlled as he pretended to be. She smiled nervously, controlling inner chaos rather well. Her heart back on the roller coaster ride bubbling about, giddy.

'It's ok… Unexpected but I get it. I guess you probably kiss Abby and Morag goodbye a lot?' Acting cool and calm was far easier than taming the tornado inside her at this very moment. His face straightened, humour vanishing, a very serious look overcoming and that darkness returning to his eyes. He shook his head but said nothing, his gaze moving to her mouth again.

Crap!

What had she said wrong? God, he made her so jittery so easily.

Without warning, barely a moment to react, he swooped down; this time more purposefully, and caught her full on the lips in a much more mature kiss. Definitely no confusion this time about what he was doing. A second of stunned delay from her and then then she responded to kiss him back. Melting together without thought.

Neither knew how or what had fuelled this, but they were full on kissing within milliseconds. Mouths opening lightly to further lock together. His tongue gently sliding against hers as they deepened the kiss erotically; her back was hard against the chipped red door with his hands pressed against the solid surface at each side of her head. Bodies apart. Not physically touching anywhere else. Just lips. Her hands were down by her sides, feeling the same chipped door under her soft palms.

It was the kind of kiss that romance books were made of, not awkward or overly soggy. A perfect fit, sensual building to a knee melting climax; a passionate kiss that sent her nerves into a million burning flames and completely lost to the taste of him. The sensation of his mouth on hers as they caressed tongues and lips, an easy fluid movement sending a thousand hot explosions through her body, melting her insides and making her crave his body all the more. There was no denying the passion between them was searing like hot pokers.

Then all too soon it was over.

He pulled away and left her reeling, fluttering her eyes open and having to steady herself against the door. He ran his hand through his cropped hair, seemingly agitated suddenly, grappling to regain control; swearing under his breath he began apologising profusely.

'Rose seriously, I have no idea where that came from, I am really sorry.' He was frowning at her, moving around nervously and all she could do was draw in breaths to try and bring her body back from the brink of fire. 'You just looked.... Inviting; gorgeous as always. Shit. That sounds so fucking pervy.' He smiled, obviously rattled and then ran another hand through that cropped hair, looking at her with some seriously cute frowns.

Rose was barely listening. Stunned into silence by the kiss. Trying to catch her breath. A kiss like that made you realise no other man's kiss would ever do or ever be any better than that.

Damn him!

'It... Was... Nice.' Rose finally managed, clearing her throat softly and still struggling to breathe normally. She could hardly tell him that he had pretty much just been the best snog of her life.

'I should go.' He averted his eyes, humour and smiles dropping away and suddenly he just seemed like he really did want to leave. His whole manner changed in an instant and Rose felt that plummet in her stomach. She had the urge to run her fingers across her kiss swollen lips but instead looped her fingers together in front of her waist.

'Okay.' She had no other response. Her voice trembling slightly with after effects still ravaging her. He looked at her again briefly, only a full on frown this time and said nothing more, turned on his heel and headed out into the garden.

She followed him out onto the path, lost for words, unable to formulate any sort of noise in protest. You didn't just walk away from a kiss like that! It was not your average weekend snog with some faceless man in a nightclub, it was the kind of kiss that you never recovered from.

What was he doing?

As though sensing her silent panic he turned at the gate. His face now the calm familiar Rob. He had rolled in that perfect control and now looked like the usually smooth Mr Munro. No sign of anything that had just happened.

'Nine am!' he lingered, focusing on her face for a moment, giving nothing away. His eyes a storming grey as though clouds were literally rolling by in their depths. She nodded, unaware of her flushed cheeks and wild seductive eyes causing his own heart to race wildly. Unable to respond in any other way, holding back from chasing him down the path and throwing herself at him.

He quickly got in his car and pulled away in reverse. A quick confident manoeuvre which only highlighted how desperate he was to leave her. Rose a chaos of confusion could do nothing but watch him leave then fall into a tangled heap on her couch moments later, unsure whether to laugh, cry, sing, dance or drown herself.

Chapter 10

It was a long dragging evening that led into a tossing endless night. She checked her phone a thousand times in case he had anything to say to her, then dying when it showed nothing on her screen. She replayed that kiss over and over in her head. Trying to remember every tiny detail of how it felt. She couldn't focus on work or anything in particular. She couldn't eat her home baked lasagne or even enjoy playing with Muffin.

Listless. Restless. Agitated.

She scooped Muffin up in her arms and laid on the couch to rub his soft velvet face against hers in a soothing manner. The lump in her chest and throat un-shiftable. She tried to watch a movie and burst into tears when the leading couple snogged passionately, before he told her he really loved her and turned it over.

She texted Abby some pointless chit chat and had a brief conversation about nothing in a bid to distract herself. Trying anything to shift her focus and calm her rattled emotions. She could not tell Abby about the kiss, she was a bit too close to Rob for this kind of talk and Rose had no idea what the heck to make of it at all.

She called her mother and had the briefest of catch ups in an attempt to distract herself.

She emptied her email inbox and threw her laptop aside impatiently. Nothing could take her focus off what he had just done to her. That kiss was the stuff romance books were built on and he had just walked off casually as though he had just kissed his gran farewell.

Picking Muffin up again, she headed through to her bedroom finally, too restless to keep trying to stay awake. She replayed every minuscule detail of his face, his look, his actions and tried to make sense of them. Torn between anger, heartbreak, a tinge of hope and torture!

'Muffin why are men so hard to figure out?' She held the little fur ball close under the duvet watching his large brown eyes. He watched her carefully giving no hint to the inner workings of the male mind.

'It's the worst kind of torture for a woman.' She explained sulkily, his little face listening intently. 'If you want to inflict pain and suffering on a future girlfriend Muffin, may I suggest leaving her in great doubt to how you feel about her.' She sighed, pulling his little face close and revelling in the warm licks he spread across her nose enthusiastically as though sensing she needed them.

'Kiss her passionately, like she's your absolute world, in a way that will ruin her for any other man and then give her the cold shoulder. Like dangling a worm on a hook. The result is a pretty messed up emotional wreck.' She sighed loudly, Muffin narrowed his eyes a little and that almost made her smile, before he turned around facing her with a little fluffy rear and a sure-fire sign he was going to sleep. His butt directly in her face; no longer interested in consoling her.

'You are a just a typical male, aren't you?' She rubbed his fur and left him in peace to roll on her back and stare into the darkness. She sighed and resigned herself to the fact that this mental turning over and dissecting wasn't helping anyone.

She finally drifted to sleep in the early hours when fatigue overtook. A welcome relief. Muffin snoring loudly on the pillow beside her and the trees casting odd shadows across her room through her thin shades. The moon was high and full and giving everything a silvery sheen that had done nothing to soothe away her turmoil.

* * *

She woke early, despite her lack of sleep and plunged herself into another bath. Even her normal relaxing bubbles and luxurious products could not bring her out of this tizzy. She just needed to see him again, see how he behaved around her. She needed to know what the hell was going on between them. If anything? To try and read his behaviour or see if he would say anything more about what had taken place.

He was literally torturing her.

She agonised over her outfit far longer than normal, relying on the non-responses from Muffin as he watched from the perch on her bed, tongue out and ears up and opted for another floaty sundress. Somewhere in the back of her mind, that little voice of stupidity.

'Well it worked yesterday!'.

She spent too much time on her hair and barely noticeable makeup and even longer on her perfume choice. She felt like a teen going on a first date and had to shake herself a million times as the clock drew nearer to nine am. Her hands trembled on her coffee mug and her eyes darted to the clock every minute in the last remaining minutes. Pacing her floor had become the only calming action this morning that gave her any sense of control. Muffin had not enjoyed being dragged out for a six am walk and was now sleeping soundly in her bed. Not offering much in the way of comfort to his frantic owner.

Finally, the familiar crunch of his tyres on the gravel out front had her spring from her perch at the kitchen table. She had to grab herself and wait for his knock on the door and calm herself down.

Okay... okay, okay, Calm and slow.

She chastised herself and her over eager nerves. She pasted on her brightest smile, walked slowly and deliberately down the hall; opening the door and almost swooned at the sight of him. He was in a dark grey hooded sweater over jeans, a navy t-shirt evident where the zipper had not been pulled all the way up. It really brought out the colour of his steel grey eyes and black hair more so than light colours did and the effects were utterly soul destroying on her already fragile heart.

He looked different today, more sinister than smooth and charming. Possibly a little tired with a slight shadow under his eyes. He hadn't shaved for once and was sporting some serious shadowy stubble that made him even sexier. His aftershave smelled divine and he looked less pulled together than normal, not the overly in control well-groomed Rob of yesterday. Shyness overtook her.

'Hey.' his thousand-watt smile as always, no change there.

'Hey.' She smiled back, feeling the tension sizzling between them. He followed her into the cramped hall, once again that awkwardness and tension looming between them. She held her hands behind her back to make sure she did not reach out and touch him as she let him in. Every one of her nerve endings urging her to do so. He seemed torn.

'About yesterday Rose. Can we just forget it? … Moment of madness? Weakness! Fatigue and sawdust drunk …' He trailed off as he manoeuvred past her in the hall, trying to pull out a response from her facial expression. There was an aura of restlessness and unease about him; his body giving off a million conflicting signals to her as his body heat began to stir up her blood from close proximity. 'I don't know what I was thinking and I don't want it to come between us.'

Inwardly dying, surprised by this turn of events, she plastered on a fake smile and nodded, trying her hardest not to react.

'I guess … Moment of something, that's for sure.' She dropped her eyes to focus on the collar of his t-shirt, her voice soft and almost deflated, trying to stop the tears coming up from deep within. She could not look him in the eye like this.

'I think we were just caught up in a brief second of craziness, from too much sun and god knows what. I'm sorry.' He sounded weird and tense. But she couldn't bring her eyes up to him, no matter how much she tried. It was taking all her energy to keep her face calm and straight.

'We won't mention it again. Say it was heat stroke or something' Her voice didn't fully conceal the emotions coursing through her this time, it was obvious she was upset, but he didn't respond. Her heart had shattered into a thousand little pieces that were filling up her hollow legs and all the while, he seemed relieved.

She was desolate; so easy to brush her off, so easy to brush that kiss off like it was nothing.

He was an asshole after all.

He gestured for her to follow him to the car and she obeyed. Grabbing her bag and avoiding looking at him anymore; she no longer wanted him near, she wanted him to go away so she could curl up on the floor and cry. A conflict of emotions battling inside of her that wasn't going to be so easy to get over.

Her mood never lifted the entire time they were driving, the car journey was strained, as was conversation and in the end, he put the radio on, allowing them both to stay silent and look at the passing scenery. A few times she thought he looked like he wanted to say something, but then he would aggressively gear shift and look away again and just concentrate on the road. She wanted to get away from him. Somehow being beside him as he expertly handled his little sports car, just made her even more heartbroken.

In the store, they selected the waxes and stain without much interaction, her answers were mostly nods or short responses and he seemed equally quiet. When she moved forward to pay for the wax stain he cut in front of her, a gentle hand on her shoulder.

'I've got this.' He smiled at her, almost as though he was trying to get her out of her funk but she just shrugged.

'It's fine, I don't need anyone to pay for things for me. I'm more than capable.' She shrugged his hand from her shoulder, hating that it's heat still affected her body and slid in front of him daintily. Smiling widely at the shop assistant while pulling her purse out. She could feel Rob still so close beside her, he hadn't moved back and she didn't care if he had taken this refusal to let him pay as rude. She didn't care if he was annoyed at her mood. Right now, she didn't like him very much at all.

She felt him finally move as she punched in her debit card pin on the machine, he seemed to take an awfully long time to walk away from her though, carrying the cans of wax and sealant and brushes. She said goodbye to the clerk and followed slowly.

The long journey back was not much better. He tried empty idle chat and was met with short uninterested replies and finally gave up. He didn't press further but retreated into silence and turned the radio up further. He seemed to sense that it was futile to try and the atmosphere between them was no longer hospitable. Some love songs came on, filling the car with soothing seductive tunes and he immediately flipped the channel.

Said it all really!

Rose continued watching the road.

* * *

Back at the cottage they were greeted by Abby on her morning visit and Rose felt relieved.

'Hey, you two; well this looks domestic. What are you doing here?' Abby grinned at her brother, who then ruffled her hair as he passed, carrying the bag of supplies. The girls followed him in.

'Slave for a day.' Rose answered as casually as she could, trying not to fixate on that pert ass walking in front of her; he reached around for her key as he got to the door and without thinking she handed it to him, their hands brushing lightly and sending another wave of fluttering tingles through her.

Jerk!

'Penny needs a man about the place to get all the hard stuff done.' Rob grinned back, Abby smiled and Rose just lowered her chin and pretended to look in her bag for something, rather than respond to him.

'I'm sure there are far better prospects than the likes of you to do that in this village.' Abby stuck her tongue out at her brother who just hauled her forward in a head lock and pulled her into the cottage with him.

'Shut up brat or I'll glue that trap shut for your cheek.' Abby was wriggling and trying to break free, squirming and cursing at his hold and even despite her low mood, Rose couldn't help the small smile that erupted over her face. She just loved the way Abby and Rob interacted, it reminded her of her own brothers and how they used to be in their teens.

Rose took Abby into the lounge as Rob moved to the garden to resume his work, away from him deliberately, so she didn't need to suffer the torture of his company anymore.

'What's up?' Abby hit her with questioning eyes the second Rob had meandered out back and out of ear shot.

'Nothing, what makes you think somethings wrong?' Rose laughed defensively and tried to make herself busy with cushion plumping and tidying the already tidy room.

'Hmmm, maybe the fact your face is tripping you, and you are being unusually quiet.' Abby raised an eyebrow her way and Rose just batted it away with a coy shrug and smile.

'Must be tired or something.' She went back to cushion plumping.

'Or Rob has done another sterling job of pissing you off... What did he do this time?' Abby wasn't slow on the uptake but Rose was not about to go down the route of telling Rob's baby sister all the sordid details of him snogging her behind his girlfriend's back.

'Seriously Abby. I'm fine, just tired from a crappy night's sleep. Was so muggy last that I just couldn't get a proper sound sleep.' She wasn't exactly lying; she was tired from lack of shut eye.

'Okay, if you say so... But if I find out he's upset you and you haven't told me, I'll kick his arse.' Abby grinned and clicked her fingers together to beckon Muffin to come to her, smiling and gushing with baby talk as the little fur ball ran to her with his tongue wagging around excitedly.

'We should walk him, he probably needs out.' Rose watched her snuggling up and figured more space between her and Mr Munro was probably a good idea, until she could reel back this funky mood and act a little more normally around him again.

* * *

The girls took Muffin on a wander out of the cottage grounds, along the edge of the main road and towards the manor. The hedgerows had been trimmed enough that walking on the grass verge was easy and Rose noted for the first time, the huge bushy trees at the manor entrance had been cut right back; the ones that had concealed Rob's car from view. You could now see the turn out clearly from the road and whoever was driving out no longer needed to edge out dangerously far. She noted it but never mentioned the change, knowing only too well that Rob must have had it cleaned up.

The sun was shining and beating down on the girls; warm air and the sounds of the countryside around them helped lift Rose's mood a little. The warmth defrosting some of the icicles stabbing at her heart.

'How's your newest commission coming along?' Abby wandered casually by the roadside, using a long piece of wild grass to hit at the bushes on the side. Muffin trotting between them happily and sniffing leaves every three steps.

'Good, I have eleven illustrations for this book and as it's a second book to one I did last year, I already have my characters sketched out and planned. It's an easy job when writers come back with sequels.' Rose beamed, talking about her work was something that always made her smile. It had taken a few years to become recognised in the children's book industry as an illustrator and she was fast becoming a known name. Her agent had lined up three more books after this and things were looking promising.

'I guess it's great having a job you can do anywhere and just mail off your art. I would love a job like that.' Abby sighed, eyes lifting at the sound of an engine coming up fast from the oncoming road.

A bright red car came hurtling along the road towards them from town, neck breaking speed and turned dramatically into the manor opening ahead of the girls. Tyres screeching on the tarmac as it rallied into the long smooth drive. Rose only caught a glimpse of the driver but it was enough to send that sinking lurch to her feet. Wild red curls and manicured eyebrows, flawless eyeliner signalling that it was Morag.

Abby muttered under her breath something illegible and picked Muffin up, hugging him close and burying her face in his soft white fur. Rose felt slightly smug at the fact Rob was safely tucked in her garden for the next few hours and not seductively wrapped in white bony arms with claw-like nails. Surely, she must know her boyfriend was not home.

Did she never phone ahead?

A few minutes later the car screeched back out of the manor entrance as the girls were still milling around the grass and headed away again at death-defying speed. A loud rumbling engine, breaking the calm silence of the summer air, the aggressive sound assaulting the peaceful atmosphere. Much like Morag's presence did whenever Rose was with Rob.

Abby grumbled and glared back along the road before putting Muffin down onto the soft grass.

'Bitch!' Abby spat at the retreating car; both girls laughed spontaneously as they caught sight of the mirrored grumpy frowns and snarling glares aimed at the red car. Almost identical faces and carried on kicking at the grass beneath their sandaled feet.

'I can't say I like her much either.' Rose sighed and then went back to following Abby.

They walked as far as the sign for town then turned and walked back. The calm time spent with her favourite girl had given her enough head space to re-evaluate things a little. Give her head some space to put things in perspective and really, Rose wasn't one to harbour moods or grudges for very long and being mad at Rob was already tiring her.

Why was she punishing him?

Yes, she was maybe smitten with him and he had kissed her, but he had not exactly avoided her afterwards. She had kissed him back, but still agreed to forget it. Hadn't she?

He hadn't led her on or been dishonest. He had come face to face, told her he didn't want it and wanted to move on and forget it. He hadn't come slinking by for a bit on the side, some secret nookie behind his crazy girlfriends back, like most men would. It had been a mistake on his part and he had admitted it. As much as it hurt, and Oh boy it hurt, she just needed to make the best of the worst and stop being pissed because he didn't feel the same way as she did. For Abby's sake and for her own sanity. She needed to stop being so over emotional and erratic with her moods when he was around, stop acting juvenile and just get over it.

* * *

He was still wiping down doors when they got back to the cottage, Abby had to get going, her visit was only a brief stop by as she passed and only popped in to tell him her plans before she left, stealing Muffin for a while so she could go walk by her new beau's farm; leaving Rose once more, alone with Rob, and suddenly feeling really stupid and foolish for this morning.

She took him out a tall cool iced drink and food in the garden as soon as she waved Abby out the door, her mood brighter and determined to be nicer; she even managed a genuine smile at him when he looked up and accepted the plate of sandwiches. He sensed the change in her and smiled back, that usual jaw-dropping smile that made her feel like melting at his feet. She moved away quickly and tried to avoid too much eye to eye contact.

'Thanks.' He smiled her way but Rose had already decided she was going to put distance between them and keep out of his way.

'You're welcome, have to thank you for all this manual labour.' She tried a soft smile to match her soft tone before going to sit down on the patio chair, pulling out her pile of magazines she had carried out and spread them on the table. Most were art supply brochures and the odd fashion mag but she intended to act normal and not sit staring and fantasising over the hunk rubbing her doors in a very sensual way today. Seeing her settle down to read, he left her alone to do so and went back to the doors.

She was not going to mope and bring her mood down on him either. Light and carefree. That was how she planned to spend her last hours with him and forget yesterday and this morning had ever happened. Life was too short for this kind of drama and she wasn't exactly a child.

She felt his gaze on her a couple of times but refused to look up. Steeling herself to stay strong and not fold; the radio was on in the garden, playing summer tunes on a low level so there was no need to talk at all and it made the whole atmosphere seem peaceful. She had nothing to say to him; not right now, not when her emotions were still unstable and raw and he seemed focused on what he was doing anyway.

She was sitting cross-legged in another of her endless collection of feminine summer dresses, her tanned legs on show from the knee down, unaware of how many times he glanced up to look. Assuming her lost in some article she was reading, poised and lost in thought. Unaware of how alert and tense she actually was. She had no idea how many times his eyes were drawn to just look her up and down before forcing himself to focus on the task at hand. She would have been slightly proud the effect her dress was having on him if she had.

His phone began ringing, breaking the calmness of the garden. The birds singing and the insects making all manner of subtle noises silenced by the shrill tone. He scooped it out of his pocket, pressed the screen and walked off into the house saying Morag's name in a neutral tone.

Rose's mood was instantly ruined again, so effortlessly, and jealousy peaked out harshly.

For god's sake. That woman! Like an eternal bad penny.

Rose wanted to throw her glass at him through the open door. It was not his fault she made her feel this way, but who else could she take it out on? Just when she thought she was getting a handle on herself, that stupid woman just had a way of making her presence known. Of course, he would have a leech of a girlfriend, he was obviously not the most faithful of guys, judging by last night and the woman probably knew it.

She tried not to eavesdrop, but the slight raise in his voice made it hard not to. He sounded annoyed. They were arguing. Somehow that made Rose feel a little bit better, trouble in paradise and all that. He moved further into the cottage, obvious he did not want Rose to hear and she could no longer strain over the side of her chair to eavesdrop anyway. She got up and walked down the end of the garden, away from the house to kill all temptation. She didn't really want to know what they were arguing about; she didn't want to hear him talking to her at all, and she just figured this was a better way to deal with it.

Admiring the fields beyond and the prettiness of the summer countryside from her vantage point, she tried to bring her focus and feelings back to calm. She didn't hear him return but she felt her skin prickling as he appeared directly behind her, wondering why he was so close. She didn't turn or say anything, assuming he would go back to the doors near the cottage or maybe start a conversation, seeing as he was intent on practically leaning into her. She almost jumped in fright as his warm arm came around her waist from behind, hooking her firmly and tugging her back with a jerk, sweeping her up in his arms and her face was instantly faced with his, extremely close. She gave out an involuntary small squeal in reaction. He had trundled her into his arms, swept her against him in a smooth move with her feet miles from the ground. His eyes were back to that storming grey, his face unreadable, Rose had no clue how to react.

He said nothing just swept her against him and caught her mouth in a kiss that melted away all resistance and rendered her completely speechless.

Rose didn't need to be told twice, or kissed twice, she kissed him back feverishly; her hand coming around his neck to pull them closer together and pushing all thoughts of his 'girlfriend' far out of her mind rather successfully. The kiss matched and exceeded the passion of the one previously and had Rose's heart pounding through her chest, his own reflected in rhythm.

While still locked to her lips with his own, he turned and marched into the cottage with her, kicking open her bedroom door; stalking in as though he had been here a million times before and dumped her on the bed in the most unceremonious way.

Not sure whether to fear for her life or be overtaken with joy, she crawled backwards, moving away so he had space to get on. He followed, climbing onto her bed, his knees planted firmly between her ankles and moved forward, catching her with one hand at the nape of her neck, he dragged her face to his and began kissing her in a way that could not be misunderstood at all. He wanted her and for some unknown reason had decided to act on it right now and with very little conversation on the matter. He was so much more forceful about it than he had been last night and it was pretty evident he wasn't changing his mind this time. Rose almost cried with happiness and tried hard to push Morag out of her head.

Things escalated quickly; from passionate hot kiss to entangled bodies rolling on the bed, hands fumbling and exploring. Clothes being ripped open frantically and shoes kicked off with wild abandon. Rose got lost in the hot craziness of it, pulled in by sheer lust in a way she never knew she could react; by something more. She was beyond lust, this feeling, the way he made her feel. She was falling in love with him, had been for weeks and she knew she was probably about to surrender in the most stupid way, but she didn't care.

As things became heated to the point that hands began sliding into undergarments, heading towards the point of no return, Rob guided Rose's hands by the wrists above her head and pinned them down to the pillow. His breathing heavy and ragged, he broke free from her kiss and rested his forehead against hers. Locking eyes; both struggling to regain composure.

'Not like this Rose.' His voice was husky and heavy, his breathing rapid; he leaned over her, caging her in and looked breath-taking. Pinned down by his body on top of hers, her lips swollen by hungry kisses and passion, her eyes questioning him defiantly; he groaned. 'As hard as it is to stop; we need to.' She could see the storm in his eyes and the battle for control in his face.

'Why?' Her voice was barely a whisper as she struggled to compose herself, trying to steady her breathing enough to formulate words. Feeling that rise of fear lifting inside and a tinge of uncertainty.

'It's complicated. I want this, I want you...I just can't right now.' He looked devastated but stayed with eyes locked, noses brushing softly. His mouth finding hers again, this time gently and only brushing, nothing more. A gentle teasing motion that was only fuelling her passion instead of calming it. 'You drive me crazy. You know that, right?' He pushed his forehead against hers and smiled but Rose only frowned back, aching with confusion.

She didn't reply, just searched his face for answers but none came. Instead, he moved off her and leaning back on his haunches, pulled her to sit up. Brushing her hair back and touching her face, she could tell he was searching for the words.

'It's Morag, isn't it?' her voice was deflated and broken and she was cursing herself internally that she was so stupid, she wasn't mistress material and as much as she wanted him she had been an idiot to be so weak. He frowned and dropped his eyes to her lap, finding her dainty hands and scooping them into his. The warmth of his skin was too alluring for her to pull away.

'Yes...But not in the way you think.' He tilted his head back towards the ceiling, as though looking for help. Searching for some sort of way to answer. Sighing with frustration and revealing his long muscular tanned neck. He was wrestling internally.

'So, tell me... I think I'm owed an explanation... Especially after this!' She nodded towards the bed, strewn with messy covers and scattered cushions. The consequence of the previous chaos.

'She loves me. 'He shrugged emptily. 'She can't get over it. She thinks she needs me; Maybe she does.' He slid off the bed, releasing Rose and leaving her feeling cold and rejected as he went to stand in the room and started fixing his clothes. Pulling the fluffy cushion into her stomach, to cuddle away the sudden shivers running through her, she watched him as he then started to pace the room.

'She's struggling right now. She has issues. We were together for a while, on and off but she can't accept that we're done and to be honest, she isn't exactly in the frame of mind right now for me to push it.' He looked towards Rose and try as she might to tell herself he was lying, she found she believed him. Relieved that here he was, telling her that Morag was not his girlfriend. Somehow it made her feel less shameful.

'So, she believes your together and you're letting her think it?... Are you sleeping with her?' She knew She had to ask. Once and for all. After being kissed that way and getting to the almost point of sex, she was owed a very clear answer.

'No. And it's not that simple. She knows we're not together, but she's trying, I mean really trying, to get me back; she's not well Rose. I think right now she's more than capable of another suicide attempt.' He assumed Abby had told her of Morag's past so didn't elaborate. His eyes were pleading, his voice strained. He had stopped pacing and returned to perch on the end of the bed. His face a picture of turmoil, his eyes storming in ways she had never seen.

'What are you saying?' She was really trying to second guess him but it was not really falling into place. Afraid to try and formulate her own answers. 'You want me to be your secret screw? Anytime your horny and I get a call, right?' She couldn't stop the frosty emotion raw in her voice. She was trying to push away this overwhelming feeling of rejection and bitterness, dejected and looking at this with scepticism.

'Rose... ' He sighed. 'It's not like that.' He shook his head. 'This!...us!... You make it near damn impossible for me to function. Looking the way, you do. Smelling the way, you do. God, even when you're mad at me like right now, all I want to do is drag you over and rip your clothes off.' He got up from the bed emphasising the fact he didn't trust himself near her.

'I was angry with her...All morning all I wanted was to get over here and see you... I wrestled all god damn night with myself. I almost drove over here a hundred times after I kissed you; I wanted to tell you all of this. I fought with her all the way back from the airport about this crap between her and I, trying to tell her, trying to make it possible to be with you. It was obvious that wasn't going to happen.' He pulled Rose closer by the hand, bridging the space with his own body and pulling her into his lap.

'I tried to think about this rationally and stop it before it got out of hand. Being with you today, knowing you were upset about it. Drove me crazy! She…Just as usual, made me so pissed, the same crap on the phone and there you were. Standing there looking soft and feminine, uncomplicated and inviting. Beautiful! I have wanted you so badly from the first moment I met you. I just went into autopilot, I just needed to wrap myself in you…To feel you… Screw the consequences. I'm so sick of fighting how I feel about you and I'm losing my mind over all of this… I'm sorry Rose…None of this is fair on you.' He buried his face in her neck and breathed her in, as though trying to make the most of the time he had left. He was making it clear that after this, they would be going nowhere.

Rose bit her lip lost in thought, absorbing everything he had just said. Tingles at knowing he wanted her too. She had never seen him this way, so far removed from the cool and in control Rob Munro.

'So, what do you want from me now Rob? It's not very clear what…? What now?' She smoothed the fluff on the pillow in her lap calmly, betraying none of the inner screaming chaos she was feeling and lifted a hand to bring his face up to hers. Tingling at the grazing of his stubbled jaw as he came up so very closely, nose to nose. The man had the ability to make her weak all right. Just being this close was making her body go into overdrive but she had to be stronger than this.

'I need time! … To figure out how to deal with this. To let her deal with the stuff going on in her life right now. I don't want to not see you, Rose, but I don't want to hurt you.' His hand moved around her hand, finding her fingers and enveloped them. 'I want you! … Just you! Just us with no complicated mess surrounding it.' Embracing her in a hug and resting his face against her ear through her loose hair, she could feel him sighing and leaning into her, breathing her in again and even though her heart was somersaulting with the realisation that he did feel the same way about her after all, it was dying with the fact it sounded very much like he was saying goodbye.

'Just not right now? Just an indefinite wait, right? Even if that takes ... A year... Two... Maybe more?' She knew she had no right to be pissed, he was really trying but her heart was aching and irrational and tears were starting to pool in her eyes. She pulled away from him and got off the bed, searching for her discarded shoes on the floor in a bid to stop the onslaught of heartbreak before he saw it. She heard him say her name but she ignored it and headed for the door. He jumped up blocking the exit and caught her in his arms.

'You think I can just forget this... Just avoid you? You have no idea what you do to me, Rose. If you did you would see how hard this is for me. I want to just tell her to go, to get over it. I want nothing more than to throw you back on that bed and finish what we started. But I'm not an asshole, as much as you think I am right now' His face portrayed every exact emotion that was also running through Rose right in that moment and she couldn't help but let out a muffled sob. A tear rolled involuntarily down her cheek and she heard an unfamiliar sound come softly from him, a regretful moan.

'Don't do that please...' His soft hushed voice was followed by his fingers tracing the tear and brushing it away. His forehead came to rest on hers, his breath warming her face. 'I just need to know that you want the same thing...? That you will give me some time...Within reason.' He pulled her into his arms, never breaking eye contact. 'I want a future with you in it, Rose. From the day I laid eyes on you, like a crazed Penelope Pitstop, all I have wanted to do was kiss you... Kiss you and strangle you at the same time. I knew from the second I met you I was not ever going to forget you. I want to date you; be with you... I just need you to wait for me.'

There was a long pause as she tried to calm her scrambling thoughts.

How could she stay mad when he was looking at her that way? Touching her like that and making her feel this way about him.

She had to think about this rationally, think about what he was saying to her. Did she want to be with him enough?

Standing in his arms, finally feeling him around her was so heady that she could not imagine letting him go now. What he was suggesting didn't work for her or her aching heart, she didn't want to go back to yesterday and being left alone by him. What had started between them wasn't that easy to just let go and she wanted to be selfish.

'I can deal with secretiveness if that's what it takes.' She hoped what she had to say would make a difference, the alternative was not an option. 'I can't deal with distance Rob… Avoidance… Don't do that to me. I can't just forget this happened and act like strangers when I see you.' More tears escaped gently down her cheek and he wiped them away again, watching her closely as she spoke. 'I don't want to wait; that would be agony.'

'I don't want to hide you! … Us! … I want you, but not in that way. Secret dates. Lying to people we know. Sneaking from your bed in the darkness. Leaving you alone. It would destroy us Rose; it would make you feel dirty and worthless. Do you think I could treat you like a mistress? A dirty secret? … I couldn't!' He frowned down at her but his arms had snaked around her firmly, his body making it clear that he wasn't ready to just let her go despite what he was saying. Rose's heart wavered.

'Then what? because I hear nothing in this that gives me any sort of clue as to how to behave. What to expect! Feel! … How long I need to pretend that you mean nothing to me. I just need some definite sort of plan to know that I won't be dangling on a hook for months. Maybe years. Waiting!' She let out another broken sob, wiping her own tear this time with the back of her hand and trying to wriggle away from him angrily. He just held her tighter and pulled her chin back to his face.

'I have no answers. I don't know what to do either, I've never been here before. I shouldn't have grabbed you and dragged you in here. I've complicated shit way more by doing this, but I just couldn't stand it anymore. Seeing you in the yanks arms that night has been eating me inside for days, seeing that asshole kiss you; I wanted to rip his throat out… I warned him off Rose. Told him to stay away… Do you know how crazy I must have seemed to show up at his hotel to threaten him? I didn't care I just wanted to make sure he never laid another hand on you.'

Rose inhaled quickly with his confession, taken so suddenly by the ridiculousness of it, she started to giggle. It was through tears and completely out of place but the need to laugh at what he said came bubbling out from some crazy neurotic place inside, despite being highly inappropriate. Laughter quickly changed to tears and found his arms wrapped back around her.

'I'm sorry.' Rob was cradling her against him once more, his own emotions as all over the place as Rose's.

'Don't be... He was an asshole.' Rose sniffed and pulled her eyes up to meet his, swallowing down more tears.

'He IS an asshole.' Rob corrected her a little sternly, his face softening and a smile breaking out over that godly perfection.

'I agree, and I didn't kiss him; he assaulted me at the front door... You had no right to be pissed at me!' Rose pouted, she wanted that made clear right now. Fully intending to get an apology out of him for his distant behaviour right after.

'It was pretty obvious you weren't into it to be fair.' Rob shrugged and caught her mouth with a surprise quick peck on the lips.

'Really?' Rose smiled.

'Really! I wasn't mad at you. I wanted to get out of here and chase that prick down. Tell him to never lay another finger on you again or I would beat him to within an inch of his life.' He shrugged. 'I did!... Then I realised it was better for all of us if I just put distance between you and I. I wasn't exactly making a great job of keeping my feelings in check when it came to you.'

'You're an idiot.' She smiled, her tears drying up, her body still on full alert seeing as it was slowly moulding to his the longer they stood here.

'Only when it comes to you!' There was a raw truth as he uttered those words. No games. No pretence, he had made his feelings clear and now it was her turn, she wasn't letting this go quite so easily and she was sure, despite his protests, that he didn't want to either.

'We take one day at a time, Rob… See how we feel…How it goes. No plans. No promises. If sneaking from my bed gets us through one day, then I say we do it.' The alternative was not bearable to her at all. She pushed down the doubts and reservations racing to the surface, assuring herself she could do this. He frowned; his eyes the darkest grey she had ever seen as he wrestled internally with his choices and regarded her brown eyes with a look of sheer longing.

'I don't know Rose…. It seems wrong to make you do this.' He pushed his forehead back against hers and locked his eyes on her mouth, she could tell he was still mulling it over, weakening to her way of thinking. Rose, feeling brave, pushed her mouth on his this time; enjoying the way he instantly responded and kissed her softly, opened his mouth to let her kiss him seductively before she pulled back.

'If I can't, I'll tell you.' She nudged him with her own forehead, smiling softly and seeing the slow defeat in that handsome face. Finally, he looked at her fully, she could see the acceptance in his eyes. Logic prevailing. Having her close to him, surrounded by the smell of her and the feel of her, he had no way to fight it.

'Like I could stay away from this?' He scooped her up from the floor into his arms, pulling out a squeal with the speed he captured her and pulled her lips to his mouth, kissing her hard; he carried her back to the bed, his mind obviously made up and her close proximity far too much of a lure to deny this. Turning his back on the hall, making her heart rate elevate and her body melt to his with the intensity of his attentions, he kicked the door firmly shut.

Chapter 11

Rose lay in bed, staring up in the semi-darkness, watching the shadows and moonlight flicker across the ceiling. Lost in euphoria with a warm muscular arm draped across her naked abdomen under the thin cotton sheets. His steady slow calm breathing, indicating he was asleep and made her body tingle all over again with the realisation that this was not a dream. She glanced down at his strong tanned back, his softly carved shoulders and long straight spine; the sheets cutting off her view at waist level and smiled. He was face down, his chiselled face partially hidden by her padded cushions, his thick black eyebrow smooth and flat with no sign of any expression, just peaceful slumber. He was the most beautiful sight to behold and Rose was glowing from every cell of her body inside and out.

She had slept a little after he had made love to her for hours. From fiery passion and raw longing to gentle affection, they had stayed in that room as shadows grew long and moonlight had overtaken. Lost in the passion they felt and undying urge to satisfy it. As a lover Rob Munro certainly did not disappoint, he had a confidence that hinted at someone who was no stranger to sex and he had skills in between the sheets. Not that she minded his obvious experience, Rose had enjoyed the benefits with multiple rewards.

He stirred, almost as if sensing her eyes on him and rolled towards her, pulling her close.

'Hungry?' He asked huskily and smiled when she nodded in reply, she was far too sated to move but if he was offering food then she would attempt to get up.

'I don't really cook much, so if you're looking for me to do it then I'm staying here.' Rose giggled and revelled in the deep soft laugh that came from him.

'Lucky for you then that I know my way around a kitchen. Besides... Seems only fair I cook for you after what you have given me for the last few hours.' He leaned in, kissing her just below the jaw where her neck met and a fresh wave of tingles erupted all over her skin. She wasn't so sure he was accurate, he had been the one making the moves.

'A man who cooks.... I may get used to that.' Rose giggled, focused on the way his fingertips had trailed across her abdomen and sent a thousand tiny fireworks through her stomach.

'Come on, keep me company while I make us food.' He pulled her up with him, taking a moment to kiss her softly and let his eyes lazily trail down her naked body before handing her a rob from behind her door. He pulled on his jeans and then hooked her hand to pull her with him to the kitchen.

He cooked her bacon and eggs while laughing and teasing one another and Rose ended up helping, despite her statement that she wouldn't cook. It was a little after midnight and together with coffee in hand they wrapped up in thick blankets and sat on the back step under the moonlight. Rob held her close under the furriness of the huge throw draped around them, naked skin on naked skin as they star gazed and sat in companionable silence for a moment.

'What made you move here?' he asked casually, nestling her against him between his legs, laying the mugs on the concrete steps beside them before sliding his arms back around her and resting his cheek against hers. She had her back to him and was watching the comets shooting by in the cloudless night sky.

'Honestly.' Rose sighed. 'I wasn't happy with my life; I just didn't feel I belonged there and memories of being here with Olivia made me hope I could be happy like that again.' She rested her head back against his neck, loving the feel of him wrapped around her and breathing in his own unique scent. Every part of her was almost singing with sheer joy.

'You will be that happy again Rose, here with me. I guarantee it' He grinned as Rose elbowed him lightly, the humour in his voice making her smile, his arrogance in that statement.

'Well you're confident, I'll give you that!' She giggled and closed her eyes as his mouth found her neck, kissing slowly to her ear and setting her skin ablaze again.

'You were really close? To Olivia I mean.' Rob continued, bringing her attention back to reality and not lost in some lusty euphoria where she had been heading. 'I remember her; I liked her a lot when I was a kid, don't think I ever came here though. She would like what you have done with it, It's really a nice little home. Very you, with your pink and girly ways.' His voice was sexy and deep with tiredness. Rose smiled and sighed down that tug of heartache that always raised when she talked of her aunt.

'She was like a second mum to me.' Roses voice trembled a little, as emotion caught in her throat, it was still hard thinking about her, the pain of missing her still so raw but somehow talking with Rob didn't feel as bad as when her mother brought her up. 'She was the one who taught me to paint, made me appreciate art and colour and well, I guess being the only niece, she just liked the company of a little girl. What with having no kids of her own. She would be happy that I put my own stamp on the cottage too, you're right.' Rob kissed her on top of the head and gave her a little squeeze feeling her sadness, able to sympathise with his own loss.

'I wonder if we ever met … As kids; while you were here.' He queried, nudging her gently and pointing up to show her a blaze of sparkling meteor high in the velvet sky. They watched it for a second before it burned out, a beautiful sight to behold.

'Maybe. I always went with her to the dances and fetes; the charity sales and church coffee mornings when I was here. I'm sure I would have remembered you though.' Rose giggled, trying to picture him as a kid and guessing he would have been memorable with that black hair and those grey eyes.

'I would have definitely remembered you.' He smiled.'I can imagine little Rose with her big brown eyes and pouty face. Pretty sure I would have tried to ask you out or felt you up at least.' He kissed her neck with a smile, squeezing her when she giggled. 'Was she happy when she left here? I heard she met some rich english guy and trotted off down south.' Rose squirmed as he breathed down onto her naked skin, the feeling of his warmth igniting so many sensations within her so easily, she wasn't sure if he was doing it on purpose but it was having an effect either way.

'Yes. She had everything she wanted; love, a beautiful home, her dogs, her cats and gorgeous countryside. Despite never having children I think she was pretty content.' Being here with him like this she could imagine the happiness Olivia felt with her husband. It made a world of difference being in the arms of a man who truly awakened you inside, the way Rob did with her.

'I'm glad she found what she had been looking for. I guess that's what we all want in this life... Tell me a little about you Rose; I mean London, that's a big move for a girl on her own when you were young and starting your career. Do you miss it at all? Don't your family want you closer to home?' He nuzzled her close, this time pulling her in so he could wrap his arms and his legs around her snuggly. Getting as much bodily contact as possible.

'I guess I thought I wanted big city lights and excitement, but when I got there I just felt alone. I hated the city, I hated the fast-paced life and shallow people...... I was always independent; having my parents around all the time was never something I thought about but somehow London just made me so homesick and miserable. Sure, I miss them, but I can always visit them or they can come here and coming back here made me feel better. They just want me to be happy, wherever that is.' She was relaxed and content, exactly where she was this very second and could not imagine ever wanting anything else than this, right now, here with him.

'You think you will be happy here? Forever?' His voice had softened, he was trying to gauge what her long-term plans were, she guessed. She wondered if his questioning was to suss out if they had a real future.

'I think so, I hope so anyway. I feel like since I came here I have finally found where I belong and I have no intention of leaving.' She raised her chin to look up at him from her angle and they smiled at one another.

'I agree, you definitely belong here... Right here.' He grinned, sliding his hands under her butt so she was lifted onto his lap in one swift move and immediately devoured by his mouth. Rose cried out in surprise and burst into giggles before she was mauled by the amorous man pulling her into him.

* * *

When they returned to bed, fed and watered he pulled her into him, tracing her curves with kisses and soon led her back into another long slow session of making love until her body had writhed and arched, giving into the crashing waves. Rose was no virgin; she had dated men in her past, but no man had ever connected with her body in so many ways, bringing her to so many levels of pleasure, so effortlessly.

Maybe this was the difference between sex and love. It catapulted all of it to a much higher level of pleasure and satisfaction. She was in no doubt after tonight that she loved him. Even though it had happened fast, she had no doubts. She had never felt this way before. Her whole being was screaming it out and she could no longer deny it. Just lying by his side listening to him breath made her feel safe and secure. Content. As though lying by his side was what she had been waiting for all these years, a homecoming. She did not want to ever lie beside anyone else. She felt as if could get lost in these moments and never wake up.

Eventually they both drifted off to sleep, exhausted and satisfied, bodies unable to stay awake and more than happy to curl up together and finally be still.

* * *

A sharp shrill ringing broke into her happy dreams to break the spell. Coming from the side of the bed he was sleeping on from the discarded jeans. She knew it wasn't her ring tone; he lifted his pillow from under his head without opening his eyes and laid it back down on top to drown it out, groaning and mumbling something incoherent. Rose smiled and let out a small giggle. It was such a boyish motion and made her love him all the more.

'What if it's Abby?' She whispered under the edge of the cushion. He didn't respond only tightened his arm over her abdomen, pulling her close against him and draped his leg over her legs under the sheets.

'Rob!!' She laughed louder 'What if it is and she actually needs you?' Rose didn't exactly want that to be true, but she also knew it wasn't exactly a normal hour for someone to be calling. It was still majorly early, so it had to be serious.

The pillow lifted as he raised his head, giving her a pained expression. Sleepy and stubbly. Complete sex appeal. His brows knitting together in a frown and his eyes palest grey, looking exhausted.

'I swear she better have broken bones and there better be a lot of blood!'. His voice was husky as he released Rose, moving across the bed on his stomach and leaning his long arm down to scoop his mobile from the jeans on the floor. Pausing to read the screen he immediately put it to his ear and greeted Abby by name.

The briefest conversation ensued, he sounded more irritated than concerned, he told her his whereabouts was his business and to stay put. Yes, he would be there soon, a few minutes. He cursed under his breath as he hung up. Throwing his phone back down on top of his pile of clothes strewn carelessly across the floor. Rose felt her heart sink.

This is what he had warned her about. Breaking the spell, life beckoning and he had to leave. He moved back towards her, placing a gentle kiss on her face, his hand tracing her shoulder and naked arm regretfully. Groaning as he moved away again, leaving Rose with that aching hollow feeling rising up inside her as he slid out of bed and hurriedly dressed. Even the sight of his naked taught body did not alleviate the mounting anxiety forming inside her. He began pulling his clothes on fast.

'Everything okay?' She didn't want to sound like a clingy whiny woman so early in whatever this was.

'I need to go home, Rose. Morag has shown up at the house drunk because I have been unreachable all afternoon and throwing another bitch fit. It's…' he paused to check his watch 'After two, so she's freaking out about where I am. Whose bed I'm…' He sighed, stopping and turning to look at her apologetically, eyes full of remorse. 'I can't leave Abby to deal with her like that, she won't calm down or leave. I'm sorry.' He looked boyishly young like this and it just tugged at her even more. He slid across the bed, fully dressed and gently kissed her on the mouth, softly yet so much longing building between them again, even in the briefest touch. He frowned as he pulled away, holding her a moment to stare at her face, words poised on his lips but she smiled and stroked his lips with her fingertip. Hushing him.

'Don't! … I agreed to this remember. Go. Do what you need to do.' She was good at pretending to be chipper and calm while inside she was disappointed, upset and frustrated. Reality returned but she wasn't going to show him that.

'I'll call you in the morning. Sweet dreams beautiful.' He kissed her on the forehead, then got up and left, grabbing his keys and phone from the bed where he had laid them. Rose watched him leave; torn between anger, sadness, and anxiety, happy and heartbreak, all at the same time and unsure whether to smile or bury her face and cry. Hearing the door click as it closed behind him, it suddenly felt so quiet and empty in the cottage. Aware that this was what it was going to be like if she continued this with him, sneaking around; lonely nights when he couldn't stay.

She didn't go back to sleep. How could she? So much had happened in the last few hours, so much turmoil and happiness. Her body had been touched and kissed in places she never knew existed. Her nerve endings tingling with the ecstasy he had given her body over and over and her heart had taken off to live on cloud nine while her brain was planting a foot in doubt and hell.

So much to process in her mind. Between complete ecstatic screaming happiness and searing 'Oh my god, why me?' pain. She could do this. She could deal with this short term. Sneaking around. Pretending to be nothing to him in public. If that is what it took to give him time to help his friend and have her come to terms with his moving on.

As long as he held her in private and kissed her like he had so many times in the last few hours, then she could deal with this right? Not being with him was more than she could bear so she would take what she could get. She didn't fully understand the dynamics when it came to Morag but she was sure he wouldn't find this necessary unless it was the only way to deal with her. She didn't want to pry, didn't want to over question the complicated relationship. All she wanted to know was that she was his and only his and Morag was nothing except a friend. They could take everything else from there.

* * *

As sleep was not on the table anymore she got up and reluctantly washed her body in a bubble bath. It seemed so wrong to wash his smell from her skin, his touch and lingering kisses. It almost felt like sacrilege but it was the only thing she could do to relax again, instead of obsessing over what he was doing right about now.

When she got out she began cleaning up the cottage, one room at a time, aware of the sun beginning to move higher, brightening the world outside as dawn approached. Songs of birds becoming louder as they awoke and started their day. The world seeming so quiet and empty. She figured doing something to keep her busy and tire her out was a better option than staring at her ceiling and torturing herself by over thinking.

Wrapped in a fluffy bathrobe she soon had the place neat and prim. Cleaning a little more thoroughly than necessary, considering she was not really an untidy person generally. She polished and even hoovered before finally coming to sit on the couch to try the morning TV programs. It was almost five am, time dragging so slowly.

He had been gone only a couple of hours and it felt like days.

Could it really be?

It felt like it should have at least been several hours and again, despite herself, she wondered what was happening at the house, tempted to reply text Abby and see if she offered any information in a roundabout way. Abby was normally up at the crack of dawn for college and would be up soon.

No!

She knew for now she had to keep Abby out of this. The girl was too open and honest, she carried everything in that readable face, one look or wink suggesting a relationship between Rob and Rose and it would cause an uproar. Rob had not elaborated on the finer details of Morag's issues or what was going on in her life but she was sure he wouldn't lie to her, that he wouldn't over dramatize or use her. He had mentioned suicide attempts; therefore, it wasn't hard to assume Morag had mental health issues, she had seen for herself how the woman could change with a drink. From cool cold temple to slurring mess, she could bet that behind the scenes there was a whole lot more going on and she had only grazed the surface.

She grabbed a hot chocolate and plate of biscuits from the kitchen before settling down to watch some old cheesy romance on the TV. The great thing about sky tv was movies on demand, heaven sent for the restless and awake at stupid o'clock; a distraction. A way to occupy her mind and hopefully she would fall asleep here and not be a train wreck of exhaustion tomorrow, god knows she hadn't slept much when Rob was in her bed either.

Just after six am her phone lit up, vibrating across the coffee table and breaking her from her semi dozing state.

'**Are you awake? Xxx**'

Rob's name illuminated above the text, sending her heart into a little flurry of fluttering's. She hesitated then grabbed it to reply.

'I am, been watching an old movie on the couch. Couldn't sleep. X' She sighed as she cradled the phone towards her, only too aware how deep she was into this relationship already and it was unnerving.

'I'm sorry I had to leave. I'm in bed and all I can think about is you there alone.'

She smiled to herself, running her thumb across his reply as she bit on her lip, her heart swelling somewhat.

'It's ok. I understand. Is everything ok now?' She missed him so badly already, it was crazy to contemplate the instant dependency on him.

'Yes. She finally passed out and I put her in the guest room, sent Abby to bed. It got ugly but she won't remember it when she wakes up. She can rant on a bit when she's that drunk.'

Rose held down the urge to throw her phone, her love-sick mood suddenly turned on its head abruptly. She knew she was being unreasonable, but the thought of him pandering to her, taking care of her, carrying her the way he had carried Rose and putting her in bed. Running to deal with his ex-girlfriend and letting her control things this way. She could not control the spikes of emotion and anger that scraped to the surface.

'Ok. I guess I will see you when I see you then?'

Did it sound bitchy?

She regretted sending it, but then changed her mind and let it go. She was upset, he had to understand that. Had to understand her disappointment at least. It would take some time to get used to this; it's not like she had anything to fall back on in her own dating experience. This was a complicated start to a new relationship and she had never dealt with anything like it.

There were a long few minutes of no reply and Rose started to regret the message fiercely.

Was this officially their first lover's tiff? Was he ignoring her?

Finally, almost ten minutes after she sent it, her phone lit up and gave her a small fright. She had been gazing into space, mulling things over and once again over analysing everything. The vibration through her hand alerted her with a jump.

'I have a confession!'

Rose felt her heart tighten as she read his reply, especially when it followed immediately with

'I told you a little white lie'.

Rose took a deep gulp holding back the urge to sob, her frayed emotions and tired mind reacting in the worst conceivable way.

Lied about what? Oh, my god!

She felt instantly sick and couldn't respond. She was terrified of what he would say.

Was Morag really his girlfriend after all? Was this all a lie to get her into bed? Had he told Morag where he had been and was now breaking it off with Rose?

Her mind was racing frantically, going over every single thing he had said to her in the last few hours. A monsoon of emotion opened and began pouring down her face, tears flowing freely.

He had looked her in the eye and told her he wanted a future with her and only her. She felt so stupid! Rose had been duped by a guy who obviously was a born womaniser, maybe it had all been lies after all.

The knock on her door startled her. It was still early, the sun barely up. She was in no state for guests but Rob's voice through the door caused her to pause, gulp down her sob and listen. Sure she just imagined it.

'Rose let me in.' He sounded normal, husky; close but seemingly normal.

She moved to the door without hesitation, inner fierce mood overtaking; ready to take him on and ask him what the hell he lied about. Tears falling down her face. Ready to confront him! Terrified to confront him!

She hauled open the door to be faced with a sight that made her heart lurch, despite herself. Too beautiful for words and it only pained her more. As soon as he saw her he dragged her into his arms.

'Baby. What is it? What's wrong?' Concern and panic fleeting across his face instantly. All she could do was wave her phone at him, swallowing her tears, flapping his hands away from her and trying not to succumb to his embrace. He caught her phone and tilted it so he could see, the screen with his text message

'I told you a little white lie'.

He read it, his face relaxing in relief, changing to a grimace, he sighed and scooped her up

'I meant I wasn't home in bed! I lied about that, I was at your door! Well walking up to it. I came across the back fields as soon as I knew you were awake. I just wanted to be back here with you already and surprise you.' He laughed apologetically, wiping her tears and covering her face with kisses and nibbles, his arms sliding around her fully and hugging the life out of her.

'I'm sorry. I didn't think you would take it any other way! ... I'm an idiot!' He found her mouth and hushed her crying. Wrapped back in his arms the tidal wave of emotion began to subside slowly and her crazy thoughts calmed at his touch. His hands cradling her hair and face.

'I thought you were going to tell me I was just a one night stand.' She broke out shakily, smiling back her tears and sniffing once more.

'I wouldn't lie to you in that way Rose...I wouldn't hurt you! You are definitely not a onetime thing, or a casual thing.... I really, really like you, I really want to have a relationship with you.' it was the way the words tumbled from his mouth. The way his normally manly face suddenly looked like a lost little boy that made her believe, stop and take stock.

He wasn't lying.

She had never seen him look sincerer as he held her face so their eyes locked. She could only see honesty in the clear greyness of those beautiful depths.

He pulled her down to the couch, stroking back her hair and gently kissing her face until he was sure she believed him. Calming her with his soft words and reassuring her that this was real for him. Finally satisfied that she was calm and happy again he relaxed, sliding off his coat and throwing his keys and phone aside on the low table by the couch.

'Come on, I'm tired and I want to sleep beside my woman.' He pulled her to her feet slowly, up to his tall height and gave her another tight embrace; his hands sliding down over her robe suggestively. He let her go, sliding her hand into his and guided her along the hall to the bedroom, stopping to peel off his hooded top and kick his trainers off as soon as he entered her room. A simple motion that sent tingles through her stomach as she watched him.

'I have not had a second of sleep since I left and I'm pretty knackered.' He turned, pulling off her robe, his eyes lighting up when he realised she was completely naked beneath it. 'Maybe not too tired.' He grinned, scooping her up and taking her back into bed. His one track mind showing her exactly what he was staying awake for.

Chapter 12

Rob woke her a couple hours later, moving over her to kiss her passionately.

'I don't want to leave beautiful, but I have a flight to catch. I need to be in Edinburgh for a meeting.' He stretched out, pulling her head to rest on his exposed chest as he leaned back against the headboard at a slight angle. Rose sighed, equally bummed that he had to go.

'You can't help being in high demand with your business.' She smiled up at him sleepily, smiling when he traced his fingers across her face, tucking back stray strands of hair.

'Sometimes all the demands on my life get on my nerves. I would rather just stay here with you indefinitely.' He smiled, moving down so he could pull her body against his in every way possible, moulding together, face to face, hooking her legs with one of his.

'What demands would those be?' She smiled playfully, lifting her chin to kiss him lightly on that sexy stubbled jawline. She heard the almost silent moan escape his throat and felt the stirrings between them arise again, now that she had found one of his weaknesses, nuzzling his neck with renewed vigour.

'I swear if you keep doing that then I will cancel my flight.' He caught her face with his hand and hit her with a toe curling kiss before drawing back and regretfully sliding out of bed. Rose sat up, drawing the sheets over her naked breasts, making herself comfy in a sitting position.

'Does being Laird take a lot of work?' She asked quizzically, intrigued by what the title actually meant. She watched him dress lazily, no hurry this time in his movements.

'Not really, it's more of an honorary title nowadays. The village don't expect much of me, but I like to stay involved; keep the place maintained and deal with minor issues. It pretty much just means I own most of the land around here and I have tenants that rely on me to keep things ticking.' He smiled back down at her as he pulled his shirt over his head, all those biceps and taut muscles moving seductively. Rose inhaled slowly, to cool her rising temperature at watching him.

'So, the dances and charity things; they're just you, staying involved?'

'I like to be part of the community, the house is big enough for events, and as I grew up with these people, I want to have a part in things. Abby and I were raised to love this village, appreciate the people as well as the surroundings and being a Munro means I carry on the tradition of making sure it continues to grow.' He had now started hauling his hooded top on and zipping it up slowly, running a hand through that sexy hair. He stopped to pull on his trainers before crawling back onto the bed and pinning Rose down with his body weight.

'You're just an all-round good guy then?' She giggled as his mouth met her neck and jawline tenderly.

'According to the town biddies I'm their favourite celebrity. They all treat me like a rock star when I'm home.' He was moving decidedly low, pushing the sheets out of his way as he got to her cleavage. Rose moaned lightly, distracted and struggling to formulate a response.

'Well it doesn't hurt that you look like one of Hollywood's sexiest men.' The giggling turned to immediate groaning as his hand slipped under the sheets and found her a little too easily.

'Is that you saying you find me sexy and good-looking Miss Turner?' He was peeling back the sheets now, gaining full access and obviously changing his mind about going so soon. She breathed in response, only able to nod as a reply, incapable of more while his hands were on her that way. Rob let her go and leaned back to settle on his legs, pulling his top and shirt back off in one easy movement.

'You make me horny as hell Rose. Don't think I have ever wanted a woman as badly as I want you.' He grinned and swooped back in, stopping the conversation with a swoony worthy kiss that sent her off the rails before moving back to gaze at her adoringly and move back to her cleavage.

'Has there been many?' It was out before her brain connected to what she was saying, instantly mortified that she would even ask him this and it seemed to stop his kissing slowly down her body, an immediate pause.

'Girlfriends or sex buddies?' He looked at up her seriously, a slight smile to his face and no obvious irritation at her question.

'Either. I mean I dated a few men in London, not many and they never went anywhere before I decided that single life was less hassle. I haven't ever had a serious relationship though.' She was blushing wildly, embarrassed by this and not sure she even wanted an answer to her question. Covering with her own rambling; Rob came back up to lay beside her, pulling her hands to his mouth and rubbing her small fingers over his chin.

'I had girlfriends on and off until Morag... She was my first meaningful relationship I guess, and after it went tits up I had to be a little more delicate with dating. She was unstable, so I kept things casual and brief the with women I saw. There's been a lot, I'm not going to lie, none lasting more than a couple of months because Morag would start to see the clues and start getting hysterical again. I hate sneaking around but it's pretty much been my dating life for a while and not one of them was ever a real girlfriend. The last one was six months ago. Morag has made it near impossible to get any breathing space since then, so I just haven't bothered.' He sighed as he watched her closely and pensively, knowing that what he was saying was hardly putting him in a good light.

'Why have you let her affect your life in this way?' She furrowed her brow. A knot of apprehension growing inside. He sighed and pondered her question for a moment before getting comfy, obvious this chat wasn't going to be brief.

'I made the mistake of starting things this way and changing it has been hard. Anytime I tried to tell her I was moving on, she relapsed. I guess after a few close calls I started figuring that pretending I had no sex life was easier than her monumentous melt downs. I always intended to try and ease her into me being with someone else, but up until now none of the women I dated were worth the hassle. It was easier to break things off when Morag started her shit than deal with her fallout.'

'Are you saying I'm worth the hassle? You told me you didn't want to sneak around with me.... But if that's what you have been doing for years then why am I different?' Rose averted her eyes to that strong neck and throat, trying to calm her over erratic heartbeats and unable to meet that steel gaze. She didn't like what he had told her, but yet a part of her liked the fact that he was this honest. Honesty meant everything.

'I knew the first time I laid eyes on you Rose, that you were different. We have something, an instant connection... A definite attraction; something rare. I didn't want you to be like every other fling I've had, I want to be with you properly and I didn't want to jade us by being the same guy I have been for years. I truly want to be out in the open with you, have Morag accept that I'm falling for someone else.' He brushed her lip with his thumb tenderly, her eyes coming to his fast.

'Falling for me? As in... Love?' She smiled up at him shyly, a grin breaking across her face and small dots of heat flushing over her cheeks. She pretty much melted into him.

'Isn't that obvious? I haven't been able to get you out of my head since I almost killed you with my car. Even spitting fire and looking murderous baby. I knew I wanted to wrap myself around you and kiss the shit out of you....... When we lost you at the dance that night I was sick to my stomach, I had no clue where you were. I have never been so worried in my life, I acted like a mad man trying to find you.' He kissed her this time, mouth in place of thumb and equally soft.

'Sounds like you have it bad.' She smiled against his mouth, her fluttering heart pounding erratically and her stomach doing somersaults.

'You may be right there. As much as I do happen to be falling under your spell, I do really have to go. Rain check on what we were in the middle of and I'll make up for it when I get back?' That easy smile and then he was up and on his feet again, retrieving his clothes and throwing her back a loaded look.

'I suppose; will really have to be something special then!' She jested, once again burrowing back into the mattress and pulling the covers around her to snuggle in.

'Dinner, movie...... Hotel after?' He cast her another look as he put his top on again, smoothing it down. 'I know a nice town about thirty miles from here that has all of the above.'

Rose's heart sank a little, it's not that she didn't want all of that; it was just she knew his mention of a town far enough away from here to do it was just another sign that this was a secret arrangement. Hiding out, dating out of town. She had to remind herself that this was temporary.

'Sure. It's a date!' She smiled, hiding how she was feeling behind it and accepted a brief peck on the lips when he was ready to go. Sighing as he straightened up, ruffled her hair affectionately and turned to go.

'I'll be back in two days; I'll call you.'

'You better.' She smiled again and with another wink and that Munro smile knocking her for six, he was out the door and gone.

* * *

Rose found transitioning back into a normal routine hard over the next few weeks. It was almost impossible. Never knowing when they could steal moments together, sneaking around in the night and his leaving before daybreak when he did stay. Out of town meet ups became a little too frequent, arriving in separate cars and leaving that way, it was really starting to get to her. In public, they acted like casual friends, in front of Abby, both so sure to keep anything hidden and would not look at one another too much.

Rob's frequent business strips cut into their time together too, so when he wasn't playing Laird in public and having to keep his distance or jetting off to deal with the Munro's family business in whisky and oil, he was committed to helping Morag. Years of being her rock and shoulder to lean on, he would accompany her to appointments and help her with museum issues; seeing as he was a silent investor. Rob's time was split up hectically, which meant finding time for them alone to just be together as a couple was proving harder than they had anticipated. A constant juggling act.

Lying to Abby was the worst part of all, although something deep down told Rose she knew more than she let on. Odd looks and knowing half smiles, occasional comments that hinted that Abby knew something but was not going to come out and say for sure. It was killing Rose inside and Rob too, both had to keep reminding themselves why she couldn't know.

They could never stay at the manor because of that and Morag, she had this highly annoying habit of popping by whenever the mood took her, day or night! She liked to pop by at every opportunity, claiming it was museum related or generally monopolising his time when he was home. The drunken episode of showing up at his house in the little hours was repeated several times; Rob telling Rose that Morag was relapsing and her mental health team were trying to get on top of her medication and mood swings. Alcohol was one of her worst vices and lately she had been drinking far more than ever before.

After three nights in a row of Morag showing up at the Manor, drunk and irrational, they had to cut down on nights he did stay with her, in case Abby was again left to deal with the aggressive woman. Rob, the eternal brotherly protector, was torn with guilt over it.

Instead of lying in bed curled in his arms and drifting off to sleep, she would have to watch him dress in the dark and leave. She had begun pretending she was asleep so she did not have to pretend to be okay with his departure. Breaking inwardly every time he leant down in the darkness to brush a kiss across her hair.

It was during a minor row over this she found out Morag had a key to the manor and had done for ten years.

'Why?' She was fuelled by frustration, over another night that he had been torn from her by his phone illuminating in the darkness. Getting up to go, getting his clothes on; same familiar scene that was replayed anytime they did steal time here together.

'Because at one point she was almost family Rose, she lived there for a while when she had nowhere else to go; it's not ever really been a great time to say, 'Oh can I have the key back.' He was pacing around equally annoyed. Aware that lately, a tension had been growing between them. Morag's antics had escalated of late and he was being pulled in two directions constantly, torn as the friend who did actually care about the woman and the boyfriend who was trying so hard to keep Rose happy.

'So she's just able to freely walk in at any time? Walk into your bedroom at any hour?' Rose could not conceal her anger and jealousy, hating that she sounded this way but breaking inside with all the recent anxiety that had built inside of her. The deceit of how they had been living.

'Obviously…Hence all the drunken appearances!' He was scrubbing his hair with his fingers, standing facing out into the garden at the window. Tense and straight. Even angry he had a way of making her feel weak at the knees.

'Take it back! Maybe then you wouldn't have to sneak out like some Casanova from my bed most nights!' She snapped, knowing she was being unfair. This is what she had agreed too but she could not keep this bubbling emotion locked down forever. It grew more and more uncontrollable as time went on and the situation didn't seem to be improving in any way.

'You think I haven't thought of that? What difference would it make? She would still show up banging down the door and setting the alarms off instead. Draw a hell of a lot more drama at stupid o'clock.

Tommy and Alice live close enough that it would become their problem too. And my fathers!' He wasn't snapping at her but he may as well have been, his voice tight and his actions agitated. This was their first real row over this.

'It feels like nothing is moving forward Rob!' Her voice shook. 'We're just brushing it aside and it feels like this is it for us.' Her voice broke as emotion hit, her bottom lip trembling so that she looked away to regain control.

His face relaxed and he turned to look at her, so many emotions passing in an instant. Mostly regret as he took her face in; closing the gap between them, he pulled her against him, his hands coming to her hair and kissing her crown gently.

'I'm sorry honey. I don't want to fight with you. I am trying Rose! I'm out of my depth with her, I feel like the older she gets the worse it is and I don't want to push her over the edge again. This is not all there is for us. I want so much more and I won't stop until I have it, but I have to be delicate with her right now. She's unwell and she's struggling.' He pulled back to lift her chin to him, bringing her eyes to his. 'I want you in my bed, by my side. I want to be able to take you out to lunch or walk around hand in hand. I want everyone to know that I'm crazy about you and a future where there is no hiding and no secrets.' He lifted her chin higher, gently with his fingers and silenced her with a long slow kiss. He had become an expert at kissing her in exactly the right way to evoke any mood he desired and right now he was trying to bring about an end to the argument. Rose was distracted enough to forget that they had not actually come to any solution or agreement over Morag's key.

Chapter 13

'Hurry up shorty, if you want to catch the bakery before it closes for lunch.' Rose pushed Abby out of the cottage door into the bright sunshine, heading for her car. They had spent the morning packing up her artwork for the courier and sketching flowers in the garden. Abby loved fine art as much as Rose and they were working on a collage together for her studio.

'Oooh, well move then. I have a severe craving for cupcakes and I promised Duncan I would save him some for later.' Abby grinned at Rose's eyeroll, Abby had been absent a lot lately due to her blossoming romance with the farm boy from the dance. Rose could only grab time with her sporadically but it did make concealing her relationship with Rob a little easier.

'What does your brother think of your new love life?' Rose pressed when they were settled in the car, Abby just smiled wickedly.

'What he doesn't know won't kill him.' Abby chuckled and pulled her bag onto her lap to check for her purse, pulling it out triumphantly and waving it around. 'You know he offered to take me to college this morning. What's that all about? Normally he's up at dawn and married to his work and you barely see him. Lately he seems to be around a lot more, although he didn't believe me that today was my day off.'

Rose's phone vibrated before she had even pulled off and her mother's face flashed on screen. She tried not to react, just slid it into her bag at her side and carried on manoeuvring out of the car park.

She had been avoiding her mother's calls lately, or passing her off with excuses that she was busy. Truth was, she just couldn't lie to her and her mother would know something was up. They hadn't spoken properly in weeks, she had no clue what to tell them about Rob, if anything and it just made things a whole lot more complicated.

'Avoiding mummy still?' Abby cut in with a knowing look and leaned back to clip her belt. They had pulled out onto the road and both girls immediately rolled down windows to let the breeze in. It was another surprisingly scorching day and shaping up to be the best summer in years.

'Who said I'm avoiding my mum?' She lied and crossed her toes childishly, accelerating as they passed the Manor opening, she still got nervous near that entrance.

'Come on, I've seen you blank that phone several times when your mothers beautiful face is on screen. What are you avoiding her for? I thought you were close.' Abby was inquisitive at the best of times, Rose's nickname for her was 'Nosey mare' as she was forever prodding for information, it only made Rose surer that Abby knew something about Rob as she never broached that subject at all.

'It's nothing, she just calls a lot and she is just a bit over protective.' Rose hated the white lie, hated that she was yet again bluffing her way out of the truth with Abby but she couldn't tell her the truth. It had gone on too long and even if she could, she didn't know how to tell her now. Abby would be crushed that she had been kept out of the loop. That Rose and Rob had been sleeping together for over a month now and had never told her.

Abby flicked through her phone and bumped on a tune loudly.

'This is my new fave.' She beamed Rose's way and started gyrating in her seat and singing along as they pulled up to the town sign and Rose followed the familiar route to the café car park, it looked unusually full as she circled for a space, noting a couple of tourist buses nearby and headed back out to the road for the next carpark at the museum.

Tourist season was starting and that's when the village would start to get busy, she hadn't been looking forward to the invasion in her corner of paradise but thankfully it would only last the summer.

Finding a space outside the museum was easy, practically at the door though; Rose couldn't help but spot Rob's car parked near the entrance and that familiar pang hit her in the stomach. He was here… With her. She knew he sometimes had business with the museum, Rob was a benefactor after all. She just didn't expect to turn around as she slid out to come face to face with him walking towards her. Morag at his side and sauntering a little too closely beside him as they approached.

'Morning' He smiled towards her, aware of eyes on them and Abby's usual presence. His face a picture of blankness and giving nothing away; he was always a little too good for Rose's liking at this causal indifference. She assumed it was honed with years of dating women quietly. She smiled tightly, trying not to look at the redhead or the figure revealing dress she was sporting today, or the way she was leaning a little too close to Rob's side. That air of ownership.

Abby slid out of the car and greeted Rob with a sisterly hug. They always showed affection to one another in small ways publicly, that highlighted the bond between them, and it made Rose envy it a little.

Okay, envy it a lot. She longed for the days when he could be that way with her in the open.

'Where're you girls off to today then?' His eyes kept coming to rest on Rose and then shifting again. He was only too aware of the way Morag was watching intently and Morag smiled at the two women in her usual fake hospitable way. A seasoned pro of social etiquette when faced with members of the public or strangers, she played her part so very well. Cool, calm and poised, as though nothing more was going on behind those narrowed green eyes; her manner giving nothing away at all. Today she was dressed for a party, even though it was around ten am, and made Rose feel plain in her white summer dress and sandals with her loose waving hair around her shoulders.

'The bakery for Abby's daily intake of cupcakes, then maybe the beach for a walk with Muffin. We're celebrating the conclusion of my commission today.' Rose was trying to sound light, trying not to focus on the hard lines of his body under his shirt and linger in the memories of what he had done to her last night. Her face must have betrayed a mere hint of what she was thinking as she caught the change of shade in his eyes and the briefest pause of his attention on her mouth. She saw the familiar glint of lust as he cleared his throat, pushing it away. Her body always so aware of his every tiny movement.

'Congrats, well done for getting them done so quick. Try not to drown my sister while you're there, I know how irritating she can be.' He was trying to lighten the mood and Abby sucker punched him lightly, a scowl on that pretty face. She had been standing glaring at Morag openly until that point, oblivious to all the passed looks between her brother and best friend.

'Screw you, asshole.' Abby laughed and ducked as he tried to catch her in a head lock. Rose watched them with a smile moving across her face, always warmed by the bond of siblings. Morag was looking cold and bored as she glared first at the sparring pair who were now dancing about then gave Rose a quick once over with a disapproving air. Rose stiffened and tried her best not to react.

Abby was trying to take another mock jab and Rob was keeping her at arm's length, teasing her and calling her names, his hand on his sister's head. He expertly ducked and dived from flailing limbs while she was calling him every name she could think of that would insult, but it only made him laugh louder. That unguarded smile causing Rose to warm up in places that brought a flush to her skin. It was in these moments when Rob lost the look of the mature business man and looked every bit the young carefree twenty-nine-year-old, years slipping away with a change of facial expression, that only made her want him more.

'It's a lovely day, isn't it?' Rose tried with the other woman, her heart beating fast and the awkwardness of being left here to stand silently facing her. Trying to drag her attention away from how hot Rob looked, fooling around with his sister so childishly.

'Hmm I guess.' Morag didn't look at her, just checked her watch for the umpteenth time and sighed loudly. She was concentrating on sending facial signals to Rob to move; making it clear she had little interest in the annoying brunette standing three feet away. Rose could feel her irritation rising. This woman was not easy to warm too and the way she was looking possessively at Rob was making her temper simmer.

'Going anywhere nice yourself?' She pressed. Really trying to make an effort, maybe if she endeared herself a little to this woman it would make things easier. On Rob. On her. Maybe if she formed a friendship then things would move along faster.

'Rob's taking me to a business brunch for the museum.' She said drily, closed off, offering no more information and shutting her down. She waved a hand at the pair who were now several feet away to attract his attention. Rob had Abby hanging upside down over his shoulder, screaming for dear life and wrinkling the hell out of his sky blue shirt and navy trousers.

'I see. Well, have a nice brunch.' Rose interjected with her most friendly smile and was met with a mask of dead pan indifference. Morag just ignored her. Rose gritted her teeth, clamped her mouth shut with the temper that was threatening to pour out and focused her eyes on that gorgeous six-foot hunk instead. He always simmered her jets.

He was obviously in a good mood. Rose knew why; they had not slept much last night, the hot humid night keeping them both awake and they had simply filled the hours with some acrobatic exercise. He had pretty much tested out every available surface in her cottage that he could prop her on and she baulked at where the heck he was getting his energy this morning, he looked anything but tired.

He had been in a lust hungry mood and had not been able to get enough of her, no matter how many times he had her. It was one of those rare nights when he had stayed until morning and his phone had not rung, even once. They had talked, made love and held one another repeatedly until sun up and he had to leave for work. She was tired this morning and her body ached, but it had all been worth it. The memories fuelling her through today and longing for later when they had arranged to meet out of town for dinner.

Rob finally dropped Abby back on her feet and hauled her over, under his arm, planting a kiss on top of her head. She was still struggling and aiming elbow jabs at his side, but he caught them expertly. He was faster and stronger than Abby and made it look easy to control the fiery demon.

'We have got to get going Rob!' Morag's voice was tight and controlled, but a mere hint of temper fraying at the edges. She was obviously bored with the company and wanted him alone once more.

'Yeah sure. Hate to love you and leave you ladies but we have a meeting.' He looked directly at Rose as he said, 'love you' lingeringly, his eyes glinting and the tiny hint of a smile tugged his mouth subtly, sending a small shiver internally through Rose's pelvis. Anticipating later when she could be alone with him. 'Behave yourselves.' He walked forward between Morag and Rose as though making to leave, so that his body brushed her lightly, his fingertips quickly tracing down the inner skin of her arm and wrist gently. A small brief touch, concealed by his body but sending a thousand tingles through Rose like a shockwave, with his eyes catching hers; that now familiar look of longing in that shielded expression. She caught Abby lifting her attention their way with a narrowed look and moved away from him quickly, face heating and cursing herself for the inability to act.

These last few weeks She had been learning how to read him a little better, recognise the tiny signs and looks that he rarely gave away for moments like this, when his act made her feel insecure.

'We shall!' Abby butted in, the strangest expression behind those eyes and she pushed her brother in the back as though telling him to hurry and leave. He batted at her head with his hand before leaning down and hitting her with a kiss on the cheek.

'Have a nice day.' Rose said quietly, to him, not Morag and met his eyes with a smile.

'You too.' He turned, a last quick look at Rose and placed a hand on the back of Morag, guiding her onward towards his parked car. Rose tried not to watch him go, tried not to let that bubble inside that was growing affect her, but she was watching a little too intensely and aware she was frowning.

'I feel the same way about her.' Abby butted into her thoughts and nudged against her. 'Slutty freak. Who dresses that way at ten in the morning?' She laughed and turned, yanking Rose by the wrist and not waiting for a response as she hauled her into the bakery.

* * *

Rose pulled up to the restaurant in her little car and stopped, parking easily in the dark but sitting a moment to check her hair and makeup with her visor light. She was meeting him here as planned, yet that heavy weight in her stomach was being stubborn and refusing to go away tonight. All day it had weighed on her, her mind, flitting back to her situation with Rob over and over and causing a deep swirling nausea making it near impossible to just relax.

She saw his car pull up in her rear-view mirror, smoothly reversing into a space across from her and waited patiently. They had gotten into a routine of meeting in car parks, always late at night, always out of town and Rose couldn't help the lump that formed in her throat. The feeling that this was what they were, at the rate things were progressing she couldn't see an end to this either.

He wrapped on her window lightly moments later, pulling her out of her own head and then opened her door to help her out with a hand.

'Hey there gorgeous.' He pulled her against him and sunk a kiss on her that helped push away all the tension and upset, normally it worked to eradicate it completely but tonight it only softened the heaviness. Tongue flicking against hers lightly and bringing out the desire to be naked with him once again.

'Hey you. How was your brunch?' She asked a little too frostily when he finally released her, she breathed in heavily, swallowed down and smiled to cover the way she said it. He narrowed his eyes on her for a brief second before turning her to walk with an arm about her shoulders, obviously dismissing it.

'Boring… Long. How was the beach?' His mouth found her temple as they walked and a small squeeze of her shoulders were all she needed to let the mood go. She would just focus on being here with him tonight, enjoy the food and his company and look forward to being alone later.

'Tiring. We stayed till mid-afternoon and then I went home for a nap, You, exhausted me.' She smiled up at him a little easier, being released as he opened the restaurant door and gently guided her in.

'I intend to do the same tonight.' He winked and this time looped her fingers in his to pull her in towards the maître de.

'You're staying tonight?' Rose blinked up at him, questioningly, knowing that his staying the night before was usually a sign that they wouldn't get to spend another full night together for at least another few days. Two in a row had almost become impossible.

'I'll try too.' He winked, hushing her as the man approached them with a smile to ask for the reservation name. Rose looked away, tears stinging her eyes, knowing that this wasn't how it should feel. That being in love and a relationship shouldn't always be so uncertain. She wanted definite plans, no broken nights and stolen moments. She wanted a proper life and relationship with him and the way things were going it was causing all sorts of doubts about their future together. None of this she could voice of course, for fear Rob would end things like he had originally wanted until Morag was well, or more able to cope with Rob having a girlfriend. Rose sighed and followed him as they were shown to their table. Pushing it all down and plastering a bright smile on her face to cover all of her heart ache.

'You look stunning tonight, you always look beautiful but especially so in that dress.' He smiled at her when they were seated, his eyes running over her appreciatively. Rose could only smile and smooth down her skirt, eyes avoiding his as she got a handle on her internal tears.

'Your sister chose it… Figured I would look good in aqua.' She smiled, pleased that her new fifties style dress was a hit. Always a lover of vintage. She pulled the menu towards her slowly and used it as a diversion from those smoky eyes.

'It won't be like this always.' His soft tone picked up her gaze to meet his, that frown and gentle expression telling her that he had sensed her upset. Knew she was having a hard time nowadays. 'I told Morag I was dating, that there had been women in the last few years…… She didn't take it so well but she also didn't erupt.' He was watching her intently, not making a move to pick up his menu.

'Does this mean things will start to change?' She enquired warily, her heart afraid to hope for anything so soon.

'Not yet, I want to get her used to the idea that there is someone… Before she finds out it's you. Before we start walking around publicly and put it in her face. I know this is shitty on you baby, but I am trying to do the right thing and protect both of your feelings.' He frowned, finally lifting his menu and opening it quickly, not really reading it either.

'How long will that take? What if she never accepts it?' Again, this same old fact, over and over in Rose's head. The what if's. Her deflated tone couldn't conceal her doubt.

'Rose look at me.' He pulled her to his gaze once more, a smile softly on that perfect mouth. 'I love you. I will do whatever it takes to make this as fast as I can, but I also can't rush things. If she harmed herself because of us, it would affect us, affect our happiness. I know you don't get why I am this way with her, but there is truly nothing there but friendship. I have known her for fifteen years, been her only friend for most of that time and been the only one who has managed to help her. Her story is complicated and heart breaking and I care about her the way I care about my sister; I'm sorry I'm not the kind of asshole who can just push her aside; even for you. I want her to be happy too.' He reached out and caught Rose's hand in his, pulling it towards him slightly, so he could rest easily and smooth her fingers with this thumb.

'I don't want you to just push her aside, I get that you care. I love that you care the way you do.... It's just so ... Frustrating!' Rose sighed. 'It's not exactly a run of the mill situation, anyone on the outside looking in would never understand any of this.'

'I only need you to understand, and to not give up on me.' He watched her, waiting for a response but Rose could only sigh heavily again.

'Look. I'm not going anywhere, let's just eat and go. I just want to be wrapped up with you and forget about her for tonight.' She pulled away from his fingers and lifted her menu once more, scanning the food quickly and trying to pick something before her mood took yet another weird turn. Her menu was whipped out of her hand, making her jump, and she was faced with him standing right beside her, hand held out.

'Come on, we can grab takeaway on the way home... I want to be alone now, not later.' He looked serious, gaze intense and she didn't hesitate. Reaching out to be pulled up out of her seat, his arm coming around her as he ushered her back in the direction they had come in. He waved the waiter away with a smile and apology and dumped a few bills on the stand as we passed by.

'Appetite is not for food.' He grinned at the other man, getting a smile in return and a knowing look as he pulled her towards the exit. Rose blushed furiously and looked down at the floor in complete mortification, hissing his name in embarrassment.

As they got to the car park, Rose went to pull away and head for her car but he pulled her back to him.

'I meant what I said in there... I love you. More than anything in the world. Trust me that this isn't all there is.' It wasn't the first time he had told her he loved her but something in the way he was intensely gazing into her eyes made it feel different, made it somehow more convincing that he wouldn't just let things go on like this.

'I love you too Rob, I just want to be happy and for us to get past this... Soon. It's not how I imagined falling in love would be.'

His fingers trailed over her face softly.

'It's not how I want it to be. Give me time, just a little more, let me try it my way for a little longer.' She nodded and let him kiss her slowly and passionately in the dark car park, when he released her he walked her to her car and deposited her inside. 'I'll follow you back to the cottage. We can phone for food when we get there, I love you.'

It was almost as if he could sense her rising insecurity tonight, or maybe just all the tension of late was bothering him too but Rose felt a little lighter with the way he was looking at her.

'Sure you can keep up?' She grinned and pulled her door shut. Starting her car with a wicked gleam in her eye and warning him that she didn't intend to drive like a lady.

Chapter 14

Rose dropped Abby off at Duncan's farm, well the gate leading to it, Muffin in tow, the girl loved stealing him to take there and not that Rose minded, he was getting the run of the countryside and socialising with Duncan's two collies which was doing wonders for the little fur ball. He was far more sociable nowadays when she took him to town and still the love of all the old women. Muffin jumped all over Rose as she clipped on his little blue leash and handed him out to Abby at the side of the car.

'I'll see you tonight then?' Rose beamed at her, watching the wriggling white ball get loose on the ground and start running around wildly, tail almost taking off with the excitement of being here. He recognised the drop off point and knew where he was going.

'Yup, I'll get Dunky to drop us off at yours around eight.' Abby leaned in and kissed Rose on the cheek, a usual farewell and turned on her heel. 'Don't forget the cakes!' She waved Rose off as she moved her car off the kerb, U turned in the road and headed back towards town with a smile and wave.Yelling out the window.

'I won't forget, going there now.' She turned away from Abby's departing figure and turned on the stereo, summer tunes bringing her mood up a little.

Abby and she had plans tonight; Rob was apparently working late and meant to be meeting a client tonight for dinner. She wouldn't see him until late, if even at all, depending on when he got finished and the last few days he had been so busy.

* * *

Rose walked in on Rob and Morag unexpectedly in the bakery, unaware that he was even back in the village this afternoon after he left for a city meeting this morning, she hadn't heard from him all day. Morag was clinging to him possessively in a way that sent Rose into a dark mood. Jealousy eating into her bitterly, the shock of walking into him here without any heads up that he was back, and the fact he was with her of all people.

Morag's hands were wandering over his upper body, the seductive way she was leaning in to talk to him quietly and that look of unconcealed desire on her face for anyone to see sent Rose into an eternal rage. Having to endure watching them from across the room as she walked up behind them to queue was more than she could bear.

'This looks cosy.' She snapped angrily, not caring what the other woman would make of it and only concerned with letting her so called boyfriend see that she was pissed.

'Rose.' Rob turned and caught her eye, a smile with a frown that portrayed he was confused with her hostility.

Are you dense?

'Who else?' She grated, shoving her hands into her bag to find her purse and praying to god they would just leave. She was beyond angry, she was inwardly seething and using her temper to keep tears at bay. She just felt like screaming at him right now and maybe batting him around the head with anything to hand. She could feel his eyes on her, probably wondering where this had come from but she didn't care. That woman was still pawing him and he was still allowing it.

'I just got back, came in to get some cakes for Ab's and you … You know your movie night…. Ran into Morag here.' He was trying to explain, without it being too obvious to Morag and she seemed to be too lost in scanning the cake board to even realise the huge tension building up between them.

'That's what I'm here for.' She said tightly, still avoiding his eyes and making it clear she wasn't being appeased in the slightest, she lifted her brow and gazed directly at Morag's hand on his chest, her hip nuzzled against him in a semi snuggle and Rob followed. Looking down he frowned and pulled himself away from her in a slow step back.

'If you're getting them then I guess I don't need too; just send Abby along with whatever you're buying.' She smiled sarcastically, turned on her heel and stormed out fast. She was sure for a moment that he would have the sense to follow her but he didn't. A glance back showed him looking her way but still firmly rooted to the spot in which she had left him and not looking like he intended to move. Rose swallowed the sob and stalked to her car in an almighty temper, tears hitting her cheeks before she even got out of the car park.

Driving back home her phone lit up on the seat beside her and despite still driving she picked it up to look.

'**What the hell was that?**' It was Rob and by the looks of things he was pissed too. If he had no clue why she was upset over this then he was a moron.

Flinging the phone down on the seat, she drove the rest of the way home stupidly fast and almost crashed into the opening of her cottage when she made a death defying turn at too high a speed. Slamming the brakes on when she pulled up to her gate, stones scattering as she skidded to a halt.

'**For someone who is just a friend, you sure spend a lot of time cuddling up with her!**'

Rose replied with blurry vision and nose running, sniffing hard as the tears fell fast and not giving one shit that she was acting like a crazed jealous psycho.

'**Are you really accusing me of fucking around with her? Of cheating on you?**'

His response was fast, obviously pissed and Rose had nothing more to say. She knew she was over reacting but she couldn't calm down.

Any woman would feel this way in her shoes, at seeing her man in the clawing hands of some snake like woman he just didn't seem to want to get rid of.

She stared at her phone for a moment and then dropped it in her lap, unsure what the hell to do. She was howling, angry, upset and yet regretted starting this stupid fight. Her head a chaos of doubts and insecurities caused by this damn infernal situation. It was destroying her sanity.

Her phone lit up and vibrated again, she looked down to see his name and picked it up to look.

'**Cancel Abby tonight, I'm coming over. We need to talk.**'

Feeling that inner pride hit, that stubborn side of her, she raised her chin and replied in impulse.

'**Sure your red head will allow you off your leash for that?**'

Rose stared at her own reply and cried some more, mentally wondering if she was about to get her period because this level of immaturity was not her and her hormones obviously had something to do with it.

''**I'm coming now. You better meet me at the cottage!**'

Rose hesitated and all her anger dissipated, sudden trepidation in place of anger now and immediate fear that he was coming, right now! She picked up her phone to tell him 'No' but something stopped her. As upset as she was, she wanted him to come. To get him away from that woman and just… She had no idea. She was too overwrought to think straight and she just couldn't get her head in gear.

Moving fast, she grabbed her phone and bag, wiped her face quickly and dived from her car. Hoping to get in the cottage before he appeared and try to look less hysterical. She got inside as she heard the rev of a familiar sporty engine heading up the gravel driveway and moved faster, pulling the door shut behind her and heading straight for the kitchen.

He didn't knock when he got to her door, just barged in, calling on her and wandered through at speed, obviously intent on finding her. She was by the cooker, trying to steady her nerves and make herself busy by wiping counter tops and moving canisters for no real reason. Spotting her he caught her shoulder and spun her to him caging her against the counter with a hand thrust at either side of her so they were nose to nose. She inhaled sharply with the anger in those steely eyes.

'What the fuck was that?' He snapped at her, no love or warmth in that face right now. Rose jutted her chin up, not afraid to meet his glare.

'You tell me.... How would you feel if I was canoodling with someone ... say, Matt ... In the bakery like that!' She jibed, sarcasm thick and eyes still streaming tears.

'Don't do that! You know it's not the fucking same. There was nothing going on... What the hell has gotten into you today?' He slammed his hand on the counter as he pushed off, putting space between them and turned his back on her.

'I hate that you let her paw all over you like that, you have no idea how it makes me feel.' She blurted out emotionally, wiping her tears on her naked wrist but it was futile.

'I would never do anything, she's harmless.... It means nothing, no different to hugging Abby or Alice or any female I know that I care about.'

'You never had sex or a relationship with Abby or Alice!' Rose snapped, fury coming from low down and angst that he couldn't see why this was different.

'For the love of god... I should have stayed at the bakery or gone home. Instead of this bullshit. This wasn't worth the drive over.' Rob had spun to face her again, pushing his butt against the opposite counter and crossing his arms menacingly over his chest.

'You're saying I'm not worth it?' She spat, tears subsiding to be replaced with irrational fury. Wounded by his inability to see why this bothered her. Rob wasn't an overly jealous guy from what she had seen and even she knew he would have flipped out if roles were reversed.

'Don't put words in my mouth, you know that's not what I said.' He was pacing angrily, his body sending out sparks of rage across the room. The atmosphere electric with two strong forces sizzling in combat, neither able to back down.

'I am pretty sure that's what you meant, even though you didn't word it that way.' Rose sobbed, hating that they were fighting but still unable to stop, hating that he was making her this mad and hysterical.

'Typical woman! Can't just take anything at face value but has to twist its meaning so she's always the victim!' He barked, once again pushing off from his stand point and pacing across the room to slam things about the worktop.

'Fuck you Rob. I AM the victim in this. Do you think I enjoy having to keep my mouth shut, every time I see you canoodling with the woman, who you claim means nothing more to you than friendship? It sure as hell did not look that way to me.' She wiped her face angrily, tears subsiding as rage became the dominant force. Hurt by his behaviour and the way he was talking to her. Yelling at her!

'Did I look like I was doing anything in return? Do you really think I have the energy to fuck both of you Rose? I spend most of my free time here with you. I'm pretty sure the amount of fucking we do is more than enough for any guy.' He spun towards her, his eyes so dark they looked terrifying.

'Is that what I am? Just someone to fuck? Someone to fill your free time?' She baulked, only taking from it what her frayed emotions would allow. Rational or not.

'For the love of god woman! You're fucking insane, you know that, right?' He stormed out of the room, exasperated, throwing his hands up aggressively as though he wanted to strangle her and stalked into the lounge, trying to reel in his temper.

Rose gasped, open mouthed disbelief that he would even say that to her.... Insane? Her? She wasn't the one snuggling up to her ex for fear the they would top themselves and allowing the person they loved to be left out in the cold. If anyone was insane then he was pointing a finger at the wrong bloody woman. Rose sniffed, a new wave of tears hitting her hard, she pulled open the door which led directly to the hall and stomped out, bypassing the lounge and heading straight for her own front door, bawling her eyes out.

She stormed out of the cottage in floods of tears, so fed up with the situation and that woman! Bruised by his words and her head a swirling mass of every emotion going crazy.

Hearing the door slam he came after her fast, catching hold before she even made it to the gate.

'Woah, stop Rose.' He grasped her wrist, tried to pull her back to him, his anger replaced with remorse and pleading. Regret at saying things in fury, at letting words tumble out without thinking.

'Go away, leave me alone.' She wrestled to get free, but he was all around her in an instant, pulling her body to his, trying to turn her face to meet his eyes.

'Baby, I'm sorry. Rose look at me. I'm sorry.' He was panicking, while she was howling and here they were, tangled and over emotional in her front garden as the sun began to go down.

'Fuck you.' She croaked, losing her strength in his tight embrace and giving in as he pulled her face to his chest.

'I love you.' Was all he could say as the last ounces of fight in her dispersed and he could finally, fully pull her into an embrace.

'If you loved me you would stop torturing me.' She sobbed quietly, her arms snaking around him despite herself. Being weak when it came to him was something that annoyed her on so many levels, but she couldn't help it.

'No more, I swear. I won't let her touch me. I won't touch her. If that's what makes you believe that there is nothing in this.' He pressed his mouth to the top of her head, breathing warmly into her scalp and she couldn't fight it anymore. Couldn't stay angry when all she wanted was to let him pull her inside and curl up to forget all of this.

'I don't know how much more of this I can endure' She stifled more tears, her voice shaky and her heart aching. Something had to give, the way things were, it seemed to be getting harder for her.

'I'll tell her.... About you. About us. Soon. I swear.' His voice broke with emotion that matched hers and she felt his body tension begin to slide away. Picking her up in his arms and holding her close so he could look her in the eye. 'I won't keep putting you through this.' He leaned in softly and captured her mouth, kissing her slowly at first and then dropping her feet to the ground gently so he could use his hands to tilt her jaw and kiss her passionately, heat building between them fast. Even more so than normal. He kissed her hard and deeply, tongues met and throats groaned, lost in each other until fever pitched so high he dragged her inside and peeled her clothes off frantically.

After they made love, he cradled her close, listening to the sound of her breathing, her head against his chest, she was lulled into silence by the steady rhythm of his heart. Both lost in thought and pondering the last few hours with a sense of foreboding.

Rob was becoming increasingly agitated; she could tell, although he tried to hide it, but it was obvious the growing tension was clawing away at both of them if today was anything to go by. Lately things had seemed strained, always an underlying atmosphere around them and it was starting to break Rose's heart. She knew this was tainting what they had and she wasn't sure anymore if they would get through this.

Chapter 15

Her newest commission work was coming on leaps and bounds, despite the shift in her relationship and the effects it was having on her mental state, already the first new illustrations had been passed off to her new contract and she only had five more to do for this book.

The book's author was ecstatic with the work so far and her agent had yet another contract already in the works! In the last few years, Rose had become a highly sought-after artist in the field of children's illustration. There was talk with her agent to move into prints for general sale of some of her most popular images in the coming year, and contract offers fast piling up for future work. Financially, Rose had a bright future and the move here was showing in her work. Her art was far easier flowing and natural since coming here. More vibrant with a lot more character and charm. Her agent had seen the change too and admired it with enthusiasm.

It was not just falling in love with Rob, it was the place, the people, Abby, her cottage! All of it just seemed to effortlessly fit like a glove and she could not imagine ever going anywhere else again. The turmoil of her love life was not distracting the need to paint and get lost in magical worlds of make believe.

She could now see why her aunt had spent her adult life here until she had married. The locals were all so welcoming and friendly. They popped by to bring her baked goods, casseroles or invites in passing, they greeted her at the coffee morning meet ups and jumble sales like an old friend or just around town.

Muffin had become somewhat of a celebrity and most of the food shops gave him a free treat on sight. The butcher kept his bones every Friday afternoon for their weekly shopping trip and everyone they met knew him by name, calling him over for a frantic clap. He even had a camaraderie with Rob, snuggling up to him whenever he was here and trying to sleep between them in bed on the rare occasions that he stayed nights.

She had never ventured near the museum again and something inside her sang with relief when she saw the banners coming down for the art exhibit when she was passing. She guessed that meant Matt had returned to the states and there would no longer always be a chance of bumping into him; free from any more awkward encounters.

The cottage was complete, in that every corner, every wall, every room was exactly how she wanted it. Her own stamp finally in place. Even the gardens under the care of her gardener Malcolm were looking full and stunning. He had surprised her with a handmade dog kennel for Muffin only days ago, painted bright white with a shiny red roof. She had been so moved by the gift she had welled up and the red of the little house had pushed her to pay him to redo her front door. It was now a shining glossy pillar box red with gleaming brass handle and letter box. The cottage was everything from her memories and more. It was complete. It was her home finally.

If only her relationship with Rob could be as effortless and uncomplicated as life here was. Maybe then she could finally shift the ever-looming grey cloud from her life and be truly happy.

It was all this clicking into place, and things coming together that made Rose even more frustrated. The one thing she wanted more than anything, was to be able to walk hand in hand with Rob into town, or stand holding his arm at the next dance or charity night. To smile when people saw them together and have everyone know she was his. The mere thought of it got to her more than she ever let on to him, for fear another huge row like the one that night would overcome them.

The longer things stayed the same, small doubts had started to creep into her mind about the situation with Morag. Doubts that they could get through this for much longer before she snapped and made Rob wonder why he was even trying anymore.

Rose had spoken to her parents on and off since moving here, through Facebook, skype and phone on occasion; before she had started to avoid the most recent calls. They had hinted several times at coming to visit for a long weekend, but so far Rose had put them off, explaining she was lost in her commission work and needed to concentrate until it was done; but they were becoming persistent.

She loved her parents. She loved her two older brothers too, but somehow coming here while things were this way felt wrong. She wanted them to meet Rob as her significant other.

How could they?

All this cloak and dagger stuff and secret love life! She didn't want to lie to them either. It was easy to exclude her love life from conversation, they didn't pry and figured she would tell them if any romance sprung up. Somehow though, face to face, she knew her mother would see it. See the look in her eye when her phone beeped. The constant checking of her watch when they had arranged to meet out of town somewhere and she was eager to leave. The restlessness when she did not hear from him as planned or he took an age to reply to her texts. The constant tension in her brow as she mulled over the lack of change in circumstances between them. She would see that her daughter was basically living the life of a glorified mistress and the thought made her sick to her stomach. This was not how she imagined finding 'The one!' would be.

* * *

Abby threw a cushion across the bed at Rose, they were sitting in her bedroom for once, instead of down at the cottage after a long morning shopping at the nearest outlet forty miles away. The bags were all strewn across the fluffy cream carpeted floor and the contents pulled here and there after they had admired and tried on several items of summer clothing. The new perfumes they had bought nestling in the covers of the luxurious bed. Rose had picked up a bottle of her favourite scent, hers dwindling low and knowing full well how much it drove Rob crazy. One of the reasons he would bury his face in her neck from behind and breath her in. He was forever telling her she smelled amazing and edible; tracing nibbles and kisses across her skin deliciously; so, she had made sure it was going to continue.

Rose had been celebrating and splashing out after a good phone meeting with her agent yesterday; some new contracts she had lined up and the news that her fee had been raised for her next two, due to high demand. Both were by authors she had previously worked for and loved that she was getting to return to once loved characters and create more scenes.

Stuffed from takeaway food and chocolate muffins, the girls had decided to make an entire day of it, to meander down to the private lounge, of which they were two. One that was grand and opulent, a huge fireplace and mantle taking over the largest golden wall of the room for guests and visiting clients. The other small cosy room, full of stuffed couches and throw pillows and the largest TV screen known to man, nestled off the large country kitchen.

It used to be Rob's office, but when he had parts of the house remodelled he had the large room put to better use and moved his office directly next to his ground floor bedroom with a joining door. They liked that it was only accessible via the kitchen and gave them a sort of cosy family room to relax and watch movies together. The girls were going to watch a succession of chick flicks in there, gorge on pizza and let the world rock on by; a perfect ending to their girly shopping day.

Rob was away again. She did not know when he would be back this time. It was an impromptu trip to sort something unforeseen and he did not know how long a resolution would take. He had flown out, heading for Glasgow in the early hours, briefly stopping by the cottage before dawn to say his goodbyes and satisfy their need for each other. Short and bittersweet moments crammed in before he headed out and long lingering kisses by her bedroom door. He had seemed stressed and distracted, but she had not pushed him to talk about it, knowing he wouldn't. Business was his forte and he was always someone who played it all close to his chest. This was fast becoming commonplace.

Her phone had lit up several times through the day with texts from him, he was missing her and the feeling was mutual. They text sporadically, nothing of value, just small talk but it was just the contact that mattered. That wherever he was she could still reach out to him; knowing he was always at the other end of the phone somehow helped her relax.

Muffin was running about crazy under Abby's bed, grabbing discarded shoes and pulling them around. The girls had given him a little too many treats today and the hyper-buzz coming off him was a little extreme. They watched him, laughing before scooping him up to belly rub the little fur ball and try to calm him down. It was the dog equivalent of a sugar rush and he was rolling around wildly, eager to play. Attacking any skin with licks and nibbles and whimpering like he was excited. She knew the rush would dive soon and he would crash out for a long nap before long.

A huge ruckus down in the hall drew the girl's attention. Alice's voice could be heard echoing in a very aggressive manner and another female voice equally angry in return. Abby groaned, sliding from her bed and moved quickly out the open door. Following Abby out onto the balcony over the grand stair, they caught sight of Morag nose to nose with dear old Alice, yelling at one another. There was a smashed vase on the floor by the wall and water and flowers everywhere. Their voices echoing loudly around the large space below them.

'Wow! What the actual hell!' Abby yelled and made her way down towards the women angrily. Rose stayed put from her high perch, unsure what to do but stay back. Out of sight and out of that woman's way.

'MORAG!' Abby yelled again, catching both women's attention and halting the argument briefly as she closed the gap between them. 'What the hell???'

'She demands to know where Mr Munro is Abby!' Alice put her hands on her hips, pushing her chin out defiantly. Rose loved that little fierce old lady. She really did look like a force to reckon with, standing there all bosom, plump floral dress and angry glare. Her grey curls bouncing in agitation. Morag was scowling at her angrily, pointing a bony finger at her in mid-air.

'This Shit again? Really?... He's not here Morag! I'm sure Alice already told you! He's gone to Glasgow for a few days.' Abby could not conceal her hatred of the other woman. Coming close to her in a defiant aggressive manner.

'LIAR!' she almost screamed in Abby's face, causing Rose to jump where she was shielded from view, her nerves tingling with the impulse to protect her friend. She swayed against the balcony, torn between staying put or going down there and getting in between them.

'He's with her. Isn't he? He's with his fucking whore!' She was spitting venom, her normally controlled face contorted and ugly. Her red-rimmed eyes narrowed and cruel.

'Here we go again!' Abby spat back 'He has NO whore Morag. Your crazy ass self and multiple fucking personalities make sure he can't do a bloody thing with his life without answering to you! You're more than enough versions of female for him to keep up with!' Abby swung away, throwing her hands up in exasperation. A sign this was a common argument and showing no ounces of fear or intimidation in the face of this angry woman.

'I'm not stupid! You think I don't know he has some slag shacked up somewhere? He's made enough hints that he was dating.... Tell me... Where has he been going lately?... Always checking his phone. Always busy running errands. Creating distance between us... Barely any time anymore to take me to the hospital or come for my therapy appointments... He missed my last flight back and I had to get a taxi home at four in the morning because I could not get hold of him and whenever I come here he is never in his own bed! Now he disappears without any word and leaves me high and dry again. I need help with the museum and he's always fucking busy! Won't answer my calls.

Leaves me lame excuses that he's in a meeting or he's dealing with a client, doesn't text me back for hours on end.' She was high pitched, closed to hysteria, rambling and Rose suddenly saw what she needed to see.

The agony of a woman in heartbreak, the pain of a man trying to pull away from her while she was clinging onto him like a lifeboat. Morag was behaving like Rose but for different reasons and a lot more extreme. Rose had felt only a margin of this ache when she had seen them together at the bakery and now seeing her here like this, she put herself in Morag's shoes for a second. If the man you were wholly dependent on and crazy in love with was trying to find happiness with another woman, then it would send you off the edge much like this. Whether you had mental health issues or not.

Abby muttered something about hardly being 'Dry' and the smell of booze. Not really helping things at all and she could see, even from up here, Morag was swaying on her feet quite drastically.

This was what he had been dealing with for god knows how long.

The elegant seductive woman from the museum, replaced with this wild-eyed, erratic mess before her. Hair tangled and unkempt. Clothes dishevelled and normally manicured nails chipped and broken. Her makeup had slid under her eyes, giving her an almost panda look, her mouth normally precision lined in red was faint and smeared, which added to the hysterical ambience. She looked like a total train wreck, the air of someone who had been scrubbing her fingers over her head and face in desperation, voice several keys higher than normal and with a slight slur. Her normally upper-class manner now rough and full of common slang and slurs; the facade well and truly slipped. She did not seem to hear Abby's insults. Lost in her manic pacing and raging as she cursed out Abby.

'Maybe he has just had enough of your bulls…' Abby continued, waving her hands dramatically and stomping closer to Morag.

'Language Abby!' Alice cut in like a motherly hen, patting the girl's shoulder and pulling her back to intervene. The voice of reason and calm in this household. Mother Alice.

'Morag?... Mr Munro left on business in the early hours. I packed his bags last night and Tommy got his car ready for an early departure. Go look at the airfield and you will find his car parked in his usual spot... There is no woman Morag! He barely has time to relax, let alone carry on some sordid affair!' Alice folded her arms under her ample bosom and tried to sound sympathetic.

Rose felt the pang of pain hit her stomach and heart in unison. Knowing that Alice was unaware, but somehow her words had struck a chord.

Was that how it would look to everyone? Is that what people would think? That she was carrying on with him behind Morag's back, having a dirty little fling? The cause of this woman's anguish?

It made her feel dirty and stricken with pain, looking at herself in a whole new light.

'I'll check alright, and I'll check his flights and make sure he was alone!!!' She was still seething and spitting feathers. Rob had mentioned that he let Morag use his private jet when needed, so the threat was probable. She didn't put it past this version of Morag to go ravage through the flight papers and check for other passengers.

'Do whatever the fuck you want, psycho, and you will pay for that!' Cut in Abby, pointing at the mess to the side of them on the floor. The remains of a crystal vase and beautiful floral selection which had been sitting in the side hall earlier.

'Shut up you jumped up little br...' Morag swung forward violently, just missing Abby by mere inches with an attempt at a slap.

'Oh no, you don't!' The voice came out of Rose without prior thought and even shocked herself. The way Morag had moved towards Abby aggressively, that look in her eye. It had impulse kicked this loud aggressive reaction from her and she was already half way down the stairs, her temper flying.

No one would lay a finger on HER Abby! Especially not this crazed hag!

'Don't you dare talk to her like that and you get the hell away from her! You lay one finger on her so help me god I will snap you like a twig!'

Astounded into silence, everyone just stared at Rose as she approached at speed. She had scaled the stair in bare feet in a matter of seconds, her hair flying wild and her temper roaring like a lioness. She bounded to push in between all the women speedily and was now only inches from Morag herself.

Morag's breathy What the F response only enraged her more.

'Who the hell do you think you are, tramp?' Morag had regained some sense of aggression and was now ready to square up to this new annoyance. From here the stench of alcohol was enough to put hairs on even Rose's chest, it was obvious Morag was more than a few bottles into a heavy drinking session, more alarmingly was that she probably drove here.

'SHUT UP!' Rose had stayed her sharp shrill voice with a palm, millimetres from Morag's face, startling her into a moment's pause. All the built-up frustration, heartache and agitation of weeks and weeks of sneaking around somehow coming tumbling out in one moment.

'Who the hell do you think you are talking too? She's Rob's sister! She's Abby Munro! She lives in this house! Who are you to disrespect her and Alice? Coming in here smashing things and raising your voice huh? Demanding to know where Rob is?? He's a grown ass man with a business to run and a life of his own. He can do whatever he damn well wants without your permission and everyone is completely sick to death of your behaviour; you're not even his girlfriend Morag!!' Rose let loose, her temper spewing out and her mouth enjoying a moment of verbal diarrhoea.

Abby and Alice stood in stunned silence, their eyes large and fixed on Rose and Morag as though time had paused; mouths agog. The normally cheerful and smiling Rose breathing fire before them was enough of a surprise to bring an unearthly moment of silence... And then Morag's voice broke

'He's my... We're supposed to be working it out...I'm trying. I'm really trying and he knows I love him. He loves me, I know he does.' The tears fell like waterfalls from her face and Rose felt immediately bad for the woman. The fire in her belly dowsing quickly when faced with genuine sadness and her own seething anger simmering down at this pathetic demonstration. But like the flick of a switch Morag seemed to get a hold of herself and snapped back into fierce anger. Rose found it hard to stay angry at this picture of genuine heartbreak, a moment of empathy cooling her down.

'What the fucking hell do you know anyway? You don't have a fucking clue what we are, so back off! It's none of your fucking business, slag! You're just his baby sister's bestie and nothing but a fucking annoying presence wherever we go.' Morag moved forward, raising her clenched fists up to her chest. The anger and violence once again threatening to explode from the red-haired woman and Rose recoiled slightly, suddenly unsure of this manic reaction, all her fire and fight gone and wasn't as quick to return the way Morag's had.

Abby sprang into immediate protector mode, screamed at Morag to leave her house.

'Get out! ... Get out! ... Crazy bitch' She was in Morag's face now, pushing Rose aside and pushing Morag back hastily. An instant reaction to defend Rose. The fiery nature of Abby only superseding Rose's previously rage.

The next few seconds went by in a haze of chaos. Rose was not sure exactly how or what happened, the pushing twosome became a threesome of hands and grabbing. Hair tugging and chaos and somehow, she was caught up in it. Her hair grabbed and yanked hard so that she was pulled in against Morag's slender frame and embroiled in a cat fight of sorts that included Abby jumping on top of Morag.

They ended up brawling in a heap on the floor, all legs and nails and screaming. Rose was slapped in the face so hard by Morag she saw stars before Abby managed to jump on her back and wrench a good amount of red curls out. Alice was trying to pull Abby away but soon felt the wrath of Morag as the old woman was smacked over the right breast with a flailing arm and dove in to join in.

Next thing Rose knew, boys were hauling them apart. Rose had seen red and was clawing and kicking at anything resembling Morag aggressively as she was drawn out of the fold.

Tommy was pulling his now animated brawling wife to one side and trying to tame her unleashed beast. She was a fierce one that little old lady. Morag was being half dragged, half escorted by two burly lads out the front door kicking and screaming back out of the house and Duncan was holding Abby's screeching fighting form around the waist. Her arms and legs flailing as she called unladylike curse names and insults after the red-haired woman.

Rose was helped to her feet by one of the returning boys, dazed from the smack in the face and a little unsteady, her hands shaking as she was ushered towards the kitchen behind Tommy and his wife. Rose had no clue who these boys were, they seemed vaguely familiar from the dance but she recognised Duncan right away.

'Girls, sit.' Alice commanded them and ushered the men out, once they were in the kitchen. Adrenalin was still coursing through their veins. Duncan kissed Abby quickly and shyly, saying something in her ear before following his friends out. She watched him go with a smile on her face that looked a lot like Rose's whenever Rob was close. She envied her for being able to freely be that way with Duncan.

'Well that was eventful. Thank God Duncan was popping by with my festival tickets.' Abby burst out laughing and ignored Alice's shake of the head. The woman turned and moved to put the kettle on and uncovered a plate of scones to bring to the table.

'Tommy will be telling me off later, hearing that ruckus from the garden, must have given him heart failure.' Alice brought over a tray of tea and cups with milk and sugar and laid them in the centre of the table.

Rose just sat, dazed by the encounter. Wondering what the hell Rob was going to say about it and unable to shake Morag from her mind. She was completely torn about what had happened.

'Rob is going to be pissed.' She said out loud without thought.

'Don't worry about it Rose' Abby smiled, catching the worried expression on the normally cheerful face. 'It isn't the first time and won't be the last. She's attacked Rob many a time. Slapped Alice here once before too, and she tried to go for me with a vase once but Rob was quick and restrained her. If you're worried he's going to be mad then fear not, he will be mega pissed at Morag for this. Not us.' Abby pulled over a cup and started making herself a sugary tea.

Alice pushed between them, lifting Rose's fingers which were cradling her burning cheek and placed a small ice pack on her skin instead, pushing her hand back against it to hold it in place with a warm smile and a pat on her shoulder.

'Keep that on to stop it from bruising.'

'Why does he put up with it?' Rose was in disbelief at her statement, but Abby didn't need to respond. Alice cut in instead, a sad look on her maternal face as she moved to a chair and slowly sank down.

'The girl has real troubles, Rose. I feel sorry for her really. Her mum killed herself when she was still a young un. Much of the same illness that Morag seems to suffer from and well that no good filthy alcoholic father started abusing her.' She looked down at her lap sadly. 'Even as a kid, she was never quite right. Something off about her emotionally, so when it came out a few years ago that she had finally spoken up, well… No one could blame her for being that way. He got five years for sexual abuse, should have been more but her testimony was weak. She was too emotional and too afraid to really tell them everything she should have.' There was a glaze of emotion in Alice's eye and Rose could tell she had probably known the girl a little more than Rose first thought. Alice had been the housekeeper here since Rob was a baby, it made sense that she had known Morag as long as Rob had, if not longer in this tiny community.

'And she ended up in the nut house for a year!' Abby chimed in, seeming a tad smug about it.

'Abby! It's a psychiatric hospital, that's not proper to call it that and please take that look off your face. No one asks to be unwell in that way!' Alice chided. The pair looked at each other with narrowed eyes. An obvious affection between the sparring pair despite her scolding.

'So, she still has to go there then?' Rose cut in as Abby made faces at Alice childishly, remembering Morag mention her appointments and therapy.

'Yes, she sees a shr…Psychiatrist!' Abby corrected herself, catching the glare from Alice across the table. 'She has a list of things going on as long as her arm. Bipolar… Some personality, anxiety thing… Lack of one more likes!' Abby mock grinned at Alice who shook her head, mock bashing Abby on the head indulgently.

'Yes, she still has to go, still has to check in every two weeks and they monitor her medication.' Alice seemed to know more than she let on and she wondered if Rob confided in this dear woman or if this was simply observation. A tug at her heart as he came to mind and another shiver of apprehension at how he was going to react. Rose pulled the pack off her face now the ice was starting to sting it.

'When she takes it!' Abby raised her eyebrows as she mumbled and took a sip of tea. Uttering something else under her breath and gaining a small slap on the hand from Alice. A look of warning before Alice pulled over two cups and made one for Rose and herself quickly, pushing the cup to Rose and tapping the ice pack with an authorative look. Rose put it back on her face obediently.

'Sadly, this morning, the behaviour is a sign she's back to not taking her medications.' Alice sighed, genuine sadness on her face. 'Poor Rob is the only one she ever listens too, ever leans on. He really is the only one who has any time for her anymore; she put's so much stress on him, the poor sod, and all he can do is try and be there for her. He has always been a decent sort of boy, looking out for everyone else instead of his own needs and she has no idea how much pressure she puts on him day after day. It's no wonder he sometimes takes a break from her.'

Rose felt the pride and pain hit equally. Torn badly.

'Has she no one else? Family?' Rose was beginning to see for the first time why Rob felt he needed to be delicate. Understood his personality enough to know he was the eternal caregiver and protector with people he felt responsible for, and if Morag was as fragile as she seemed to be then it was no wonder he was treating her with kid gloves in this way. He had never told her any of this, not that she had asked, but still. This was far worse than anything Rose could have figured out.

'Not anymore. Those that didn't walk away, she pushed away. Been a long time coming to that breakdown she had. Pushed every single soul away and just clung to him like he was a raft, her only lifeline. I could see he was struggling but he never let her down, just pushed on and tried to help her find her feet again.' Alice looked pensive. Abby was now restlessly moving in her chair and slid her mug across the table, cutting in.

'No one can deal with her erratic behaviour. So, no one wants to know anymore. She's reckless. Swings from purrs to scratches without warning. Drinks a lot of alcohol a lot of the time, despite it making her act like an arse, likes to smash things and lash out but then cries for days. Makes him feel shitty for everything she does; blames him. She holds it over him. Threatens suicide and breaks her heart in front of him, knowing he has no resistance to girls crying. She knows how to play him like a fucking violin.' Abby was starting to look irritated, the subject beginning to piss her off. 'He's the reason she even has a bloody job; our money is what keeps that museum open and her position permanent. She couldn't run a mile let alone a museum alone; he does more for that place than she's capable of. Do you know that it was him that started off the exhibitions every month to bring newcomers in? The new displays, switching it up. He has enough to deal with, yet he also has to find the time to run over there and deal with stuff she should be doing for that place' Abby pushed back in her chair angrily, hiding none of the contempt she had for the red head.

'And they're not still... You know...Romantic?' She knew she shouldn't be prying like this, acting like she didn't trust or believe him. She knew he had told her so many times and doubting him was stupid, but she had to understand if there were any other motives, such as deep-rooted feelings that he would never admit to her. She had been afraid of that for weeks now when trying to figure this out.

'No. Not on his part. Not since she told him she was having his baby a few years back. They got engaged. He really was going to make a go of it and do the right thing, typical Rob. They had been on and off for years and we all knew that he didn't really want to marry her. More off than on but he always still tried to help her. Turned out to be nothing but a lie to make him marry her and it all blew up in her face.' Abby sighed, twisting her cup around in agitation.

Alice got up to clear the table and the worktops, knowing this part of the conversation was a little too personal for her liking. Abby lost in thought was still talking without hindrance.

'Totally destroyed him you know. Not just that the baby wasn't real, but the lying, the pretence. The way, that no matter what he had done for her over the years, she still could do that to him.' She shrugged. 'I don't think he ever looked at her the same again and she's been trying ever since to make him love her; to get him back. Always hanging over him and pretending she's still his girlfriend. I don't think he even notices it anymore, he's that used to it.' She pushed her cup away, obviously irritating herself with fidgeting. 'He told me he really believes she would kill herself if he found someone else. She really is that obsessed with him… He would never forgive himself if she did. He feels responsible all the time for how she's as it is.'

Rose had no words, her head swirling with all of it. The complicated mess that it was. The way her heart felt like piercing hot needles were being pushed in all over its surface at the thought he had once felt something for that woman.

Had he ever really loved her? The way he told Rose he felt for her?

The thought that she had deeply hurt him and still he had this crazy duty to look after her, to be the rock in her life no matter what she did to him, made her heart ache.

Did he still have feelings for her?

The heaviness of the situation started the small tear in her heart but the flood of information had ripped it wide open. This was why he could never open up and tell her the true extent of the issue. It was vast! This was not a situation that would just get better anytime soon. This was not something he could softly get her used too. Morag was really ill. Seriously properly long term and medicated ill and had a past that would destroy most people! She was far more dependent on him than even Rose thought possible and this thing they had…This always, never ending, waiting for the impossible thing...It was not going to get better any time soon. Morag was never going to get better. She was so in love with Rob that it clouded everything she did and felt, she was delusional and lost in make believe that he was still hers.

How could that ever change in their situation? How could it when it was hanging on a thread dependent of this sick woman's mental state?

Real mental health issues, a real diagnosed, something wrong, sickness. Someone who was properly not capable of being held accountable for her actions. The irrational mind and erratic behaviour. The agony she must go through every day. It made Rose feel sick to her stomach for the woman and she barely knew her.

What must Rob, her friend, her ex-lover feel when he looked at her?

He knew she was barely hanging on and he was all that was keeping her afloat. This was not short term, this was forever.

She couldn't do this!

And the sudden heart stopping realisation that she could not go on another second, knowing this was the reality, caused her to break inside like a shattered mirror. This was not the path to happy ever after. If he tore out Morag's heart to be with her it would forever, follow them. If he delayed telling Morag the truth and they carried on this way it would destroy them, it already was. There was no getting around this undeniable truth. There was no solution that involved Rob and Rose being together.

Chapter 16

Rose went home later that afternoon, feigning a headache and apologising to Abby for ruining their plans, but she just needed to be alone to think. Everything she had learned about Morag was swirling in her head and her heart was breaking into a thousand pieces with all of it.

It tainted everything she did for the next few hours. Took all enjoyment from her life. Her mind, a swirling mass of conflicting thoughts and emotions, robbing her of her sanity, and as much as she tried to put on a brave face, even Muffin was sensing something was wrong. Following her around needily and whining up at her every time she sat still.

She pushed her phone into her bag on silence and ignored his texts, ignored when he called her later that night, unable to bear the sound of his voice. Unable to look at his name on the screen. Her heart prickling and heavy with the realisation that it was never going to work, that seeing Morag that way, seeing the extent of what he was dealing with, just put an end to everything.

She couldn't do this anymore and it was going to be the hardest thing she had ever done in her life; she needed to break things off, for her own sanity and for him too. This relationship was on a one-way road to destruction and if they kept going on this way she would end up hating him or vice versa. Morag was always going to come between them and Rose deserved more. She wanted normal; love; a relationship and happy endings. Kids, marriage, a life. None of that was possible if things were always going to be this way.

She tried to resist the temptation to read his texts but weakness got the better of her. She missed him more than she could bear and she knew she was only delaying the moment that would cut her heart out. Mostly they were just updates on his trip and that he missed her. That he would catch her when she was not busy. He would just assume she was with Abby and couldn't answer, or was in her studio where she never took her phone so she had peace.

The normal tone of his messages ripped her heart out, she felt like she was dying inside, he had no clue about the change in her and what was coming and the thought of hurting him only made her ache more. She sat staring at it numbly, tears pouring down her face as her phone vibrated again.

Another text, asking if she was upset with him as she was not responding. It had been a couple of hours and he knew she usually responded eventually when it came to him. Even if she was with Abby; she never usually just blanked him completely. She stifled a sob as another text hit her screen.

'I think I get it Rose... I spoke to Abby. Talk to me baby. xxx'

He was making this so much harder already and she had not even told him. She was losing resolve to stay strong and wait for his return to do this face to face. She couldn't keep ignoring him, it wasn't fair. He had done nothing to deserve this.

'Is there nothing I can say?' He barely left a minute between texts, sensing some how he would get no response. She bit her lip, holding back the tears inside, hurting so much more now that he knew what she was thinking. He knew her well enough to be able to piece it together.

He would have known from a brief conversation in which Abby would have told him about Morag's visit. She would have told him about the fight and the following conversation. What Abby had told her about Morag and their past; Abby told Rob everything. She had no secrets. Part of why she loved the girl was becauseshe was honest and open with everyone. He would have guessed at what she was thinking, maybe even coming to the same conclusion a million times before himself. The fact that this situation had no end. That their future was as bleak as the last few weeks had been. That sneaking around would always be part of the relationship and Morag would always be there, always in the way. That it was not about needing more time, Morag was never going to be ready.

She picked up her phone, her will breaking and the need to reply to him overwhelming her.

'I can't do this anymore.' She had no idea how else to say this, even typing those few words was breaking her heart into a million pieces; she needed to say more but she had no idea how to tell him that she needed to walk away for her own sake. She typed another text immediately, feeling the need to try, afraid to let him respond when she had so much more she wanted him to hear first.

'I have thought about this all afternoon and it just keeps coming around in circles. It's ripping my heart out but I need to end this Rob, before it destroys us. I love you so much but this is killing us and it's not working.'

There was a long pause, her hands trembling. Reminiscent of the first time she ever texted him weeks ago about being her slave for a day, but this time it was far more devastating. Far more real. She knew that his response was going to tear her apart. Her mind was made up and even though she was dying inside she knew it was the only way.

She sat with her phone in hand for over ten minutes waiting. Barely breathing, unable to look at anything else. Tense at his lack of response but knowing she could not keep sending messages into the emptiness and crying silently as her body wracked with pain.

Finally, her phone vibrated and she turned it over with trembling hands.

'I know! I have known for a while; I said it would destroy us. I have felt us falling apart more and more the longer we go on. I won't try Rose, I love you too much to make this harder for you. I don't want to get to the stage where you hate or resent

me for it, just know I'm always there if you need me. No matter what. Xxx I love you Penelope. Always.'

It was the worst goodbye she had ever had in her life; this was not how she had wanted it; she wanted to feel him against her one more time. To feel his arm's pull tight around her and push away the world for one last moment. To have their one last time, so she could cling onto him and burnish those memories into her brain for eternity.

She slid down onto the couch, dropping her phone silently. She had nothing she could say to him that would make any difference now and her mind was so overwrought that typing would have been impossible. She rested her head against the arm and let the flood of gut wrenching pain and heartfelt sobs wrack her body. She had no more fight left in her anymore. She had literally just ripped out her own heart and stamped it to absolute death.

She laid on that couch and let the despair take over for the longest time, until the sun disappeared and she was left in only a moon lit room.

When she finally had the strength to pull herself up from the couch, the rage within her caused her to lash out and swipe the mantle clear of frames, crashing and smashing to the ground in an emotional release.

He hadn't even fought for her. Just let her go. Just like that. Just a couple of texts and it was all over.

Had she ever really been anything more than a distraction for him?

Crumbling back into a sodden sobbing heap she stayed that way cradling her legs as Muffin tried to click the tears from her hot cheeks until the sun was long gone.

* * *

Rose was always good at hiding her feelings when life called upon her too, despite feeling dead inside. Walking around like a lifeless zombie, yet still functioning among the living. Managing smiles for the postman; managing idle chit chat when she popped into the grocery shop for milk and the bakery for bread. Looking like she was rested and healthy under her amazing makeup skills.

Even Abby could not tell really that her world had come crashing down, breaking into a million sharp pieces on the floor and her shell was nothing more than a robotic presence. That her dark circles from lack of sleep and shadows from lack of appetite were well and truly concealed thanks to Estee Lauder.

Life just carried on around her as before; people still shone and smiled and the sun still held high in the sky. Even the news reported that this had been their longest hottest summer in recent years and that the country was enjoying the gorgeous weather. Everyone was happy and bright and moving on in life... While Rose was just trying to breathe.

Her parents had finally twisted her arm and arranged a visit, despite all her protests and excuses to put them off. Caught in her weakened state so that she couldn't argue as effectively as she would normally. Didn't want too. She didn't need to anymore, it was not like she had a reason for them to meet Rob Munro. No secret romances or lies, just Rose and Muffin and same old. Same old.

* * *

Abby came by in a super hyper state after Rose came off the phone with her mother that afternoon, she had rung three times in two days, overexcited with the plans for their visit. The Manor was hosting the annual summer fete and that meant a lot of great family fun through the day, stalls, games and pony rides; then at night, a glitzy drink and dance. Abby was bouncing and excited and trying to describe the excellence to be had as it was the highlight of the year and she was really looking forward to it.

Rose wanted to refuse. Abby staring at her with open-eyed enthusiasm only made her feel more pressured into an agreement; she groaned when she realised it was the same weekend as her parents visit and they would not let her bypass a night at the manor. It was all her mum had gushed about on the phone when she first found out Abby and Rose were such good friends.

Her mum had somewhat of a star struck condition concerning the Munro family and their huge house; Olivia's stories always being a favourite of hers. That was all she needed. Her arm well and truly twisted, she could not find a good enough excuse to bypass the event altogether without making it obvious to Abby that something was clearly off.

That something being Rob!

Rose made sure she never brought Rob up in conversation but sometimes Abby did. It was only natural, seeing as he was the centre of her world. Her big brother and protector, he made sure everything in Abby's life went smoothly and happily along; always checking in. Thanks to Abby's idle chit chat, Rose learned that he had extended his trip by a week or two in Glasgow; telling Abby he had some things he needed to deal with.

Rose had wondered if he was taking time out to let things simmer away between them. Distance to let it all drift away in the breeze.

Was he giving her time to get over it or was he simply avoiding her?

Shrugging it away and ignoring the feeling of emptiness; she was getting better at locking down her brain whenever he surfaced, to avoid any unnecessary breakdowns. Somehow even apart, it still felt worse knowing he was so far away even still. Hundreds of miles between them. She threw herself head first into trying to forget him.

It helped being dragged around by Abby that week to take a break from her work room after many a night doing nothing else but drawing. They headed out for short trips almost every day, enjoying the glorious sunshine and pretending to be tourists while Abby had a break from college.

They had visited every beauty spot in a sixty-mile radius that week, as though Abby sensed that her friend needed to be saved from her own thoughts. Abby was intuitive and although she had sussed something was going on, she never pried. Knowing when Rose needed to talk she would, so she was doing what she could on a lack of information and trying to keep her friend busy.

They had hit the beach, castles, the zoo, petting farms and museums. It had been eventful and tiring and had helped keep her mind occupied just enough to get through the days. She was thankful for that anyway.

Even though she knew he wouldn't contact her she found herself checking her phone more than she should, every time that ache of disappointment followed by anger at her own pathetic-ness. She tried to bury it deep in her bag and ignore it, but her fingers would creep down anxiously and check regardless; she would scold herself at the wave of hurt when she saw nothing but her familiar screen saver.

Rose just needed to forget him, put her head down and work hard in the hopes it would get easier in time. She had enough work to make sure she could be distracted for several months if needed.

Her agent had already overnighted new forms to sign and notes to go over for her next book. All she had to do was pack and send these final pieces in cardboard rolls ready for the printing company to turn them into luscious glossy children's books. Her heart had not been in it anymore, but you could not tell by looking at them at all. Still vibrant, fun and whimsical and very much in her trademark style. She envied the young and their ability to look at her pictures in awe and bewilderment lost in the fairy stories and characters. She could sure use being lost in a fairy-tale about now.

* * *

Muffin whined by the door, indicating he needed to go out for a toilet break, she checked her watch realising it had gone after eleven pm and was pitch black outside. Knowing he wouldn't do his business out in the garden, she had no alternative but to walk the little fur ball. She needed a break, her back and neck aching from scooping over her technical desk when she was putting the final details on her last piece. A walk was maybe not a bad idea, some air and a little stroll would make her feel ready for bed. Lately sleeping had been near impossible, so her nights had gotten later and later, working until fatigue took over.

She rummaged in the kitchen for a torch and headed out in a woolly cardigan and slip on shoes with her normally light summer dress, Muffin on the leash in hand. The night air was thick and dark. A little too humid and stuffy but the moon was up and full in the cloudless sky, casting a lot more light than normal, she held the torch out in front of her illuminating the ground, avoiding large stones and tree roots as they made their way towards the main road. There was a slight breeze in the air making the trees rustle, the faint sound of the river nearby adding to the mysterious atmosphere.

Muffin sniffed at the overgrown bushes at the sides but seemed intent on holding in his business until he had been a proper walk. Straining to pull her towards the main entrance, he was restless and whiny. She cursed him under her breath, tucking the doggy bags into her pocket again. Sometimes he was just a stubborn miniature mule. He did not even seem like he wanted to go potty anymore as she headed out of the gravel road, expecting to take a turn to the left and use the grass verge out of town, but stopped in alarm at the dark car parked just off the entranceway. Muffin began excitedly yapping, his tail flying wildly and spinning around in circles pulling the leash tightly. It looked abandoned. Two wheels up on the grass verge just at the start of the turning into the cottage. She recognised it at once and felt her heartbeat start to quicken and her nerves take over; that sinking feeling of dread overcoming her.

She heard him before she saw him.

Rob!

'Down here.'

Jumping out of her skin, she slid around the car cautiously, realising he was at the back wheel changing a flat tyre. His jacket was off, his white shirt sleeves rolled up and he was expertly using a tyre iron to tighten wheel nuts back on the new wheel, the flat one laying on the grass beside the car. Muffin lunged forward at him, covering his hands and wrists with fevered licks as he ruffled his tiny head. Rob took a second to pick him up for a belly rub before letting him back down and keeping his gaze averted.

'Hey,' She sounded as awkward as she felt and physically sick to her stomach, looking at him longingly. She knew the first time seeing him again would be hard but she had not counted on it being this much agony. She pulled Muffins leash back as he again tried to climb onto Rob's lap and he sat obediently on the grass verge, wide eyed, that wild little face alert and happy at the sight of his master. Traitorous little beast.

Rob glanced up, his normally clean-shaven, tanned face was stubbled and tired and he gave a quick smile. It didn't reach his eyes and he didn't stray on her face for more than a mere second. It had the same effect as poking something sharp in her heart.

'Hey… I'm done, so will be out of your way in a sec.' He stood up, using a rag to clean his filthy hands, effortlessly scooped up the ruined tyre and popped it in the boot. She was struggling for words, trying to find something to say and desperate to drag out this brief encounter now that she was faced with him. Seeing him only highlighted just how much she missed him, just how much she loved him.

'I thought you were still in Glasgow?' She said shyly, her voice a little fragile and low, he just seemed normal and distant.

'My flight got in an hour ago. This is me just getting home.' He still didn't look her way, concentrating on putting tools back into a little compartment on the boot floor. He sounded emotionless, no warmth in his voice, no anger either; just indifference. It was sheer agony, being this close and not being able to throw herself into his strong arms when he looked as handsome as always and it only pained her more that he was acting like she didn't mean anything to him.

'Right! of course… Did you get things sorted out then? On your trip?' She sounded odd even to herself, trying to hard not to react to him. He shut the boot

'All that I could sort, yeah.' The disinterest and coldness was causing Rose to well up inside. The urge to cry growing stronger and stronger and she felt stupid. She had chosen this; this was her doing, not his, and he was only acting like she should have been. Keeping his distance. It shouldn't be ripping her open like this, he was being civil and not being an asshole, but it hurt like crazy.

He stopped as he got to his driver door and looked down at Muffin for a moment's pause, and then finally at Rose.

'Don't go too far. It's late and although rural, you never know who is out here Penny.'

It was too much, that little piece of concern, even if he did use that awful pet name. Still, the protector; and she was rendered unable to talk. Afraid that trying to answer would cause a breakdown in front of him, she faked a quick smile and nodded, turning away quickly with an awkward wave.

Without looking back, she headed away from the car. Fighting the urge to turn back with all her might, she pushed on, tears now streaming down her face and trying to block out the hum of his car behind her.

Rob watched her walk off in his rear-view mirror for a few seconds, adjusting his mirror to watch her out of sight before heading off and going home.

Rose felt her strength going with the car as it faded away.

Muffin refused to do anything more than scent every bush they passed in the twenty minutes she dragged him around. He kept pausing and straining to look down the road to the way he had driven off and it only angered her. She grew agitated and huffily pulled him back towards the cottage. The tears finally dry and instead the return of numbness and misery.

He had looked every bit as good as her memories. Smelled his familiar scent in the air and the sight of his bare arms and tanned skin flexing as he tightened the wheel nuts had made her long painfully to reach out and touch him. The detailed memories of how his hands had felt on her body and that deep caressing voice. She could not shake the cold blank expression on his beautiful face or the lack of any love in his controlled voice, knowing fine well that she was torturing herself!

She pushed open the cottage door and turned on the lights angrily.

Maybe this is what she needed!

To see him again.

To get over the first shock and see that he was happy to move on; to actually feel that it was over and see with her own eyes his disinterest in her; some sort of closure.

He was behaving as she expected he would. Back to being strangers who occasionally nodded in passing. All back down to business as though she had never been more to him than his sisters friend. One thing for sure, he wasn't suffering the way Rose was at having ended things. He seemed like he always seemed.

Absolutely fucking normal.

She threw herself down in bed after settling Muffin into his and stared at the ceiling, pushing thoughts of him aside and tossing around. She could not get comfy, every part of this room reminded her of him even if he didn't deserve her obsessing over him. Her sheets, although fresh, still held his scent faintly. Maybe it was not the bed, maybe it was the air around her and the way her ceiling danced with moonlit shadows, even reminding her of lying awake listening to him breathe in his sleep so many times during stolen moments together.

'Argggh!'

Frustrated, she threw off the sheets and got back up, pacing and hating everything around her.

Was this how it was? In books and movies and life? Is this what getting over someone was like? Someone who you thought really was your forever?

It was horrible and cruel. Like some sort of mental torture! She picked up the phone by her bed, seeing its blank screen staring back at her mockingly and threw it at the wall.

'I hate you!!!... I hate you!!... I HATE YOUUU... I Hate...' She broke down into sobs, falling back onto the bed and curling into the foetal position. Talking out loud through a flood of tears, full of self-pity and despair.

'I'm losing my mind...I'm going insane... Is this how she feels? Is this how you make her feel, knowing she isn't wanted?'

Slow painful agony and torture.

'Like she can't breathe! Like she's having her insides twisted and pulled apart slowly. She's seeping away into non-existence...That she cannot function or go on... Or live?'

She closed her eye's feeling the hot tears change course and trickle down her cheeks towards her ears as she lay flat on her back. Somehow soothing. Morag came into her mind's eye clear as day.

The first time she laid eyes on her, when she was the hot seductive picture of perfect manicure and control. That alluring demeanour, she had seemed like a woman who got everything she wanted with little effort. Domineering and confident. It was all a facade. A lie. A face she showed the world when really, inside she was broken and aching and drowning in her own despair. She was a first-class actress and the world her stage.

For the first time, Rose felt compassion for the woman, instead of hatred and resentment. She could relate to the despair of dangling on a precipice, not knowing how to feel or act when the man you were devoted too was just indifferent. To have your heart trodden down until it resembled nothing more than ground meat.

She felt ashamed.

She felt lost.

Chapter 17

Morning light woke her ungratefully, still curled on top of her bed sheets, her face sore from dry tears and her feet ice cold from sleeping without covering. She felt like she had the worst hangover from hell and groaned when she saw the time. She had promised to help at the coffee morning today. The little old ladies had talked her into it, asking her to bring Muffin for some granny love and she hadn't been able to refuse. As if by coincidence the rap on her door by an over happy Abby just added to her groans, she sunk face down back onto the bed, allowing herself to slide off to her feet. The effort of moving almost unbearable. She was fatigued.

'I'm coming!' She half yelled, half mumbled as she dragged herself to let her in.

'Oh my god, Rose, it's after nine for goodness sakes. We need to get there for half past! Dressed. Now!' Abby was bounding around, overly energetic for her liking and pushing her back into the cottage.

Rose caught sight of her dishevelled appearance in the mirror, catching the bed hair, pale face and over red tear stains and tried to wipe them away about the same time Abby caught her tired eyes in the mirror.

'You okay? Look if your sick I can just tell…'

'No! no. no. It's okay. I'm okay. Bad night. Stomach upset or something like that. Honest I'm all good.' She lied and tried the happy face she had been wearing lately but could not muster the energy. 'I just need to freshen up.'

'Look, go have a bath, I'll call Nancy and tell her were running late; you need more than a freshen up.' Abby blinked at her rather dubiously and fished her mobile out of her bag.

Rose gave her an appreciative smile and headed to the bathroom turning on the taps, glad to be able to lock herself in; she sat on the toilet lid as her bubbles grew and filled the bath and steam started to cloud the air. She just needed to scrape herself together.

She was over the worst, right? She had hit all time low and had the night from hell. It could only get better than this. She had seen him now. That first encounter over and it could only get easier now... Should, get easier.

* * *

The sun, as usual, was splitting the trees as they drove to town. Rose felt more human after her bath and she had even dragged out her baby pink sundress and shoes in a bid to feel more like her old self. Willing herself to get back on that horse by wearing her favourite outfit. She was stronger than this.

Abby had forced her to eat some toast before they left, resulting in being almost an hour late. It had been an effort, her appetite non-existent but she had felt better for it.

The church was mobbed by the time the girls walked through the door, always the highlight of the week for all the old timers. The noise in the high-ceilinged hall, echoing loudly and drowning out the radio playing tunes in the corner. The smell of air freshener, baked goods and mustiness, something she had found in every church she had ever been too. Tinted with strong coffee and old lady perfume.

Every little round table was crowded with elderly folks, with varying shades of lilac perms and balding heads and the sight of Muffin trotting in among the tables sent off a lot of crooning and kissing as they scooped him up and passed him about, plying him with cake crumbs and milk. He was in his element, his little pink tongue flapping at faces and hands excitedly. Muffin was somewhat of a celebrity in this village, everyone knew him by sight and everyone knew his name and weakness for cake.

Nancy, the church group leader, pulled them over and showed them where to stand. She was a stout little lady with grey hair in a bun and air of old school mistress. Her spectacles perched low on her nose. They would be serving endless cups of tea and coffee to the old timers while Nancy oversaw the book sale set out on several tables at the far end. Rose was relieved to be given such a menial task that required no thought. At least she could manage to stand and smile, the busyness of the room making silent thought impossible.

This is what she needed. Mindless tasks surrounded by noise and bustle. Plenty of life and laughing.

Even in here the sun was shining through the tall arched windows and warming the air to an almost stuffy heat. Glad of her sundress and naked arms and legs, she pitied Abby and her choice of jeans and sweater.

* * *

The morning went fast, with the hustle and bustle and busy chatter, Rose felt like her face was going to seize with her smile ache. When Abby began to fade from the heat she sent her to go and help with the flower sale outside, assuring her she could manage coffee and tea service for a couple of hours more alone. Nancy agreed to find Abby a t-shirt in the lost and found box, giving her some relief and glad Donald the little old man out front would have help.

She watched the room fill some more through the day, as younger mums with kids in prams and teenage boys and girls came and went. This little community really was something she loved to be part of, age didn't stop them all from taking part and everyone made an effort to come to things like this, all intermingling and everyone just chatted to everyone. She stood watching the hubbub and happy laughter, envious of all the seemingly content faces. It lifted her spirits to be part of this. It was much needed therapy.

Nancy soon came over to give her some relief and point out her overly blushed cheeks a little after three. She was not aware of just how hot she had become, stuck in behind the steaming kettles and hot water boilers. Sending her to go get some air and take a break with a box of sandwiches and bottle of juice. She thanked the woman and headed out a side door that had been left open to help air flow through the room.

The exit took her to the back of the church, a small courtyard like area with paved ground and neat trim hedges all around. She sat on the nearby bench and ate her food quietly, revelling in the head space and cool air which was rejuvenating her. She had built up enough of a hunger that she had wanted to eat.

See she was already improving.

Enjoying the gentle breeze in the shade, she was looking around the peaceful courtyard, the noise from inside a lot more muffled out here. It gave the spot an ambience of seclusion and peacefulness.

Discarding her packaging in the nearby bin and smoothing the crumbs from her dress she noticed a small half concealed arch at the far end calling to her nosiness, intertwined with the high bushes. Heading through into luscious green lawn she realised quite suddenly where she was.

This was the path from Munro manor to the church when it had been Munro chapel. The private path which had once been used to let the family come and go. The house loomed up ahead in front of her, only minutes away. She had never seen the house from this side angle before and it suddenly felt alien and daunting to her. It looked so gothic and intimidating, even in the bright light of day.

Turning to go back she was distracted by the glint from something by the house, shining right at her face which made her turn to glimpse again. Seeing Morag's red car turning in at the front and out of sight, she turned back towards the church cursing inwardly and trying to ignore that heavy pit that erupted in her belly and spread to her heart.

It killed her mood instantly, her slight almost happy mood was now back to doom and gloom and cursing the sun. Heading back into the church with her eyes trailing the ground she walked slap bang into a hard, warm, wall.

'Ooowwww' Looking up and rubbing her shoulder, which took the brunt of the impact, she met familiar steel grey eyes and tanned skin in a very jaw dropping six-foot frame.

Fuck.

'Sorry. Guess neither of us was looking where we were going.' He smiled, but it didn't reach his eyes and she moved back, giving him room to pass but he didn't move forward. She was still rubbing her shoulder trying to calm her over racing heart and realised he was staring at her oddly.

'What? What is it?' Suddenly panicking. Wondering if there was something on her face or if there was a bug climbing about on her. She had a morbid fear of bugs.

Was she drooling? Scowling? She knew she wasn't crying… Just yet!

'Nothing!… Just…' He was looking her up and down, at her dress slowly, lost in his own head, the one she was wearing the first time she ever met him with a faraway look in his eyes. 'You look nice.' It came out as an emotionless empty compliment. He gave a short smile then immediately straightened and moved past her, turning to face her slightly as he did so and giving her one last look. Unreadable… Like always! Just like Rob.

He had moved out without touching her and despite it being the last thing she wanted, it felt horrible. To be so close and yet to be so far apart. She tried to shake it off as he left via the entrance, noticing he was carrying an empty crate in one hand. Looking back at the tables she saw the new pile of cream cakes and muffins and figured he had brought them down.

Unable to resist the urge she walked back out the open door and saw him disappear through the arch towards the house. Stopping herself and pulling back into the church; that same feeling of deflation. She hated this. The way her body jumped on high alert and crazy agony at seeing him, then crashed into despair when they parted ways.

Would she ever get used to this?

Back at her table, she figured that Morag had probably dropped him here with the new cakes and went up to the house to wait for him. She guessed it was easier for him to then walk up directly through the grounds in less than a couple of minutes and get back to her than have her wait out front among milling crowds and endless parked cars. That thought hurt her way more than she should have let it.

* * *

The girls heaved a sigh of relief when they were finally finished. The room had started to empty and the girls helped clear tables and chairs and returned the normal empty hall back to its former glory. It was not an overly huge a room but large enough for most of the little clubs to meet and greet and some of the local schools to put on plays. It had nothing to the size of the rooms at the manor. Nothing she had ever seen could ever compare to that big old house.

It was still early in the day when they were done so Abby suggested they take Muffin up to the house and use the pool. Muffin had been occupied all day by eager fans and he looked ready to sleep for a week, his little head was bobbing with the effort to keep awake as Rose picked him up to stroke that tiny velvet muzzle. He was too tired to attempt any sort of licking and just rested his tiny face against her bosom.

'You have a pool? Where? Rose laughed in disbelief. 'I have been in your garden remember? In your house! I have never seen anything remotely pool like in all that time!'

Abby tilted her head. 'That's the beauty of the big house. So many secret places.' She laughed, explaining there was a building fifty yards from the house on the grounds that sported a pool and sauna, concealed by trees. 'It was one of dad's indulgences, he practically lives in the sauna nowadays.'

'Sounds perfect Abs, there is nothing I can imagine I would love more right now.' She was attempting to peel her dress strap from her clammy skin.

Abby pulled Rose after her, towards the car. 'Come on, we will take your car up so later you don't need to come for it, we can leave Muffin with Alice, you know how she loves him.' Rose could not argue. The thought of a nice cool swim in this sticky heat actually sounded amazing. She needed to cool off and relax after that hard shift as tea maid. Nothing sounded better than peeling off sticky clothes in this humidity and diving into cool clear water.

Well, something else would have sounded good but that ship had now sailed.

It did not take long to get the car out of the church car park and navigate along a side private road straight to the house with Abby's direction. Realising this was where she had seen Morag drive earlier, it somehow felt wrong.

They parked up at the front of the house in the usual wide open car park by the main entrance and Abby dashed inside to grab swimwear and deposit a now sleeping Muffin with Alice in the kitchen to be pampered some more. Rose made excuses and stayed outside, gesturing towards the red car next to Robs and Abby shrugged. She assumed Rose was hinting about the drama and their tiffle with Morag and dashed inside cluelessly.

She didn't want to see him or her, if she was being honest, and she certainly didn't want to see them together.

Rose meandered towards the flower bed and looked at the delicate white Roses all in full bloom waiting for her, lost in thought. Trying to keep her crazy pounding heart and trembling nerves under control.

'Urge to climb in and take a nap?' the humour of the familiar voice made her freeze, her heart crashing heavily into her rib cage. Slowly turning to see Rob leaning in the open door against the thick rustic frame lazily. He looked effortlessly masculine, his muscles on show under a t-shirt that did little to hide his body. One arm raised over his head as he leant in and made it even more pronounced. That little peek of skin at the waist line where the hem was pulled up.

'Funny!' Rose regained her equilibrium quickly as she wandered to the next bush, putting more distance between them, afraid he would see the way her body was starting to react.

'I know you and Rose bushes... Flower baby.' There was something unreadable in his voice but Rose averted her gaze to some small pink Roses further along and tried to keep her voice steady.

'Only when I'm under the influence.' She shrugged 'The rest of the time, I just like to admire them.'

'You look nice today, really pretty.' He sounded genuine, he was trying to be light and upbeat but she could hear the deeper tone in his voice. He had already told her that at the church but the way he said it this time did funny things to her insides. There was a brief silence as they looked at one another for a moment before she lost her bravado and looked back at the flowers.

'Rose?...' The way he almost whispered her name caused her to turn without thinking, a soft unreadable look flashing between them, but he backed off as Abby came racing through. Stopping to throw a kiss on his cheek and waving two sets of bikinis in her hand and towels in the other

'Darling brother, we're going to use the pool!' She was giddy and happy. Rob was eyeing up the skimpy costumes in her hand and looking back and forth at Rose. His expression unreadable once more and that dead pan mask back in place. His gaze lingered longer than necessary on her for a second and caused the familiar tingles and shivers to begin creeping over her.

Still he could affect her this way.

'Sure, just as long as you don't annoy dad. He went for a sauna about twenty minutes ago. I saw him trailing across the lawn in his white robe.' Rob ruffled Abby's hair and pushed her onwards out the door. She skipped down the steps towards Rose with a smile.

Abby grabbed Rose's hand as she danced by, twirling her around and jerking her in the direction intended at the same time. Her skirt flying up lightly with the twirl she did and her hair following. She couldn't help but give out a little squeal and laugh as she did so.

Abby the ever-fun loving child.

She caught Rob's expression, just a fleeting moment.

Remembrance, maybe?

Clouded dark grey eyes and a pained expression. He watched them leave via the side of the house until they were out of sight but she resisted the urge to look back at him, aware of his eyes still following them and wrecking her nerves once more.

The pool house was not far across the lawn, to the sheltered side of the house. Concealed by trees and bushes, it was almost like a secret little building and Rose could see why it was hard to find if you didn't know it was there.

Once inside it reminded her of an expensive public pool. Tiled from floor to ceiling in hues of sea green and mint, with the unmistakeable strong smell of chlorine and that echoing sound of water. The blue-green pool was full to the brim with inviting cool clear water, Abby checked the temperature panel on the wall and smiled.

'Perfect!' She pointed towards the far end and two sets of doors. 'Left is to the changing room. Right is to the sauna and my dad is most likely asleep in there, so I better go check.' She handed the black bikini set to Rose with the towels and sent her towards the shiny white door while she took a detour and knocked on the other. A deep smooth voice so like Rob's called out and invited her in and Abby slid in, casting a wave and gesturing one minute to Rose.

Rose opened the changing room door and slid inside, faced with a row of wood clad changing rooms with swinging doors. There was a bench along one wal,l lined with mirrors and silver hooks and a vanity with a couple of hair dryers, a basket of assorted toiletries, a single enclosed shower and bathroom in one corner. She opened the first door into one of the trio of small changing rooms and began to undress.

The bikini was a tad skimpy for her fuller figure than Abby's, but it still covered her modestly. Catching sight of herself in the mirror she felt rather indecent. It was not her normal style for sure, riskier and naughtier than what she liked to throw on, but as she was in a private pool with her best friend, she figured it didn't matter.

Abby walked in and wolf whistled

'Check you! Sexy!'

'Thanks' Rose laughed.

'Think Rob would have some sort of caveman moment if he saw you in that.' Abby winked devilishly and Rose felt that moment of fear colour her cheeks.

'Shut up.' Rose laughed, trying to conceal her guilt and wondering why Abby would even think Rob would care. A small doubt about what she knew passed her mind fleetingly and she pushed it away as stupid. Abby obviously didn't know, not that there was anything to know anymore anyway.

Abby picked the same dressing room she had just vacated and threw clothes over the upper wall beside Rose's. Sporting a similar style of bikini in bright turquoise, somehow Abby looked more covered. Her slimmer figure and smaller bust made it less revealing.

'My dad's going to come for a wee swim for a few minutes to meet you.' She grinned. 'He says he's sick of hearing about the amazing Rose and wants a face to the name, he remembers you as a kid but wants to know you as a lassie now apparently.' She laughed childishly 'Dunno, who's been telling him nice things, cos I told him how boring you were.' She laughed again, ducking as Rose threw one of the towels at her.

'I have no idea why I hang out with you sometimes. You're an actual brat!'

'You cannot resist me sweetheart.' Abby grinned cheekily. Blowing a kiss her way and patting Rose on the butt to get her out of the changing room.

'Come on.' Rose led the way back to the pool, keen to be submerged before this man saw her in all her curves and glory. She felt a little too naked as she slid into the cool water easily, loving how it felt on her clammy skin and weary bones. She would have to make Abby bring her here more often. This is exactly what she needed after everything in the last few days. Always a lover of the water; sliding under and relaxing to the cooler temperature, she swam an easy length before this long-awaited stranger made his appearance. He was not what Rose expected.

Memories of Hamish years ago had always seen him a big figure; huge grey beard, dressed in kilts and sporrans at dances. As a child, he had seemed like a big hairy bear of a man, always loud and alive, full of life. But the tall large man sporting bright red shorts, coming from the sauna, struck more of a muscular, older version of Rob than memory served her. His once huge grey beard gone and smooth-shaven face. Chiselled jaw line still evident despite his age and wrinkles. His grey hair tamed and shorter; he used to wear it shoulder length in all its curly wildness, and actually for a man in his later years, still handsome. Still full of life and vitality. The faded grey eyes were a shock to Rose. So familiar and so unexpected to see in a different face, looking so weary and dull.

Yes, he was aged and not so firm and fit as his son but the resemblance was striking. He was so like Rob in mannerisms and voice too as he slid into the pool and approached the pair.

Brief introductions and small talk had them all relaxing quickly, the easy-going nature she remembered so well and deep hearty laugh. Rose could not stop being mesmerised by the similarities, wondering if this was how Rob would look in years to come. It was obvious both his children had inherited his genes, good looks, good bone structure. Abby's green eyes, the only part of her mother that was obvious and the straight black hair of both her children. They both had Hamish Munro's smooth confidence and easy manner. Rose liked him instantly. He had charm and a quick wit, a great sense of humour. His affection for Abby was obvious as the pair verbally sparred like a comedy act.

They splashed in the water for a good fifteen minutes just laughing and joking before he looked her in the eye, making her feel like a ten-year-old child again. A serious expression on his face as though he was scrutinising or appraising her.

Abby climbed out to go use the bathroom, leaving them alone for a few minutes.

'He told me about you two, you know?' Hamish didn't hesitate, no sense of accusation in his tone, just a warm smile as he tread water, facing her.

Roses look of panic and confusion obvious, she began to try and formulate a response but he put his hand up.

'Hush now, I'm aware Abby has no idea, don't worry; I will leave that up to you or Rob to tell her in time. I just wanted to say I agree with you. Ending it! That's no way for you to live. No way to treat the girl he says he loves and that I think my son's an idiot, I think he knows it too.' He moved forward giving her shoulder a small squeeze and an apologetic look. Reassuringly fatherly and Rose sighed, relaxing a little.

'I don't know what to say.' She truly had not expected this. 'I didn't see a happy ending the way things were going, or even a change in the future.' She felt a tear hit her eye and a lump forming in her threat and pushed them down again.

'Just tell me, lassie… Do you love him?' He was still close, their voices hushed with a hopeful look in his eye.

'Yes, I do.' She looked forlorn but could not lie about this, especially not to this kind hearted man. It felt good to finally be able to speak to someone about it, it had been ripping her apart inside for days.

'Well, at least there is that. He knows he's being an idiot. Just don't rule him out forever. Sometimes Rob can be stubborn like his mother. Trying to do what's best for everyone else.' Hamish moved back a little, giving her space and glanced to the door to check Abby was still not returning.

'You can say that again.' She smiled sadly.

'Sometimes it takes him a little while to figure out what needs to be done when it comes to his own needs. Don't you wait on him! He needs to see that he's lost you before he can really get that head out of his ass. Don't make things easy on him, like you were... Won't change otherwise.' They heard Abby flushing the toilet and he moved forward to pat her again, warmly. She smiled as he reached forward and kissed her cheek with a wink, moving back before swimming to the side and climbing out with a backwards wave.

'Now if you don't mind, this old man needs to get back into the warm air before my legs give way. Not quite as virile as I used to be and the sauna is much more my style.' He grinned, throwing a wave and stopping to kiss Abby on the forehead as she emerged from the changing room once again.

'Bye.' Rose called after him, watching Abby slide back into the water gracefully.

Rose felt cold with the immobility in the water but a small warm glow inside her began to spread. A feeling of something fuzzy and gentle and hopeful.

He had told his father about them. Told his father he loved her. Talked about them despite all the secretiveness... He had told his dad! Surely that counted for something?

It had given her enough of a warm glow deep inside she felt her face warm and her limbs loosen up with some inner hopeful tingling.

* * *

They stayed in the pool for an hour. Seeing Hamish Munro again before he left, midway through splashing and carry on and laughing at his awful jokes. He really was a lovely man and the wink he threw at Rose made her feel for the first time in weeks a tad better. Like a warm gesture from a kind stranger that could brighten your day.

Maybe it was more than the wink. Maybe it was what he had said to her.

Chapter 18

The girls spent the rest of the day at the cottage in Rose's work room, she had been glad of being able to go straight to the car when Abby went in for Muffin and even more glad to see Morag's car was nowhere to be seen anymore.

At the cottage, she had been teaching Abby about illustrating whimsical creatures and magical forests, watercolour and the use of inks and pens in her work; together they had been creating some little art pieces for Abby's room. Magical Unicorn and princess style pictures in soft tones and muted colours.

There was something relaxing and healing about sitting side by side in silence and painting, the companionship of another artist in the way her aunt and she had sat as a child. She realised just in that tiny moment why her aunt had loved bringing her here and it pained her to think of her again. She had got so good at pushing it away. Forcing the memories down until she could deal with the pain, but today she felt more able to let them linger for a moment. Reminisce and remember her. Picture her sweet face and her long flowing dark hair that she loved to wear down; it still hurt a lot but not in the heart-wrenching, breath stopping way it had after the funeral.

She watched Abby, engrossed in her painting; her eyes watching the way her brush flowed on paper, the gentle tilt of her head and the innocent chew on her lip and felt an overwhelming maternal surge.

Rose had never had a sister. She had two brothers she rarely saw but she had never had someone she loved to death the way she loved this girl. Not since her aunt. Not in this way. A real friend but something more; a sisterly protective love, she knew she would beat down walls to look after her no matter how things ended with her brother.

Abby felt her gaze and glanced up smiling at her. There was something in that trusting look, the eyes full of affection, trust and happiness and mutual love that instantly broke her. Out of nowhere the sob flew from her throat and the tears fell like a waterfall that had just erupted from a damn and she just could not contain it.

Maybe it was the meeting with Rob's father and his words, maybe it was having no one to talk to about this and bottling it up inside for days on end. Maybe it was allowing the thoughts of her aunt to overwhelm her in that moment, making her fragile or maybe it was the exhaustion from lack of sleep and a hellish night, but whatever reason; it came crashing out like an eruption and she could not stop.

* * *

Two hours later, calm and curled on the couch, surrounded by screwed up tissue Rose was sat with a snuffly nose and puffy eyes. Her skin sore from repeated wiping and she was cradling a cup of cocoa as Abby sat perched on the arm of the chair, watching her studiously. The picture of calm wisdom despite the fact Rose had told her everything.

Abby had not flown into a rage, angry at the lies and the deceit or betrayal of both brother and best friend. She had not stormed out or cried and gone off on one. She had instead wrapped her friend in a hug and let her talk and sob until there was nothing more to say. Nodding and stroking her hair; she had told her she knew deep down something was going on between them. Gut instinct. Knowing both of them well enough to see the subtle signs and she wasn't mad at either of them. She was hurt, but she understood why they hadn't told her; Abby herself admitted it would have been used as a weapon the first-time Morag riled her, she was just glad she finally knew. That she finally had the whole picture instead of hopeful suspicion and half guessed facts.

'What now?' She watched Rose take sips of her soothing drink, a look of compassion on her beautiful face, but Rose shrugged.

'I try and get over him I guess.' Even saying it aloud hurt.

'I can't believe it had been going on that long and I had no clue, looking back though it's so obvious. Rob has been unusually happy the last few weeks, overly nice and loving and well he was just damned more fun to be around. Until this past week that is.... He's back to being a crabbit arse. I could arrange her disappearance.' Abby broke into a wide grin and winked, that same wink bestowed earlier by her father. 'You know how much I love that wretch and well, we are rich enough!'

Rose smiled, feeling lighter and drained. She shook her head.

'If it's meant to be Abby then she wouldn't be an issue. He would make it work. I would have made it work. It wouldn't have ended the way it did.' She needed to accept part blame in this. It was not all on him.

'No! If he loved you then he wouldn't have let her come between you. He would have been honest from day one and made you feel like you mattered more than she did. He's an arse and a half for how he handled this.'

'You know it's not that simple. Morag is his friend and she is fragile. Despite everything, all my pain and tears... He was only trying to be a good guy, Ab's.' Rose nudged Abby with her foot, to pull that scowl from her face. 'It's not his fault that Morag's unwell, he just got into a place that he couldn't get out of so easily and I stupidly agreed to play along. I thought I could handle it... I thought it would be different and he just needed a little time.' Both girls sighed loudly.

Abby looked down at her feet, curled on the couch, equally frustrated; seeing the situation from Rob's viewpoint and trying to empathise.

'Maybe not being with you will change things, Rose...? He seems...' She was grasping the air for the right words. 'Different!'

She huffed, 'I don't know! With him, it's always hard. He's not easy to read, always keeps everything close to his chest, but he's off; moods and general air around him. Since he came back he is just so agitated; jogging way more at night than ever before. Spending a lot of time in his office; narky as fuck and seems to lose his temper way too easily with me lately. More so than ever before.' She slid down into the couch a little more, her feet mingling with Roses. 'Knowing what I know now, I would say he's hurting... In that manly, quiet, strong-faced guy, kinda way! You know when they act like there all cool and don't care shit! I've never seen Rob broken hearted but I'm guessing it looks a lot like this.' She laid her head on the arm of the couch and pulled a fluffy cushion between her knees.

'Maybe... But it doesn't make me feel better Abby. It doesn't change how things are, how impossible it is to even try again.' Rose threw a gentle smile at her friend, pulling the cushion from her and cuddling it herself. All this talk of Rob had her heart aching badly and she wanted nothing more than for his arms to be around her right now.

'Maybe not right now it doesn't, but Rob is hardly the type to sit back and let things he wants slide away.' Abby stretched her arms out into the air, exhaled as she stretched her limbs.

'Maybe that's the problem...? Maybe he didn't want me enough? Maybe, despite thinking I would be different than those other women, he just realised I wasn't and it was just another casual fling.' A tear rolled down her cheek, her insides aching and Abby pulled her over into an almost headlock embrace and patted her back, meaning she was pulled forward almost to lie on top of the girl. It was incredibly uncomfortable and awkward.

'Don't ever say that! Any guy who did not want you with his whole heart and soul is a fucking moron. Brother or not I'll slap his big dumb head into...'

'No!!' the sudden spring backwards sent them both flailing, close to the edge of the couch and grasping to stay upright, sheer panic on Rose's face.

'You CANNOT! I repeat CANNOT! Let on you that know anything Abby. Promise me? If he knew I told you after promising I would tell no one...'

'Heck No! That idiot brother of mine deserves no loyalty now Rose. You're done with him and your promise ended when you broke up! You already told me my dad knows, so its okay for him to tell someone, but not you? How is that fair then? It's not and right now I am so severely pissed at him.' Abby was back to scowling, scrambling to sit up and sit rigidly.

'You can't hate your brother on my account, He loves you and you love him. You adore him! I don't want this to affect you Abby, to come between you.'

'I don't hate him. I'm mad at him. I'm severely raging at him for letting this happen. For you getting hurt... It's HER I hate!'

They both sat back silent and broody, looking at one another, with minds whizzing, gears and wheels turning. A smile slowly broke out on the younger girls face that started to take over, reaching her mischievous glittering eyes.

'What?' Rose knew that look only too well and sighed suspiciously. The plan hatching smirk! Abby licked her lips looking smug.

'What does every wronged heroine do in every chick flick and soppy book since the start of time when the hero breaks her heart?' She beamed knowingly.

'Cry and hide in her mansion, looking beautifully distressed and eating ice cream?' Rose sighed hopefully, knowing full well Abby was plan forming in that quick head and she probably wouldn't like it.

'Screw that! Shut up and err NO...They spruce up. Push up their boobs and get out there, acting like the world's their oyster and way more fish in the sea!' She exclaimed triumphantly as thought she had just found the cure to cancer.

'I'm not ready to go fishing Abby.' Rose said flatly and returned to picking fluff from her dress.

'You're not going to be fishing, my empty-headed love...It's never about getting under a new man, is it? It's about getting over one! It's about torturing the old one!' Abby prodded her annoyingly in the shoulder to get her undivided attention.

'You lost me.' Rose just blinked, deadpan.

Abby jumped up onto the arm, perching her butt rather tediously for emphasis and leant in with a wickedly childish smile

'You look amazing, right? Swan about carefree and non-broken hearted. You see him and you're like 'Yeah whatever'... It drives him crazy. He will pine over you and long for what he has lost; if you look broken hearted then he feels better, right? Because he knows you're in as much pain as he is and it makes him feel better. You look over it, act on it and he goes into meltdown. Starts acting like a crazy fool to get you back and maybe finally dump the red head in the river.' Abby all but licked her finger and sizzled it in the air as though she had found the answer to all her prayers. Rose was not so sure.

'And you learned this from where? A Danielle Steele novel? This is real life Abby and he's not some dim-witted moron who would fall for games like that. I don't play games and I don't want to start now.' She felt irritated and got up to start clearing up the sea of tissues and empty mugs. This was what having a childlike best mate was really like.

'He's male! There all pretty typical from what I've seen.' Abby huffed, annoyed that her plan was not being met with smiles and thumbs up.

'At the grand old age of nineteen may I add!' Rose shuffled her off the arm and started rearranging cushions distractedly. Trying not to be moody with her best friend.

'Shut up old fogey. I'm sure I know as much as your twenty-seven-year-old ass!'

'Look I'm tired, Abby. It's been a hell of a week and a hell of a day. I can't think about this right now and I just want to stop. Turn on a movie, we will raid the freezer for ice cream and you can crash in my bed tonight.' She glanced at her watch seeing the late hour and hoped to god this would appease her. She also didn't want to face the night alone in an empty bed when she was feeling this fragile.

'Okay, okay boss.' She smiled. 'But I get to pick though and this is not end of conversation! It's just to be continued!... I need to go text that ass and tell him I'm staying!'

Rose sent her a mock-pained look as the girl slid out her phone from her bag and rolled her eyes.

'Only thirty new messages from Duncan. Jeez, that boy is in love!' Her cheeks tinted red and delight shone through, despite her mocking him.

'It's going well then?' Rose had an armful of trash and crockery as she moved through to the kitchen to discard it all. 'I think he will be pulling out a ring in no time!' She jested.

'You think?' Abby looked hopeful then brushed it away, making jokes about him just being her 'hoe' of the minute and nothing more than a toy boy. Rose wasn't fooled and saw the look on her face when she was typing replies to him and ending them with a dozen kisses. Moments later she came through to join Rose in the kitchen both simultaneously nosing in the freezer, searching for that elusive ice cream

'Asshole asked if I wanted to be picked up.' Abby butted in while moving around food in the freezer.

'You mean Rob?' Rose sighed, hating that even his name on her lips caused her heart to contract bitterly.

'I mean what I said. And I told him NO. That were getting a stripper and some vodka shots and later you're going to be eating ice cream off his six pack.'

'ABBY!' Rose sent the boxes of frozen food she was moving aside, flying everywhere.

'He said to have a nice time!' Abby giggled and scooped down to retrieve the boxes and bags.

'You actual brat! I thought you were serious for a minute.' Rose's elevated heart rate was not seeing the funny side just yet.

'What do you care what he thinks...? His loss!' Abby shrugged 'If he's stupid enough to lose you then he deserves to be tortured.'

'You told him the truth though, right?' Rose ignored those last comments.

'I told him we're having a girly night in and I'm staying, okay?' Rolling her eyes and mocking a huff, Abby elbowed her friend gently. Rose relieved, nodded and bopped her on the head with the now located strawberry ice cream.

* * *

Having Abby on side and always there to talk made an enormous difference to Rose's state of mind. As though some of the burden and heartbreak had been shared, allowing space to breathe. To be able to get some perspective. Maybe it was having someone she could joke about things with and make light of the heartbreak, that in a way helped ease the pain. Or maybe it was just not being alone with her own thoughts, going crazy and not being able to vent.

Abby had upped a gear in terms of keeping her friend occupied and between work, and her little friend, she was rarely lost for something to do. The days had flown by far quicker and thankfully run ins with Rob had been non-existent for the past couple of weeks. Apparently, he had thrown himself head first into work and had been gone on a lot of trips. In a way, and this upset, it made Rose feel better, she was glad he wasn't around to run into and wasn't spending his time with Morag, but at the same time she was broken over the fact that he was simply moving on with his life and didn't seem to miss her at all. There had been no contact.

Her parents were arriving today, in time for the fete tomorrow, and to be honest, Rose was looking forward to their arrival more than she could ever remember. She had missed them a lot more since moving here than she ever had in London and when you were feeling low and vulnerable, you could really use your parent's cuddles. She put it down to the over emotional rollercoaster ride she had been on lately and looked forward to seeing them.

They were booked into a small guest house a few miles away, seeing as there was no longer a guest room in the cottage. She had offered them her room and she would have taken the couch but they refused. They wanted to visit in style and treat it like a proper holiday weekend. They had chosen a beautiful guest house with great reviews online, close enough to spend a load of time with Rose but far enough to not be breathing down on her the entire time they were here. She had to admit that she liked that idea more than cohabiting and being cramped up when she was still nursing a broken heart.

They finally arrived mid-morning and showered her with cuddles and kisses, admiring and complimenting the cottage as she showed them around and smothering Muffin in kisses. Muffin had been a gift from her mother when she had left to live in London. One of her mother's own dog's offspring, so they had genuine love for the little fur ball. They loved to see how much he had grown since the last time they saw him and as always lavished him with treats and gifts and another dog bed. This was as close to grandkids as her parents had so far and it showed.

After the initial welcoming excitement had calmed down, tea and cakes consumed and generally getting used to seeing one another again and catching, they headed to town. They had planned to walk on this gloriously beautiful day, conversation never drying up where her mother was concerned. The sun was still high but the overall heat was becoming cooler as weeks went on. Soon it would be colder and darker and winter would start moving in.

Her mother had brought her a beautiful sundress to add to her ever-growing collection, which she was now wearing proudly. It floated around her legs as she walked in a beautiful subtle floral print on a buttercream base. It was strappy and floaty and feminine and made Rose feel like a princess. A new dress could always lift her mood; her mother knew what she liked only too well and it warmed her heart that she would still buy clothes for her.

They met Abby at the opening to the manor as planned and together they all walked into town along the grass verge of the main road. As usual, the road rarely had much traffic and was a pleasant walk. They had left Muffin home chewing on a new pig's ear and trying out his new over fluffy, over plumped dog bed with matching blanket.

Her parents immediately adored Abby, finding conversation easy and quizzing the girl on her studies and home life.

Rose's dad was a lot like Hamish Munro in that he was large and grey haired and loved to joke. Abby immediately struck up a great camaraderie and the pair of them had Rose and her mother in stitches as they arrived in the town centre. A shared sense of humour and irresistibly funny together.

Wandering into the centre of town to the desired destination, Rose took the lead, looking back towards her little brood as they continued to chat; right into Bella's bakery. Turning to scope the tables for free seats, her face immediately fell as she was greeted by Rob and Morag standing at the counter, both backs to her and oblivious to her sudden appearance.

Here we go again!

She felt her insides droop, Morag had her arms entwined around Rob's Left arm as he tapped his wallet on the counter. Distracted while she talked, he was looking straight ahead at the wall of prices and cake lists, with a stance that suggested he was uptight. Probably a dreadful day at work or Morag giving him a hard time over something pointless. Rose's stomach dropped, the colour instantly draining from her face and leaving an icy coldness to spread throughout her body.

Her sudden stop caused Abby to walk right into the back of her with a massive muffled 'Ooooft' noise, sending Ross sprawling forward and having to grab a nearby chair to steady herself. Rose's dad laughed and skipped around the pair, pulling her mother out of the way to avoid a further collision and just making it even more obvious they were all there. Rob turned, as did Morag, to see what the weird noise was.

Locking eyes for a mere second as she straightened herself up and fixed her twisted dress, she looked away and headed towards the nearest empty table she could, hearing Abby awkwardly introducing her brother to Rose's parents. Rob's smooth charming voice and easy manner as her parents warmed up to him gave absolutely nothing away and even Abby sounded convincingly normal.

Way to go Laird!

She had known they would instantly love him, it had been inevitable and today was the last thing she could deal with. Morag's high pitch purr was in full swing as she managed to sound very much like the lady in control, the one Rose had met at the museum so long ago. Mask fully stuck on today then.

Rose bit her lip, unable to turn around, but instead started to lay her bag on the chair and pull seats out for her family. Concentrating on breathing and keeping her legs from buckling under her. Seeing him was one thing, but seeing him with a serpent wrapped around his body was unbearable. Rose hated the fact that even after a couple of weeks she still went to pieces at his presence.

Abby appeared immediately, trying to catch her eyes and smiling to cover Rose's obvious loss of mood as she too slid off her bag and propped it on one of the seats and moved the menu cards off the table. Her parents were at the counter with Rob and Morag, ordering coffees and cakes, completely oblivious to anything going on before them.

'Smile, sit up and dazzle.' Abby warned under her breath and kept her eyes firmly on Rose so she could glance over her head at the group behind.

'Easier said than done.' Rose whispered back, aware her cheeks were heating and her hands had started to tremble.

'Go to the ladies' room and powder your nose, take a minute to gather yourself.' Abby smiled softly, eyes motioning widely that she had a chance to escape for a minute before they came over.

Rose sent her a silent thank you before retreating to the lady's room to pull herself together and take some deep breaths with her head between her knees. Her hands were shaking, her skin had lost all colour.

Damn her, for leaving her bag and blusher compacts out at the table.

Instead, she patted cool water on her face and tried to pinch some blush back into her cheeks, bringing back some much needed colour to them and smoothing back the wild look as best as she could.

Upon emerging from the bathroom Rose groaned inwardly. Her parents had managed to convince Rob and Morag to sit at the table next to theirs or had simply followed him to sit down and were all chatting warmly. Like some scene from a cheesy soap; she had the urge to go back to the bathroom and stay there. Abby looked tense and agitated, tapping her foot against the leg of the table and casting Rob some crazy looks. Silent scorn that either he was expertly ignoring or simply wasn't seeing.

Shit, shit, shit.

Rose, taking one last calming breath and plastering a fake smile on her face, ventured out and sat next to Abby as casually as she could muster. Aware that this meant her seat was directly in line with Rob's, making them close enough to touch if she moved too far back or to the side. She felt instantly awkward and wanted the floor to open up and swallow her whole.

This could only happen to her.

She felt eyes on her as she settled herself and fixed her dress, but didn't dare glance up to look. She could feel the heat coming from his side and smell the familiar scent as she tried to keep focus on her mother and keep up with conversation.

Her mother was engaged with extreme interest in a topic with Morag, something to do with her museum and some ancient Scottish relic. Her mother being an ex-history teacher was lapping it up and looked like she wouldn't be letting the woman leave anytime soon. Rose was impressed that she had managed to engage that woman in any form of conversation if she was being honest. She was not the overly chatty type and had given Rose the distinct impression in the past that she didn't like woman at all.

If only her mother knew what a traitor that made her.

Her father was engaging Rob in a conversation about the estate and tomorrow's fete, while Abby was throwing worried glances at Rose and trying to silently signal her.

How could he just sit there? So normal and unaffected. Relaxed and sociable, acting like nothing had ever happened between them?

Abby, silent and broody was again sending some sort of subliminal messages to her but she just could not think straight. Turning her silver ring on her finger and trying to look interested. Trying to act unaffected. Trying to behave in a normal manner as though she was merely listening to the conversation and not on the verge of an all-out emotional meltdown

The girl at the counter shouted on Munro and Turner, signalling both their orders were ready and Rose jumped up.

'I'll get it Dad, you sit right there.' She gushed a little too enthusiastically and sped to the counter in the hopes of making it before Rob even got up.

Rob unfortunately was almost as fast as her, got up and followed her a little too closely. Aware of him right behind her, she wanted to run but that would have been ridiculous.

The two trays of cups and plates with steaming liquid and delicious pastries were slid in front of them as they stood side by side, reaching the counter together. Close enough to hear each other breath but a hairline crack between them so they did not touch. Rose kept her eyes front and centre even when he leant in close, reaching for his tray, brushing his tanned arm against her naked skin. She bit her lip, unable to move until he had stepped back and grabbed her tray. Her hands were shaking so badly she knew she could not lift it. She just wanted him to go back to the table but she could still feel him behind her, close enough to feel his breath near her hair.

What was he doing? Watching her?

'I've got it, Rose.' His voice was right behind her and tickled her hair.

He reached around her, taking the tray with one hand. Once again, their skin meeting softly and lifting it out over her head expertly and steadily. She hated that it left a lingering sensation of warmth on her arm, something else to torture her mercilessly.

One tray balanced precariously in each hand, he threw her an unreadable look and smile and gestured they go back to the table with a head nod. She followed like a dumb, mute, puppy dog. Walking behind him the short few steps and taking in his broad back, smooth t-shirt and jean clad rear. She wanted to cry.

Sliding the trays onto the two tables he was standing in her way so she could not sit, but had to wait. Like some naughty school girl outside the head office unsure how to act or what to do, she fidgeted with her ring once again. He moved aside, stopping to pull out her chair he had pushed in when putting their tray down. She avoided his eye contact sliding into the chair and avoiding another touch for fear she may cry as he gently pushed her back in.

This whole scene felt so surreal. Like she was in some weird dream and melted clocks and flying pigs should float by any minute.

Abby was unreadable. A dark look in her normally glittery green eyes.

Seems she has Rob's great skill there.

Morag and her mother still monopolising conversation and had moved to Robert the Bruce's era.

For the love of god, mother! Realise this Satan's beast is the enemy and set her free!

Her father made some joke about Rose as she tuned back in, realising he was talking to Rob about her. Abby had joined in, completely ignoring Morag who had finally shut up and was listening with a bored expression. Her mother reminiscing about some vague memory of Rose when her aunt had owned the cottage. Some affectionate childhood story in which Rose starred in all her youthful cuteness.

Rose just cringed.

For god's sake. Could this be any worse?

She felt his chair shift forward so he could better look at her father, obviously interested in what he had to say, this meant he leant in and rested his arm across the back of her chair casually. His forearm grazing her exposed back and shoulder. She froze at the sudden electric touch, finding words hard to form as she tried to answer something her mother had said, well, she was looking towards her expectantly as though she had asked something of Rose. She simply had no clue and had been out of whack with the entire conversation, only aware of his close proximity and what it was doing to her. It was sheer agony.

Grabbing her mug, she instead took a mouthful of coffee trying to drown it out, nodding and shrugging simultaneously in hopes it answered her mother. She used eating her pecan pastry as an excuse to stay zoned out and try and ignore his constant skin on skin heat. She wasn't even hungry, but it was better than nothing.

'Seems she always liked rambling in the gardens then.' Was all she heard in that familiar deep tone and turned around rapidly, catching the devilish look in his eye, she was suddenly aware that they were regaling the night of her disappearance after the ball. Morag was glaring at her nails, her mouth pursed tight and tapping her foot against her other leg in an irritated fashion. Her temper simmering beneath those glittering narrowed eyes.

At least there was some good coming from this meeting. Morag's irritation.

His arm came up and around her front unexpectedly, across her chest and gave her a squeeze as he continued. An easy nothing sort of gesture but it was devastating to her and her breath caught in her throat, causing her face to immediately flame.

'Scared the crap out of us and really, all she was doing was taking a nap in the rose bushes, like some Disney princess.' He laughed, his voice and closeness again tickling her hair and neck, making her crazy.

Her father erupted in laughter, claiming 'like mother, like daughter' as Rob returned his arm to its previous position. Maybe also aware of the heat growing between them at the slightest touch.

What in the actual hell was he doing? In which world did he live?

Laying his hands on her so effortlessly. Sitting cosying up to the parents of the girl whose heart you have broken. Your mistress. Non-mistress. Whatever the hell she was, sitting there fuming. No sense that this was the most uncomfortable awkward situation ever.

She felt her temper rising. Both at being the topic of conversation and by the absurdity of it all. She pushed her chair back, giving off a loud scrape and knocking his arm off ungraciously.

'Mum, I'll be back in few minutes I need to get something from around the corner… A book! I forgot I said I would pick it up from Mary's book shop today.' She tapped her watch, trying to be convincing. Her mum looked surprised and raised an eyebrow but nodded with a smile as Rose excused herself, avoiding Rob's eye and slid out from behind the table. Abby started to come but she gestured not to. She sat back down, lifting her phone and giving Rose a look that she understood.

'Pass my bag mum, I need the receipt in case the other girl is on the desk instead.' Rose smiled calmly, hiding her eternal wall of pain and needing her bag to get her phone.

Her mum passed her the bag and she turned, walking out quickly before anyone else could delay her; she needed space. She didn't care what it looked like to him, she just needed to get away from that completely absurd scene, away from the proximity of him and his arm against her back.

Hauling out her phone she texted Abby that she needed a few minutes to clear her head and not to worry. The air felt good and so as not to be truly lying to her parents, she ducked into the bookshop and began looking for a title she would normally buy.

She was shaking all over. Feeling the rising knot in her stomach as she tried for the millionth time in the last few weeks to calm the inner storm.

Deep breaths Rose. Deep slow and steady. Feel the air around you and nice calm steady breaths.

Pulling a random art book from the shelf she headed to the counter and paid for it without really opening it.

'I've suggested we go take a walk.'

The text beeped.

'Soon as your back we leave, okay?'

She loved Abby. She replied with an Okay.

'Told them I felt a bit queasy in here. Even Rob believed me, although he has gone into protective brother mode and offered to drive me home. Ughhh!'

'Okay Ab's, I'm coming now x'

She knew she could count on her favourite girl to rescue her and upon returning she did not even have to venture inside far. Abby was hauling them out, yelling goodbyes to the unwanted's and pushing Rose back out into the street in a rather boorish fashion. Mumbling curse words under her breath and masking them with a huge smile. Her cheekiness as always, bringing Rose back to a happier place.

Her parents did not seem any wiser to the craziness that had just gone on before them and scooping her book from her hand her mother admired her choice. Rose smiled, faking interest in the artist and some vague reason she wanted it. Noticing it was a contemporary artist and almost frowned that she would even buy it, her mother didn't seem to notice.

Chapter 19

Back home alone, Rose collapsed into her couch and let out a frustrated 'grahhhh' noise loudly, startling Muffin from his nap.

Her parents had stuck around most of the day and left after having dinner in the cottage. They had spent a majorly long time making small talk and praising the new Laird, how handsome and charismatic he was, and how very sophisticated his girlfriend seemed to be. Rose had wanted to stab her own eyes out with a fork but had managed to smile sweetly, nod and not say anything that would give them any suspicions.

She had not been much good at keeping the conversation in neutral territory when all her parents wanted to do was gush over their idea of a celebrity around here.

Abby had gone after lunch, making strangling gestures towards her parent's backs and laughing as Rose threw a mock kick up her butt. Finally, glad to be alone to let the madness process and her brain have some much needed quiet. Muffin was sound asleep again and exhausted after her father had walked his little legs off, so he did not even need out for a walk. Regardless, she pulled on her sandals and ventured outside. The need for air and calm peace around her, now that she had long awaited breathing space.

The walk was what she needed now, to soothe her frazzled brain as the sun lowered in the sky, making the light around her dull and grey tinted. The flies were not so bad tonight and even bare armed she was not being bothered by them.

She walked out of the gravel road, onto the main road and began walking away from the manor entrance. She needed to put as much distance between her and his abode as she could tonight. Away from town and out towards the town limits. She had no intention of walking far or any inclination of where she was heading but she just needed to walk. To feel nothing. Just concentrate on footsteps on grass in the cool silent air, looking at the scenery. A chance to clear her mind and let the chaos of the day evaporate, take a minute for herself. She scooped up a long piece of grass, using it to trail along the flower heads absently and push at items of interest on the ground. Losing track of time or distance she just kept on going, wanting this short-lived feeling of calm to continue.

The road sign over her head indicated she had come a few miles and it was getting darker faster. Looking back where she had come from she immediately regretted it as it occurred to her she had no torch and the road was not lit at all. By the time she got even halfway back she wouldn't be able to see even a foot in front of her. The nights here moving in fast and thick with the lack of suburban lighting and the road was not heavily used, so traffic could not even light her way.

God dammit Rose.

Heading for home, she tried to quicken her pace from the gentle meander to a much more purposeful step. If she hurried maybe there would be enough light to see her most of the way back.

She was wrong.

Pitch blackness surrounded her only thirty-five minutes later and she still had over a mile to go. The air had cooled enough to make her skin goosebump all over and the sounds of wildlife and bats in the surrounding hedgerows had started to freak her out. Cursing internally at her own stupidity, she kept on. Knowing home was a straight road and she would get there if she kept on. She just kept moving and taking steady steps. She had not even lifted her mobile phone!

Another couple of metres down the road she saw headlights coming towards her and moved into the grass verge again. She had been walking on the road so as to avoid tripping but could not be sure the driver would see her and moved over. She stumbled slightly on the kerb and righted herself on the grass, smoothing down her dress as the headlights passed, facing away from the road and then continuing onward when she knew she could move back to the roadside.

Her heart dipped into fear as she heard the car skid to a halt and start reversing at speed, panic moving in and moving straight back to the grass verge.

Shit!

Even though heinous murders and rapes were not the norm up here, she was aware this was exactly the kind of situation women found themselves in when they least expected it. She looked around, trying to make out an escape route but could only see a wall of darkness around her.

Picking up the pace, she tried to hurry forward but the car came level with her and skidded to a stop. The overwhelming fear made her feel almost faint and about to break into a run, eyeing the ground for any signs of rocks or sticks to defend herself.

'Rose? Is that you?'

She paused mid inhale, body getting ready to scream and blinked instead. Knowing that voice a little too well.

She looked down at the open window as the interior light was flicked on, a wave of relief washing over her, followed by a wave of 'Oh fuck.' Rob was frowning at her from the inside of his black car and Rose couldn't do anything except stare right back.

'Get in!' It wasn't a question, it was a command. She was too scared from freaking herself out to argue and slid into his sports car, unable to look at him as she clipped on the belt. Relief short lived as she saw the glint of temper in his dark eyes.

'For the love of god woman! What are you doing out here in the pitch black?' Rob's voice was majorly gruff.

'Taking a walk.' She stared out her window as he pulled off, once again that usual internal rhumba starting at his close proximity.

Damn him for the way he made her react!

'In that?' He nodded haughtily at her light weight dress, she glared at him and caught him looking her dress up and down, her bare shoulders and neck.

'Why not?'

He gritted his teeth, flexing his jaw and never responded. Just looked for a cut off in the road to turn around and head back to her cottage in a smooth manoeuvre.

Sitting in the dark, illuminated only by dashboard lights she felt cocooned with him in a little black box. He expertly spun the car around, shifting gear and heading back. He was a capable confident driver and somehow that just added to his list of charms that made her feel like throwing her shoes at him. His posture tense and unreadable as he kept his eyes on the road.

'Going somewhere nice?' Rose said airily.

None of her business, but well, she decided to be as intrusive and rude as him for a change.

'Nope! Just picking something up.' He retorted drily.

'At…' She glanced at the clock on the dashboard, shocked at the time. 'Ten pm at night?' Her voice was dripping with sarcasm. Feeding on his snarky atmosphere.

'Managed to pick you up at that time, didn't I?'

His jaw was set in a stubborn 'don't push me' kind of mood. Something had obviously killed his earlier chatty and cheerful mood from the bakery. She turned away, giving up as he turned into her road, all too soon the cottage illuminated in his headlights, not that she felt relief at seeing it suddenly.

'Thanks!' It wasn't grateful thanks, but more of a 'thanks for nothing' kind of throwback, fuelled by his mood and bristling her own temper. Turning to slide out of her seat and pushing the door open, he suddenly grabbed her wrist, his grip tight but not aggressive. He didn't turn to look at her, just clenched jaw, gritted teeth, staring head

'I'm trying to make this easy on both of us Rose. Trying to be civil when we see each other out and about; It would help if you got with the programme and stopped acting like a moody kid.' His voice was calm, but there was anger in its depths. She shook him off angrily, feeling like her wrist was burning with the contact.

'I don't think cosying up to my parents with the girlfriend in tow is something I can 'get' with! But thanks anyway!' Stung by his words, she didn't wait for a response, just swung her legs out and stormed towards the cottage, slamming the unlocked door behind her dramatically. She stood inside pressing her back against the closed wooden door, heart pounding in her chest, wondering if he would follow her, scared that he would but heartbroken that he might not. She swallowed back a sob as the roar of his engine indicated the speed at which he had reversed out of there.

Chapter 20

Her parents picked her up for the fete at ten am. Dressed in a long white summer dress, her hair piled on top of her head loosely and gold sandals. She felt fighting fit to take on Mr Munro should the need arise. She had spent the night tossing and turning in anger, adamant he wouldn't do this to her anymore. She was not going to be a victim and if he wanted to act like they never happened and all were cosy friends then so be it! He did not have a problem with acting like they had never meant a thing to each other and it was time she followed suit.

Abby had been on the phone this morning after receiving her texts and fuelling her rage with news that Morag had stayed at the manor last night. So now she knew what he had been out picking up and judging by the fact he had her stay indicated maybe he was sleeping with the red head after all.

It really was over. Done and dusted. She was not going to let this affect her anymore.

* * *

Arriving at the estate the view was magnificent. The large gardens full of stalls and tents, a miniature fun park and pony rides. Bright banners hung from trees, and flags, and bunting, draped from tent to tent. The place was so magical and whimsical that Rose almost forgot her rage for a moment. It was like being transported to a magical vintage fair.

It did not take long to get it back when she saw Rob and Morag casually walking together from one of the beer tents dressed in smart summer clothes. Steeling her heart against the thundering beat, she stuck out her chin defiantly and plastered a smile on her face.

Not today Munro!

Abby, seeing where her glare was focused, pulled Rose in the opposite direction quickly, to one of the shoot a duck stalls to vent her anger. Handing her the pink fluffy bear, the stall owner admired her ability to knock down every target she had aimed for and Rose fired back that having a black soul made of rage did the trick. He had waved her away laughing at the non-joke. Clueless to the fact she had envisioned every duck to be Rob's head.

'She was a world class sniper before she retired.' Abby grinned at him and got a hearty laugh in return.

'Yeah, I'm sure, Abby.' He handed her a lollipop for her wit and waved the girls off to try their luck at the next stall.

Abby was good medicine. Pulling her and her parents around, making them get involved in games and races. Plying them with beer and booze and generally making Rose's mood lift by the hour. Everyone needed a pick me up like Abby in their life.

'Ooh look, a wandering bit of eye candy to sweep Abby off her feet.' Rose nudged her in the back to point out the approaching tall blonde. Abby turned, turning a nice shade of blush and started fixing her hair enthusiastically.

'Eyes off Turner, he's my eye candy.' She winked Rose's way.

Duncan joined them and the fun, disappearing every now and then to catch his friends; Abby cuddling up to him at every opportunity and smothering him with affectionate kisses. Rose had felt a twinge of envy but could not feel happier for her. She liked to see Abby happy and Duncan seemed to do everything in his power to make her that way.

They rode a carousel and then hit the dodgems, acting like children again, before trying their hand at 'Hit the Vicar' on the cream cake throwing stall. The 'Vicar' was really one of the town farmers in a costume and Rose got a perfect bullseye. Screaming in laughter as her Dad proudly announced he taught her how to throw. Her mother was having an amazing time at trying her hand at every event and making it clear Rose actually took after her mother, both sporting winning teddy bears before long.

She had drunk a bit much already and was feeling giddy and light. For once her emotions flitting away and giving her room to have some fun. She felt reckless and high, throwing caution to the wind and trying every drink handed to her in the various tents offering home brewed beers, wine, and even the cocktail bar. Her parents had wandered off to have a break from the bustling crowds and left Abby and her to meander without them.

As the day drew on, her hyper-energy began to fade, so instead she began to fuel it with fruit punch and vodka juices at a more alarming rate. Ignoring Abby's warning about drinking in the sun, she carried on regardless; she was making a point to herself.

The point was that she could be free and have fun and ignore the idiot and his crazy sidekick today. She could smile and be merry, even with them at the same event and just get over it! They had seen them in passing in the distance throughout the day. This was her way of proving to herself that she didn't need him!

Her parents, on arriving back seemed equally tipsy and unaware of the extent of her drunkenness. Abby was finding time to sneak behind a tent with Duncan momentarily and had stopped giving her a tough time for ten minutes.

'Ahh, loves young dream.' She thought dryly as she watched them sneak off together enviously. Alcohol tainting her mood with a touch of sour, that tiny sadness creeping into her slowly.

He will only break your heart Abby! They all do!

* * *

Drunken wandering caused a lot of bobbing in and out and around people before long, losing her little group in a crowd of eager teens, Rose found herself wandering alone behind one of the large beer tents, tripping over some already legless men propped up sleeping by the entrances. She tried to take a shortcut between tents but found it too tight a gap and headed back the way she came. Only they had moved off somewhere else. She had truly lost them now.

The busyness of the grounds was overwhelming, crowds had come in all morning and the park was so mobbed that she had no way to navigate, unable to see through at the stalls or tents to recognise where she was. Just a wave of endless people blocking her view.

The drink and sun combination was really hitting her now and her head was beginning to swim. She didn't feel so good anymore and the panic and overwhelming need to cry at the sudden lonesomeness was bubbling up inside like a freight train heading for a tunnel exit. She reached down looking for her bag and her phone realising she had handed it to her mother to hold when they had hit the carousel and not taken it back.

Damn it!

It would still be hung across her mum's dainty shoulders holding all of her much-needed gadgets.

Someone bumped into her, knocking her forward violently and sending her into an inevitable forward fall, Rose flailing her hands to catch something stable knew she was going to end up in the dirt face first. Hard warm arms broke her fall, pulling her quickly into a safe circle and pulled her upright, away from pushy people and into a safe haven of hard muscle and warm arms.

'You okay?' Rob's voice like a torturous warm tide.

She didn't want him to touch her, didn't want his help. This was just getting to be too typical.

'Leave me alone.' She snapped a tad too aggressively. She tried to break free of his grip but he easily pulled her back again. Her drunkenness giving him extreme manageability over her.

'Rose come on, let me help you.' Exasperated by her fighting and twisting, he led the way, keeping a firm grip around her shoulders with one arm while his other grasped her wrist tightly so she couldn't break free or fall again. He found a quiet clearing and set her down on a fruit crate between two large white tents rather unceremoniously and stood back, giving her space. She avoided looking at him, feeling the emotion bubbling further up her throat and instead glared frostily at his loafers.

'I'll go find one of them and bring them here. You stay put and catch your breath.' He sounded normal, again with the lack of emotion and general dead pan tone.

'Don't bother! I'll find them myself!' She snapped and got up, attempting to storm past him but again he caught her, pulling her back with a little too much ease.

'Look, it's pretty obvious you have had too much to drink. You were about to get trampled to death out there. Sit here and let me go find Ab's or your dad.'

'What do you care?' She spat at him angrily, trying to throw his hands off again but failing as he just renewed his hold elsewhere. This was too easy for him and she was getting exasperated beyond control.

'Fucks sake Rose!' She had never heard him lose his cool so quickly before; It made her stop. In fact, she had only ever once seen him angry like this and that had ended up… well in her bed in his arms. He looked over her head as though checking to see who could see them then lifted her face with his fingers, cupping her jaw and stroking back tendrils of hair. His flash of anger dissipating as quickly as it had arisen.

'We both know I care; and the extent in which I care about you.' His mouth came close to hers, his voice sincere and soft. Too familiar. Too intimate. It was too much, too close, too soon and Rose broke into sobs uncontrollably. She heard him curse under his breath as he pulled her into his embrace, resting his chin on the top of her hair and stroking her back lightly.

'Don't cry. I can't stand it when you cry, baby.' He sighed heavily and squeezed her a little more.

'I hate you.' She didn't try to break free anymore, too exhausted to do anything but cry against his strong chest, enclosed in his warmth. Knowing she should push him away but wanting the comfort only he could give. She had dreamed of being in his arms again, so many times and nothing compared to the reality. The swaying of the world around her making her feel hopeless.

'I hate me too!' It was almost a whisper and despite herself Rose nuzzled closer and breathed him in. Bittersweet pain shooting through her heart as memory collided with reality and the fact she was still hopelessly in love with him.

They stood that way motionless for a few minutes before he tilted her face back, wiping the tears and standing her back on her own weight. His eyes locked on hers and he sighed, flexing his jaw but saying nothing. So much in those stormy eyes yet as always, unreadable. He just looked like her dreams, so effortlessly handsome. Holding her this way, and so close to him she didn't know why she had been foolish enough to ever let herself fall so badly for him. It was obvious she was never going to get over him, not anytime soon anyway.

Rose didn't know what came over her, maybe it was the alcohol, maybe it was the fact she was a total emotional mess and he was looking at her so intensely, only inches from her face. The fact all she could think about was how much she loved and missed him, how much her body yearned for his touch but she leant up, on tiptoes even in heels, and kissed him.

He didn't immediately pull away but he didn't fully respond. Just caught her face with his hand, holding their mouths together for a moment, almost as though he wanted to savour the touch before pulling away. Resting his forehead on hers and closing his eyes. His voice sounded full of regret and raw emotion.

'You're drunk Rose.' The husky way he brought her back to reality to see the face of his refusal sent her overboard. Feeling burned from the rejection, crippling pain searing her already fragile heart, she slapped his hand away from her face, shoving him from her hard in his chest. He barely moved so she backed away angrily instead.

'I hate you! Just stay the hell away from me … For the rest of my life!' Her voice broke, tears stinging her eyes. Practically spitting with anger and hysteria but she managed, ducking away from his attempt at catching her again and moving with sudden speed despite her spinning head between the tents.

'ROSE?' He called after her, but she put her head down and just pushed on running.

She broke free into the crowd and was lost in the sea of faces before he could catch up. Falling into people and tripping over ropes and occasional children. She fell flat on her knees submerged from his view by the people around; cursing and pulling herself up with the aid of a lovely couple, she looked down at the grass stained mess of her dress and began to laugh manically.

This just summed up her life lately. Every bloody moment of this dreadful bloody hour summed up in the sad grass stained and torn dress.

Feeling warm hands on her arms she spun around ready to slap him in the face for following her and was met with Abby's green sparkling eyes instead. Immediate concern replaced joy and the quick glance up and down.

'What the hell happened, what's wrong?' Abby went to wipe Rose's tear stained face but Rose shook her head as her mother appeared behind Abby and hushed her with a look.

Abby, pulling a tissue from her bag began wiping her friend's face and gestured towards a large sign indicating toilets, shielding her from her mother's eyes; she nodded, moving fast. They left her parents and Duncan at the ice cream stand while Abby hauled her towards the quiet of the mobile bathrooms on trailers.

Checking no one was in the first cubicle she dragged her in and handed her a bottle of water. Pushing her down on the closed loo and shaking her head with a 'what shall we do with you' expression.

'Oh Abby.' Rose burst into another torrent of tears, unleashing it all and felt her friend come down to cradle her head.

Talk to me Rose.' Abby lifted her chin with a concerned frown.

Chapter 21

'So, he didn't kiss you back?' Abby was still limiting the damage to Rose's make up with Kleenex and water, brushing her hair out and trying to bring some sense of normal back to her ravaged look. Kneeling in front of her in the tight cubicle.

'No... Yes... No... I don't know!' She was sitting on the toilet lid, no longer crying, having recapped the sorry tale already.

'Well he either did or he didn't!' Abby rummaged for a lip balm and started using it on Rose's mouth.

'He stopped me, but not like right away. He didn't pull away, he just held me a second, mouth to mouth. Like a kiss but not an open mouth let's take it further kiss. Just lips pressed on lips. Just sort of stopped and waited for a second to pull away.' Rose sighed and took the balm herself to apply a generous layer, her mouth felt swollen from repeated lip biting when she had been howling her eyes out.

'So, he did kiss you, he just didn't let it get out of hand?' Abby said thoughtfully.

'I think he was more concerned with the fact I was drunk and emotional and he was trying to not make me worse.'

'I have nothing!' Abby slid down onto the floor in the tiny space. 'Honestly I have no idea what the heck it even means. Without seeing how he was or anything. It's Rob... He is sometimes a complete enigma to me.' Abby sighed.

'Thanks. He's your brother!' Rose raised her palms in exasperation, if his sister had no clue what went on his head, then how would she?

'Maybe he wanted to kiss you back but he just knew he couldn't.' She raised an eyebrow, a helpful one to that charming voice.

'Maybe he just didn't want too and tried to spare my embarrassment.' Again, Rose sighed, deflated and fast sobering up.

'I thought you were done with him, Rose? Why did you even try?'

'I don't know...I wasn't thinking about it, he was just being soo...'

'Like when you were together?' Abby blinked at her sympathetically, a hand coming to brush hair from her face and behind her ear.

'Yes. I just wanted a moment of that back. I miss him so much it hurts.' She dropped her gaze to the floor, shame washing over her at her stupid move. 'I really am pathetic, aren't I?' A single hot tear escaped her eye and rolled down her now blushed, clean cheek. Abby moved towards her, dabbing at it with her tissue.

'Your broken-hearted Rose! Not pathetic... Just struggling and all of this is enough to make any woman break.'

'Why can't he just keep his distance...? He's always there. Always showing up to torture me! Always with her.' She pulled the tissue from her friend and began shredding it between her fingers.

'Maybe it's time you let me talk to him?' Her green eyes tinged with hope, she really wanted to end the way her friend was suffering but Rose shook her head.

'I'll be okay... I don't want you two falling out over this. I don't see that it would help in anyway, just cause drama Ab's.' She took a deep breath and straightened up purposefully 'I'm going to go home and sleep this off. I'll feel better! More in control. Less emotional. I promise! I just need time to get myself together and stop being so god damn stupid over him, I just need to accept that it's done and get used to the fact we live in a tiny village and will see each other often.'

Abby looked doubtful but held her tongue and got up, squeezing together to pull open the small cubicle door. She watched her friend with an aching heart, knowing she was falling apart slowly and there was nothing she could do.

Her brother had a lot to answer for.

* * *

Her parents agreed that Rose needed some respite from the sun and alcohol and to have a sleep, assuming she had taken a turn of illness in the bathroom from too much of both. Her naked arms and cheeks were itchier red than blushing sun-kissed now and she looked weary and tired, only cementing the belief she had mild sun stroke and not heart break.

Abby promised to take care of them but they brushed her away, assuring her at their age they did not need babysitters. As she kissed them goodbye near the fete entrance her mother pulled her close with purpose

'Whoever he is! He's an idiot and you deserve far more.' She kissed her hard on the cheek, smoothing back her hair and bringing her daughter's eyes to her maternal gaze. 'We love you Darling, don't forget that.'

Rose was shocked into silence, aware that her mother had a lot more insight than she had given her credit for. She felt the lump in her throat tighten and pushed down another sob. Hugging her mum tightly, she left them to go return to the fun of the day.

She was sobering up now, but still had a slight unsteadiness to her walk, feeling more Bambi-esk than drunken mess now. She headed through the arch made from white balloons indicating the way out. Her mind set on walking home and getting away from all this craziness.

She heard him call her name as she let a small group of kids slide by in front of her and felt herself instantly bristle inside.

For God's sake!

Closing her eyes to regain her composure and fix a calm look on her face she turned towards his approaching frame. As always, devastatingly handsome and effortlessly casual. As always appearing to make her agony endless.

'I've been looking for you.' He said quickly, a strained tone to his voice, possibly a slight edge and she hated the way his mere presence seemed to drown out everything around her like an all-consuming black hole.

'You found me.' She kept her tone even, unreadable.

An old Rob trick.

'I wanted to make sure you were okay.' He was looking her over, appraising her calmer appearance and newly fixed make up. Probably wondering if he had imagined the whole thing.

'Just dandy.' She gestured down her length as if to say 'See.'

'You look better.' He sounded overly bright now, appearing friendly and upbeat. She was trying to focus on other things, using any passing person as an excuse to break away from his intense gaze and smile 'hello' in passing.

'You mean I'm sobering up?' She inwardly chastised herself for the tinge of bitchiness in her tone, knowing it would just ignite another argument. She just needed him to turn around and walk away, leave her alone.

'I mean less upset.' His tone gave her nothing but his eyes had become fixed to her face and his body a little too close for comfort.

'I got over it!' She crossed her arms defensively across her chest, holding them. Praying he would get to the point and end this agony, this polite pretend friend's conversation that had absolutely no point at all.

He didn't say anything, just stood looking at her until the uneasiness forced her to speak instead.

'Look, I'm going home! I don't feel great and I need to lay down. So, if you don't mind.' She gestured for him to give her space as she moved to turn away, but he stopped her.

'I'll drive you. It's a bit of a walk if you're feeling ill.' His hand on her upper arm seemed to burn.

'No. It's okay... You need to stop okay?' She pulled her arm away from his hand, moving out of his reach.

'Stop?' He seemed to reel back slightly, confused.

'This!... This coming to me. Talking to me. Seeing me around and acting like were mates and you can just come over and act normal!' She hadn't wanted to lose her cool and hushed her tones as more people passed, she wanted him to move back and give her space. His closeness suffocating her, making it hard to think straight. She just couldn't control it anymore and he just wouldn't let her go.

'I'm trying to make it easier on you. On both of us.' He said defensively in a lowered voice, more people moving past them and breaking his gaze for a second.

'Well you're not okay... You're making it worse!'

'I'm sorry, that's not my intention.' He lifted his eyes from her and was instead lost in a gaze over her head, a faraway look in his eyes. A troubled expression on his face and then a sudden statement she hadn't expected 'I just... Miss you!' It was so quiet it was almost inaudible but she heard it and it sent a breaking pain through every cell of her body. Seeing for the first time a slight hint of sadness in that calm controlled face.

She lost all traces of anger and instead just felt broken, that she had been hating him for being able to move on and here he was looking as sad as her; then in a fleeting moment, it was gone. He cleared his throat and his face returned to unreadable coolness. Return to typical Rob. A look of determination taking its place.

'I'm still driving you home, though.' He said with more strength to his voice.

She moved to argue but he slid his hand into hers, interlocking fingers in a way too intimate hold and pulled her in the direction of the manor, ignoring her protests. Cutting along the outside of the fete in full swing, his hot warm strong hand holding her in an inescapable grip and his stride pulling her onwards whether she wanted to or not. Trying to pull his hand off and free hers, he only tightened and fighting was futile. She had no choice but be pulled along.

'Did everything I say just get lost on you?' She snapped, becoming breathless with the effort of his fast pace in heels on grass.

'Nope.' He was in stubborn, clamped down mode. Unreasonable Rob had returned and she knew this side to him too well.

'Then how is running me home helping?' She gasped and tried to steady her pace to meet his. He did not respond, just pulled her past groups of smiling people, picking up eyebrows in interest as he dragged her by, leading the way purposefully.

'Rob? Everyone's looking.' She was starting to become aware of the little whispers as they passed, the fleeting looks and eyebrows raised, but he just shrugged. For the first time in a long time, he did not care at all. She realised with a huge sadness this was the first time he had held her hand in this way in public, first show of something more between them and it was only because they no longer were. She followed obediently willing him to let go, aware of the amount of people around who turned to look now and willing him to give her breathing time to settle again with a less fast pace.

'Rob?' Morag's voice shrilled over the crowd from the distance towards them but he did not react. He did not even look her way. It repeated, this time higher pitched and annoyed and he turned in irritation without breaking his pace. Waving her a gesture, indicating five minutes and the briefest of glances, she seemed stunned into silence, stopping her pursuit. Rob carried on unphased and Rose's skin felt like it was flaming. She was sure her blush had enveloped her entire face as she averted her eyes, avoiding the other woman's nasty glare.

'Rob? Really I... ' He cut her off mid-sentence, pulling her closer as they approached the gravel of the sweeping drive at the front of the house. His phone started ringing in his back pocket intrusively, pulling it from its nestling place she could see Morag's name flashing boldly but he clicked the screen, switched off the phone and put it back in his pocket. Still holding her hand, he led her to his car neatly tucked under trees. The shade of the huge oak concealing it.

Pulling his keys and remotely unlocking it with a beep he pulled her to the passenger side and gently deposited her in the car, leaned in and clipped her seat belt over her; his face so close she could almost kiss him. He looked at her for a brief moment although said nothing and closed the door. Still not saying a word he walked around and joined her in the driver's seat, within seconds they were heading down the long smooth road to the manor gates avoiding meandering people in their Sunday clothes. She watched his profile, feeling for the first time since knowing him that she was unsure as to what he was doing.

The journey was short and silent. He seemed to be concentrating on the road and she was unsure as to what to say, the roar and hum of his powerful car adding to the tension between them. He pulled into the cottage, stopping swiftly by the gate and jumped out as she was unbuckling her belt. Coming around to open her door as she slid up, aware of his closeness and tensed. His expanse of muscle and presence blocking her way., affecting her ability to breathe.

'Thanks for the lift.' All her fight had deserted her. She was now just very confused and feeling really unsure as to how to behave. He did not move, still blocking her escape.

'Look. This is hard for me too. Can we talk? Just for a few minutes. In private, inside. I swear I'll behave.' That hint of humour in his eyes. Her head was screaming 'No!' but her heart was already leading him into the cottage, melting down into her stomach weakly.

Did she have no self-control left at all?

* * *

He stood in the living room, filling the space, so familiar yet so out of place now. Obviously uneasy. Rose moved to the kitchen and filled the kettle, unsure what else to do or how to behave now that they were both in here alone. Her whole being paused momentarily, waiting for him to make the first move. To say something first.

Fixing her hair with her fingers and smoothing her dress, trying to catch her reflection in the chrome of the kettle to wipe any make up smudges from under her eyes, she made herself a little less wild and more presentable. The alcohol in her blood was fast dispersing and the new adrenaline coursing instead had sobered her up greatly.

Walking back through she found him sitting in the armchair, perched on the front of the seat holding a framed picture of Abby and Rose on an outing. It was one she loved dearly, wrapped in each other's arms with huge smiles on both of their faces. He looked up at her as she approached, sliding the picture back onto the small side table with a lingering look. He seemed ready to say something, his whole manner screamed it so she waited quietly.

'I regret the way it ended Rose…I shouldn't have let it happen that way. We should have at least talked about it face to face first, talked when I got back.' He dropped his hands between his legs, resting his elbows on his knees and hunched a little. So much strength in that body that it was distracting her.

She bit her lip, quietly studying his face, sensing he had more to say and unsure what to even respond anyway.

'I stayed away longer than I needed too. I figured we could both use the thinking space.' He stood up, walking to the mantle, resting his one arm on the top and gazing down into the stacked wood, ready for colder nights moving in. 'When I saw you that night. I should have done this then but I couldn't trust myself. It was too soon. I wasn't ready to see you.' He glanced over at her, checking for her response and making sure she was listening.

Of course, she was!

He watched her walk to the couch and sit down gently. Unsteady on her feet and in need of a little support, careful movements under his scrutiny and unsure how to feel.

'I acted like an idiot. You deserved more.' Walking back towards her, he kneeled in front of her at her feet, taking her dainty soft hands in his 'I owed you more.' She looked away, unable to keep control while he looked at her like that. Her bottom lip trembling so that she put it between her teeth to quell the urge to break.

'Rose? I am sorry I really am. I understand why it couldn't work. I agree. If things had kept going the same way it would have ended us anyway.' His voice was strained and husky.

It didn't make it hurt any less with him saying the words, it just caused her eyes to fill with tears. Seeing her pain, he got up, moving to beside her on the couch and pulled her against his side. His arm loosely around her shoulders, his chin resting on her head.

'I don't want to think about tomorrow or the next day when it comes to you. It's too hard to imagine. I was trying to take each day and moment as it came. Trying to deal with it the best way I could so that I could still function. When I saw you I couldn't help myself, I just wanted to reach out!' Rose was trying not to melt into his arms and body, trying not to lose her mind at his closeness and warmth.

'I can't do it that way Rob.' She couldn't bring herself to face him, still staring blankly at the window away from him, feeling his heart beating through the wall of his chest and trying not to get lost in his arms. 'It's too hard. '

Even sitting here like this was a horrible bittersweet pain.

'I know!... That's why I came here... To end this the right way Rose. To set the ground rules...I think we both need to lay things out on the table. To have you tell me what you need to make this easier on you.' It was a simple request, a mature request but somehow it was sheer agony having him talk to her about the breakup this way. So calm and final, his tone even and sure. No hint of tears in the way she was falling apart.

She thought for a moment, taking her time to really think about what she needed from him, pushing herself to be rational. He waited, guessing her silence was because she was trying to figure it out.

'I need us to avoid each other until I can stand being around you.' She pulled away from him and dried her eyes. Standing up to take position at the mantle as he had previously done and telling herself distance was what she needed to do this, his touch was still too potent. 'I need you to stop laying hands on me so effortlessly when all your touch does is make me want to crumble and cry.' She glanced at him, watching him silently agreeing, reluctance on his face. 'I need to not see you wrapped in her arms wherever I turn.'

'There's still nothing between her and I. I promise.' He cut in quickly, seriousness on his face and in his tone.

'It doesn't make it easier seeing her all over you though.' After all she was the reason her heart was shattered into a million tiny flakes.

'Agreed.' His voice steady and determined, he leant forward, again resting elbows on his knees and studying her face. 'It will get easier Rose.'

'Don't!' She stalked away from him to the far window, smoothing back the drapes to stare into the garden. 'I don't need to hear statements like that for a start. Not from you!'

Her body bristled and exploded in goose bumps as she felt him move up behind her unexpectedly. His torso brushing her back lightly as his hand came up to slide down a strand of loose hair. They both knew there was nothing more that could be said and this was just prolonging the pain.

'I will do whatever it takes. Whatever you want. I don't want to hurt you anymore than I have already.' He turned her slowly to face him, coming close enough to almost touch noses. Gazing at her as he pulled together his own thoughts. 'Is that all? Nothing else you need from me?'

She shrugged, unsure what else he could do to make the pain go away but at least it was a start.

'There's one thing that I want… Something that I think we both need. To say goodbye properly. To always remember, even when you're looking at me like you hate me.' He smiled softly, his hand coming to her cheek gently. His eyes fully locked on hers and sending a thousand tiny fireworks across her skin. Her body trembled in anticipation.

'What?' Her breathless response indicated she already knew the answer as he moved in towards her, slowly tilting her chin and first rubbing his nose against hers. Lingering to breathe her in and looking into her dark brown eyes. He bent down towards her, kissing her slowly, gently at first and full of meaning. A slow brushing together, a parting of lips as he moved in and captured her fully. Deepening the kiss as his arms moved around her to completely encircle her against him.

It was one of those long slow tender kisses you read about in romance novels. So much more meaningful than hot fiery open-mouthed snogs. This was the kind of kiss you remembered for a lifetime, that plagued your sleep in those restless dark nights when you least wanted it too. Their mouths fitting perfectly, effortless motion and the deepest rising of emotion from the pit of her stomach.

It was the worst kind of goodbye, because it only highlighted the perfection in their compatibility. She had longed for the touch of his lips again. Ached to feel him around her in that soft tender way, cradling her and making her feel safe and loved. She didn't want it to end and it seemed neither did he. They kissed until tears began to slip down her cheeks and then some before he finally broke away. Smoothing back her hair and wiping the wetness from her face. His eyes raw with emotion, he stared into her eyes for a long moment, his thumb brushing her cheek as he cradled her face one last time. Pulling back regretfully, slowly as though he just couldn't let her go willingly and then he turned and left without a backwards glance, almost as though he couldn't.

Leaving her feeling cold and empty and desolate.

Rose opened the floodgate and cried in a way she thought she had exhausted over the weeks.

Chapter 22

Despite the heartache and the torrential flood of tears she had finally drifted to sleep, curled on her bed, hugging fluffy cushions with Muffin laid across her hair. The last traces of alcohol finally dispersing into her bloodstream and sleeping away all the misery.

Her phone ringing had awoken her and disorientated she clambered up, looking for the shrill tone to shut it off. Her phone was still in her bag in the kitchen where she had left it and the walk through barefoot fully woke her up.

Dammit.

She had a tonne of missed calls from her mother and several texts from Abby. It was getting late and checking the time on the phone she realised she should be getting dressed for the party. It was incredibly late already but she no longer wanted to go.

Calling her mother back and hearing the slurring merry tones and background noise she realised that they had not left the fete to get ready but had simply followed the crowds into the manor straight from the activities as soon as the doors had opened. Abby had informed her, by yelling in the rear that most of the partygoers were still in shorts and sundresses and to hurry back just as she was. She was missing the time of her life. Abby also sounded suitably merry, her words slightly slurring.

She looked at her stained white dress and slid it off. Replacing it with a short black floaty dress that could be passed off as formal or casual with the change of shoes and make up. She fixed her hair into a messy up do and reapplied her makeup to look sultrier and more formal than her daily light touch. She looked better, less tired and frayed. Even the bags under her eyes were temporarily absent after a decent amount of shut eye.

She slipped on moderate heals but then thought better of the look, opting for flats and no jewellery. Didn't want to overdo it if everyone else was still in their outdoor outfits. It was borderline casual/formal and gave her an air of sophistication. Garden party glam.

She really did not feel up to this. Although the mirror told her otherwise. The memory of his kiss still lingering on her lips, her heart still fragile. She pushed it all down deep into the pit of her stomach, closing off her mind and gave herself that mental shake she needed. She had been getting better at this. She couldn't let her parents down. Or Abby!

Realising she could not drive, she managed to catch a lift from passing party goers heading to the party. They welcomed her into the car with bright smiles, complimenting how pretty she looked. All familiar faces scrubbed clean and sparkling for the night ahead. The fete, despite the growing darkness was still busy with teens and younger kids and the odd adult. Fairy lights illuminating the stands now and screams of delight still to be heard. It would carry on for a while out here. The fun and chaos still brewing between those too young to go to the dance.

A new large white tent had been erected on one of the cleared lawns and it seemed an underage disco was starting to get going. The DJ visible in the open doorway behind a large flashing podium, beats and thumps in time to his nodding head. Many suitable adults in yellow vests with various positions emblazoned across their backs overseeing the rabble of kids running in the flapping entranceway. She recognised no one and carried on past them.

Abby was waiting outside for her and broke into huge smiles at seeing Rose's arrival.

'Hey you, god you missed so much fun!' Abby looped arms with her and started pulling her along towards the still busy gardens.

'What exactly did I miss?' Rose hoped it was something involving Morag and a disabling fall, then chastised herself for even thinking that way.

'Your parents got so very drunk that I had to send them to the house to nap it off in the guest rooms. Think your mum was about ready to lay down in the middle of the garden.' Abby grinned but Rose just groaned in embarrassment, even at this age, her parents still had that ability.

'Then I'm glad I missed it.' Abby was guiding Rose on through the remains of the fete which still looked in full swing.

'Well, I doubt they are any more sober, last time I saw them my dad had cordoned them off in the lounge and was popping open his whiskey collection. Seems being your parents meant they're his new best friends.'

'Abby I'm scared to see the state of them, I thought parents calmed down by this age.' Rose giggled at the thought of the three of them up to no good.

'Mine certainly didn't, he's already been around the dancefloor twirling that god damn kilt and I can guarantee he will be up again soon.' Despite the cringey way she was saying it, there was also a hint of pride in Abby's voice.

Duncan looked smart and handsome in a shirt and navy trousers as they approached him in the hall and Abby was almost glowing with pride as she let go of Rose to give him a kiss on the lips softly. They made a gorgeous couple. Unconcealed infatuation was written across both of their young faces. Neither could stop looking at one another and the subtle touches between trailing hands were not overly concealed.

Rose couldn't deny the look of uncomplicated love between them. Again, that tiny surge of envy tried to surface but she pushed it down, deep into the recess of her mind and pulled a smile back on her face.

'I'll catch you up laters, Rose needs a guided tour.' Abby winked at him, before releasing him and returning to Rose's arm.

'You look very nice Duncan, very smart and handsome.' Rose smiled at the boy, she didn't know him well, but what she did know of him was all good. He seemed good for Abby and the affection was genuine.

'Thank you Rose, you girls look lovely too and many a head will turn tonight.' He smiled, a hint of red creeping up his cheeks and then he was turning to his friends and gone. Abby's eyes following him out of sight with a satisfied sigh that just screamed 'My boyfriend's so dreamy.'

Rose was quickly dragged around and introduced to several members of the family Munro who had come for the party. After all, this was their annual event. A chance to get together and have a good old knees up. It was apparently one of the few times a year that so many of them gathered under the roof of this old house and she had already lost count of the number of Munro's she had met.

Abby dragged her over to a group of men, all equally handsome in fitted shirts and casual jeans, beers in hand. All in their late twenties. They looked like a typical bunch of guys out for a drink any given weekend in any city.

'This lot are my adopted brothers. Well except those two, who are actually my cousins.' She gestured towards two black haired, well-built men, to the rear who raised their bottles of beer in unison. They bore a striking resemblance to Rob and Hamish and it was a little distracting. She took a moment to glance over the fact the Munro Gene was obviously very strong. Neither had those clear grey eyes, though.

They all shook her hand one after the other, as Abby graced her with names, smiling and kissing her cheek, introducing themselves by short nicknames instead, none of which were obvious but she didn't like to ask. They had the manners of the old fashioned, despite their youthfulness.

'This is Rob's crew!' She laughed and waved an airy hand in a half circle at the men.

'Talking of which, where is he?' One of the tall dark-haired cousins piped in and nudged Ab's in the shoulder with his bottle.

'God knows! He was milling around somewhere in the hall earlier.' She passed Rose a quick glance as though this little piece of information would upset her but strangely Rose felt okay. Earlier at the cottage had somehow helped her heart a little. Abby continued with her introductions.

'They all went to school together and this one… ' She pulled the arm of a tall blonde. 'Is Damien. Rob's best mate and all round geekazoid. Watch him he's a creep.' she was grinning wildly, obviously in jest as he bopped her on the head with his beer and grinned. He was slim and athletic looking with baby blue eyes and a soft sort of gentleness to his face. His blonde hair flopping over his forehead lightly that reminded her of Duncan.

He looked much younger than his age and Rose felt an instant fondness for him. He reached forward taking her hand and placing a gentle mock kiss and bow upon her fingers, she laughed at the motion, enjoying the company of these good-humoured fellows.

'I'm the better looking one.' He winked; she smiled seeing that he was not serious.

'I think you'll find Rob wears that crown.' Another of the men cut in and was met with immediate mumbles.

'Err no, I think I'm the one the ladies prefer.' Another hit into the conversation and soon all of them were arguing over who had more sexual prowess and appeal, loudly and messily as they all shoved and poked at one another. Rose listened and laughed at the comedy of it.

She had never thought of Rob being one of the lads and having a group of mates like this. It somehow seemed at odds with the smooth mature businessman who ran around overseeing so much. Just another layer to his complex self. She could not imagine him among them or even how he would behave surrounded by these jocular blokes.

One of the men tugged Abby's cheek in a little squeeze and she batted them away. Obvious that she had known all of these men for a very long time. They were teasing her about her height and obvious maturing. Pointing out her boobs had 'come in', becoming a woman instead of a 'wee lass'.

'Get lost, perves.' Abby slapped away hands that were ruffling her hair, poking her in the face and generally teasing the hell out of her.

'She's one of the women now, guess we had all better be nicer to her seeing as she's turning into a stunner and lost the pigtailed knobbly kneed look.' Her cousin jested, the one she had learned was called Gavin.

Taking a cue from what was said, one of the other men mock knelt on one knee, proposing marriage and sending Abby into a laughing fit.

'Shut up you nonce.' Abby squealed, batting him away before he scooped her up and threw her over his back effortlessly. Rose could not help but let their infectious fun and laughter filter through and she felt better than she had in weeks. They had an energy that was catching, an easiness and light humour you had to get caught up in.

Damien leaned in purposefully while Abby was being swung around like a rag doll.

'Is a dance later out of the question?' He seemed shy and sincere and Rose smiled genuinely.

'Of course I'll dance with you, Damien. It would be nice.' he smiled, lowering his eyes and raising his beer in a laddish gesture. A gentled head nod, a little worse for the wear already.

Back on her feet and looking completely breathless, Abby pulled Rose off to find her parents and save them from her dad once more. Getting respite from the rowdy men and managing to calm her hair back into a sleek style.

Soon enough, they were back in fighting form and already boogying on the dancefloor. Rose cringed at the sight of her parents trying to do the time warp, joined by the now transformed man of the hour Hamish Munro and smiled affectionately. She could not help but laugh, watching the antics as she crossed towards them. Her parents looked so alive and young and were obviously having an amazing time.

'R'ooo'se.' Her mother squealed at seeing her, a little girlishly, an obvious slur to her speech. She embraced her with kisses on both cheeks.

'Mum.... Dad.... Mr Munro.' Rose nodded and smiled at all of them.

'You look so much better, and very beautiful.' Her mother stroked back her hair from her face in her usual maternal manner and then pinched her cheek. 'Showing him what you're worth!' She winked, cheekily grinning and turning back to re-join her dancing partners. Rose sighed and resisted the urge to eyeroll. Rarely had she seen her parents drink and right now she had no desire to get caught up with them while she was very much sober.

Abby coaxed Rose into a little five-minute dance and twirl, to appease the old folks, before they left them all to it and headed to the pop-up bar. In great need of something cool in her parched throat; it was stuffy in here already and was only half filled with hot bodies.

'Just a coke Ab's!' She stayed her hand as she gestured the barman.

'You sure?'

'Yeah, I want to stay clear-headed. I still feel a tiny bit fragile. No more booze for me right now, okay?' she squeezed her hand gently and smiled warmly, knowing that staying sober when she would ultimately see Rob again would be for the best. She would need to handle seeing him with Morag, no doubt, and she didn't want a repeat of earlier.

'Okay dokely lovely!' Abby ordered them two cokes, deciding to join her friend's sobriety for the time being. A show of support.

The hall was fast filling up and Rose caught glimpses of Rob across the room unexpectedly. She had, for once, not been looking for him but still her eyes had managed to find him amid a sea of faces. He saw her too, but true to his word he did not react but kept his distance, smiling briefly at her and turning away. It didn't feel good but it felt safer than having him approach. Her eyes lingered on his wide shoulders and dark shirt a little longer that she should have and she had to physically pull her gaze away, chastising herself inwardly.

Oh god, how much she missed him.

Morag sashayed in across the floor as though to serve as a reminder as to why Rose should keep her distance, her casual outfit from earlier replaced with a figure hugging short black dress and killer platform heels. All evidence of anger and crazy safely locked down as she headed straight for Rob's side. Rose swallowed hard and bit on her lip to quell all the emotions swirling inside of her. Unable to stop looking her way.

There was a look on Morag's face that was hard to translate and a few words in Rob's ear, pressed close enough to him to make it obvious she was not entirely amused. The tension in both of their body language told Rose that she wasn't being friendly. He turned shrugging her hands off his arm, saying something to her. Close to her face, almost nose to nose before turning and leaving her standing there alone.

To anyone else it looked like a domestic between lovers and that only irritated Rose more, she instantly wondered how many people in this town thought that Morag was his girlfriend.

Morag turned, scanning the crowd, possibly checking if anyone had seen the interaction, only now she looked livid. Realising there was an audience, she threw back her hair, pasting on a bright fake smile and picked at the canopies on the table. She glared at his back as he stalked away towards the group of men Rose had met earlier and was greeted with a beer and a chorus of a lot 'Yay's', back slapping and male bonding ensuing.

Rose knew she shouldn't be watching and staring but something in the little scene had made her feel better. Slightly triumphant despite not even knowing what it was about. Just seeing him push off her normally wandering hands and putting distance between them was enough to lighten the heavy thud in her chest, enough to make her relax a little.

She watched him being enveloped into the masculine group, laughing and joking, clinking beer bottles and behaving like lads did on a night out. He looked younger, carefree and so unlike his normal 'all business' self. Still the best looking of the group of men, she noted. Oblivious to the seething stares being cast at him mere feet away by his red headed serpent.

It helped that Morag was angry and storming away; her chin held high and daggers flying from those slanted eyes and a deep frown.

Maybe tonight Rose would get a chance to relax without being assaulted by the view of Morag feeling Rob up and acting like she owned him.

Abby caught her arm, bringing her back to the present and yanked her towards the dance floor as her favourite song came on. Relieving her of her drink as they passed the last table, she swung her into a clearing with little protest.

The floor was already busy but there was still room to move and Rose fell into the beat of the music effortlessly. One thing she had always been good at was dancing. In fact, she loved to dance and could already feel her tension lifting and floating up into the high ceiling. Duncan appeared behind Abby and began shimmying and sashaying with her, receiving a gentle shove in the chest and a mock telling off. He leant down, giving Abby a kiss briefly on her lips, his hand wandering over the girl's backside sneakily then moved off to re-join his friends dancing nearby. She smiled at him, her eyes shining with love.

'He's a really nice guy you know?' Rose yelled over the music.

'I know!' Abby had not torn her gaze from the tall boy across the floor, obviously smitten with the tall sturdy frame and light hair '. He even gets on with Rob, which I have to say is a bonus. I was sure Rob was going to take his head off when I finally admitted we were dating.'

'He's definitely a keeper then!' Rose laughed as Abby turned back her way, a strange misty look in the glittering cheeky eyes.

'I love him Rose!' Her eyes filled with emotion and her cheeks flushed. It was almost as though she had been afraid to say it aloud and it scared her.

'Tell me something I don't know!' She shook her head, grabbing Abby and spinning her round, killing the conversation as the music upped a gear and a dance tune blended in effortlessly. Somehow the sound got louder so talking was impossible.

They danced until their feet ached, stopping only briefly to sip their drinks and scream to another favoured tune. Abby and Rose were well matched in dancing skill and enthusiasm and she really was having a good time. Even with Rob in full view, with his group of men chugging down beer and talking to one another with animated gestures. Rose was enjoying herself.

The goodbye at the cottage. The lack of serpent by his side. It all felt somehow more bearable. She could do this if she set her mind to it and kept a reign on these damn emotions.

Her parents appeared and danced terribly besides them for two songs before admitting defeat and heading off to find a comfy chair among the sea of faces. Not that Rose was complaining, it had been excruciating and she wondered if she would ever become the kind of parent who embarrassed her kids that way. They really did think they were Torvill and Dean.

The hall was mobbed! The lights had been lowered to darkness and the twinkling fairy lights and disco balls were creating a moving pattern across the mass of bodies. It was almost magical.

A softer song blended in, slowing the tempo and bringing the chaos of hyper-dancing down to a calmer movement like a wave across the floor. The air around them quietening slightly as the pace was dropped. Duncan appeared, pulling Abby towards him and Rose turned to head off in search of food, not wanting to be a third wheel just as Damien appeared before her, mock bowing and offering his hand out towards her.

'My lady, I would like to have that dance now.' He smiled shyly.

'Of course, kind sir.' Rose grinned and curtsied, joining in the game, accepting his warm gesture and let him lead her back to the floor to take up a slow dance waltz position.

He was a good dancer, a strong leader and effortlessly moved her in time to the music. Swaying gently. There was something sweet about him, almost childish, and she would never have put Rob and Damien together as best friends, they were like chalk and cheese.

'You're a great dancer you know?' He smiled down at her from his tall height. 'I could see you from over there.' He motioned to where they had all been congregated earlier and she resisted the urge to look over, afraid she would catch Rob's eye. Afraid it would make her feel as uncomfortable as the night she had danced with Matt, but Damien was completely different.

'Thanks! You're not so bad yourself.' her smile was genuine as she did mean every word.

'You look really pretty you know. It's a nice dress. Makes you stand out. Classier than most of the girls here.' He was sincere and sweet but Rose didn't like where this conversation was heading. The nervousness of his facial expressions, despite being well and truly drunk and the slow creep of colour across his cheeks. She could tell his brain was whirring and clicking, trying to carry out whatever plan he had souped up mid-dance. She had that anxious feeling building inside, suddenly aware that this majorly drunk man was going to make a move on her after all. His eyes glued to her mouth in that undeniable way.

Shit! Rob's best friend of all people!

She felt her face strain with the effort to keep smiling and tried to put some distance between them. A hard task when he was holding onto her like his life depended on it as he was practically sweating nerves. It was obvious that being best friends they obviously had a similar taste in women.

But what about loyalty?

Rose found that distasteful.

Looking around briefly, trying to catch Abby's eye, she was aware he was still talking but she was no longer listening. Nodding and raising her eyebrows as though she was responding to the brief conversation Damien seemed to be having with her as she looked for an easy escape route that wouldn't embarrass him. She was too late and saw the kiss coming in advance, turning her face evasively. Damien, being slower than her, planted his lips firmly on her cheek realising he had missed his target he looked embarrassed and his cheeks started to redden. He made another move forward, more certain of the mark this time and assuming his drunkenness had been the cause. This time he had an intense purposeful look in his eyes as he descended again.

Roses facial expression and raised hand stayed his advances. She looked around fleetingly unsure what to do next.

Rose caught Rob's eye directly through the crowd, feeling that overwhelming surge of panic rising. Aware that he had probably seen the awkward encounter but his face gave nothing away. He just stood pouring beer into his mouth from his glass bottle, his eyes steadfast on hers and almost statue like in his pose. The man next to him unaware he had lost his interest in their conversation.

'Look Damien. You're really lovely! You are! It's just...' Rose dragged her focus back to the task at hand, faced with a floundering man who was obviously mortified at her rejection.

'Shit, you have a boyfriend, don't you?' He frowned hard, hands moving around nervously as they were standing still in the middle of the moving dancefloor, no longer touching.

Rose felt confused. For his best mate, he obviously had no clue that Rose and Rob had once been lovers. That it had only been recent and things were obviously still raw between them.

'Not exactly, but I'm still getting over someone.' Rose smiled gently, Damian was still standing close but it became obvious the rejection had him looking for an easy escape. She could see his eyes flicking to the sides, looking for a way out and that surge of embarrassment staining his upper cheeks and forehead. Rose felt immediately sorry for him.

'Do you mind if we sit down, my feet are aching from all the dancing.' She said softly, patting him gently. It was a little white lie to save his grace as much as hers. Relieved and almost grateful, he gave her another mock bow and let her walk off before turning, walking back to the podium area and being enveloped back into the group of men.

Rob was still glancing her way between responding to his friends, his eyes never leaving her as she made her way off the floor. He smiled at something that was said to him, that thousand-watt killer smile, but it didn't seem to reach his eyes. He seemed to be fully focused on what had just taken place down here on the floor instead and now that it was over he stopped looking her way and turned his back. The jovial noise echoing her way and a hint of his laugh. It sounded genuine despite his previous manner.

Rose literally could not handle another episode like that today. She felt like she had been on way too many rollercoaster rides lately, it was becoming way too familiar a feeling. And what she needed was a long evening of carefree emotionless fun that didn't involve advances from men or watchful eyes that made her feel guilty.

The entrance hall, bustling with people was quieter than the dance hall, venturing out she found her parents perched on a love seat by the main stair chatting to another elderly couple on a matching couch. The relief washed over her and she slid on to perch beside her mum, welcomed with a motherly arm slid around her back. A simple gesture bringing back her childhood memories of her mum reading to her.

It was safer out here, no more men to try and seduce her, no bodies bumping and grinding around her and no more staring eyes watching her every move and making her feel guilty even when she was doing nothing wrong.

She soon bored of the conversation, though, the rotational planning of a vegetable garden was not something she would ever find passion in and the call of some great music beckoned her. Abby would be done with smooching as this was a firm favourite, she was always singing it in the car on full blast. Just the beat alone had her hurrying back to find her friend.

She went back in search of her, grabbing a glass of bubbly from a passing waiter.

One wouldn't hurt!

Chapter 23

Being sober among drunk people was getting dull. She needed a little boost to get through the party and get her happy back on. Right now, she needed some merry, downing it quickly and discarding it on a table.

Abby saw her and screamed in delight, yanking her onto the dance floor and immediately assaulting her with a shimmying butt to butt rubbing in time to the music. Rose slapped her on the rear and shoved her off laughing, she could feel the electric excitement returning with the beat to a fabulous song.

A couple of the men with Damien were dancing nearby and turned to encourage a group dance; Abby immediately jumping on the back of one of her cousins and rubbing his hair messily, shouting something about cowboys. She had obviously been downing shots in Rose's absence. Rose tried to stay a little demurer but with the blink of an eye, one of the men had sidled closer, scooping his arm round her waist and trying to thrust a thigh between her knees and throwing her about like a rag. He seemed intent on some groin to groin rotating.

For the love of god!! Were all his friends in heat?

Trying to untangle herself was almost impossible. As soon as she managed to turn away, making it look like an expert dance move, the other guy moved in, almost pinning her bust to his chest and tipping her back. His hands sliding over her back and ass.

She immediately felt her skin crawl with the unwanted touch, overly sexual dance moves were not her forte and she had no clue how to get out of this. She literally wanted to scream. She was internally cringing every time she felt a hand placed on her seductively or her body was crushed to his in a manner befitting the bedroom.

Drunken north men with hot blood and absolutely no inhibitions. It was like being back in the stone age with cavemen trying to drag women back to their lairs. Abby seemingly oblivious, was still perched on the back of a rugged looking male and being bounced around like a child. Screaming in delight, her hands waving in the air in time to the music and singing along wholeheartedly.

There was no way out and Rose felt her panic rising. The crowds moving in as this song was pretty damn popular and alcohol fuelled. Dancing always encouraged some pelvic grinding from randy drunks and she felt like they were closing in around her. His hands were devouring her no matter how much she tried to pull them off, even slapping him away only seemed to encourage his antics. She shrugged and twisted and tried with all her might to untangle herself from the mess of hands and body. He was like a man-child and this was all a game of 'grope the lassie'. She managed to break free turning to face her assaulter.

It was in an instant. The body that flattened against her back. The hands finding her hips and moving her in time to the music away from creeping hands and overzealous pelvic thrusts that she instantly knew his touch. The familiar heat and slip into safety and security like a warm wave had smoothed over her, shielding her from unwanted attention and creating a safe haven. Her eyes closing at the sensation of having him touch her again.

How much she had longed to feel him around her again.

He was saving her. She couldn't be mad at the way he was doing it. The effortless rhythm and easy way he was dancing behind her, holding her to him so it was clear to his 'mates' she was off limits. They took the hint, turning to another gyrating woman nearby and leaving him to carry on moving with her. The song was the kind that demanded sexual swaying and a lot of suggestive shimmies and grinding. She didn't want to turn and look at him or pull away, she just wanted to pretend this was okay and enjoy the moment. Not break the spell with reality. Pretend for the sake of being saved. Relieved that he had actually come to her this time.

The way he slid her up and down and moved in time, his jaw against her cheek. His breath on her face. The way he was making every inch of her tingle by just being held against him. Her back against his chest and her head against his throat and jaw. Her hair falling down around her shoulders; the pin up do, long falling down. It was the most erotic highly charged feeling in the world. She knew it was stupid, but for once, her mind was not battling her emotions and the longing to stay this way was winning out.

The darkness of the hall and the flashing lights somehow made this okay. Surreal. Getting lost in the music, she lifted her arms, letting his hands slide up from waist scuffing the edges of her breasts and up her outstretched arms. Her senses reacting with hot burning sensations going off inside of her. He turned her, her arms falling down around his neck as he Patrick Swayze style moved into her. His mouth coming dangerously close, his eyes focused heavily on hers. Pushing her thighs apart with his and moving into her snugly, a perfect fit, their bodies sexually moving 'a la Dirty Dancing'. She could sense the hardness against her pelvis that he was just as turned on as she was yet neither broke away.

He had moves she would give him that much. An unexpected great dancer.

Fully controlling her body with every tiny movement, she was breathless and lost in the moment. He tilted her back easily and his breath skirted her cleavage. Rose was ignoring the screaming voice within that this was not what they had agreed on, that this was only going to hurt her more in the long run but It was over too soon, as the tempo changed and the bodies around them cheered and began jumping up and down to a new dance beat.

He still had her against his hard taut form, both their chests rapidly moving and eyes locked. He didn't speak, just a final stroke on her cheek with the back of his fingers. His breath tinged with alcohol, his mouth moved dangerously close to her lips for a mere second until she could feel his shallow breath against them, her own lips parting in anticipation. His dark storming eyes moving down to focus on their soft fullness, his slight jaw movement and the tension appearing in his face signalled he was contemplating kissing her but stopped himself. She wanted him to kiss her. Her whole body was screaming out for it and she could feel both of their elevated heartbeats pounding erratically in unison.

She was so weak.

He let go of her, obviously reeling in his senses and realising this was dumb; he turned and walked off, leaving her alone amid the sea of bouncing bodies. Like suddenly being plunged into an icy bath. The sagging of her insides and the jelly legs gave her no choice but to stagger to the nearest chair and sit down.

She couldn't think straight, she didn't want too. Her body still tingling and her pulse racing. She had known his touch instantly. Felt his familiar warmth and she had let him take control of her body without hesitation. She was her own worst enemy when it came to him and this only proved it. He could have done anything to her in that moment and she would have let him. She was still reeling and sizzling from the effect he had on her.

Did she have no self-control or self-worth?

The message to his friends was loud and clear and they didn't try again. Even Damien, who had returned to join a non-contact dance seemed to be keeping his distance. One of the burly men winked at her when he caught her looking towards where Rob was standing with his back to them; he had a beer in hand and lost in conversation with some other man. Completely recovered and unfazed by what had just taken place on the dance floor. He was the picture of control once again and acting like Rose didn't exist.

It upset her greatly and she pushed it away, down towards the hard wooden floor strewn with empty paper cups and streamers squashed flat by thumping feet.

Knowing he was nearby, in view and Morag'less, ready to save her at a moment's notice had made her feel better, despite the dance-floor moments. All the earlier agreements forgotten temporarily, she couldn't be mad for what he had done.

How could she when she had so wantonly reacted to him. She had hardly pushed him off, had she?

Pushing down the feelings of warning, she relaxed into enjoying her night. What was left of it, one eye always checking where he was. Aware and highly sensitive to his whereabouts.

* * *

Danced to death, exhausted and carrying their shoes; the girls staggered out of the hall in the small hours. The night had carried on uneventfully and it was now moving into the early morning. Many of the party goers had dwindled away, leaving only the hardcore drinkers behind in the hall. Streamers clinging in their hair and smelling strongly of the alcohol stench that was mainly coming from Abby, they were trying to work their way out to the main sweeping stair.

Her parents had left hours ago in a taxi back to their hotel, their age getting the better of them. Hamish, on the other hand, had out danced them all and was still in there leading the remaining party animals to a Runrig song.

Despite swearing she wouldn't drink more, Rose had ended up drinking a decent amount. Fuelled by her high adrenaline, willingness to drown out the memory of Rob's body against hers and her better mood, she was more than a little tipsy.

Morag had not even managed to lower the tone in her short brief appearances. She had another verbal tiff with Rob in a dark corner of the room, seemingly unimpressed with something he was or wasn't doing and left in a blaze of drama just before one am. They had been too far away to really hear anything said but the heated expressions and arm waving made it clear that it was another 'domestic'. She hated the way Rob and Morag looked like a blazing couple having another lovers tiff. Hated the way the woman monopolised his attention at every chance she got and felt she had the right to fight with him this way in public. It just highlighted why she had ended things and it broke her heart.

Abby had one arm draped around her friend's shoulders, obviously unable to walk without assistance but Rose was bearing her weight. The girl kept falling over nothing and could no longer string a coherent sentence together.

'I am putting you to bed miss!' Rose was struggling to keep her upright.

'Jus aswerl I live in here then innit!' Abby drunkenly slurred, gesturing towards a bathroom door off to the side.

'You actually live up there!' Rose pointed to the sweeping stair. 'And I somehow have to get you up there.' She glanced around for some help, spotting Duncan asleep and propped by a door. He was in a far worse state than Abby and would be useless in assisting them. Rose half dragged her to the stair and attempted to climb. More of a two up, three backwards kind of motion and kept having to swoop lower to pull her back onto her shoulder every few seconds. Abby's grip as loose and uncoordinated as the girl herself.

'Have I told yuhhh…? Really cos arrr mean it babe… Have I told yurrr…? Rosy, I lurve you.'

'I love you too Abby.' Rose laughed once again, finding them stepping backwards down two steps and making little progress. Abby was a terrible drunk. 'I would love you more if you could walk though, or maybe climb stairs.' Her own tipsy mind finding the motion they were creating was not helping her own state.

'Here. I've got her!' Rob cut in from behind, lifting Abby easily up in his arms as though she were a mere child and heading up the stair with Rose in tow to the girl's bedroom.

She helped him get the now unconscious girl up along the hall to Abby's room and into bed, pulling off her shoes and jewellery in the darkened space, noting that he was swaying slightly even in the dimness. Not his usual full 'compos mentos' self either, but hiding it well.

He was almost as drunk as Abby, yet being a seasoned pro meant he was still functioning in the land of the living. His strong form in the darkness and the mix of alcohol and aftershave making him seem more manly and sexual than normal. Rose had to move away from him, aware she was losing her resolve and the longing to touch him was killing her as he tended to his motionless sister, so gentle and caring as he tucked her into bed. He turned, satisfied that Abby was asleep and bumped into Rose behind him awkwardly as she tried to figure out where to stand.

His hands immediately went to her waist as he steadied her against him but he didn't release her, instead, he pulled her forward so their bodies met softly, her breasts against his torso; the heat from his body surging through the thin cotton of his dark shirt. She was too drunk for this and did not have any defences left at all to fight him off, not that she wanted too.

His hot hands on her body just served to remind her of how much she wanted his touch, his closeness and instead focused on his eyes and the way they were devouring her. He walked forward, moving her back until the cool smooth wall of Abby's room came up against her back unexpectedly, giving her no escape. His body pressed to hers and moving in closely to her face. The closeness and intimacy of his actions causing her breath to evade her.

'Rob?' There was no conviction in her breathy whisper. It sounded more like an invitation, sensing that he wasn't going to just let her go anytime soon, her heart rate elevated and her legs turned to jelly.

'Tell me NO and I'll stop. I'll let you go and walk away.' He was breathing so close to her, his hands now on her naked thighs below her short dress, moving up under her dress slowly, erotically. He had decided this was not going to stay platonic or safe and she was mesmerised by him, her mind racing and unable to focus on anything but the heat of those flat palms moving up under the hem of her dress and setting her skin a light.

'Your drunk. I'm drunk. This would be…' She could not even formulate any form of rejection, her brain wildly clutching at straws as her eyes tore at his mouth, her own mouth practically begging him to kiss her. She knew she was lost and this resisting was futile, all night her body had been aching for him after the dancefloor and now she was finally getting her heart's desire.

'Tell me you don't want too, that you don't miss me as much as I miss you!' It was almost as though he was begging her to stop him, aware that he no longer had the control to stop himself. She couldn't formulate a response, her mind a chaos of contradicting thoughts and emotions. She wanted him. Her body on fire with desire and longing. His closeness blocking out any rational thought and the burning ache and longing from lack of his body against hers. The slow build of tension between them all day building to this very moment. His mouth was close enough to almost feel, his eyes locked with hers, full of lust and disregard for the consequences. Her mind still scrambling to be logical, to get some control of herself.

'We're in Abby's room, she might see us.' Was the only reason she could find to object but it fell on deaf ears. He had given her enough opportunity to push him away, his lust taking over, assured by the fact she wanted this too. He lifted her up against the wall, pushing against her so she stayed balanced while he pulled her legs around his waist slowly and surely, taking the time to stare deeply into her eyes. Her body was reacting like it always did when he was against her. Opening like a flower to envelope him in her warmth, surging heat emanating from her need. Giving into him, she arched her back, hands sliding along that jawline, her lips finding his mouth and hungrily plunging straight in. Crushing and purposeful, the desire and need in him making it almost animal as he responded to her instantly.

His hands moved under the thin fabric of her lace panties, looking for her and she groaned as he found the source of his intent, falling against him weakly. Pleasure sweeping through every cell of her being and only pushing her to kiss him more vehemently, biting his lip and savouring the way he teased her tongue with his.

She was already close to orgasm and he had barely touched her, heightened senses, the slow build to this moment and weeks of not being connected to his body. Moving closer, Rose drowned out her voice of reason easily, giving into the extreme hunger within for him. Not wanting to listen to that inner voice anymore. She was pulling his shirt open, the buttons coming away easily, her hand ravaging his shoulders and chest, cupping behind that strong tanned neck to pull him closer.

Pulling her from the wall, he walked in the darkness, straight into Abby's bathroom and kicked the door shut behind them. Within moments he had her on the floor, pulling off clothes, lost in fevered kisses, hands rambling over one another. It was not like anything they had done to each other before. There was an urgency and desperate need fuelled by sizzling desire and some sort of crazed frenzy in what they were doing as though they could not stand to deny it for another second.

It was hot, fast and crazy. Lost in drunken abandon, feverishly turned on by each other and hell bent on having their way, satisfying the all-encompassing hunger inside of them and throwing caution to the wind. Fuelled by the clouded logic of alcohol.

She had never been taken by him this way and she writhed around in ecstasy forcing the inner voices and warnings out of her skull. Pushing down the doubts and instead submerging in the feeling of him all around her, within her. Begging him to push harder, faster and he obliged. His hands finding her wrists and pinning them above her head as they both climaxed in unison. It was so earth shattering it was almost violent. She was more vocal than she could ever remember and he was equally matching her. All inhibitions were gone as they finally slumped together on the cold tiled floor, breathless and tingling yet buzzing with satisfaction.

Blissfully stilled and laid over her in her arms, his face resting in the nape of her neck, breathing hard and purposely. His heart beat was pounding ecstatically through her own. Illuminated by moonlight and the coming of dawn.

'I'm sorry Rose.' His voice gentle; regretful. He leaned up over her on his arms, meeting her eyes, full of remorse and sadness. 'I shouldn't have done this. I shouldn't have pushed you into this.'

'You didn't force me, Rob, I wanted this.' Her face was flushed and hot and just his gaze alone was affecting her breathing. She knew that letting him go again was going to be even harder so instead just focused on the here and now and not the later.

'I didn't give you much choice, though.' He looked down at her mouth and gave out a small pained groan, breathlessly screwing up his brow. 'I can't do this!' Genuine pain in his statement as he slid back and off her, leaving her feeling cold and suddenly shy about being naked on the floor. She sat up quickly, pulling her dress to cover what she could, looking up at him questioningly with wide eyes, fear lingering in the back of her throat.

'Can't do what?' She asked quietly, nerves spreading through her stomach.

'I can't stay away from you. I can't not touch you. You drive me crazy Rose. I feel like I'm going slowly insane and all I ever think about is you, like this. What it's like to touch you. Kiss you. Make love to you. Over and over, every god damn second and I feel like I'm losing my mind... I need you... Losing you has been the second single most awful thing that has ever happened to me, next to losing mum to cancer and I can't just keep on pretending that I'm not falling apart without you.' His pained expression made her heart ache.

'Rob... ' The emotion of his outburst had caused a lump in her chest and her throat, she felt the tears welling up inside and yet she could not formulate a sentence. He crumpled against her once more, pulling her into him in a crushing agonising way. The force of his own emotions evident for once.

'I love you so much. This is killing me. I feel like I have lost all control of everything and only you can fix me.' His voice was strained with emotion, pleading her, begging. 'Rose give me another chance?

Another go at fixing this, please? I will literally do anything you ask… Whatever that is… I swear, I'll do absolutely anything for you baby.' He pulled back to lock eyes with her again. looking for the first time since she had known him like a lost soul. All evidence of the calm controlled Munro gone. Just painful honesty and genuine fear that she might turn him down.

She couldn't resist him. She didn't have the strength to reject him, she did not want too; he had always had her heart and she needed him just as badly. She could feel her cheeks wet with her own tears, unaware they had started falling and closed her eyes to his touch as he began to brush them away tenderly, kissing her softly where he dried them from her skin.

'I need time to take all of this in, time to think.' She knew that wasn't true, her body was screaming to stay joined with him but nothing had changed in their situation, she knew she should be pushing him away but she was clinging on.

'When I left the cottage today, I had every intention of doing as you asked.' He brought a hand up to her face and traced her lips softly. 'But every time I see you, all rational thought goes out the window. I can't think straight. Whenever you're around the blinkers go on and I just want to be near you. I want to touch you, want to hear your voice and have you look at me. I just react… I can't go on like this another day Rose, I have never felt this way in my life about anyone and I'm dying without you. There has to be chance for us, we fit perfectly.'

She leant up, kissing him gently on the mouth, untangling his hands from her hair and pulling them to her mouth so she could gently rub them against her lips once more. Softly stroking his skin against hers as her mind tried to calm the chaos and torment of being torn.

'I am not going to lie, I have been going through hell too. I miss you so much that I can barely breathe most days. But nothing has changed. Morag is still swanning around acting like you're her possession and she doesn't seem any more mentally stable.' She looked up at him imploringly.

'At least give me a chance to talk this through with you, let me try and change things. Figure out where to go from here that involves you being with me and not apart, not sleeping in separate beds and acting like strangers in passing. I don't want that with you anymore.'

She closed her eyes knowing that all resolve had long since left her, she nodded gently, she would give him that, time to talk this through, time to listen to what he wanted to say and if he could change the way things had been. She felt his breath on her cheek as he moved in again, brushing his lips across her temple, feeling his body relax over her as he slowly pushed her back down to lay flat on the floor and nudged a knee between her legs.

'Rob?' She pulled away and caught his gaze. 'We can't stay here like this'

'I could stay this way forever!' His voice soft and full of meaning. Still focusing on her face, his fingers tracing her cheekbone.

'We're on your sister's bathroom floor. It's not even locked and she's like ten feet away.' She laughed lightly, suddenly wracked with guilt that they had done this with her unconscious in the next room. Rob swooped up towards the door, stretching out and flipped the cold steel latch over.

'It is now!' He grinned and planted a kiss back on her mouth. Firm and sure and acting like reconciliation was a done deal in his head. She laughed, shaking her head and shifted under him, pushing him off so they understood this was not what it was, not yet. He rolled over , mock clutching his heart, feigned agony and ducking as she batted him with a hand towel that had fallen on the floor during their chaotic entrance.

'Get up, I'm not talking here while you are naked on your sister's floor.' She scolded lightly and began pulling her scattered belongings together.

'I meant it Rose.' His face was calm and serious as he watched her pulling on her clothes. 'Us! I want that more than I want anything… I want to try again. I will do whatever it takes this time. I swear. Morag doesn't get priority over you anymore baby.'

Rose sighed heavily, knowing that the conversation that was coming was going to be hard, she had no idea how he expected to play this out but she was willing. She missed him more than was bearable and having sex again had only cemented the fact that she was not going to ever get over him.

'We get out of here and we go somewhere that Abby is not snoring six feet away from first. We talk. We figure this out…Okay?' She glanced back at him, nodding at his trousers slewn across the tub.

He nodded, a hopeful look on his face and pulled the rest of his discarded clothes up from the floor. He knew better than to argue when he was coming out on top.

Chapter 24

Sneaking from the room and along the dark hall had felt like being naughty kids, sneaking out after dark. There were still people meandering in the hall below, remnants of the party goers and waiting staff picking up discarded glasses. He had her hand tucked neatly inside his, pulling her along in the shadows, a simple possessive gesture; his large form and strength making her feel small and fragile. She felt like a teen sneaking from her parent's house with a rogue boyfriend and it somehow felt exciting and right, especially when that rogue man was six feet of pure sexy gorgeousness and smelled amazing.

The hall, open on one side to a huge balcony that overlooked the main grand entrance was illuminating some of the ceiling and areas below, but here none of the lights had been put on, creating a dark passage to move unseen. They stuck to the wall in the shadows, hurrying along. Pulling her behind him, he opened a door at the end of the corridor and pulled her inside, both stifling giggles, still as drunk as they had been.

It somehow felt different this time already, just the fact he was sneaking her around his house at a very public affair and not caring who caught them was stark contrast to before. Everything had changed, she could feel it in the atmosphere between them, in the way he was being. He looked younger, more carefree.

Maybe it was because of the alcohol, but she didn't ponder to think about it.

The room was a beautiful opulent suite with huge canopied bed and luxurious bedding in shades of creams and peaches. It was obvious this had been his mother's influence, so much in Abby's taste only more mature and sophisticated.

Latching the lock on the door closed he caught her and pulled her against the hard wooden surface, planting his mouth firmly on hers, making it clear he wasn't about to go back to keeping his distance, but she resisted, pushing him away playfully and putting up a warning finger at his lips with a stern look. He groaned, reaching for her again but she skirted away out of reach and climbed on the bed with a shake of the head.

He took the hint and rested back against the door, watching her with a look of amusement on his face. Folding his arms across his wide chest

'It's like that, is it?' He smiled lazily, his mood a lot better than previous weeks.

'We agreed to go elsewhere… To talk!' She slid off her shoes, getting comfy against the overstuffed cushions and watched him shrug off the door and follow her to the bed. Kicking off his shoes too, he climbed up, laying down beside her, his hand trailing across her lap to tangle in her fingers possessively, despite her trying to keep this 'talk' uncomplicated she didn't have the will power to remove his hand.

'I meant it. It's not because I'm drunk Rose…I got this drunk because of you… This insane ability you have to make me feel like I'm free falling whenever you're around and I've lost all control…' He looked up at her sheepishly, his eyes for once reflecting just how much he was missing her. 'I want to try this again. I know things have to be different and I want them to be. I was an idiot to make you feel like you did, I should never have treated you like a secret that I was ashamed of. Every fight we had, I knew it was my fault, that I was losing you. So god damn stubborn and sure I could do it a better way… One where we all walked away happy.' He let go of her hand and instead slid his hands around her waist and tugged her closer, pulling her to lay beside him so he could hook her with his legs and nuzzle into her neck to breathe her in. 'I miss you so god damn much.' He sighed heavily.

She looked at him thoughtfully, so many objections rising about the situation that had not changed but willing to listen, unsure what else to do.

'Go on.' She said quietly, wanting to hear exactly how this was going to be different.

'It won't be the same, Rose. I'm not that stupid to think I could ask you to do that again. To go backwards to a situation that was hurting you. I don't want too. I'm not ashamed of us, the exact opposite in fact; I want everyone to know you're mine, that I'm the luckiest guy in the world and show you off. After tonight, I think it's pretty obvious I better make that clear so no more of my mates try it on. Honest to god you just attract every male eye in a fifty-mile radius.' He lifted his chin from the hollow of her neck and glanced at her, a small glimmer of humour in his eye. 'No more hiding baby, no more acting like we don't mean anything to one another. I love you and I want everyone to know it.'

'What about Morag? What do you intend to do about her, her illness.' She was quietly taking all of this in, her face devoid of emotion and trying so hard to give her brain some quiet to really process it all.

'I can't let her dictate my life forever. It's not going to be easy but I can't do this anymore; I kept putting her feelings before yours. I see that now and I will never do that again. Losing you Rose, was like a huge punch in the stomach. It's the wakeup call I needed… I can live with her hating me but I can't live without you… I won't live without you.' He laid on his back, pulling her hand onto his chest and gazed at the canopy overhead. 'She's not getting any better. She could be this way for the rest of my life; I'm not willing to hold my breath in the hopes she moves on and lose everything I want. Everything I need! I won't risk losing you again.'

Rose silently watched him. Pulling together her thoughts, her brain in a whirlwind, afraid to commit just yet, afraid to say everything he wanted to hear as her heart was still afraid of being hurt by him again.

'How do you think she will react?' She instead responded, knowing she needed to just let this all sink in. It felt too right laid here with him, his hands on her and cosily snuggled on a bed. She couldn't lose sight of things, she needed to be rational and think about this properly, knowing that maybe he wouldn't be quite so sure in morning light when faced with a tearful Morag.

'Badly. That's what I'm worried about. She has tried before, in the past, to harm herself when I broke up with her a long time ago. There is always that fear hanging over me that this time she will succeed.' He sighed and squeezed her fingers firmly, tugging her ever closer as though it was just not enough.

Rose did not answer but just slid down the bed further so she was eye level with him and turned towards him, pulling his hand to her mouth and gently touching it against her lips, her usual mannerism when she needed his touch. He turned, meeting her gaze.

'You didn't give me an answer Penelope!' He kissed her fingertips gently that were on the back of his own hands. He knew he didn't really need one, lying here beside him looking at him like that. He knew he had never lost her. And it only made him hate himself more knowing that he had put her through hell yet she could still look at him with open-eyed trust and devotion. She had no clue how just a look from her could change his whole day, his whole life.

'I think I may run off with Damien instead. He's far less complicated!' She smiled wickedly and broke into howls as he quickly rolled on top of her, torturing her with tickles and threatening to break his face.

'Damien could never keep up with you! You need a real man with a high sex drive and patience of a saint Penelope. Besides, I would never allow any other man to get near you in that way. You're mine baby, from now until eternity.' He buried his face in her neck again, feeling her hair on his skin and breathing her in. She jabbed him lightly in the stomach laughing at his gentle jerk reaction.

'Why did you never tell him about us?' He had ceased abusing her and was instead burying his face in her neck, trying to provoke a different kind of bed rolling.

'Who?' He didn't raise his head. Trailing kisses across her throat and down lower to the dress neckline, pulling the thin material down slowly exposing more skin to devour.

'Your best friend! Damien! You know the dude that I only just met!' Rose laughed and tugged her dress back in place, he just paused and looked up smiling

'Is this because he tried to seduce you on the dancefloor? Should I be worried and maybe actually go break his neck right now?' Rob moved back enough so that he could lean up a little and gaze fully at her face. She raised her eyebrows and pulled her bodice up to cover the cleavage he was exposing once more with that sneaky hand. A look of mock seriousness on her gentle face.

'Okay. okay.' He raised his palms in defence and flopped back on the cushions in mock defeat. Sighing heavily at being refused what he really wanted to continue. His libido always ever ready because she made him crazy hot, pretty much all the time.

'Damien and I are not so much the inseparable pair we used to be. Truth be told, I barely see him and we barely call each other much anymore; we're guys and we just grew apart. Not just him, the whole group of us did. He moved away and we lost touch! I see them a few times a year and we get drunk and hang out.' He shrugged. 'After my mum died I just grew up a lot faster than they did. I had responsibilities to deal with and he's not someone I would tell anymore; I guess I tell my dad the things I used to tell my mates instead... And don't think I let it slide about the dancefloor either, missy!'

'Excuse me! I did nothing!' She gently slapped him in the chest and rolled again towards him getting comfy. His hand immediately coming to play with her hair by her face. Looking at her intently.

'Still wanted to break his nose, though, then Gav's and Mickeys too.' He nuzzled into her jawline, trailing small kisses along the length before coming to the corner of her mouth.

'You seriously have a lot of aggression, don't you? Always wanting to physically assault people.' Rose turned to him, planting a quick chaste kiss on the mouth that was teasing her and moving away again to continue conversation.

'Only when it comes to other guys trying to touch you I do.' Once again, he leaned over her, hand coming to rest on her cheek a moment. Staring at her silently, thoughtfully

'I love you Rose. More than anything in the world. More than life.' His eyes were cool calm and pale. She had learned over the weeks that this was when he was at his most unguarded, most sincere and honest. His eyes an eternal glimpse into his soul. It was so unexpected amid their gentle banter that it caused an immediate lump in her throat, tears pricked her eyes.

'I love you too Rob. If we do this again it can't be the same, I couldn't go through that again. Don't hurt me.' She hadn't meant to say all of that, but in a way, she wanted to tell him she was his. That she wanted him more than anything and was willing to let him try again. Another go at trying to fix this mess they had made; that she needed him just as much as he needed her, maybe more.

'You're my heart baby. Hurting you is like stabbing myself in the chest. I won't do that to us anymore. I swear.'

He swooped down, kissing her in the way he had done so in the cottage earlier that day, except this time instead of painful goodbye it held far more meaning. Soft and full of longing and promise. No sexual innuendo behind it, just the desire to kiss away all the memories of her heartbreak. To be lost in her and to let her lose herself in him. It was a silent promise, wiping out all the pain of the last few weeks that he wouldn't let her go this time.

Chapter 25

They slept in the bed wrapped in each other's arms until the sun streamed in the window only a few hours later. They had given up on talking with that kiss, falling easily into the passion that was always sparking between them. Fully immersed in each other and not letting tomorrow take up any more time; aware that they would have to let things play out to see what the future held for them.

Rose was the first to wake with a start, forgetting where she was and sighing contentedly when she saw his sleeping form beside her. Face down on his stomach, his face turned towards her so his nose touched her hair, his arm tossed casually over her waist. His favourite way to sleep.

God, she had missed seeing him that way and it made her heart glow brightly. He woke, feeling her movement in the bed and hauled her in for a sleepy cuddle without opening his eyes or even raising his head. Murmuring at her to go back to sleep but she shook her head.

'I think I need to eat! Shower at least, I feel woozy and grubby.' Her hangover was barely kicking in so she still had the tipsy feeling and alert awareness of pre-hangover. She stroked his eyebrow, watching his peaceful face adoringly, so still and free from tension and stress. Achingly handsome. Opening his eyes slowly a wide cheeky grin spreading across his face

'Now a shower sounds fun!' That tone and wink hinted at less cleaning and more getting dirty.

'Is that all you ever think about?' She laughed, pushing his wandering hand off her pelvic bone, throwing back the covers boldly. No qualms at being naked in front of him anymore.

'I'm male! It's all we all ever think about, besides with you walking around looking like that... Can you blame me?'

She laughed, her face breaking into a genuine smile from ear to ear, she secretly liked that he never tired of sex when it came to her.

'We need a battle plan of action! Or at least I need to know what I am supposed to be doing or telling your sister when she sees me walking around in last night's dress at stupid o'clock.' Rose sighed and reached for the throw on the floor to use as a make shift bathrobe.

'Firstly, she stays in bed till late when she's been a dirty drunk so she won't be seeing you anytime soon. Secondly, you won't be in last night's dress as I'm taking you to my room and keeping you as my prisoner and naked. It may involve various degrees of torture.' He had slid up behind her, sitting against her back, twirling her hair in his fingers. 'And we will be testing out the spaciousness of my shower in the name of ergonomics. You have no idea how many times I have imagined you in there with me.' He was grinning at her now, one arm propping him up on the bed casually so he could lean in and kiss her neck. His lusty glint brazenly obvious.

'I'm being serious.' She laughed pulling his hand out of her hair and kissing his fingertips. 'Last time we snuck around, hiding out, and I never stayed here. This all feels weird for me. Not to mention seeing Alice and Tommy wandering about this morning with the clean-up crew.'

'This isn't last time.' His face was serious as he drew her with him, back across the bed, pulling her flat onto the mattress so he could lean over, moving over her effortlessly.

'No hiding, remember? Today we go test my bed springs. A lot! Try out the shower and maybe if you're lucky... My office too. I am pretty sure there are a few places in there I could bend you over.' He planted a kiss on the hollow of her neck and pushed her ankles apart with a foot, meeting with no resistance. 'I have a lot of making up to do for weeks apart.'

'Rob as good as all that sounds, I have one little issue.' She was finding it hard to resist, hard to formulate words when her body was already yielding to his.

'Mmmmmm?' He was lost in her skin, trailing downwards towards her cleavage, obviously engrossed with his task.

'My parents!'

He stopped. Sighing. Amazing how two little words could have the same effects as a bucket of icy cold water.

'I'm supposed to be meeting them for breakfast and take them sight-seeing while they're here.' She laughed as he collapsed hopelessly on top of her over dramatically. Sighing and acting like a child who has just had their plans spoiled.

'I would invite you but my mum is pretty sure you're marrying some skinny redhead and might think I'm a dirty whore. She really does not encourage side chicks in a relationship.' Rose giggled.

'So, we put her right!' He caught her eye, complete seriousness. No mockery or jest.

'She thinks the guy who broke my heart is an idiot!' She touched his stubbly jaw affectionately. 'She doesn't know his name only that he's a moron, and probably wouldn't like me showing up with him for cosy family time.'

'She had a point, but see, I'm not an idiot anymore and your heart's no longer broken! I am however much more intent on breaking this bed right now than letting you go anywhere.' He had moved back and was trying to nibble her neck again, Rose inhaling with exasperation of his one track mind.

'She's not as easy swayed as I am.' She doubted molesting her mother would work in quite the same way.

'I don't expect her to be.' He kissed her nose, realising molesting Rose was going nowhere without this little chat first. 'Look I'm not expecting her to warmly embrace me. If you don't want to do this then we won't. But if you do… Then I'll take whatever happens. I'm a big boy and I own my mistakes.'

'Even if she yells at you and calls me a slut?'

'She better not! I'm the only one who gets to call you that.' That twinkle back in his eye, his hands caressing her body again. She batted him away again, that hopeless smile across her face at his lack of seriousness over such a critical issue.

'I think I want to do this… I've never lied to them about anything serious and the last couple of months have been torture.'

'Might explain the craziness in the bakery the other day and your fast exit.' He interjected with a wicked smile.

'I don't think they noticed. They are not the most observant.' Rose eye-rolled at him and had to yet again remove that wandering hand from her breasts.

'Were you running away from me Penny?' He teased, leaning in to brush lips again. She sighed and smiled. He was constantly like a dog in heat, unable to control his hands or mouth.

'Do you blame me? Even after dumping your ass. I couldn't get you to keep your hands to yourself! You still can't, while supposedly talking things through!' She chastised warmly, sinking back into the bed as his mouth made another trip across her chest naughtily.

'It's not my fault your irresistible. I'm the victim in all this. Unable to stop myself when I see you.' He scooped her hands up and pinned them to the pillow over her head, giving him free rein to dive into her neck again and obviously fed up with her thwarting his advances. 'I'm a hot-blooded male and you just make me worse. I think I may need some sort of therapy… Sex addicts anonymous.' He had upped a gear and was now moving in against her, his body meeting her teasingly, nudging her legs open and sliding the throw away from between them. Roses breathing getting shallower as her body core heated up.

The quiet chap on the door stilled their heavy petting abruptly.

The look of 'Oh shit' on Rose's face, her eyes wide and the slow gasp she let out caused Rob to laugh and then cover his mouth. They felt like naughty kids who had been caught in the cookie jar, trying to keep quiet and listen. He cleared his throat and called out

'What is it?'. His attempt at a normal voice failed, deep and husky and obviously not hiding what he was up to.

Abby's voice muffled grumpily

'Rob? Why are you in mum's old room?' She sounded still very drunk and irritable.

'Go away, I'll tell you later.' Rob was eager to continue where he left off and back to licking Rose across her cleavage and nuzzling lower still.

'Rose, tell my asshole brother to put you down for five minutes.' Abby yawned, Rob's look of surprise made Rose cringe guiltily. Recoiling into the pillows a little. A sheepish smile on her face.

'Rob…I kinda told your sister everything. I mean not last night obviously, but everything before.' She whispered, biting on her lip and hoping he wouldn't go mad. He cocked his head to the side, looking unimpressed but amused, a raised eyebrow. 'She is, now go away as I'm keeping her busy.'

Abby's whoop noise startled them both before she wrapped the door tunefully.

'Well tell her in future, the discarded black lingerie on the hall floor outside the door is like a big arrow pointing out her sins.'

Rose recoiled in shame.

She had wondered where they had gone last night, when moving from bathroom to bedroom. Rob had picked them up and triumphantly yet clumsily tucked them into his back pocket of his jeans, claiming they were his 'souvenir'. Not noticing that he had obviously dropped them in the darkness of the hall somewhere and left them behind.

'Abby?' Rob shouted, almost an afterthought as her footsteps could be heard trailing away.

'What?' Was the grumpy response, at a distance.

'Why are you up so early and looking for me?' Rob was now leaning higher, straining to hear over the top of Rose, she couldn't resist running her fingertips across that expanse of muscled torso and slight scattering on hair teasingly. Smiling at the way he tensed and pushed against her.

'The house phone to our private rooms has been ringing nonstop, the one in my room almost met the wall. I assume it's for you!' There was no phone in here so they had been blissfully unaware.

It was barely six thirty am.

'Shit...... Cheers Ab's. Go back to bed, I'll deal with it.' Rob slid off the bed, Abby's mumbles fading away with some incoherent response and pulled his clothes off the floor, searching for his phone. Switching it on he found a dozen voicemails and sat down looking agitated, his shoulders rolling as he tried to remove the return of tension.

'And so it begins!' He grimaced, showing her Morag's name next to every single one from around four am. 'Won't be long before she's here in person. It's a little pattern she likes to go through. The calls get more constant right before she shows up.'

'Shall I leave?' She moved to get up but he shook his head, reaching out to her instead. Pulling her close to him and burying his face in the curve of her stomach.

'No. Come on, we'll go to my room...When she shows up just stay out of sight. I'm hoping we're gone before she shows up and Abby can tell her I had a breakfast appointment that I already left for. I need to be sober to tell her about us and just want this day to enjoy having you back before it all explodes.' He slid his arm around her, pulling her into his lap and kissing her lightly. 'It's way too early to deal with this shit just yet, besides, we were in the middle of something.'

He picked her up, turning her back towards the bed and slid her on, pulling her knees apart so he could slide between them easily. Resistance was futile and his mouth was already surrounding her nipple erotically.

Chapter 26

They were not so lucky.

Rose was laying on his bed wearing one of his t-shirts and pushing the remains of food around her plate absently, trying not to listen to the commotion. He had been out in the hall from the second he had heard her car screech up. The shouting had calmed down but the ringing of something smashing had turned Rose's blood cold. Afraid to venture out and wondering if Abby was hiding out too.

Her phone was dead and she didn't want to get off the bed to find Rob's charger for fear any noise would bring the hurtling suspicious women running down this hall. She knew she was being stupid. He wouldn't let her in here but after seeing that woman in a half full manic blow out once before, she felt uneasy. The pain of that slap was easy recalled to her cheek.

It was still early, they had barely come in here after making eggs in the kitchen together. He had kept her upstairs for another hour after Abby had interrupted, making sure neither of them was leaving that room until fully satisfied. Her body was still tingling in places that made her blush. Her skin still flushed all over.

In the kitchen, it had been romantic and easy. Dressed in his shirt while he stood topless, tanned and sexy, moving seamlessly from cooker to cupboards together as though they did it every day. They had walked out carrying plates and mugs to his bed, laying them down so he could kiss her briefly, admiring her in his clothes, his hands reaching under the shirt longingly. It seemed no matter how hard he tried he could never fully satisfy the craving he had for Rose. And he wasn't against trying repeatedly.

He hard cursed at the familiar hum of the bright red car, despite trying to return her calls to stave her off and meeting voicemail. He pulled on a t-shirt and told her to stay put and now here she was, stuck here, unable to call her parents or check the time. Unable to go anywhere except the bathroom or his office from the internal doors. Afraid to do either.

The noise had abated completely and she wondered if they were even still out there in the main hall. This was complete agony, sitting in suspense waiting and listening to nothing but silence. Staff to do the mass clear up would be arriving soon and he had told her Alice normally came in to spring clean his rooms when he had got up and out for the day.

How was that going to look, finding her sitting here in nothing more than his shirt?

She didn't need to ponder over it for long.

Abby slid in with a rucksack in hand, her face a picture of happiness.

'I figured you would need clothes and an escape route!' Her grin barely concealed as she took in her friend's rosy cheeks, glowing complexion and brothers shirt from the night before. A knowing eyebrow raise.

'Are they still out there?' Rose started towards the bag Abby had thrown onto the bed, grateful of the contents, pulling out toiletries and casual clothes. Abby tossed the trainers from her other hand and shook her head.

'He took her to the formal lounge. Stupid bitch and all the bloody noise, I was almost asleep again before she showed up. The doors shut so you can pretty much escape.' She clocked Rose's hesitation 'What's wrong?'

'He's meant to be coming with me to meet Mum and Dad for breakfast.' Rose felt stupid and selfish. 'It's just, with her here. I don't want to just leave!'

'So, meeting with the rents eh? Things have changed I see. If Rob says he's coming then trust me he will be there. Just leave him a note with the when and where and soon as he gets rid of the crazy witch he will be right along.' Abby was slurring her words slightly, obviously still drunk. Rose looked doubtful, knowing that dealing with Morag could take far longer this morning judging by his intentions made clear last night.

'I need to go home. My parents will be showing up there to get me and I have no idea what time it even is'

'Its eight twenty five¡ chipped in Abby glancing at her watch. Rubbing her eyes and gawking at the early hour. She was still a little drunk from the night before and had not even begun to feel the effects of her hangover yet. Rose, however, had the familiar sore head and fuzzy mouth of suffering, she sighed, knowing that waiting would be pointless. If she left now and walked home she would have an hour to get bathed and pull herself together before they showed up.

Muffin would be desperate for his morning walk to relieve his business too. She also did not want her parents knowing she had slept here with him. Once it was clear Rob and Rose were a couple, the thought of them knowing she had not come home was a little too embarrassing. They were still her parents after all. She did not want them looking at her with the knowledge she had spent the night writhing and moaning under his naked body. Despite her age!

'Ok, Abby. I need paper and pen, my phones dead.' She was pulling on her friend's clothes and trainers as Abby slid her a notebook and expensive fountain pen and stood to yawn as Rose left Rob a brief note. It felt weird to be the one sneaking out for a change. Another shift in reality.

'I shall be going back to bed after you're gone!' She scratched her head, picking up her friends discarded dress and shoes from the floor stuffing them into the rucksack. 'I hope you remembered your underwear this time!'

'Firmly back where they belong!' She smiled flashing a lace edge above the sweat pant waistline.

'So, you and him? it's all back on, right? This isn't just a drunken fuck?' Abby cocked her head to the side and regarded her seriously.

'Right and No, please don't call it that.' Rose grimaced at her friends and her choice of vocabulary. Squirming under her intense scrutiny.

'And psycho?'

'Abby don't use that word either. He's going to tell her. He's going to try anyway. I guess her showing up means maybe sooner, rather than later.'

Abby looked impressed and gave her friend a hug before leading her down the hall and quietly across the main floor to the front door. Rose aware she was tiptoeing on the marble. Alice appeared from another door, apron on and duster in hand.

'Morning girls. You two are up early!' She was twinkling and fresh despite being one of the merry partyers long after the majority left. Abby mumbled some incoherent nonsense and Alice smiled as though she understood, although she clearly hadn't.

'Did you have a wonderful time Rose? Saw you dancing with a few of those handsome men, lucky thing.' She winked cheekily, obviously assuming Rose had slept in Abby's room with her and waved her off when she slid out the door moments later with a red-faced smile as way of an answer.

Abby walked her down the drive a little way, still wearing last night's clothes and fluffy slippers. She looked a lot worse for the wear out in the early morning sunlight.

'I'll text you in a bit and let you know if he's got away from her okay'.' She squinted at the sun and shielded her eyes.

'It's okay Abby. Just go back to bed. If he doesn't text me or show up I'll know why and I'm okay with it, honest. It's different this time. I trust him.' She smiled convincingly. Crossing her fingers inside that this time was going to be different, that he wouldn't let her down anymore.

'Okay, but don't take any shit, this time, Rose. Brother or not, I will still cut off his balls if he fucks your head over again.' Her angry frown and fist raising were a little too adorable to be threatening.

'Nice Abby. Very classy!' Rose leant in, kissing her on the cheek affectionately and headed off down towards the long sweeping drive.

* * *

The walk home in the calm early day sun was exactly what she needed. Everything seemed so surreal and dreamy and she needed the walk, to not only wake her up but to accept this was real. That everything she remembered had happened. That her now blooming, bouncing happy heart was not some mythical illusion about to be shattered by waking up.

Muffin practically devoured her on sight and only made it as far as the grass by the door before releasing a night's worth of doggy gifts. Rose was now feeling fragile and nauseous from alcohol consumption and could barely scoop it up into one of her doggy bags. Throwing the little fur ball a pained look and making disgusted noises. He just ignored her, sniffing at some flowers.

Rose was really beginning to suffer and the thought of breakfast was no longer appealing. The awful after effects of alcohol reminding her why she did not drink very often. Her phone was on charge and had enough power to switch on now.

No messages from her parents yet so she left it plugged in and ran herself a bath. Her usual bath bomb dumped in and turning to a foaming lathering cream in the hot water. Even the strong normally favourite scent was making her queasy. This was going to be a long painful day; swallowing some aspirin and sipping water as she sat on the bath edge, she slowly peeled off the clothes, feeling the weariness of aching muscles. Overused in dancing and after hour workouts with Rob.

He knew how to make her body respond, finding positions she would never have dreamed of. Seeing some faint marks on her thighs and wrists from their over enthusiastic bathroom reunion made her smile, casting her mind back to the hazy memories. That scene was one for the keepsake chest and there was no way now she was going to let him go now.

The water although a little hot was a welcome soothing relief. Relaxing in and letting all the night's smells and aches soak away. She could sleep in this bath this way right now, exhaustion finally catching up with her.

Muffin snuffled in the open door sniffing her clothes on the floor, wagging his tail at Abby's scent. Rose watched him contentedly, smiling before closing her eyes and laying her head back. She had no intention of moving for quite some time. All she wanted to do was revel in her thoughts and feelings and ponder how everything had changed literally overnight! Enjoy the soothing water around her and nap.

Her mother sent a text at nine fifty am, informing her that instead of breakfast they would do a late afternoon lunch. Alcohol was the devils work and neither of them were fit to go anywhere so early. Rose was relieved and amused. Not only did she feel like death and gladly swapped her dress for sweatpants and a baggy shirt but she had not heard from Rob and was beginning to seriously worry.

Concern had been building in the pit of her stomach for the last half hour. Unshakeable anxiety gnawing away. The lack of contact nibbling at her nerves no matter how much she tried to ignore it. She did not want to bother Abby, knowing she would be asleep by now and most likely dead to the world and any beeping of phones.

By eleven am she was pacing the house, looking for things to occupy herself and she had managed to fight the urge to text or call him. She needed to let him do this, give him space and time. It was complicated and delicate. He needed time to sort things out. Maybe Morag had taken it badly, far worse than he had predicted. Maybe she had broken down sobbing and he could not get away.

Maybe she had tried to hurt herself?

Oh god, what if she had done something stupid?

Rob would be absolutely devastated. The thought sent a ball of choking panic up her throat. Her body shivering involuntarily.

Another long agonising fifteen minutes later and the temptation was too much. She couldn't stand it anymore, her mind racing with crazy thoughts and scenarios that all resulted in Morag's death. She picked up her new fully charged phone and sent him a text

'Is everything okay?'

She sounded calmer than she felt.

She needed to be rational about this. If Morag had done something foolish then he would have contacted her by now. It was more likely the silence meant they were still going around in circles in that room. She knew there was a chance he wouldn't respond if that was the case. Knowing that it was most likely his phone was still in his room where she had been and he was still in the lounge with Morag. She bit her lip feeling frustrated. Looking at the time again she figured Abby might be up and chanced it

'Hey girl. Any word?'

When her phone rang she almost dropped it in anticipation but felt disappointment when she saw 'Mum' flashing on the screen

'Hey Mum,' she sounded deflated.

'Hiya darling. I'm sorry to do this love but your dad's not too well. Can't keep much down. Do you mind if we rain check today and we will pop over tonight with some takeaway and a movie? Let him recover a bit. One last night together before we head home tomorrow?' She sounded genuinely disappointed but Rose was monumentally relieved.

'Aww Mum. Sure… It's okay. Tell dad to stay off of Mr Munro's whisky next time.' she laughed as her mum agreed.

They chatted briefly, vague small talk about the rest of Rose's night at the party and Rose held back the urge to tell her about Rob. She did not want to do this over the phone and right now she wasn't even sure Rob would make an appearance before they left tomorrow. It could wait until she knew what was going on with him and Morag, right now it was all up in the air in her head.

Saying their goodbyes moments later she ended the call and looked at her blank screen.

Fuck.

No texts or voicemails. Muffin was scraping at the door and Rose wondered if a walk to the manor was maybe an idea.

Would he be mad if she showed up?

Surely if Morag was still there she could just go straight to Abby's room and act like that was her purpose after all. He would never be mad at her for coming back. She was being stupid. He had not wanted her to leave in the first place, she needed to keep reminding herself that things had changed. Hopefully for the better.

Her stomach fluttered with nerves, torn between walking up there and seeing for herself and staying here waiting endlessly. Somehow unable to concentrate on anything else. She rang Abby's phone in one last attempt to get a response but it went straight to answer machine, indicating she had it switched off.

'God's sake Abby!' She cursed at her, knowing it was not her fault. She was probably asleep.

She swallowed her nerve and rang Rob's phone. It rang out as she had expected, most likely nowhere near him or even within ear shot. It just frustrated her even more. This wall of silence.

'Come on Muffin my lovely. I actually cannot sit here agonising any longer.' She slid up, pulling off her casual clothes and headed to her room for a change of outfit. She still had to look good, even if he had seen her in all shades of naked.

* * *

The walk took far longer than any other time she had used this route. Or so it felt. Muffin walking slow or stopping to sniff for an age at seemingly nothing and she was beginning to get ratty with him. Knowing it was not on him that she was feeling this impatient, it was making her equally guilty and when his soft little face looked up with big brown eyes innocently, she cursed herself and told him he was a good boy.

Even with the manor in sight, it seemed to take forever to walk up the drive. Up the long grey steps and finally knock on the door. Morag's car was still parked in the middle in an abandoned fashion but Rob's car was nowhere to be seen. This little detail made her uneasy and her mouth dry with anxiety.

'Don't jump to conclusions.' She chastised herself inwardly as Alice answered the door with a bright smile and beckoned her in warmly.

'They're not here Rose. But I'm waiting on them calling if you want to wait. Abby promised to call as soon as she could and it's been a while since they left.' She said warmly, assuming Rose had a clue what she was on about.

Confused and feeling a tad betrayed stupidly, her nerves tight and fraying. A huge sense of foreboding weighing heavily upon her.

'Where are they?' She asked quietly, emotion threatening.

'There all at the hospital. Had a bit of a mishap here earlier. Morag did herself a nasty turn!' Alice frowned, realising Rose had no clue and guided her inside with a gentle hand.

Rose physically paled, her stomach lurching as she grasped Alice's arm.

Chapter 27

'What happened? Is Rob okay? Is Abby?'

'Calm down. Now hush my dear.' She took hold of Rose's now shaking hands and pulled her towards the kitchen. Making kissing noises for Muffin to follow them. The smell of baking bread failing to wash over her with any kind of calming effect

'Both are fine. It was that stupid wretched woman and her love of smashing the blooming vases.' She sat Rose in a chair and moved away to fill the kettle. 'Cut her arm open quite badly and left blood all over the lounge rug that I'm going to have to clean up.'

'Oh my god!' She laid her face on the table, suddenly feeling faint. Muffin sensing her distress pawed at her ankle before laying across her feet protectively. Small whimpers as he continued to glance up at her.

'Its okay dear. Rob was quick off the mark. Bound it up and held it tight. Abby had been out here when she heard the smash and the screams, in the kitchen with me. She helped get her in his car and they rushed off. Abby told me to man the phone for her call.'

She placed some cups out neatly, getting them ready for the boiling water. Rose could hear every movement and noise, still holding her head on the table while nausea and dizziness passed. Her breathing shallow and her thoughts frantic.

What the hell had that stupid woman done? Oh, my god...Rob.

She felt sick to her stomach with the realisation that this is what he had been afraid of all along.

'Quite a bit of drama. Abby said she would call with an update as soon as she could.'

Rose lifted her head unsure how to feel. She took the mug of tea gratefully and sipped down its hot liquid. Thankful for the excuse not to talk, thankful for a task that focused her frantic brain.

Alice was clearing plates and washing dishes in the sink, chatting away about the state of the lounge and speculating on this morning's row. Rose watched her in disbelief, almost deaf to her words and lost in her own scrambled brain.

How could she be so calm?

'It's odd, but I assumed things were long dead with those two… But he had obviously had her stay the night in his bed, judging by the mess of it, the extra towels on the bathroom floor and the two plates of breakfast left sitting on his bed.'

Rose felt her face colour and tried not to react. Willing the old woman to stop talking.

'Not that it's my business, even if it's just sex. He should never confuse things that way with her, it explains all the recent outbursts if he's been sleeping with her again and leading her astray.' Alice carried on, oblivious to Rose's pale pallor and wide eyes, or the way she was staring at her hands in a bid to stay quiet.

'She thinks he's seeing another woman behind her back.' Alice looked her way with a raised eyebrow. Rose almost choked on her tea. The flush of guilt creeping up her neck.

'I think she might be right you know?' Alice winked merrily. 'Should have seen the mess of his mother's bedroom. Someone had certainly been having a good time in there last night. And it was not red hair on the pillows. Nooo, it was a brunette. I know it was Rob who had used the room as only him and Abby have keys, besides me. It stays locked and Abby has jet black hair.'

Rose inwardly cringed. Plastering a smile on her deeply blushing face and wriggling uncomfortably in her seat. Making sure not to draw attention to her hair by touching it.

'Not that I blame him mind. He's told her a million times that there's nothing between them that's serious. He's dated women in the past on and off but I don't think she had the inkling like she does now, following him around moping and crying. He needs to get on with his own life and just be done with her. A nice girl and a family. Not all this drama.'

'Hmm.' Was the only reply Rose could formulate for fear her voice would betray her. Her head racing and face burning with shame and guilt.

The phone shrieked like a welcome alarm on the kitchen wall and Rose resisted the urge to jump up and answer. Instead, having to sit and pretend she was not dying to grab at it. Alice was so slow to answer, drying her hands first that she was almost in hysterics with anticipation.

Greeting Abby on the line she hummed and ahhed as she listened and asked some brief questions on Morag's state. Rose was tapping both foot and hand against the table, trying not to chew her nails or wrestle the phone from her.

'Oh, and Rose has come by to see you.' She added as an afterthought, stopping to listen to the response, smiling she turned holding out the cordless handset towards her. Rose wanted to snatch it manically but instead, she smiled and deliberately took it gently and calmly. Her hands still trembling.

'Rose?'

'Hey Ab's. Yeah, it's me. Alice told me what happened.' Rose gushed down the phone, finally relieved to have made contact with one of them.

'Oh my god, Rose, it was awful. So much blood. I nearly puked!' Her voice was weak and shaky and she was in obvious distress.

'How is she now? How's Rob?' Rose couldn't conceal her concern, tears prickling her eyes and her hands shaking violently.

'They have her in with them. We were not allowed past the waiting room so we don't know. Rob has been trying to find out for the last hour but no word, she's in surgery apparently. I had to come find a payphone as my mobile is totally dead and he doesn't even have his here. He's quiet… Worried I guess, and not saying much.'

'I have been so worried, when I didn't hear from either of you, I didn't know what to think.'

She saw Alice raise her eyebrows in interest from the corner of her eye.

'I'll tell Rob you're at the house. He will want to call. He's been major stressed at not being able to contact you. Neither of us had either your home phone number or your mobile with us and your cottage isn't listed.' Abby sounded tired and so far away, the hospital was a good thirty to forty minute drive away.

'Okay. Please keep us updated Ab's. I'll stay here until your back so you can call me, so he can call me.' Rose tried to lower her voice but she could see Alice had the hearing of a hawk.

'Okay. I better go. I'm running out of money, I'll call soon, when I get more change.'

They said their goodbyes and Rose returned the phone to its cradle quietly. Relieved that the people she loved were okay but frustrated at not being able to talk freely or to him. She just wanted to hear his voice so badly right now, know that he was okay.

Alice smiled and offered some words of comfort about no news sometimes being no big deal. Busy hospitals and short staffed. Waiting times being hours long. Rose listened, only half taking it in and drinking the new mug of tea placed before her on the scrubbed pine table, unaware that she had already emptied her last one. The older lady began making some homemade soup in silence as Rose sat gazing blankly, obviously lost in thought.

She jumped when the phone rang again and without thinking jumped up to answer it saying his name before he spoke. Not caring that Alice expression was that of someone putting two and two together and getting a satisfied conclusion of four. A knowing smile spreading across her face.

'Baby, I am so glad to hear your voice.' He sounded tired and stressed. 'I'm so sorry about standing you up, I had no idea how the hell to get hold of you to let you know.' He sounded tired, exhausted if she was being honest and yet relieved to hear her finally.

'It's okay, my parents bailed on me with hangovers, I'm seeing them tonight. I am just so relieved to know what's going on.' Her voice was strained, hushing to avoid Alice's ears and desperately wanting to be able to talk freely.

'I just want to be there with you right now, wrapped in your arms and lost in the feel of you baby.' His husky tone and betrayal of emotion sent tingles along her spine. Rose face and neck warmed and she tried to hide by turning towards the kitchen door, aware Alice had become extremely interested in this phone call.

'Umm so any news on Morag?' Rose was trying to make it clear she wasn't able to talk.

'I guess you're not alone?' Rob was quick on the uptake.

'Sure, Alice is taking great care of me, plying me with tea.' Brightly casting a smile towards the lady, making it clear that she could not openly say what she wanted too. After a pause, he told her to take the phone to his room, to tell her she was to go find something for him.

'Okay sure...Uhuh I'll go now.'

She covered the phone telling Alice she had to go retrieve something for Rob and headed off down the small hall, motioning for Muffin to stay under the table. She fumbled with his bedroom door handle. Once inside, concealed in the familiar closed room and free from prying ears she sat on the bed and sighed with relief. It felt better being surrounded by his smell, his things, Away from eyes and ears.

'I'm alone now. God Rob, I was so worried when I didn't hear from you. I felt so frantic. What happened?' Her voice was shaking, matching her hands and at least in here she felt able to be herself.

'I'm sorry baby...It was all my fault, Rose. I told her I was seeing someone, that I was in love with someone.' He sounded odd, tired and deflated. 'I told her I couldn't go on like this anymore and that she had to stop, that she had to let me go.' He sighed down the line, obviously torn up from events.

'She smashed something? Flipped out?' Rose questioned quietly, trying to picture it, sensing he needed to get this off his chest.

'I was hungover and pissed that here I was dealing with this shit again, making you hide out like some dirty bit on the side in my room and I was tactless. I spat it out in anger. I handled it really badly.' His voice had an edge to it, stressed anger, maybe annoyance at how it had panned out.

'Rob, you can't blame yourself. You are stuck in an awful situation and you have the patience of a saint dealing with her this way all the time.' Rose soothed, her voice strained with the effort of not crying for him.

He sighed. Murmuring that he had no patience left anymore. His unfamiliar tone bringing a lump to her throat at his obvious lacklustre. He was spent. He sounded so fed up with everything and she ached to hold him and wipe it all away.

'Tell me what happened. Talk to me Rob. I just want to hear your voice. I miss you.'

'I miss you more.' That cheeky hint of a smile invaded his tone for a second and was followed by another heavy sigh.

'You know she burst in manically going off on one this morning? Well she pretty much carried on after, ranting and raving and smashing another vase in the hall. She was pissed about my distance at the dance, pissed that my phone was off all night.' He sighed again 'Same shit, just another day.'

'She was drunk, she drove over here in that state?' Rose questioned in disbelief.

'Yeah, another thing she spat at me, accusing me of not caring about, that she had to drive over drunk because I wouldn't answer her calls. She wanted to know who my whore was, wanted to know how long I had been cheating on her and I just couldn't be assed with the shit anymore. I lost my temper and told her to fuck off.' There was a silent pause and then a sardonic laugh. 'I just realised how done with all of it I was, how she just made me see in that moment how differently I felt for you. I told her to get back on her meds and to go sleep it off.'

'I'm guessing she didn't take that well at all?' Rose sighed, knowing his gentle handling he normally displayed had obviously been lacking.

'No. She started sobbing and pulling at me to hold her, trying to force me into an embrace. All I could think about was you and how much it upset you letting her paw at me. I shoved her away, not wanting anyone else to be wrapped up in my arms besides you. I just couldn't do it anymore Rose, the pretence, the patience I have had to have and all the while you have put up with so god damn much.'

'It wasn't your fault, you didn't make her this way.' Rose tried to soothe him, his voice was still husky and strained.

'She asked me if I still loved her. I was pissed, agitated and I told her I didn't. Not anymore. That my heart belonged to the girl I wanted to be with and she was waiting for me. That I needed to go.' Again, he paused, she could imagine him rubbing his face with tiredness, maybe even scratching his fingers through that dark cropped hair. 'She flipped out. Threw things, attempted to slap at me and just kept screaming abuse at me. She walked off, pulling at her hair and sobbing.... I thought she was going to calm down but instead turned to the nearest side table, wiping the contents off with a crashing sweep. Glass and ceramic smashing and flying in every direction, pushing over tables. Screaming out loud how much she hated me. I tried to grab her from behind but she broke free, lashing out at me, the air, anything close. Like a wild animal, feral and vicious and hell bent on causing harm to anything that came near her.'

'Jesus. I have no clue what to say to that.' Rose's face flushed, hit with visions of Morag in all her fiery fury and tear stained manic behaviour. She shivered as it came clear and pushed it away.

'She ran forward when she squirmed loose, falling to her knees, she landed in front of the long low glass coffee table in the centre of the couches and without hesitation just smashed both her fists and arms through. It was like she just lost the plot, I saw it happen in slow motion yet I couldn't do anything about it, she completely just lost it. Then there was blood, a heck of a lot of blood, pouring everywhere and I just went into auto pilot. I don't even remember getting her here.' By the end of his sentence his voice was strained, a sign he was getting emotional. Neither said anything or made any noise for a moment, lost in the seriousness of it.

'Baby.' Was the only thing Rose could finally say, aware of tears falling down her face and sniffed them back.

'I haven't seen her since they took her and told me she would most likely go straight into surgery. I have no idea what's going on. It was bad Rose. The cuts were deep and long, she lost a huge amount of blood. The first hour here all I could do was console Abby. I think she's in shock and well she's never been good with blood and I had her holding Morag's wrists all the way here, while I drove like a crazy man. I am pretty sure I was still too drunk to be fucking driving; so stupid with my baby sister in the car.'

'Rob. I don't know what to say.' She was wiping the tears feeling a huge amount of guilt wracking through her. She just wanted to be there with him, wrapping her arms around him tightly and convincing him that this was not his fault, he sounded so defeated and deflated.

'You don't need to. Just hearing your voice is enough. I miss you so badly right now. I would give anything to be laid in bed with you and have none of this ever happen.' His voice was strained, he sounded ravaged which was never a good sign with him, the master of hiding his feelings normally.

'I miss you too. I want to be there with you so much right now... What happens now? Do you just wait? They have given no clue to what's happening?' Rose was trying to be logical and calm, trying to focus on details to still her washing machine nerves.

'They took her into emergency surgery, I know that much. I'm guessing the operation is dependent on how much they have to repair. How easily they can stop the bleeding. It wasn't just one or two huge lacerations Rose. There was a mess of slices and cuts on both arms, wrists and hands. That was a toughened table. It should never have broken as easily as it did.'

Rose felt physically sick. This was all her fault. Her silence told him what she was thinking and he gently chided her for feeling responsible. Assuring her this had been no one's fault, his at most, but mainly a freak accident.

'I should have handled things better with her long before now. I should have cut the ties years ago and let her move on.' He said regretfully.

'You weren't to know back then that it would evolve to how she is now, you only did what you thought was best.' She didn't want him to take blame right now, whether it was true or not.

'I should never have made you hide, I should have at least told her from the start that I was falling for you. Been honest about what you were to me and maybe it would have been different.'

'Or maybe you would have been sat in the hospital back then instead of now.' Rose interjected, knowing that this could have happened either way. Morag was more than in love with him, she was obsessively glued to his very being and she would never have taken it well at any time.

'No matter what the outcome of this, I'm not going back to how it was. I told you it would be different and regardless to Morag, it will be. I won't hide us anymore Rose. I want the world to know how crazy I am for you and nothing is going to stand in my way.'

His words soothed her. His steady manner returning and voice steadying. Calming her tears and making her long for his presence even more. Her rock. Even when surrounded by the chaos he was still making her feel better.

When they regretfully ended the call, he told her he loved her. He had run out of change and Abby had appeared motioning him from the door. He had to go. Rose felt so torn. Not wanting to hang up but wanting him to go and see if there was word. Aching that he had to go, she told him she would be waiting for him no matter how long it took. Waiting here for him. He told her that was the only thing keeping him going and they disconnected.

Wandering back from his room she found Alice had moved to the grand lounge. The noise of a vacuum humming loudly in the large room and she followed, unable to be alone right now.

The sight before her caused a fresh batch of tears. The broken chaos around the side of the room and the centre smashed table. Alice was concentrating on the small trinkets and frames below the huge window which had been Morag's first wave of destruction. She was using the hoover nozzle to collect the fine broken glass and china from the surface picking through and removing large chunks and dropping them into a basket on the floor. Seeing Rose, she cut off the hoover.

'She did it proper this time, didn't she?' She gave her a supportive half smile. Rose nodded in response, her eyes coming to rest on the pool of blood by the table legs and the sheer volume of it. Causing her to shiver and wrap her arms around herself; the splattering and smears on the metal frame and the glass on the floor below. Fixated and unaware of the fresh tears rolling down her face.

Alice was immediately by her side offering a handful of tissues from a gold carved box.

'Don't you be blaming yourself now.' She patted her back gently and gave her a half hug.

Rose glanced at the wise woman questioningly

'Oh, Rose. I know it's none of my business. 'She lifted up a tendril of Rose's hair and winked 'Pretty brown hair you have, matches that pretty face.' It was followed by a knowing smile.

She felt her cheeks colour.

'I don't know why I didn't see it before? It's pretty obvious now. The way he lights up whenever you're around. The way he reacts at the mere mention of you and the way you reacted that morning when Morag flipped out. I have seen him with women before Rose, in passing, and I have never seen him linger on every word the way he does with you. I'm just amazed I didn't put the puzzle together before.' Her little speech interrupted by the doorbell, she squeezed Rose's arm and left her alone. Left alone with her thoughts and the sight before her.

Chapter 28

Her parents had been more than understanding. Surprisingly. Briefly telling them of events on the phone and they had appeared at the manor as it grew darker outside, not even questioning why Rose would be waiting here.

She had heard from Rob a handful of times in the last hours, all calls brief due to having to keep going back to check for updates on her condition, the phone a bit of a walk back to the ward. Morag was out of surgery and in recovery and he was waiting to see her, waiting for the sedatives to wear off. He wanted to see to her before he left and came home, so he was hanging about endlessly waiting.

They all ate dinner with Alice and Tommy. Courtesy of her parents appearing with a huge Domino's pizza and a can of food for Muffin. Alice had shown them all into the cosy TV lounge by the kitchen after and left them to it, alone at last and sitting face to face. Rose had finally told them everything, feeling unable to continue without being honest.

It had been so much easier than she could have imagined. From therir first few weeks sneaking around, to the break up over Morag's mental state and finally leading up to the events this morning. She had of course skimmed over the dirty details of how many times she had ended up naked with Rob Munro but they got the just of the situation.

Her dad had been silent and thoughtful. Her mother more verbal and breaking in with small remarks and all the right noises of a protective mother hen. She was more sympathetic to Rob's part than Rose had expected.

The end result was that both had suspected something was going on with Rob and their daughter already. Her behaviour at the bakery barely masking it, and neither had wanted to question her. The chemistry between them was apparently undeniable and Rob's attention to her a little bit of a giveaway that they were more than they pretended to be.

Imparting their words of wisdom, they had sat and mulled through all of it with her, their blessing, despite all the heartache she had suffered in recent weeks and finally their love in the form of supportive hugs and kisses before they finally left. She had told them she was tired, she wouldn't wait up for him but go to bed and wanted to sleep off her hangover.

Really, she had just wanted to be alone to wait by the phone and hope he came back sooner rather than later, he had her mobile number now and she had been keeping one eye glued firmly to it.

She gave them the cottage keys so they did not have to go all the way back to the hotel and so they could take Muffin home with them to his own familiar surroundings to settle. She wanted them close by tonight, in case she needed to see them but far enough to give her breathing space. They finally left. Promising to come back before they had to start home the next day.

Rose watched them drive off from the open door, feeling a little vulnerable. The moon now high in the sky and the air dark and twinkling; It was late and it had been almost two hours since he had last called. Abby was apparently asleep under some plastic chairs in the waiting room by then and suffering an awful hangover and the after effects of shock. He had been waiting to see Morag, talking to staff and trying to catch some sleep in the hard-backed chairs and sounded even worse than before. His own hangover and fatigue setting in amongst stress and worry.

Unable to keep pacing the halls erratically, she slid into Rob's room, turned on his tv and channel hopped for a while. The feel of his bed around her offering comfort, knowing he would come back at some point.

Alice had left some time ago to go home to her little cottage nearby with Tommy, showing Rose how to set the alarm and lock up. Her daughter, who normally cooked for the big house was away so that left this big old empty place with only Rose in it, like being locked in a big empty museum for a night. Eerie and echoey and a tad uncomfortable considering she had only just got back with Rob less than twenty-four hours ago and here she was alone in his huge house and nestled in his bed.

Stripping off and pulling on one of Rob's t-shirts for comfort in lack of his actual self, she climbed into bed. She wanted to stay awake for his return but the combination of tiredness, remains of a hangover and all the emotional turmoil had her drifting off before long, despite her efforts not too.

* * *

She awoke to warm arms pulling her against a hard, hot body, under the covers. Startled momentarily but immediately soothed by his familiar scent and touch, she would recognise anywhere. She reached up to wrap her arms around his neck, feeling him sigh and relax, burying his face in her neck and catching her naked legs in his. The room was pitch black.

'This feels too good. It's what I have been needing all day.' He murmured from the hollow of her throat. His voice soft and full of exhaustion. She could already sense the way his body had sagged against her and his eyes were closed. 'You don't know what it feels like to come home and find you here in my bed. I don't ever want it any other way.'

'I think I do.' She kissed his head through his ruffled hair softly, equally overjoyed at finding herself back in his embrace, so much better than the dreams she had been having about him.

She had so many questions, but she could see he needed sleep more than she needed answers right now. Curling around one another, she closed her own eyes and found falling back into slumber effortless now he was home right beside her finally. Wrapped in his secure, safe arms. Warm and peaceful, the steady breath and heartbeat lulling her into sleep.

* * *

They slept late. Alice had opened the door a crack only, early in the day and seeing them both curled up sound asleep had retracted and gone about her business in another room. A small smile spreading across her face.

He was the first to wake. Planting soft kisses on her face and bringing her round gently. Smiling when she opened her eyes sleepily and looked at him. Momentarily forgetting everything, she smiled back and accepted his soft kiss on her lips as his hand moved across her body suggestively. She knew resistance was pointless and before long that shirt was laying crumpled on the floor beside his discarded clothes from his return home.

Afterwards, she lay in his arms looking at the ceiling. He was twirling her hair absent-mindedly, staring at the same spot above them.

'She's going to be kept in for a few weeks.' He sighed. 'They managed to patch up most of the damage. She will need more surgery today and she's got to see the plastic surgeon for the damage to her tendons and to handle the excessive scarring. Mostly though they're keeping her admitted until a bed in the psychiatric ward opens.'

Rose glanced at him seriously, baulking at the words.

'Voluntary... She told them she had caused her wounds on purpose.' He sighed again obviously in turmoil. 'She's classed as a suicide threat so they will keep her in for evaluation and some sessions with a therapist.' He sighed.

'How did she seem?' Rose pushed gently, not sure how to feel about this whole thing but still a smidgen of empathy for the other woman breaking through.

'Drugged! I only got to see her briefly when they settled her in the ward. She was still not fully out of sedation. Coherent enough to only have a few words before they made me leave.' Rob stilled his hand, entangled with her hair and brought her temple to his mouth, kissing her softly, almost absentmindedly.

'Did she say much?'

'Only that she was sorry and did I still love her?' He cursed under his breath. 'I had no idea where to go with that, so I just told her I would come back and see her in a couple days. After surgery and when she was more lucid.' He turned, kissing Rose on the temple again, somehow finding some solace in this little act. 'Then I left!' He sighed heavily, both silent. Rob mulling over events and Rose processing it.

'Abby?' Rose looked up at his perfect profile in afterthought, realising he hadn't mentioned bringing her home or even how she was. His rested relaxed features and morning dark stubble showing along his jaw gave him a rougher sexy look. He looked better now, earlier he had seemed so uptight. Strained. But making love to her had obviously been the release he had been aching for.

'I put her in bed. She was practically a zombie. Doubt she will surface much today, she was in a bit of a mess for a few hours. Tears. Exhaustion. I think she may sleep the day away.' He pulled his arm out from behind her head and made to get up. He seemed restless again and she couldn't help the feeling of anxiety at him getting up.

'I need to go see my dad for a bit Rose. Tell him what's happened. He won't be happy if he finds out from someone else.' He leant down, kissing her on the forehead before scooping up his clothes and heading into the bathroom to get ready.

She lay watching the door close softly, feeling numb and quiet. Unable to really process anything right now because it felt like everything was in limbo. Standing on a precipice, looking into a deep cavern. She felt restless too. Glancing at the time she too got up, pulling on clothes and brushing her hair best she could with fingers.

He appeared. Looking her up and down questioningly, a tinge of disappointment on his face.

'My parents! They leave today and I really need to go see them. They're at the cottage!' She reminded him with a smile.

He looked thoughtful, crossing the room and pulling her into him, touching noses and just looking at each other silently for a moment, before he broke the spell with a kiss. A long lingering, 'I need you' sort of a kiss. Then broke the romance of it by slapping her on the butt rather loudly and throwing a cheeky raise of the eyebrows and melting smile her way before heading out the door. He motioned a phone with his hand to his ear and she nodded.

It was only when she walked out the door of the hall that she realised she had walked here. She had no car parked outside.

Dammit.

She was still tired and did not really want to walk home, her body was suffering from days of broken sleep and far too much exertion at Rob's hands.

Standing in the open front door she pulled out her phone, ready to ask her dad to come get her when she felt him behind her again. His presence always alerting her body in heightened ways.

'Changed your mind? The lure of my bed a little too much for you?' His arms moving easily to her waist and around her body.

'No.' She laughed, enjoying his breath on her neck. 'Laziness and calling for Daddy Cab.' She waved her phone, showing her dad's name on the screen. He leant down ending the call before it started to ring.

'I'll take you home.' He cut in instead.

'No. Rob, go see your dad. Honestly, I can get him to come and…'

Bringing his face to her cheek from behind as he leant forward, she heard the jingle of keys as he slid his hand from his back pocket. Holding them in front of her face suggestively.

'So, take my car and come get me when I'm done.' She paused, staring at the small bunch of keys, the shining expensive logo on the keyring and hesitated. Sparkling in the morning sun like an expensive trinket.

'I can't! It's too much. It costs a bomb. It's your pride and joy.' She rattled off apprehensively, suddenly extremely nervous.

'Planning on writing it off, are you?' He kept the keys in front of her face, waiting for her to take them. Both standing motionless as they sparkled in the sunlight.

'No. It's just its really fast. I'm used to my mini and it's... Well it's a sports car! She knew she was panicking.

'You CAN drive them like any other car you know?' He was being persistent, her arguments pointless as she reluctantly took the keys from him.

'Don't you have a Range Rover laying around. You know like normal Lairds and highland people have?'

He shook the keys suggestively in her hands as though motioning that this was what she was getting and he wasn't listening to arguments.

'Fine! But if I damage it, scratch it or break it, you just remember you pushed me into driving it.' She mused, her hands trembling a little at being trusted with his prized possession.

He turned her slowly and placed a long kiss on her mouth, fingers trailing down her throat and back up again to her jawline seductively.

'It's only a car, and yeah I left my Range Rover packed up with my tartan pants and bagpipes... I'm expecting some sort of scratching or breaking Penelope as I've seen you drive, remember!' He laughed at her as she moved back in mock anger, a comical frown on her face and batted him in the stomach. Pulling her back into a headlock and planting a kiss on her head, he turned her, moving her forward out the door with a gentle shove.

'Besides, there are ways in which you can make up for any damage that I would be highly open to.' He grinned after her as she waved him away and shook her head. Exasperated with his one-track mind yet secretly pleased that by lending her his car he was showing that the relationship between them was not going to be a secret anymore. Anyone out on the road knew his car and everyone knew he never loaned it to anyone.

The car made her nervous as soon as she slid into the driver's seat. The smooth soft leather and moulded shape holding her strangely; she adjusted the seat and mirrors, glancing to make sure he had gone back inside, not wanting to be watched. She was already nervous enough in the sleek black cockpit of the car. The sea of buttons and gadgets illuminated in the gloom under the deeply tinted windows. It felt like being inside a very modern spaceship. A highly expensive modern spaceship. The hum and power of the engine caused her nerves to start, she could tell from even the feel beneath her hands and feet that this was more car than she had ever driven and lost her nerve. Her stomach lurching.

A small shake and internal pep talk had her reversing slowly and carefully, afraid to put her foot down and moved gently into position to then head down the drive. She kept telling herself the cottage was not far and out loud to her reflection in the mirror that she would never drive this beast again. On the straight road she relaxed a little; this wasn't so bad once you got used to it. The smooth purring drive, the roar, anytime you accelerated. Rose realised how sensitive the pedals were and trod gently, trying to ignore the huge price tag on the car. Keeping below the speed limit, she felt relief at the sight of her turn in and indicated. He could keep his car to himself in future, her hands were clammy with the effort of not killing herself.

Parking the sleek car easily behind her parent's and making sure to lock it up carefully, she slid the keys into her jeans. Her feet back on the real ground felt surreal after the purring vibration of power. Welcoming. She didn't know what men's obsession with cars like that was all about. She felt a nervous wreck. Somewhat awed at his lack of fear and his ability to drive it around casually.

Muffin greeted her ecstatically as soon as she entered the front door. It felt like she had been gone for days. The warmth and cosy sight of her cottage instantly relaxing her. Her parents were in the kitchen making breakfast and called out their greetings at the sound of her. It did not take long to bring them up to speed on Morag.

'Has he gone back to the hospital then? her mother enquired. A look of interest and accusation on her face. Unsure how to take it.

'No. He's gone to tell his father what's gone on. He doesn't live in the manor anymore but in one of the fishing crofts nearby.' Her mother of course intrigued by that tit bit of information then had to drag out the details of why the father had left his own home. Nodding understandingly when she told them that the tragic death of their mother had a devastating effect on the man.

'Still likes a good shindig, though!' Her father chimed in, rubbing his still recovering belly. He still looked a bit peaky from the day before.

Chapter 29

They ate together on the couch, morning TV droning on in the background as they chatted lightly about nothing in particular. Muffin was gnawing on a bone she had been keeping in the fridge from friday's butcher trip.

Her phone vibrated across the table, Rob's name beaming on its screen and making her heart swell, she excused herself, taking it to her room before answering him.

'Hey beautiful.' That familiar wash of coming home at the sound of his voice, Rose gushed.

'Hey handsome.' She replied, smiling like a loony, aware how easily he could make her feel this way. Just a call and two little words.

'Is it okay to head down and finally meet my future in-laws? You know as the idiot who broke their daughters heart instead of the Laird.' He sounded more upbeat than this morning, his normal humour present in that sexy voice. Rose giggled.

'Only if you're prepared to be interrogated and made to explain yourself in detail. My mother isn't the push over that I am.' She warned lightly, knowing that despite saying it jokingly, there was a little truth to it.

'Don't worry I brushed up on my spy torture evasion techniques, I'm ready for it baby. Damien is bringing me down in a few minutes. He popped by to say goodbye.'

'Tell him I said goodbye too.' She replied coquettishly with a smile on her lips.

'Don't make me hurt him.' Rob threatened in humour, hinting that he had not forgotten Damien's attempt on Rose at the dance.

'Oh weesht, you know it's only ever been you.' Rose sighed. 'Hurry up and stop making me wait.' She giggled girlishly.

'You're wish is my command gorgeous, and it will always only ever be me, baby.' He ended the call with a goodbye and Rose rolled her eyes with a happy grin. Her heart was beating fast to the thought of him and her parents meeting again in this way, knowing the truth finally, but she was also just eager to see him again. She hated when they were apart, more so now than before after losing him for so long.

Moments later the car tyres on gravel alerted her to his arrival. That surge of anticipation rising in her stomach, she rushed to the door to answer it as he chapped lightly, being pulled out the door slightly by him so he could kiss her without her parent's keen eyes. Leaning close to her ear and keeping his voice for her ears only he muttered huskily.

'Best friend brought up to speed and dutifully warned off. He apologises profusely for trying to steal my girl and told me to man up and make my claim public.' He smiled, brushing her temple with a kiss and winking at her amused expression. She shook her head as she brushed past, leading the way to where her parents were waiting, jumping slightly as his hand pinched her butt from behind. She glared at him and put distance between them as they met her parents in the lounge.

It was tense at first; her mother grilling him unashamedly. Wanting to know what his intentions were with her daughter after Morag was stable enough to come out. Chiding him over the whole messy situation and the stupidity of thinking he could carry on a secret romance in a town as small as this.

Rob took it all on the chin like a trooper, he explained, he apologised and he even asked for their forgiveness. Rose stayed tense and silent, perched on the arm of his chair and bit her lip nervously. Feeling much like the teen who first brought a boy home.

Finally, they made their peace. Her father, the strong silent type, nodding and listening intently. It was excruciating for her to sit watching, listening, but Rob was used to difficult board meetings and awkward clientele. Smooth, confident and calm. He never fluttered an eyelash, fully aware that this relationship depended on winning them over. Knowing that it mattered to Rose.

Finally satisfied and allowing Rose to let out her breath and relax, they all seemed to sigh and sit back a little.

'Well, if you love her and the nonsense of hiding her is over, then I can only say that we approve.' Her mother injected and got to her feet, extending a palm to Rob, who obediently took it and stood up. Her mother hugged him and gave him a mock slap on his shoulder. 'Don't hurt my baby again or you will see the lioness come out in me and you won't like it.' She threatened, her little face full of raised eyebrow seriousness. Rose giggled and Rob merely bowed his head to meet her small height.

'I don't intend to hurt her again, or lose her, so mama lion can retire.' He grinned back and then was met with Rose's father standing to give him a manly pat on the back.

'Welcome to the family son, my condolences on being lumbered with a Turner woman… They are very trying on your nerves but wholly worthwhile.' He winked and gained his own slap in the shoulder from Rose's mother.

'We're beyond worth it, you will never find any woman quite so special as us.' She pouted. Rob turned, catching Roses eye with a heart stopping smile.

'I already know that.' He moved forward towards her, catching her wrist and tugging her to his chest, placing a light kiss on her cheek and embarrassing her completely in front of her parents. Her mother made it worse by 'ahhhhiiiing' loudly and then thankfully they all sat down, only this time Rob pulled her onto his lap onto his chair and wouldn't let her escape, her face instantly flushing with colour.

She suggested they all go out for lunch before her parent's departure, the confines of the small cottage and tense last hour suffocating her. She needed breathing space and a new setting, she also didn't like the way her parents were watching Rob snuggle her into his lap, completely unaffected because they were not his parents. Not that she thought he would be embarrassed, even in front of Hamish, he just didn't seem to be the kind of man who was phased that way; but to her, Rose would always be her parent's little girl and she didn't like to shatter their illusion.

Her parents loved this idea of a final outing, and on Rob's suggestion chose a nice garden centre a couple mile away. It was all arranged. They would go in their own car, easier that way to leave from the lunch and go check out of their boarding house before the trip home. Rose would come with Rob, him back at the wheel of his purring beast. Thankfully, and some alone time once more. She needed that right now, more than ever.

Less than half an hour later and snugly buckled in his passenger seat he reversed out, letting her parents manoeuvre and turn out of the car park first; they turned around the small space and headed out down the long gravel road. Looking back as they headed out Rob unclipped his belt, pulling the handbrake on. Rose frowned, confused at what he was doing.

'I've been dying to do this for almost two hours.' He dived across, pulling her forward and kissing her passionately up against her seat. Straining across the gear stick in an awkward manner with his hand cupping her jaw, while the other leant on the back of her head rest, holding on so he could pull his weight towards her. Her hands came up to cradle his face and lose herself in a kiss that had become a necessity to her. The familiar surge of heat rising inside her erotically and pulled away, breathing heavily.

'Stop that or I'll never make it through lunch Mr Munro.' She laughed, gently shoving him away as he playfully tried to catch the side of her face with his mouth.

'If only your parents knew what kind of things their little angel got up to in my bed!' He grinned, sitting back and putting his belt back on, Rose tamed her hair and tried to calm the blush that had developed across her cheeks with that heated encounter.

'They would never believe you. I'm too innocent and pure!' She blinked into the mirror on the sun visor, casting him a sweet look.

He had expertly swung the car round the gravel park tightly and was now following in pursuit of her parents, gaining on their little green car up ahead on the straight main road. He looked across at her smiling

'You are you know?'

She cocked her head quizzically, showing a doubtful expression but he looked serious.

'No, I'm not.' She giggled and carried on fluffing her hair before closing the visor and nestling back in her moulded seat.

'You have this innocence about you. Naivety… It makes you vulnerable and childlike sometimes… Pure!' He was eyeing her speculatively, all serious and thoughtful.

'I'm not sure that's a compliment.' She laughed but his face stayed steady.

'Trust me, it's one of the many reasons I go crazy over you. Angelic, beautiful, gentle girl in floaty feminine dresses…Smelling like cakes and berries… Always smiling and gracefully unaware of how stunning you are. Brings out the protector in me! But once you're in my bed a wild little hellcat! That Penelope you keep hidden deep down sure shows up then, with a fiery little mix of irresistible and sexy… You know that, right?'

'Not really.' She shrugged, still giggling at his description and feeling a little smug at how he saw her. Warm inside and a little gooey.

'Well, you are! Sometimes you remind me of Abby… A petulant kid with big Bambi eyes and the ability to wrap me around your little finger. But other times you're more capable, stronger and more stubborn. Iron-willed and able to do just fine on your own; you made it abundantly clear that you didn't need me and it hurt like hell. Sometimes you make me want to throw you over my shoulder and drag you to bed. Sometimes I just want to throttle you.'

'Charming! .... I did need you though, I just wasn't going to let you know that while you were the reason I was heartbroken.' She smiled softly this time, sliding a hand to his thigh and giving him a soft reassuring squeeze. Their eyes met briefly, so full of unspoken messages.

He had overtaken her parents to lead the way to their destination, still glancing at her as she watched his face, he was glancing into his mirrors and checking the road expertly between every longing look at her.

'I won't ever break your heart again, I want you to need me as much as I need you. I want to know that you can't function without me... I sure as hell can't function without you.' He winked, lightening the heavy tone of their conversation a little.

'Sounds like your smitten if you ask me Mr Munro.' She teased, following suit.

'You don't know the half of it!' Something in the serious tone of his voice and the glint of honesty in his eye sent a shiver down her spine. 'I wouldn't have just let you go, Rose. If we hadn't...? I didn't see a future without you in it! Even when you told me to stay away. I always knew that no matter what I would try and get you back... No matter how long it took... I knew from the first second there was never going to be anyone else for me. I didn't just fall for you, I completely crashed head first with no hope of recovery.'

Her eyes started to well up with emotion, her smile hard to maintain with the urge to cry at just how sweet he could be, just how much he could tug her heart. He reached out, touching her face gently with the backs of his fingers; his eyes warm as he focused on her emotions bubbling forth. His eyes glancing back and forth to the road and on her sporadically.

'Rob, I feel the same.' She sniffed back a tear, catching his fingers on her face and rubbing her cheek against them soothingly. She loved to feel his hands on her face.

'I love you more than I have ever loved anyone in my life. This isn't just some passing fad or casual romance.'

'What? You love me even more than your car?' She winked in jest, blinking back the tears. 'It isn't for me either Rob. I knew from that first week, you had me under a spell and I had no defence against you.' She was looking away again, shyly, dabbing her eyes with her sleeve now.

'I'll marry you, Rose. When we're ready. When I've fixed this mess that I created.'

She turned back to him quickly. Mildly shocked but in a good way and caught his eye. Both smiled in unison as he reached out, gently squeezing her knee before changing gear. The warmth of emotion and happiness tingling through her, making her feel like she was walking on clouds.

She would marry him too; there was nothing more that she could ever want than that. There was no thinking about it, no hesitation.

'Mrs Rose Munro does have a nice kind of sound to it.' She smiled at him and was rewarded with the biggest grin back at her, those grey eyes, pale and seductive.

The garden centre was not far and they soon pulled into the car park with her parents close behind.

It was a quaint little white farm house with shiny large conservatories added on the front and side of the main door, creating a shop and cafe. The grounds to the left full of huge plastic and sheet greenhouses and signs for several types of plants leading down winding flower edged paths. It had a whimsical old-world quality and was utterly adorable.

He casually draped his arm around her as he walked, their bodies side by side and him leading the way into the warm sunny tea room. An easy fluid movement that made her feel light and happy. She was liking this new dimension to what they had. Being in public and being treated like his girlfriend was an improvement and she felt pride as some young women at a nearby table glanced his way appreciatively. One nudging the other to point out the hunk who had just sauntered in. Not that she could blame them, he really was eye candy even dressed in casual clothes and trainers.

It smelled of freshly baked cakes and homemade soup. Warm and inviting and already half full for the time of day. The tables layered with cloth and lace coverings and bunches of fresh flowers in assorted little glass vases on each table.

* * *

An hour later, stuffed and still sitting lazily around their little pretty white table, empty sandwich plates and soup bowls littering the surface, they finished their hot drinks. Both women sore from laughing, the men keeping them amused and in hysterics for most of the meal.

Rose could tell her father and Rob liked one other a heck of a lot. The easy jocularity and pet names that had developed over the food. Her father now calling him 'Robster' and Rob jokingly referring to him as 'The old man' and 'Dad-in-law'. It was easy and unforced.

Rose had felt a huge warmth enveloping her through the meal and catching her mother's warm look only made her feel better. He had won them over, well and truly. Of course, it had helped that he had literally doted on her in front of them, pulling her chair out for her to sit and handing her napkins to cover her lap when food was served. Reaching over and taking her hand every time he pushed his cup aside, playing with her fingers absentmindedly and drawing them to his mouth gently anytime he thought her parents were not looking. Feeding her some of his food automatically when it arrived so she could try it and throwing her small smiles and winks throughout the lunch. Such a natural unforced behaviour for him. Ever attentive, the way he always was when he had her alone but her mother's keen eye had taken note. Rose aware of the ever-watching eyes and satisfied smiles.

All too soon they were saying their goodbyes at the car. Her mother embracing her and imparting whispered words of love and advice on handling her new man.

'Don't let him forget what he has! Never be taken for granted and if he does you remind him of your worth with a swift kick out the door.' She winked, turning to kiss him on the cheek. 'And to you Rob...Never stop treating her like a princess, even when she isn't wearing her crown.'

Rob kissed her mum on the cheek, agreeing that he would always treat her like his queen. Her father squeezed her tight and planted a kiss on top of her head, agreeing with what her mother said.

'She will always be our princess, couldn't be happier to be handing her off to a man who recognises that.' He winked knowingly and patted Rob warmly on the shoulder. They agreed to not wait so long next time and finally left the two lovebirds alone to watch them drive off. Waving until they were out of sight.

Although she had loved having them here, the relief at them leaving was evident. She could relax again; she could be alone with her tall muscular hunk and free to let his hands wander once more without parental watchful eyes. He had behaved so gentlemanly in front of her parents and she knew how much self-control it must have taken.

Without warning he scooped her up over his shoulder, causing her to let out a squeal and headed briskly across the car park to his car, keys already out and remote unlocking at a distance.

'Rob?!?!' She squealed in protest, squirming on his shoulder and trying to get free, sure every eye in the café was now focused on the car park.

'I told you, didn't I? The urge to throw you over my shoulder and drag you to bed… It's not my fault!'

Chapter 30

The next few days passed quickly. They spent every possible moment they could together when he was not working and she was not starting her new sketches or paintings for her current commission. They ate, bathed and slept together every night. Whether at the cottage or at the manor. She already loved bubble baths, but using the grand sized bath in his mother's old suite and luxuriating with him was absolute heaven. Of course, it always led to other things usually midway through but at least it was clean fun.

She had even spent time in the pool alone with him, locking the main door in case anyone came down and taking delight in getting her naked and breathless in both the pool and the sauna. He was even more lust fuelled now that she was no longer a secret than the previous early days. Something she had not thought possible or had predicted.

She was beginning to see a side to him that was irresistible. Instead of dark looks and stress of their earlier relationship and stolen moments, he was more carefree and relaxed. Happy to laze around the manor with her watching old soppy films or take Abby and Rose on shopping trips out of town. He always had to have some sort of contact, even when sitting casually at dinner. Feet together or elbows together, and if she was too far away he would pull her whole chair closer just to feel her beside him.

Things had shifted a lot in their relationship in that he held her hand in public wherever they went and took delight in as many outings as he could fit in between work and travel. He didn't care who saw them. He seemed proud to show her off. Proud to have men appreciate her beauty and see his strong arm always around her protectively. Most of the town had now seen them canoodling and holding arms or hands, he couldn't go anywhere without the urge to grope her in some way or kiss her and those that hadn't had soon learned of their blossoming romance from the village grapevine.

That was the downside of a tight-knit small community. No one seemed surprised to see them together after a few days, news hitting and filtering through. Not a single backwards glance was cast or raised eyebrow at their inability to keep their hands to themselves after a while. It was taking some getting used too, no longer having to look around and see who was watching and Rose was relieved that no one made any comments about Morag.

Rob had rung the hospital daily, checking on Morag's progress and being told she was not allowed any visitors until the psychiatrist felt she was more emotionally stable. Her arms and wounds were healing nicely with no complications. The damage to her tendons repaired. He had a feeling she was refusing to see him.

He tried to pass it off easily, but Rose wasn't fooled. Morag was besotted with Rob so refusing to see him was a pretty major deal; she knew he was worrying about where that would lead. He didn't talk about it though. Rob was always someone who kept all worries and problems deep inside and dealt with it alone. She had not cracked that wall just yet.

She knew his new-found inhibition was in part because Morag was not here and had no idea what he was doing in her absence. Offering him a small freedom he had not had in a very long time, making him more relaxed. She knew he was making the most of it before he had to face the reality of her release and like a timer on countdown; Rose was only too aware that the sand was pouring away slowly.

Abby was around a lot less lately. Her own relationship had stepped up a gear and much to Rob's displeasure she had begun spending nights at Duncan's family farm. Cosy Sunday dinners with his parents and siblings, spending her free time helping down at their farm shop. They had agreed on a future family dinner with them at the manor soon and Rose had sensed his tension when Abby had announced the plan. It was looking serious and he did not like it one bit.

Rose missed her but she relished the extra time she got to spend alone with Rob; savouring every moment this time around, feeling like she really was in a proper relationship and not just stealing moments together; everything felt different and right. She was so much happier.

Muffin had become so accustomed to the manor, and the lap of Alice, that he wagged excitedly the second he would see the sweeping drive and towering wooden front door. His little tongue flopping out of his mouth and ears perked with sheer delight. Tail whipping ecstatically.

Hamish had even come into the house for dinner a couple of times, finally getting to openly bask in the sight of his son and his lady. They had a night with all five of them for dinner, Rose and Rob and Abby with Duncan at Hamish's request. A pleasant relaxed dinner, enjoying the easy banter between them all.

He teased and chided Rob affectionately when they moved to the lounge with coffee and Abby had taken Duncan to her room upon arrival.

'I'm happy for you laddie, finally saw sense and held onto this woman with all you got. Knew it wouldn't take you long to give in and go after her.' He winked at Rose and shoved his son in the shoulder playfully.

Rob didn't respond, he just pulled Rose closer by the hand so she nuzzled against him on the couch and kissed her softly on the cheek. A warm affection in his eyes that showed he agreed with everything his father was saying.

'He couldn't resist me.' Rose giggled playfully and curled up closer, sliding her arms through his and nestling her face against his arm. He slid it out and put it around her instead, so she could lay her cheek on his chest and rest his chin on top of her head.

'You should have seen the state of him in my croft most nights, cradling a whiskey and crying into his old dad's belly.' He laughed, and dodged the throw pillow Rob threw his way.

'Thanks for ruining the manly image my beautiful girl had of me. Dad!' Rob was grinning but Hamish only shook his head.

It somehow made Rose feel glowy inside that he had suffered as much as she had through their break up. Mending those memories, a little.

'Nothing could ruin that.' Rose fluttered at him affectionately but Rob only frowned.

'I honestly cannot tell if you're being serious or playing along with him right now.' He smiled at her and tried to gaze into her head a little intensely.

'Guess you will never know.' She winked in jest, then squealed when he pulled her onto his lap to nibble, diving in at her neck and shoulders, restraining her effortlessly with sheer muscle.

'Children, you're making your old man blush. Take it to a bedroom.' Hamish laughed again and they both returned to previous seating positions, Rose trying to smooth her dress out and untangle her hair from her necklace. Rob casually slumped back into holding her close.

'Soon enough, old man. Right now, we're picking a movie and having family time with you, seeing as you're a lonely old senile who could use the company.' Rob grinned at his father and received a mock bop on the head as thanks. Smiles all round as Alice appeared with the pre-planned popcorn and milkshakes all round.

* * *

It was now mid-week and they were lazily laying across his bed semi-dressed. They had been naked only an hour before, sweaty and caught up with each other beneath the sheets in their favourite past time. Now they were cooling off and lost in work.

Rose had a sketchbook, laying down on the end of his duvet and was stretched out on her stomach, wearing one of his shirts, her body still tingling and relaxed and lost in drawing out some character ideas. Rob was sitting at the head of the bed, the length of him down her side, his covered feet level with her shoulders. He had his outstretched hand laid across her naked legs protectively; topless and covered by the sheet of the bed from the waist down; he was reading through papers he needed to sign off on; a frown of concentration on his face. Lately, he had been frowning a lot more when he was working or reading his papers, sitting over his laptop or on his phone.

They had left the TV playing, an old movie, set down low in the background, adding to the peaceful atmosphere and contentment; Muffin was curled under the bed on his thick plush rug and snoring softly. It had been a long day for them both concerning work and now here, unwinding after food, sex and showering, in that order in this comfortable silence; Rose felt like she was exactly where she belonged.

Rob leant forward, gently slapping her butt and announcing he had to go make a call. Lifting his paperwork and dumping it ceremoniously on the side table. He pulled out one stapled file and tossed it over the top of her, nearer the door, so it landed on the bed closer to his office. She threw a loose cushion at him as he passed. The sheet sliding from his naked body, affording her a moment to admire him as he walked around the bed. She sighed deeply, inwardly cursing his distraction and tried to bring her focus back to the drawings at hand. Aware of how easily he made her blood pressure rise as he pulled some clothes out of his long wardrobe and began getting dressed.

'You need clothes to make a call?' She smiled, rolling onto her back on the bed, twisting her hair with one hand and watching him pull on a t-shirt which clung to his muscular shoulders and back.

'I find that I feel a little less weird talking business with clothes on. Especially when it's to my fifty-year-old male solicitor…Plus naked conference calls tend to put off the clients when it's video chat.' He walked back to the bed scooping down to plant a soft kiss on her lips upside down, then another lower down on her exposed cleavage.

'Besides, I may be a while. The contracts they sent require some minor changes before I sign off on them. That means calls to set up a board meeting too. My assistant will not be pleased to hear from me at this time of day.' He frowned and lingered a moment to trail some more kisses across her cleavage.

Rose put on her most believable petted lip and frown face, fluttering sad eyes at him. Knowing that this had proven a very useful tool many times over, when she wanted something from him in recent days. It was usually more naked time, just as it was now.

'I know baby, but it's either I do this now via telephone or I leave it and get hauled in for a directors meeting when the construction is stopped.' He let his fingers trail her collar bone, pushing back the thin material of his own pinstripe shirt on her body. She always looked good in his clothes and he found it hard to resist her creamy skin. She had only buttoned it up part way and he exposed more skin by pulling an extra button loose

'I suppose it could wait an extra hour.' That devilish gleam in his eyes as his fingers traced down over her naked breast was a sign she had won him over effortlessly. She bit her lip and moved up the bed slightly, moving her legs seductively, causing him to groan.

'Jesus Rose! When the business goes tits up I'll only have you to blame.' He pulled his t-shirt back over his head, leaning down to capture her mouth and remove the shirt that was barely concealing the rest of her nakedness slowly. Sliding over her on the bed, moving over her neck, kissing it erotically and pinning her hands by her head. Rose completely surrendered to him.

The phone on the bedside table began ringing loudly, vibrating clumsily and he let out an agitated moan before moving off her to retrieve his mobile. He pressed the screen and informed them it was Rob Munro in his clipped business tone.

Rose sat up and pulled the shirt back on reluctantly; the look on his face signalling the end of playtime. He cursed under his breath and turned, walking off into his office via the adjoining door wearing only sweatpants, his fingertips trailing down her long leg and foot as he passed by. Her gaze following the tanned width of his muscular shoulders disappointedly, at the expanse of smooth skin crying out for her to touch it.

She could tell by the tone of his voice it was about the construction he had been overseeing for the past few weeks. He didn't sound impressed. He had briefly told her about it only the day before.

One of their breweries had expanded, setting up in another location in France. They had merged with a vineyard and had plans for some sort of hybrid alcohol. The new building being held up by so many white flags and papers by the french officials. Safety issues, problems in the contracts; he had been minorly stressing over it, and his workload the past couple of days seemed to have doubled.

She wandered into the office, handing him his t-shirt and kissing him on the cheek before turning and starting to walk back to the bedroom. Catching her by the shirt hem, he pulled her back, sliding a hand up her exposed neck and along her jaw, cupping her under her ear lightly. He pulled her forward, brushing his mouth against hers mid-sentence and mouthing a 'sorry'. Obvious disappointment on his face that he was going to be a while.

She could tell!

Once he had that business face on he was pretty much stuck there until he resolved whatever needed to be resolved. No point lying around here listening to him getting frustrated on the phone. She would go down to the cottage and collect some of her watercolours and pens. Make a start on one of her illustrations at the kitchen table until he was done.

Seeing her pulling on clothes as she passed the open door he covered his phone

'Where are you going?' He frowned her way.

'To the cottage for supplies, I have some illustrations I could be doing while you're busy. I won't be long.' She smiled back at him, pulling her dress over her head awkwardly.

He gestured for her to come to him again with a nod and even though he was still talking to someone on the other end of his call he stood up to meet her, planting a soft kiss on her mouth, this time parting her lips and letting their tongues softly graze. A slight second of erotica but enough to bring the heat back up her chest and neck, her body sizzling for him. His eyes landed on her mouth, running a thumb across the fullness of her lips, a brief glimmer of matched longing before returning to his seat and lifting the lid on his laptop.

He had once told her that he liked to leave her wanting when they parted, as he knew it meant she would hurry back. That had made her laugh but he had proven many a time it was true. Right now, she wanted nothing more than that kiss to be continued.

The drive to the cottage in the fading sun with Muffin felt good. She felt happier than she could ever recall ever feeling, despite the issue with Morag on hiatus and still in the back of her mind, she was glowing with contentment nowadays. Her skin radiant from endless hours of making love most nights. This never-ending craving for one another only worsening the more they partook.

She knew things had changed and wouldn't go back to what they had been now, so much had happened. Rob's attitude about Morag had changed too, he pushed any talk of her out of the conversation when she arose and seemed happy for the time being to forget her existence.

Well, now every single soul in the town knew she was Rob's girlfriend it wouldn't be long before the woman's reappearance would have to be dealt with and all the fall out that came with it.

The cottage as always, welcomed her warmly with an instant feeling of home and safety. She loved this place and knew no matter what happened with Rob she would never sell it; always keep this little treasure as her haven and hideaway should she ever need it. Just as it had been for her aunt Olivia.

Pulling out a large black holdall she packed a lot of art supplies and tools, found the notes and papers she had printed off; outlining specifics and the manuscript for the book she was creating images for. She took her time, enjoying the sanctuary of her little house. Muffin exploring his familiar domain, like being back home after moving out. Your old bedroom a familiar place to relax and just breathe, like a warm hug.

Packing some of her clothes and toiletries in an overnight bag, she grabbed Muffins fluffy bed and food bowls while she was here. She knew by now that Rob would expect her to stay with him tonight; he liked waking up with her by his side and after a continuous few nights together they had both taken it for granted they would sleep wherever they ended up together. Be it here or at his. With his workload the last few days, it made more sense for him to be near his home office, to deal with things there.

By the time she dragged herself away from the cottage and made the short trip back to the manor she had been gone for the best part of an hour. Letting herself in the main door, now he had given her a key, she was surprised to see him standing in the hall. His butt perched on a side table with a look of stress on his face.

Was he waiting for her?

He would have heard her car pull up from his office which overlooked the entrance. He seemed relieved to see her and immediately walked over to relieve her of the bags.

'What's wrong?' She asked cautiously, a little unnerved by his serious expression and sombre stance.

'I had a call while you were gone!... From the hospital... Morag's asked to see me.' He searched her face for a reaction but she kept it steady, despite the drop in her heart or the increased speed of its beat. She knew it shouldn't affect her but the flip in her stomach and the ice cold feeling of dread caught her out of nowhere.

'Oh!'

He kissed her on the cheek quickly, a dark look crossing his face and relieving her of her luggage. He led the way to his room, dumping her bags on the bed before turning back to face her, pulling her against him softly.

'We both know I need to do this Rose. If we are to carry on the way it's been the last couple of weeks, then I need to see her. It's been hanging in the air, over us... Lingering and waiting...Unfinished!' He said softly, still standing close.

'I know.' Her lip trembled, feeling insecure suddenly. Rob seeing the tiny tremor of emotion, cupped her face kissing her lightly on the mouth, staying close and brushing noses.

'I love you. Nothing's going to change. I won't let it.' He nuzzled her softly.

'I love you.' She smiled softly, unable to let him go. The sense of foreboding moving over her and taking small steady breaths to push away the growing tide of anxiety. Sensing her vulnerability, he scooped her up in his arms and hugged her in close. Squeezing her a little too tightly and lifting her off her feet. He made a strange 'argh' noise in his throat which caused her to giggle unguardedly, her eyes coming to his as her arms slid around his neck, relaxing her a little.

'So god damn much that sometimes I could squeeze the life out of you.' He jested and brought her nose to touch his, eyes locked and still holding her a foot above the ground.

'Please don't, I happen to like breathing.' She giggled and kissed him this time, opening her mouth to feel his tongue against hers, the soft way he could devour her mouth.

Placing her gently on his bed and planting another chaste kiss on her mouth, he stayed against her for a few moments, his hands brushing back her hair, neither saying anything. He let her go and slid away as she fell back to sit on the bed, watching him. He picked Muffin up from the floor, rubbing the little fluff ball before placing him on her lap

'He will take care of you until I'm back. If I go now I'll get back before dark. It's a bit of a drive.'

Rose watched him change into jeans and a shirt silently. A million emotions running through her, yet none visible on her face. He seemed as uptight as she was and when he finally slipped on some boots and grabbed his mobile phone to go he stopped and looked at her.

'Don't worry Rose. Nothing can ever take you away from me ever again… I'll never let it happen… I promise!' He scooped down planting soft short kisses across her face, bordering on a humorous game as she started batting them off her eyelids, ear and nose, before turning and leaving. Leaving her unable to breathe from laughing.

'Rob!'

He paused by the door, leaning back in to look at her, his eyebrows raised questioningly. The half-smile still on his face from his teasing her.

'I will be at the cottage. No point milling about here feeling useless. I feel better down there when you're not here.' She smiled; her eyes trying to devour every detail of him as though he wasn't coming back. She knew she was being stupid but the anxiety growing inside was stubborn.

'Okay, baby. I'll come there when I'm done. Keep the bed warm for me.' He winked and blew her a kiss before disappearing. Despite his jocular manner, she had seen the storm brewing in his eyes. The stress straining across his brow, leaving her feeling uptight, anxious, and extremely nauseous.

Chapter 31

It hadn't taken her long to put everything back in her car. She had grabbed Muffin and headed back down, relief washing over her like a warm hug when she walked back through its welcoming door once again.

The nights were getting colder and not having the fancy heating of the manor house, she occupied her mind by setting up the fires in the living room and bedroom. Having never really started a log fire in her life it took a good chunk of time and effort. All her direction from Abby completely forgotten. Good old google to help her do something that should have been straightforward, YouTube came to the rescue several times.

Before long the house was cosy and romantic. The flickering flames in the darkening room, entrancing, and helping to smooth her rattled nerves and unease. She made herself some tea and raided the fridge for snacks.

Channel hopping the TV for some background noise, she felt restless. Doubting she would be able to work, she set about pulling her art supplies out anyway and set up a small table at the couch. She didn't want to work in her little closed room; the fire more welcoming and giving her a sense of security. Helping to thaw that icy grip which had taken hold in her stomach.

After three hours, she pushed the table away, dissatisfied with everything she had painted and sketched. Her mind was just not focused and her heart not in it. She checked her watch for the millionth time and admitting defeat, decided she should go to bed. It was dark outside and he still had not appeared, no contact at all which was just not like him.

Muffin only ventured into the garden for a last pee before settling in bed, he seemed unaware of Rose's disappointment and absent focus, happily settling down to sleep almost immediately. She checked her phone, once again sighing at the lack of calls or texts and pondered over sending him one.

If he was in the hospital it would be off anyway, so there was no point. He had told her he would come here, so he would, he had obviously been held up. His silence unusual compared to how he had been of late. She would just leave the door unlocked for him; cursing herself for still not finding the second key to give him. She had misplaced it her first week here and knowing he could get in anytime, locked or not would have made her feel better right now.

Killing time by making herself some hot cocoa and cleansing her face carefully, she was well aware she was delaying getting into bed. Hoping he would just appear and she felt stupid. It was less than three weeks and already it was like she couldn't function without him here.

When had she become so hopeless? Is this what it was like when you met 'the one'? You became so joined at the hip that survival apart was futile.

She finally climbed into bed wearing a satin and lace, sexy and extremely skimpy, nightdress. A self-indulgent purchase when she had first got together with Rob and had never worn. It was strappy, revealing in places where see through lace panels were strategically placed and despite his lack of appearance, she put it on for his benefit. Once again feeling stupid and pushing it away in her mind that she was being pathetic.

She was barely asleep when she heard him coming through the front door. Her heart skipped a beat at the noise of the intruder before fully realising he was home and flipping in joy. She heard him fumble with her keys in the door that had been hanging inside, locking them in and signalling he was here to stay. The rush of relief washing over her was warming, and at the same time sent tingles through her, unsure whether to get up and greet him or stay laying in the dark. Rose decided on the latter and laid still, waiting quietly. Eyes glued to the door, trying to adjust.

She heard him trip and curse in the hall, he obviously thought she was asleep so was not switching on any lights. She smiled. Just his presence was enough to lift her whole mood and chase away all anxiety. The waiting endlessly now forgotten.

Stumbling into the bedroom, she could hear him pulling off his clothes and boots, dumping them on the chair by the dresser. Could smell his familiar exotic scent surrounding him in the air as he pulled back the covers, feeling across the bed for her and slid in, moving close and pulling her over so he could wrap her in his arms and legs. Feeling the smooth satin of her nightdress, he slid his hands over her body appreciatively, hearing her inhale lightly in response. She could never fight the responses her body made involuntarily when he touched her.

'Rose, are you awake?' his mouth was mere millimetres from hers, his breath warming her lips seductively.

'Mmmm hmmm.' she didn't want to admit she was wide awake and listening to him fumbling around in the dark clumsily. She tried to sound sleepy. He turned her on her side gently, facing her away so he could pull her into his stomach to spoon her. This was not a usual Rob move when he had her in a bed. He was more of wandering hands and removing her clothes as soon as he had her alone kind of guy. Even tired in the middle of the night, surrounded by darkness.

'What's wrong?' She whispered softly, catching his hands around her and pulling them to her lips. He sighed heavily. His body collapsing against her needily.

'It went pretty badly, I'm tired and stressed. It's nothing.' He buried his face in the back of her neck, sighing once again and sagging into the embrace as though it was just what he needed.

'Tell me.' she squeezed his hands encouragingly, not wanting to leave this alone, knowing she would never sleep if he didn't tell her now. He paused. Gathering his thoughts for a moment as though contemplating it.

'Now?' He asked dubiously, obviously not really wanting to talk it over. Typically, Rob.

'What better time?' She encouraged, pulling his arms tighter around her upper body and pushing her butt back into his groin a little more snuggly. He cleared his throat and paused for a second, she could feel his hesitation but he must have thought better of it and gave in.

'She was upright anyway, awake and more together. At first, I didn't think she even remembered what had happened. She just acted like everything was normal.'

Rose listened intently, knowing to stay quiet and let him work through it.

He nuzzled further into the back of her, his breath sending tingles down her back. 'She seemed happy to see me. More calm and I don't know…? Stable? We talked about what the surgeon had said, what other surgeries she still had to get. She seemed okay.'

He released Rose, pulling himself to sit up in the bed restlessly. The subject hard and he always felt more in control when she was not so close, tugging at his nerve endings and feeling so sexy in her silky lingerie. Propping cushions up behind him and laying a hand on her thigh possessively. Still needing that contact between them.

The sudden parting caused a feeling of dread to come crawling back inside Rose's stomach, pushing it aside, she turned over so she was facing his body, but stayed laying down; gently tracing his abdomen muscles with her fingertips in the dark. Feeling him tense softly as he reacted to the light tickles and just needing to have that intimacy with this subject between them.

'I asked her if she wanted to talk about things; about what happened at the house, trying to guide the subject to what started it all… You and I! At first, she kept apologising, asking me to forget it.' He reached up rubbing his eyes, sighing again and obviously already agitated with the memories. His voice was husky and his mood unreadable; she could feel the tension in his body building.

'Go on…' She coaxed gently, afraid he would clam up and tell her to go to sleep instead.

'I pushed it. Didn't I? I had to keep going. I should have read the signals that it was too soon. We ended up arguing; she remembered all right. Accusing me of the same shit, the same accusation, the same jealous blind fury. She told me I was to end it with my 'whore'! '

Rose froze. Her hand staying on his stomach.

No progress in this messy situation.

He reached down, catching her hand and pulling it against him, knowing her silence did not mean she was not reacting inside.

'I told her that wasn't going to happen. Not to call you a whore. I guess I just didn't realise how little patience I have left for her. How much I've changed towards her? I said things I would never have said three months ago. I just lost it with her.'

His heartbeat had accelerated slightly, obviously remembering the event clearly, part regret, part anger and getting worked up.

'What did she say?' Rose almost held her breath.

'She cried a lot. Typical Morag fashion! Sobbing and howling and trying to throw anything she could reach. Everything I said just made it worse and they ended up asking me to leave!…I left the hospital in such a rage Rose. With her. At myself! I couldn't come back here and have you upset by the way I was being. I needed to clear my head, so I went for a drive to calm down. I ended up driving to the coast and just taking it out on flooring it across the beaches while the tide was out.' He kissed her fingers softly, running them across his mouth. 'I'm sorry I didn't call, I just needed to think! Needed to calm down. My car looks like it's been rallied through a swamp.'

She sat up, reaching for him. Feeling in the dark the way to his face and gently kissed his cheek as she manoeuvred beside him.

'You did your best Rob. Most men would have never tried to help her the way you have. Stuck around and tried to support her. To help her get well. They would have cut their losses a long time ago and turned their back on her.' She slid her arms around his neck and rested her forehead against his.

'Maybe that's the point? If I had walked away years ago, maybe now she would have moved on with her life and got over it? Maybe I'm the reason she's so messed up now?' He sounded deflated.

'It's not you that's doing this Rob...It's us and what we have. If I had never come here, you wouldn't be going through all this.'

'That's not true Rose. Don't ever say that... You're not the first girl I have been with in the last fifteen years. I just tried to carry on living a life without directly hurting her and hiding when I should have just been honest. I should have done this years ago... This is my fault!'

'That's why you were so good at sneaking around! MI5 style.' She had tried to sound light and teasing but there was a rawness in her voice.

'I hate that I lowered you to that, Rose. I hated that it felt the same way as all those meaningless affairs. Every time I was with you it just tore at me that I was making you hide, I never wanted it for you.' He pulled her body over his so she straddled him, sliding his arms around her waist so he could pull her as close as possible, gazing at her in the darkness, only able to make out the briefest of features.

'I guess somehow she felt the change in you. You said she started getting worse after we met.'

'Sixth sense or some crazy woman's intuition. The accusations that I was screwing around started only days after I met you. I hadn't even done anything.'

'You must have done something to make her feel like there was someone else?' She was listening to the slow steady beat of his heart beneath his skin, lulling her into a sense of calm.

'I guess. Maybe it was the fact I couldn't get you out of my head. I was distracted a lot, unfocused and all over the place. I guess that screamed out that there was a woman involved.'

Rose felt her heart warm, she loved nothing more than have him admit how crazy for her he was. She felt the same way.

'It's kind of sad. For her I mean. She wants you so badly and yet she's never been able to really have the part that she thinks she needs.'

'And therein lies my dilemma... My guilt.' Rob heaved a heavy inhale and rolled his shoulders to release some of his building tension.

'You didn't ask for this Rob... I can see why she wouldn't be able to let you go. I wouldn't be able to either.'

'I get it. Because it's how I feel about you. And it only makes me feel even more shitty. Because I know how much I would fall apart if it were me and you had fallen in love with someone else.' He pulled her in tighter, kissing her fore head softly. 'It doesn't bear thinking about.' He murmured softly, a hint of anguish in his voice.

They both fell into silence reflecting on what he had said as he reached up, pinching his face at his forehead and flexing his shoulders painfully, for a second time. Rose felt a tug at her heart and began kneading his large shoulders to help alleviate the niggles.

'Maybe it's time to stop thinking about it. For now anyway? Sleep on it?' Rose suggested, sensing his agitation had climbed a little too high.

'I'm sorry baby. I'm seriously worked up and stressed. Her! work! I feel like I'm just letting you down with this entire fucked up situation!' He sighed heavily and brought her chin up with his fingers so he could kiss her on the lips, a gentle quick grazing of mouths.

'Rob?'

'What baby?'

Rose wiggled her hips suggestively. 'I happen to know a cure for your kind of stress.' She whispered seductively, sliding the nightdress up slowly and revealing her naked body in the dark. His hands following the curves she was revealing yet he didn't really respond as he normally did.

'Rose?'

She faltered, aware that he wasn't following through with any sexual advances, just gazing at her in the darkness. Motionless and lost in thought.

'What?' She felt nervous now, awkward, rejected. Like a distance was opening between them and unsure if she should move off him, admit defeat at trying to seduce him. Trying not to overthink it or take it personally.

There was a short silence, she could not make out his face in the gloomy light, only the sound of his breathing and aware that his face was still close to her own and he hadn't broken that intense gaze. Rose's own heart rate had elevated and her palms were getting distinctly clammy.

'Marry me?' He breathed it so gently she almost thought she imagined it.

'What?' She breathed in surprise.

'Rose. I want you... No, I NEED you to be my wife?' His voice was suddenly stronger, more serious and no hint of hesitation. 'I know I said I would wait until I fixed this mess, but I can't. I need you to know that I'm not going anywhere, that I'm yours and only yours and that for me this is everything. I want us to be real, living together in the manor. The full shebang... Dog, kids, happy ever after... I want it all with you. Will you marry me baby, and make me the happiest guy alive?'

Rose couldn't hold back the sudden onslaught of tears rolling down her cheeks and the quaver in her voice as she tried to form a reply, nodding her head like a child and almost unable to speak. Emotion swamping every cell with an overwhelming force. Her hands trembling, she cradled his face tenderly, pulling his mouth close to hers.

'Yes... Yes... I will.' Her voice was shaking, sniffing back the tears as he tried to wipe them away. She could make out a grin in the darkness. He pulled her forward, catching her mouth with his, and rolled her onto her side, dragging her down onto the bed and covering her with his semi naked body.

'I'm not asking you because of seeing her or a sense of duty or guilt... I'm asking because I've wanted to ask you for weeks and never seemed to find the right moment. I'm sick of waiting.' He was rubbing noses with her, stroking her face and planting small kisses across her face greedily.

'So you ask me when I'm semi naked and trying to turn you on?... You realise I'll have to censor the story when I tell our future children!' She laughed, twisting to free her face from his barrage.

'I like you naked and trying to turn me on. Seemed like the perfect moment to me.' He laughed, all his stress and tension gone, as though it had floated away on this cloud of happy they had just created.

'Maybe we should do a PG rerun for any future storytelling, though?' He was trying to find her eyes in the dark. Calming down his need to eat her alive. 'You know like the whole down on one knee, clothed and far away from a bed. Don't really want you having to tell your mother that I did not do it in a manner fit for a princess!' He was still smiling and Rose was beaming right back.

'I'd never tire of you asking me. So, I'm all for it.' She giggled, kissing him hard and pulling away to just gaze at him lovingly.

'It would maybe give me a chance to actually bring the ring next time.'

She paused, tilting her head and running her fingers over his jawline, minorly surprised.

'There's a ring?'

'Of course, there's a ring. You think I would plan to ask you and not have a ring ready?... It belonged to my mother, it's a tradition in our family that the Lairds wife wears this ring until we have a grown-up son of our own.'

Rose felt the butterflies in her stomach. The flip of her heart as memory brought up the images of the beautiful vintage ring Abby had shown to her.

'I've seen it... Abby showed it to me a while ago... It's beautiful Rob, it really is.' Rose gushed, still tearful, but in a happy elated and bursting with joy kind of way.

'Beautiful ring for the most beautiful girl; it's now yours.' He did not seem surprised at her admission.

'Do I need to wait till you re-propose? You know in the PG version?' She giggled, feeling his mouth on her shoulder once more, tracing her collarbone with kisses

'We could always get dressed and go get it now. Moonlit proposal in the gardens?' His voice was husky but serious.

'Tempted! And I mean majorly tempted but I would rather something else in the moonlight right now.' Rose giggled naughtily, tracing his strong shoulders and walking her fingertips down over his chest and abdomen suggestively. He found her mouth, hushing anymore talk and kissing her in a way that had her begging for more.

'I think you're right. It can wait till tomorrow!'

He moved her further down the bed easily, covering her with his body and mouth. Devouring her with the hunger of a man who had been deprived for weeks.

Chapter 32

When she awoke next morning, the memories of their night flooded back, causing a huge wave of elation and a smile to break over her face. She sat up with a start and planted a kiss on his cheek excitedly. All the vigour and energy of an excited child on Christmas morning.

'You asked me to marry you!' She declared in a bright cheerful voice, to no one in particular.

'I did!' Came the mumble from the pillow beside her; still half asleep, his eyes firmly closed and obviously unwilling to open. His body laid out in its normal pose and looking lifeless. She slid out of bed, pulling on a robe and almost danced into the kitchen, humming to herself loudly as she went.

Filling the kettle, clattering cups noisily and noting the sun was coming out and hinting at a beautiful day. The birds already singing. She was buzzing with life and energy, whipping open the blinds to let the early light beam in.

Rob staggered through moments later, eyes half shut and rubbing them childishly. His naked torso looking tanned and firm with jeans lazily pulled on, the waist still unbuttoned. The scattering of hair across his chest and snaking down below the denim like an invite. His normally cropped and styled hair looking a tad bed ruffled and sexy along with morning stubble.

'If this is a wake-up call to go get your ring then I'm not going anywhere until I've had coffee.' He groaned huskily, almost staggering to the kitchen table.

She spun around, planting a kiss on his mouth in passing as she headed to the fridge and ran a hand across his abdomen, making him flinch as it tickled. She laughed lightly, aware of how boyish and fragile he seemed today.

'Nope. I just woke up wide awake and happy. Wonder why?' She giggled merrily.

'It has to be a woman thing.' He groaned, grinning her way and reaching for the nearby chair, sliding in before planting his arms and face on the table. 'What time even is it?'

She watched him stifle a yawn with his fist and ruffled his black hair on passing, back to the counter. Her mood infectious.

'It's six am.' The kettle clicked, drawing her focus back to her task.

'Jesus Rose!' Another yawn. 'You realise I've had about four hours sleep if even that.' She had to admit he did look utterly exhausted.

'Go back to bed then, I didn't tell you to get up.' She smiled while pouring the water into the mugs.

'You're going to be the death of me, woman! I doubt I'll get much sleep with you Snow Whiting it around the kitchen.' He sounded grumpy but he was watching her with a smile on that gorgeous face and resting his chin in the crook of his elbow.

'Snow what'ing it?' She frowned and slid a mug in front of him.

'You're seconds away from dancing in the flower beds and talking to birds. Your mum was onto something when she called you a princess.' He sat up wearily and gratefully took a gulp of the hot liquid, grimacing and laying his head back down.

'Maybe I have something I'm happy about... You, on the other hand, are a bit lack lustre darling. Having second thoughts?' She was only half teasing as she moved to him, mock pinching at his cheek.

'Never! But... I may have to tie you down and gag you if you're going to continue waking at dawn to sing at the rising sun.' He reached out, pulling her into his lap playfully as he sat up. 'Give me time to wake up. I'll show you how happy I am... Again!'

'I'm serious. Go back to bed. You look shattered' She kissed him lightly but he shook his head and took another gulp of coffee.

'I'm up now anyway. I want that ring on your hand and I have so much to sort out today. It's not a bad thing getting an early start... I also want to go see my dad and Abby. Tell them face to face that they're going to have a new Munro in the family.' He caught her mouth and firmly planted a hard kiss on it, making it clear he was not having second thoughts.

'Abby will start planning the wedding immediately, you know this, right?' Rose breathlessly pulled away. He shrugged.

'Need to start sometime.'

'I think waiting for the ring to hit the finger is usually the order of events.'

'It will be on that finger before normal people start getting out of bed at a normal hour. That much I can promise you.' He stood up, lifting her with him and depositing her on her bare feet. A hand cupping her butt as he slid past. Taking his coffee mug with him through to the lounge and sliding onto the couch. 'We'll go to the house and get it before I do anything else. Sooner it's on your finger the sooner I'll feel like I've done this right. Then we can tell the family together, later.' He stretched out his arm to her as she slid down beside him. Balancing her cup carefully and allowing him to nestle her into him.

'I'm not harassing you to do that Rob.' She smiled up adoringly, so enamoured with him right now it was almost painful.

'I want to see it on your hand. Make it more real.' He pushed his forehead against hers, nudging her gently and smiling.

'It is real.'

'I just want to make it official okay? I almost lost you baby, this matters to me.'

'Okay.' She let him kiss her slowly, lingering together for a moment before breaking apart to smile.

They both turned and watched Muffin as he strolled in lazily, stretching out before making a quizzical yawn sound. Also protesting at the early hour.

'I need to figure out what I'm going to do about Morag too.' He kissed Rose's temple through her hair, a little habit she was starting to notice he did when he mentioned the red head. Like a little gentle assurance for Rose's benefit.

'There's nothing you can do while she's in there Rob; maybe the time to let things sink in and talking to the therapists will help.' She looked up at him wide eyed and hopeful.

'Maybe!'

He kissed her forehead now she was facing him, draining his cup and jumping to his feet, turning to hold out a hand to her.

'Come on Miss infectious. You want a ring on your hand then you better get dressed. I have plans for you in a really large shower cubicle in my room.'

* * *

They snuck into the house, aware of the early hour. Headed down the hall and let themselves into his room quietly; Muffin running off to find his usual space in the cosy room by the kitchen, knowing he had left something tasty under the couch. Rose stood awkwardly by the bed as he walked to the drawer and began moving clothes aside to locate the box she had held in her hand weeks ago. Awed at the fact that back then she had held it and wondered what it would be like to be the girl Rob gave it too, and now here she was.

Finding it easily, he turned to her smiling and slid down on one knee smoothly, A smile on that perfect face and eyes locked on hers, he took her hand and pulled her closer. Cracking open the box to reveal the beautiful sparkling heirloom.

'I love you more than life Rose. I can't imagine a life without you and I don't want too. Marry me.... Make me the happiest guy alive.

I will always love and cherish you, protect you over all others baby. Trust me to make you happy and I swear I will never stop trying too.'

She slid down to her knees, smiling tearfully and nodding. As overwhelmed as the first time he had proposed, she was too overcome to reach out and take it, waiting instead for him to remove it from its velvet cushion and slide it on her hand.

Surprisingly it fit perfectly and shone even more brilliantly against her ivory skin, taking her breath away. The soft silver and sparkling diamonds and pink stone looked as though they had always belonged on her hand. She was in love with it and would cherish it always.

They both stared at the ring now in its place silently. Both aware that this was a huge moment for them. The beginning of a life together.

Promises! A future! Children!...Eternity together.

She cried; not out of any sense of sadness but extreme happiness. Allowing him to pull her up to him, his eyes full of raw emotion.

'To us! For the rest of our lives Rose. It's us against the world.' He cradled her face against his throat.

'To us!' She had agreed, feeling the warmth of his fingers tracing her tears away and knowing this is what she had been looking for her whole life. Rob was everything she needed. Savouring the minutes they sat on the floor and just let it all sink in.

True to his word, it did not take him long to coax her into the shower and have his wicked way with her. One thing she could always count on was his never ending high libido, his insatiable need to have her naked and pressed under him in at every opportunity. And today he was in more high spirits and good form.

They ended up back in bed, despite his intentions to get an early start, the shower session bringing out a need in them both to sleep some more; wrapped up in naked cosiness. He woke and left her asleep, leaving her a note that he had gone to see his father and had work related errands to do. She was dead to the world, unaware of his kissing her face and gently stroking her hair before he left.

Rose finally stirred mid-morning, read his note and ventured into the kitchen in search of coffee and toast; Alice warmly greeted her in passing, informing her Abby had left for the day too. She had college this morning. The close of the term was fast approaching for Abby and soon would be done for good.

The large empty kitchen and bare tile floors were a welcome sight; glad to be alone once more. She loved the old-fashioned country units, homely aged room and thick pine central island. The large brick fireplace still off at one end with the original hooks, metal oven and bars from when this big old house had used it as the main cooking stove. She loved the cream ceramic containers, holding baking powders and spices that brought such gorgeous smells under the experienced hands of the delightful housekeeper.

She loved Alice to death, but this morning found her feeling unwilling to engage in small talk. She had kept her hands by her side, not drawing attention to her new precious addition. Feeling funny about telling her before he did; about telling anyone before Abby or her parents knew.

It wasn't something you casually announced over the phone or in passing, not for her anyway. She wanted him beside her when they told the people that mattered. Cradling her cup and lost in thought, unaware of her surroundings. The memories of last night niggling at her, pulling her in two directions.

Happiness and complete euphoria, then dread and unease at the unresolved.

She knew she shouldn't let it stain her happy mood. He would take care of it. He always took care of everything. It was what he did... But this time was different. She tried to push down the building tension into the pit of her stomach and shake it away.

Maybe it was the admission that in the past he had let relationships end so as to avoid any unnecessary drama. Appease Morag and keep her happy. Maybe it was that despite everything all these years, Morag had remained constant when everyone else had been left on the sidelines of his life. Or maybe it was just the fear of how Morag would react when she found out Rose was the future Mrs Munro and wearing a ring that Morag had never been allowed.

* * *

Back at the cottage an hour later, only half emerged in her work; checking her phone absently and wondering how his day was going; she knew he had a busy day so did not expect him to call or text her randomly until he had got through his to do list. He rarely did when he was at work, knowing how much of an easy distraction she was. How easy it was to drop everything for the lure of her body against his. He also knew she would be lost in her own work, deadlines to meet.

Today she was feeling fragile. Her emotions on edge and aware that this neediness and insecurity was out of character. Especially after he had proposed to her. She could not get any more of a reason to feel secure than a man asking you to share his life for an eternity and proclaim undying love.

Muffin, who normally left her alone and opted for the fireside rug, was curled round her feet indicating he too could sense her tension.

What was wrong with her? This should be the happiest day of her life!

Instead, it was clouded with an overwhelming nervousness, feeling on edge and unable to formulate a reason. She knew it wasn't the engagement, she had no doubts. She loved him more than enough and she was ecstatic. She wanted nothing more in the world than to be his for an eternity. To have a life with him and a future with children and a real home together.

But it was un-hide able and final!

Not merely a blossoming romance anymore, a real bound together for life kind of symbol. One that everyone would know about soon enough. Words spreading like wildfire in this county. The seriousness of his intentions would make its way to that curly red head in no time and that was the route of her anxiety.

Having her know that he had been sleeping with someone was one thing; dating someone. But having her know he had asked Rose to marry him was a whole different ball park. She wasn't a minor threat or accused affair anymore. She was the person destroying all Morag's hopes and illusions. A real threat not to be taken lightly or passed off as a whore. Someone to be despised. Someone to be blamed for the loss of any hope of a future between them.

The mood followed her, ever present, causing her jitters and making her hands clumsy and uncoordinated. Dropping her pens and brushes so many times, even knocking her water jar at one point soaking a piece she had barely started and cursing out loud. Burying her face in her hands for the umpteenth time that day, she just wanted it to be over, back in bed, surrounded by him, to start again. She was a nervous wreck and knew deep down it was the real reason she had not wanted Alice to see her ring. To congratulate her and dance with joy at the news, which she knew she would have. Alice had made it clear so many times over the last weeks that she was in full support of Rose and Rob as a couple.

Walking Muffin for the fifth time that day had offered no comfort and she sighed with both relief and dread as she caught sight of Abby walking down the gravel road towards her. Dressed in black jeans, a floaty top and heavy cardigan with her silky black hair in a messy ponytail. Dragging a large portfolio folder in one hand and steadying her shoulder bag with the other. The girl flashed her a huge smile and closed the gap between them.

'Afternoon lovely!' it felt like an age since they had been alone.

'Hey, Ab's.' Genuine happiness at her appearance. That immediate flow of warm affection.

'No Rob lurking in the background then?'

Rose smiled at the cheekiness in her childlike tone and twinkling eyes, looking up in mock surprise as Abby gently sucker punched her.

'No Duncan hiding in the bushes?' She jibed back, pushing her shoulder playfully.

'Touché!'

They both laughed and hugged briefly before stepping apart. Pulling back to look at one another, Abby halted, her face instantly dropping, a strange look of calculation followed by realisation as she reached again for Rose's hand and grabbed it to her eye level.

'Oh my god!' The straight face suddenly illuminated with undeniable joy. 'When?'

Rose laughed, glad to have had the task of announcing taken away from her, out of her control. No longer having to ponder or decide about what to do.

'Last night.' She couldn't help but beam and admire the sparkling beauty nestled delicately on her hand.

'I need details!' Abby hauled Rose into another stronger hug and danced her around in a circle affectionately. Her hyper-ness infectious.

'I'm pretty sure you don't want the details Ab's! But there's a PG version for innocent ears.' She laughed out loud, instantly breathless from Abby's shenanigans.

'You hussy!' Abby giggled, leading her by the hand towards the door. Scooping for a second to ruffle Muffins fluffy head.

'I'm sorry Ab's but I can't help myself. It's those Munro genes, they're irresistible to me.' She jested

'I guess that's why he was texting me this morning, asking if he could take me to college!' She reflected. 'I was already on the bus. He said he'd see me tonight!'

'Sorry!' Rose looked remorseful, wondering if he had wanted to see Abby's reaction first hand

'Oh shoosh. I'm glad I found out this way. Means I can torture him later, acting dumb and drag it out. Like to see him tongue-tied and awkward when it comes to talking about his feelings pah!'

'Really? I've never seen him that way.' Rose grinned, disbelief on her pretty features.

'You're not his baby sister, whom he assumes is an innocent child minded, air head. He still acts like I should be in nappies. He also doesn't like to appear anything but strong and capable in front of me! None of that gushy love chat!' Abby rolled her eyes and immediately looked as young as she claimed she wasn't.

Rose smiled to herself, never thinking he had different faces for different people. Realising with Abby he had taken over the role of protector and father figure when their lives had fallen apart and their own father had recoiled in his own sadness. It made sense. With her, he was never afraid to tell her how he felt. Well, most of the time.

'Does my dad know?' Abby blinked up at her, pushing her bags onto the couch and kicking off her shoes.

'I think so. He got up this morning to see him before leaving for work so I'm assuming he would have told him then.' Although she thought back to Rob's 'we will tell the family later' comment this morning.

'He will be happy. He's been rooting for you from day one apparently. He told me that Rob pretty much ended up there on a daily basis when you broke up. They have always had that male closeness thing. Turns to him when he's got crap going on. Too alike!' Abby threw herself on the couch and sprawled out.

'Well that makes two of you then.' Rose winked and tried to haul Abby back to her feet by the arm. 'Come eat with me.'

* * *

The girls sat at the kitchen table eating the remains of their sandwiches and sipping tea. Abby had immediately gone into excited 'Maid of honour' mode. Pulling out a pad and pens and trying to engage Rose in making a to do list.

Rose had declined at first, trying to tell her that her own family did not even know yet, but it was pointless. Her enthusiasm and flow of beautiful ideas and vision drawing Rose in. She had told her to take creative control if she was that impatient, that Rose and Rob would happily look over her ideas together. An excuse to not get caught up in table runners and floral arrangements via Google on Abby's phone.

'Oh, you would look beautiful in a vintage lace wedding dress Rose. You're so effortlessly romantic looking, I think it would suit you.'

'Ummm, thanks.' She wasn't sure what that meant, but laughed, feeling lighter than she had all day. Letting herself relax into the fact that this was actually real and enjoying it briefly when surrounded by the infectiousness that was Abby's way.

Abby hauled out her tablet from her bag. Anxious for a bigger screen than her mobile afforded and began scrolling google for bridal websites and examples of elegant dresses. Rose had been right about one thing. Abby would have this wedding planned before the week ended.

Feeling that familiar flutter of dread, she got up to shake it free, pulling some cookies from the bread bin and sliding them on the table. Abby was engrossed on Pinterest, already creating her 'inspiration board' of fabulous garden weddings and rustic centre pieces. Chatter bubbling forth of how amazing a wedding marquee would look on the south lawn behind the house. Rose smiled watching her. Wishing she could feel the same enthusiasm and dive right in, helping choose out the biggest day of her life. Yet all she could think about was Morag.

Her tumbling fiery red wild hair. Her darkening green eyes and smooth creamy freckle-spattered face. Like a looming serpent in her mind's eye, devouring her in one easy strike. A growing presence, reaching up over her and shadowing everything else out of her mind like a thick black toxic smoke.

She knew one thing for sure… There had to be some sort of climax to come from all this build up and it only made her feel weak at the knees, shivers and goose bumps running uneasily up her spine. Her chest heavy with the foreboding and anticipation.

Chapter 33

Rose stayed at the cottage when Abby left later that day, Rose told her she needed to work on more sketches but the truth was she needed alone time to try and get this overwhelming funk out of her system.

Rob had called late in the day, apologising to her for not calling, work had intervened, mucked up his plans, had kept him glued to the phone most of the day and he had to head into Inverness for an unplanned meeting with his solicitor and then onto his office in the city and the drive was long and laborious.

He wouldn't be back till extremely late and he told her not to wait up for him, apologising profusely for being so lame on the official first day of their engagement and making her giggle.

Disappointed and listless when she hung up. She hated feeling so out of whack. She had been holding her breath, waiting for his appearance to make her feel better. Today had dragged endlessly and been emotionally draining too.

Rose took a long soak in the tub, ordered take away for dinner and put on a smoochy movie before bed to relax her a little, but her ever rambling brain had stayed with her. That feeling of dread in the back of her mind. It seemed to be making its new home in there and she longed to go back to yesterday when it hadn't eaten so deeply at her.

Rob awakened her in the dark that night, that familiar hot body reaching for her smooth skin and soft curves. Bringing her to a surge of moans and tidal waves expertly before long as way of a hello and a sorry for being absent all day. Their bodies arching together and crashing down in a satisfied groan; she clung to him, the tears pricking her eyes at the perfection of it. Like some sort of dream in the darkness that she never wanted to wake from. He knew how to touch her, how to bring her to the heights of ecstasy so easily, as though she had been made for his touch alone. He knew instinctively how to make her forget everything for a while with the briefest motions, but it never lasted. Her mind would soon let the fears and doubts creep back in, once her waves subsided and the tingles dulled.

Rob was equally quiet afterwards; pensive in his mood, holding her gently and brushing her face with kisses before pulling her into an easy cuddle so that they could fall asleep. Her head resting on his strong chest and it wasn't long before they were both asleep.

He had again risen and left early, leaving her to sleep once more. The briefest kiss and murmur in her ear that he had to go as she hazily tried to focus on his face. It felt like a dream. When she finally woke fully, the absence of his body in her bed had her wondering if it had all been a dream.

Had she gone to sleep alone? Dreamed of his presence and woken up alone again? Had it all been wishful thinking?

The single baby pink rose laid across his dented pillow beside her, told her otherwise. She couldn't help the smile that broke across her face. Sitting up she could see the vase with the remaining roses displayed on her vanity. A single white envelope leaning against the frosted glass stem. The name 'Penelope' scrawled across in his bold neat handwriting.

Sliding from the sheets quickly, she almost leapt to reach the smooth white envelope, pulling it open carelessly. It was a glossy leaflet of a French cottage set in sunny surroundings and heavy fruit trees. A yellow post-it note on the front with his familiar script.

'Fancy a weekend away?'

Rose pulled open the folded brochure, glancing at the stunning countryside and beautiful house, french décor, with its own outdoor hot tub. Her heart lifting and a smile spreading over her face, letting the excitement drown out the dread to be replaced with happiness. Of course, she knew he would have seen that hot tub and had ideas of christening it. Overcome with elation, Rose scrambled to the bedside and reached for her mobile phone.

'Hiya baby.' His voice like a warm wave running over her, he always sounded even more sexy on the phone.

'A strange man crept into my dreams, made love to me and turned into a bunch of pink roses.' She giggled merrily down the phone. Rob laughed, that husky deep male tone that almost always made her toes curl.

'Asshole. A real man would have hung around for you to wake up.' He laughed again softly. 'Did you get my note? Sorry I couldn't wait, I'm currently sat in the waiting room of an investors office, before a meeting that will no doubt give me brain ache.' He sighed, his assistants voice in the background talking to someone else, shrill and efficient and seemed to distract him for a second.

'It's okay. I understand that your job takes you away a lot, I'm getting used to it. This villa looks beautiful and definitely something I want to do.' She closed her eyes to bring his face to her mind's eye, aching for him a little more than normal this morning.

'It's a combo of work and pleasure, I need to go there to check on construction and figured you might want to come, the villa is part of the vineyard and a perk of investing. The hot tub looks mighty fine… Spacious.' That suggestive tone had her imagining a naughty look in his eye and she beamed even brighter.

'I knew that would be your first thought… Sex in the tub. You're terrible but I love you.'

'I'm male, we really do think about sex like every five seconds. More so since I met you.'

'Hmmmm, well I suppose I don't mind if naughty weekends away in gorgeous villas are the result.' Rose rolled onto her side in bed, holding the phone close and running her fingers over the rose on the pillow, she could hear the voice of his prim assistant calling out his name efficiently in the background.

'Baby I need to go, meetings about to start. I'll see you tonight. I love you!' He rushed it out as though he was clambering up and getting his self together, Rose sighed feeling that same deflation at not seeing him properly.

'I'll be at the cottage. I love you too.' With that she hung up and sighed heavily, pushing the rose around and trying once again to get this horrible feeling out of the pit of her stomach.

* * *

When he came home later that day, he stopped at the cottage, his unbuttoned shirt and loose tie giving him an air of magazine model. He had dark grey tailored trousers on over smart expensive black shoes but he had pulled his shirt loose at the waist messily. Dropping his jacket over the couch.

He casually meandered into the room where she was attempting to put the finishing details to a little forest scene. The illustrations were similar in concept to her last in that it was a woodland set fairy-tale book but instead of gnomes and cute shaggy wildlife, it was all floral fairies and pixies, insects and small furry rodents. He leant down, kissing the back of her exposed neck, her hair piled messily on top of her head to keep it out of her way, admiring her work. She stopped, arching back and raising her face to meet his for a mouth to mouth kiss, savouring the way he always made her feel so desirable with the briefest of touches.

'I had a call today! Let's talk about it through in the other room.' He looked at her warily, she could already sense the tension in his voice, he pulled her lazily from her chair and led her to the lounge. His calm manner and fluid movements easily guiding her onto the seat with him. Kicking off his shoes as she loosened his smooth tie fully and pulled it from around his neck, discarding it on the nearest table neatly. He sighed pulling her in for a slow long kiss, his hands moving up around her neck and jawline gently before breaking away, holding her captive, his fingers tracing her lips. His head cushioned in the padded couch his eyes fixed on their progress.

'Your call?' She breathed softly. Mesmerised by the erotic hypnotics of the movement and trying to push away the niggles, she stilled as he took a deep meaningful breath, letting it out slowly

'Morag is being released!' He frowned at her, pausing all movement.

She felt her face drop before she could counteract the reaction but his hand smoothing over her frown told her it was okay. He felt the same way.

'What now?' She sounded childlike, his face closed a little, his eyes far away and dark. Tensing his jaw as he thought about it and shrugged, unable to really formulate the right response.

'I make sure she understands how things are now. What you are to me. That things are different and I won't be so readily available to shoulder her woes and meltdowns anymore.' Rob pulled her closer on top of him so she laid out, moulding his body and nestling her face against his chest. 'I told you that it would be different, it will be.'

Rose sat motionless and silent. Numb and unsure how to calm the sea of thoughts washing over her like a tidal wave. Somehow knowing that Morag had been under lock and key, unable to come out. Overseen by professionals and people taking care of her. It had given her peace of mind. Breathing space to carry on unchecked. Affording them to feel like they could carry on unaffected, lost in the fantasy of it. She had known that eventually this would come up and he would have to deal with the fallout at some point, but now it was finally here and Rose wasn't ready. He broke the silence and her train of thoughts.

'Tell me what you want me to do?' He was looking deep into her eyes. 'How I should play this?' He really had no clue anymore. He was looking for insight. Knowing that his way of dealing with it so far had only made things worse.

'I don't know Rob. I don't know her. I don't know how to deal with her or understand how to even start dealing with her.' She bit her lip thoughtfully, holding in the urge to cry. 'You need to speak to her again. Try once more. Maybe now she's back on her medication it will be easier. Calmer?' She lifted her chin so she could appraise his face, her heart thundering through her chest and her skin prickling with anxiety.

'I need to tell her about this before anyone else does too.' Rob scooped up her hand, turning her ring in his fingers slowly; his eyes a dark cloudy grey. Pulling her fingers to his mouth to brush against his lips, they both jumped as his phone shrilled out painfully, vibrating beside them on the table.

'Jesus. Abby!' He glanced at the screen. 'Talk about timing!' Sliding up from him so he could answer the phone Rose moved to the kitchen to fill the kettle and give him a minute. She needed a moment herself to think about things. Her head a whirlwind as she tried to formulate some kind of plan of action. Coming up empty.

She knew he had to be delicate, gentle, and maybe that's what this needed. Time and careful handling. An understanding that this woman was not some evil monster, but a broken and sad person, with real problems. Real trauma in her past and no one else to turn too. Maybe by ignoring that all this time had somehow made it worse for the other woman. No more pandering, but yet, a little more understanding and empathy involved in explaining that he was with Rose now. Maybe for a while, they could go back to staying out of sight, not rubbing it in the woman's face. Let her get used to the new order of things for a while before they started venturing out publicly again.

She heard the tone of his voice change and the obvious volume rise brought her attention up. Standing still. A prickle running up her spine as she listened intently. He seemed agitated with his sister, the noise of him getting off the couch and pacing around as he continued to talk.

The kettle clicked, drawing her attention and forcing her to concentrate on making the two steaming mugs of coffee. Trying to find a task and give him space, she rummaged the fridge finding cooked chicken, leftover salad, pasta and coleslaw and began to plate up instead. He rarely got angry with Abby but when he did it was best to give them a wide berth to bang it out between them.

He appeared at the door as she slid everything on the table moments later. That dark look and stormy eyes indicating he was not happy; he threw his phone on the table absently, sending it skimming between the plates and came to rest on the back of one of the chairs. Flexing his upper arms and hunching his strong shoulders moodily

'That god damn girl!' He was more than angry. The darkness of his eyes almost sinister.

'What's she done?' She coaxed gently, uptight at his severe mood change, continuing to set the plates, mugs and cutlery out before them. Trying to still her thumping heart, her gut giving her warnings.

'What have THEY done more like!' He pulled out the chair, sliding in and resting his elbows on the table, his hands coming to his temples and sighing dramatically.

'Okay, what have THEY done?' She asked again, stopping to lean on the chair and look at him fully.

'They decided we should have an engagement party… a surprise! Family and close friends, right?' He picked up his phone and began picking at a corner of his case in agitation.

'Right?' She wasn't sure why that was that much of a huge deal apart from the fact she still had not worked out the details of telling her own family, and his had sort of found out thanks to Abby.

'Wrong! The town bugle got wind somehow. Little old women and their insane need to gossip and pretty soon like wildfire the whole town is chipping in, inviting the entire north of Scotland. Abby realising what a fucking idiotic thing it was decided to fess up.' He dropped his phone and dragged over his mug of coffee, using it to cradle his hands around something as though envisioning his sister's neck. 'It's turned into this huge elaborate party, much like the one we're still recovering from. I'm still finding stray party poppers and plastic cups around the manor.' His voice was still husky, irate and deep.

'You're worried Morag will get wind and take this much worse?' Rose soothed, starting to piece together how awful this would be for her to find out this way.

'I'm not worried she finds out! I know for a fact she will. I'm the Laird and this is a small country town baby… I'm big news and that makes you and I newsworthy. Every local rag and radio will be practically headlining it. Makes a change from wool prices and oil rig strikes.'

Rose sat down slowly, letting it all sink in.

'Oh god.' Was all she could say as she thought about how cruel it would be to hear the man you were crazy for was getting married over a radio show.

'It's not that I don't want her to know. It's the way she finds out that matters. I owe her at least that much! I've been the only constant friend in her life since we were kids and to let her find out via the grapevine or media would be the shittest thing to do to her.' He was visibly frustrated, tension oozing from every pore. Rose couldn't agree more.

'What are you going to do?'

'I'm going to have to be the one to bring her home from the hospital, before this goes public.' He was angrily tapping his fingers now on the handle of the cup, trying to form some sort of strategy in his mind. 'I'll just have to tell her. Deal with the outburst once I get her home. Hope that it's not as bad as I suspect it's going to be.' He cursed Abby again. 'My father has been just as bad! He's been dishing out the cheques and making calls, arranging the whole damn thing. He knows what we're dealing with; It's like he's trying to force my hand where Morag's concerned.' He sighed again, letting go of his mug to again cradle his temples.

Rose was speechless, trying to find comforting words and wisdom, watching him wrestle with his own thoughts and anger before her. He picked up his mug and drank a large mouthful. His face calming as he pulled back inwards, the return of blank-faced control that signalled Rob going into all business mode.

Pulling his plate towards him he attempted to eat and pushed it back away moments later, apologising softly. Rose shrugged, smiling understandably. Reaching out to take his hands and watching him carefully; he gripped her fingers gently before getting up and leaving the room.

His manner was making her uneasy, a feeling rising inside her, instinct telling her she would be spending the evening alone. He returned a few minutes later confirming her fears. Shoes back on. Shirt rolled up at the sleeves and tucked in.

'I'm sorry baby. I need to go stop my dad form making this any worse. Give Abby hell and call the hospital for release details. I need some time to think things through and calm down. I don't want to inflict this mood on you.' He scooped his phone from the table.

She nodded numbly, unable to meet his eyes, pushing her food around the plate absently. Apologising again, he came around the table kissing her on top of the head.

'I'll stay at the manor tonight and get some work done after I've dealt with this shit. I'll text you.'

Rose made a face of protest but he seemed to avoid recognition. Turning to pick up Muffin and lavish quick affection on him before sending him on his way again. She wanted to cry.

Rob was doing what he did best; closing ranks, shutting her out and taking control of something messy. Abby had told her a million times that it's how he had dealt with their mother's death, how he dealt with anything that he felt responsible for and now here she was at the receiving end and she wanted to shake him.

She heard the door of the cottage close softly, moments later, and her heart deflated hugely. Trying not to be angry at him but unable to push the heartache and disappointment away. She knew that she had nothing to feel insecure about, he had proven that to her a hundred times over already, but closing her out over this stupid woman was not exactly helping her mental state right now.

The way he was being over the other woman finding out, although frustrating was also something she understood. It's who he was. Carer. Protector. Shoulder to lean on. He wasn't an asshole who just hurt those he cared about. He was someone who stood up and took control when everything was falling apart, someone who tried to smooth it over and hold it all together. The way he had done when his mother had passed; everyone looked up to him, relied on him. People in town came to him for advice and help endlessly and greeted him like a celebrity or a film star. It was because he was a good person, always finding the time to really listen to them and help in any way he could. He had an aura of control and wisdom that he could make everything better. Honest and never motivated by anything other than genuine care.

He had been in that woman's life for half of his own; once teen lovers. He had stood by her when her world had crumbled, loved her once, as much as that pained Rose to admit. Her own mother passing away early on, leaving her alone and defenceless and he had held her hand in the agonising court case against her abusive father, been the only constant when she had broken down; destroyed by the events of her own life. He hadn't turned his back on her after her lies and attempted suicide. He had pushed his own anger and hurt aside and been that strength for her once again. Patient and steady no matter how much she had acted out and fallen apart.

She knew this wasn't easy for him; he would be intentionally looking her in the face and destroying what was left of her heart with what he had to say. Someone who he had sheltered and protected endlessly and it went against every one of his instincts to be the reason she may never recover. She understood his need for some head space. It was an almighty labyrinth of complication, overwhelming him but it didn't make Rose feel any better, despite knowing all of that.

Rob didn't call or text that evening, and he didn't crawl into her bed in the night as Rose had hoped. Sleeping with the door unlocked in the off chance he would appear. She had left him alone, unsure how to navigate this, even though she felt like she knew him in ways no one else did, the reality was that they still had so much to learn about each other. Parts of their personalities and lives, they had only grazed the surface of. She had never seen him this way except when she had exited his life, didn't know how to comfort him or make him talk about what he was thinking. He was so used to dealing with things alone. The eternal strong rock everyone turned to and letting her help him was not something he was used too.

The reality that they had only known one another a few short months and this whirlwind that had taken over her life, was less time than most people spent on first dates and casual fooling around, still trying to figure out if they even liked who they were seeing. Somehow, they had bypassed all of it, going straight in for the kill; both knowing from the first moments that this was different.

She wouldn't change it though. She wouldn't have him any other way, didn't need to take things slow and waste time playing games and acting cool. It seemed he had been on the same page and when you found something that earth shattering it only made sense to dive right in.

* * *

He texted her the next morning as she was climbing into the bath, informing her that he would be gone most of the day and had to be at the hospital in the late afternoon to be there for Morag's release. Apologised for not texting last night, he had been caught up with work.

Rose didn't respond, a lump in her throat at his tone, something distant and impersonal in his text, she wavered over the call button but something held her back. Knowing that he would have called if he had wanted to talk, suddenly unsure how to read him. Trying not to be that desperate clingy woman who needed constant reassurance.

There was no mention of how it had gone with his father. If he had seen Abby. No conversation, just bare facts and plans and nothing personal. She was trying not to feel hurt by it, but it was taking all her willpower.

After a morning of no more calls or texts, she took herself out of town to try and ignore things for a while, ignore that he was pretty much blanking her out while he dealt with Morag. It was an hour's drive to a huge shopping complex filled with designer outlets and fashion boutiques but she needed the distraction. Abby also appeared to be avoiding her, texts this morning unanswered, no doubt afraid of some sort of backlash or upset and she hadn't the energy to really chit chat today. Lost in her own problems.

Her mother had left her several voicemails over the last few days and she hadn't returned any. She wanted to tell them so badly, but she knew the lingering Morag problem would be her first question and she had no definite updates.

Why was it never straightforward? Had she been a truly awful child and now karma was getting its own back on her?

She couldn't help herself but check her phone quickly every time she opened her bag to retrieve her purse or replace it. He had never gone this long without some sort of affectionate text. it just felt so out of character as though he was miles away. It felt like they were fighting even though nothing had happened between them and she knew that he was just behaving in the only way he knew. Closing everyone out emotionally until he got a better handle on things.

Abby had previously told her this, a million times, but being in the midst of it first hand was blotting out any rational thought. Aware how easily one person could alter your entire mood, she tried not to think about him, but that was like willing your heart to stop beating for a moment.

Rose threw handful of bags in her car, after splashing out on dresses and shoes. She was a woman who shopped when she was stressed, it was the only kind of therapy that actually helped. She had eaten lunch at a small cafe and even browsed the art store, stocking up on some inks and supplies.

Finally, seeing her mother's name flashing on the phone for the third time that day she gave in and answered, trying to mask the weird tone in her voice with a bright smile.

'Hello stranger, we've been trying to reach you for days. Is everything okay?' Her mum sounded worried and it only made Rose feel even more guilty and uptight than she was already.

'Sorry mum, things have been hectic. Work; fitting in Rob, and things I just had to do.' She hated lying to her, but sometimes it was a necessity.

'You sound tired darling, stressed. Are you sure everything is okay? You and Rob are okay, right?' Her mother hadn't been fooled, sensing the turmoil in her fake happy tone.

'No, we're fine. Better than fine. I'm just having one of those days, honest. I'm out shopping and it's made me tired. Walked around too many shops.' Rose was torn, whether to tell her mother over the phone or do what she intended and video call them with Rob by her side. She bit her lip, in complete turmoil and tempted to just tell them.

'Better than fine? That sounds a little interesting.'

Her mum cut into her train of thoughts and it just slipped out, completely of its own accord and completely shocked Rose.

'He asked me to marry him!'

Rose inhaled sharply, trying to figure out what the hell had made her blurt it out like that. Smiling, she had to pull the phone away from her ear as her mother screeched in happiness. She could picture her rushing to her father's side, she could hear her loudly repeating it to him with all the excitement of a child going to Disneyland.

'Please tell me you said YES!' Her mother squawked down the line and Rose burst into giggles.

'What do YOU think?' She shook her head and once again her mother went off on another little happy squealing run around her livingroom. She could always count on her mother to raise her mood anyway. Even when, right now, her fiancée was doing a great job at making her feel left out in the cold.

'Does this mean the situation with that girl is finally sorted out?'

Her mother very successfully burst her little glowing bubble in one sentence; Rose sighed and looked towards the roof of her car interior.

'It's getting there, she gets out of the hospital in a couple of days.' This time she did manage to hide the emotion from her tone and surprised even herself with how normal and upbeat she had sounded.

'Well, I guess that's good, right? I hope you can all just move on with this, you're all adults after all.' Rose bit her lip to quell a response, not liking the reprimanding edge to her mother's voice. Last thing Rose needed right now was any sort of row with her mother over how Rob had handled things so far.

'Right.' She finally ground out. 'Look Mum I need to run, I have to get back to the village for Abby, so I need to be off.' Rose was sickly sweet, fluttering her lashes even though her mother couldn't see them.

'Oh, Okay darling. We will call you later. We have plans to start.... A wedding to look forward too.' She was back to sheer happiness and bliss and Rose finally said goodbyes with a little more warmth.

Chapter 34

Rose carried on with her shopping and meandering in town, making the most of the long drive here and not really wanting to go back to the cottage to stare at the clock and obsess over Rob's absence.

He called late afternoon, her heart lurching and fingers pressed into her palm, willing him to make her feel better as his name flashed on the screen, but he didn't. He was cool and distant on the phone, informing her they needed to rain check their trip. That the french meeting had been delayed and it was for the best, seeing as he had to collect Morag on the day they would have been leaving; tomorrow. He still had some things up in the air with the construction and told her he would probably be late and to not expect him, he would stay at the manor, collect Morag in the morning and be flying out early afternoon for Glasgow. He would call to let her know how it went with Morag and be back late Saturday, or early Sunday and would come by the cottage on Sunday when he got back.

She felt the anger rising as he spoke. He was not going to come near her for at least three whole days. No affection in his tone; No, 'I love you' or 'sorry'. Just all business. Cool calm and unreadable, pushing her out still and not even realising how much of an asshole he was being.

Sensing her tone change and her cool response to him, he got irritated; a crack in the mask, but instead of remorse it only seemed to make him push her further away.

'Sure, whatever. I'll patiently wait at the cottage like a good little puppy.' She snapped angrily, her mood completely nose diving.

'You know it's not like that. I have to work, I have shit that I have to deal with.' He snapped right back, bruising her already fragile heart.

'Really? What overnight too, as it pretty much feels like you're avoiding me right now.'

'I wasn't aware we had to be glued together. You're being needy and ridiculous Rose. I need to go, I have a client waiting.'

His words stung, Rose lifted her chin defiantly and snapped.

'You know what... Fucking go. Do whatever the hell you need to do.' She wasn't normally one to swear but then normally Rob wasn't like this and making her feel slightly hysterical. She hung up on him dramatically and threw her phone in her open bag aggressively.

Rose fought back the tears, aware she was sitting in public at a coffee shop table. People around her glancing her way, obviously catching snippets of the one-sided conversation. She did not care how wild-eyed and upset she looked. She did not care that people were staring.

She composed an angry text and failed to send, losing courage and instead stalking to her car to cry. She knew from his brief conversation he was home at the manor to get changed and collect some papers. She was almost home, she had only stopped in to kill time and get a coffee. She could be there in ten minutes or less; confront him face to face and fix this. Face this. Have it out!

He couldn't just leave it like this and go out of town.

How could he go from obsessively wanting her every second to not seeing her in days?

She drove manically, her eyes blurry with tears and panic, wanting to get there before he left. She had no idea what she would say but she was drowning and clutching on for dear life. A huge sense of injustice building inside of her at his behaviour.

She had barely parked her car, leaving it half abandoned behind his, absentmindedly blocking it in in case he left before she caught him and practically ran up the main stair, bursting in. A faint thought about the irony of acting like Morag crossed her mind, and headed straight for his room.

He was in his office, sliding papers into a folder and picking up his phone. Wearing a smooth tailored navy suit and looking all business as usual. Cold and controlled. Seeing her storm in he seemed to instantly bristle and put up a staying hand as though she were nothing more than a misbehaving child.

'Not now Rose. I'm in a rush. I can't deal with some female meltdown right this second.' He didn't even look her in the eye, just carried on gathering his things.

'What the hell Rob? It's not Morag you're dealing with!' She felt her anger taking hold, aching by his manner and words; her emotions all over the place. Her self-control fleeing at his cold annoyed glare, as eyes darkened, trying to brush past her motioning he was late by tapping his watch and sighing loudly.

'I think all women have tendencies towards the dramatic.' He muttered.

'Stop it! Stop treating me like some unimportant crazy woman!' Rose snapped, tears brimming in her eyes and on the verge of complete hysteria, she really had no idea who this version was or why he was being this way.

This wasn't Rob, this wasn't the guy who told her she was his heart.

'I told you on the phone Rose. I can't deal with this right now. Things have gone to shit with the french project. I have been pulled into an emergency meeting by the board of directors in Glasgow; my ass is being dragged over coals for this... I am aware that shit is about to go down when I collect Morag this evening; Abby's having some hormonal tantrum and hiding out at her boyfriend's acting like a twelve-year-old and the phone has been ringing non-stop with local reporters looking for quotes on my happy engagement...I'm currently keeping a distance from my own father after the worst fight I have ever had with him and the last thing I need is for you to turn all crazy irrational and needy when I seriously cannot handle any fucking more.'

He had never shouted at her that way before. Never spoken to her that way. His words stinging her cruelly, his eyes narrowed and dark and anger bristling from him so that she could feel static in the air.

'Don't you dare!' She spat at him, tears blinding her and all logic and reasoning being drowned out by heart ache. 'Don't make me feel like I'm some sort of lunatic making life worse for you. Some emotional bunny boiler!'

'Right now, this whole mess is making everything worse for me. You're only the tip of the iceberg.' He replied coolly, still not meeting her eye.

'You can't just drop me when things get hard. Pushing me out. It's not fair, it's not how a relationship works!' Her voice was getting louder, her grip on rational behaviour slipping.

'I told you I would see you Sunday...How is that pushing you out? We don't need to spend every second together Rose. We're not married YET!' Piercing words. He was talking through gritted teeth trying to control his temper, although it seemed he too was losing that battle.

Who was this guy?

She didn't know this man standing there coldly looking at her like that, talking to her like that, looking at her like she was insane...Like she was some irritation he couldn't deal with, that he would rather be eating glass than having a conversation with her... That she was an unwelcome drama, like a fly buzzing around his face...Like she was Morag!

Rose snapped, pulling his arm as he tried to brush past her and catapulting him to face her with unexpected strength as he was caught off guard.

'Let me make this easier for you then, shall I?' Making a move to pull the ring from her hand he gripped it, covering her fingers. His large hand dwarfing hers with a tension that sent electric fire between them.

'If that comes off, it stays off, Rose! I don't do threats and emotional blackmail just so you can make a point.' His eyes were dark and sinister, a complete battle of wills. Seriousness like she had never seen before.

Wounded and silenced by this stranger before her, heart tearing in two. Rose chucked off his grip erratically, pulling off the ring and throwing it at him dramatically with false bravado. Blinded by rage. It whizzed past his shoulder disappearing into the room behind with a sort of an anti-climactic result. He did not falter or break his glare on her face. Just snarled a little as though he honestly wanted to tell her to go to hell.

'Screw you!' Rose blurted out with tears streaming down her face, she shoved him aside as hard as she could. Spitting back over her shoulder as she flew to the door that he no longer needed to break his precious Morag's heart over a wedding that was never going to happen. Another woman left on the side-lines he could forget about. That she had obviously never been worth the hassle.

He didn't follow.

* * *

She barely saw the road ahead. Barely functioning, yet still managing to swing her car into the cottage car park. She was livid and heartbroken all at the same time. Crying as though in extreme pain. Her hand throbbing where she had violently dragged the snug ring off.

Looking down at her trembling hands and the red marks she had left along her finger. Everything was bubbling up and pouring out all at once; all the tension and drama and anxiety of the last weeks. All the insecure doubts and niggling worries. They had been a melting pot of molten lava exploding all over her life and coming out in that room with him.

She was no better than Morag. What made her any different?

Some irrational needy woman, losing her shit over a couple of days apart. She knew it was about more than that. Knew it had been eating inside of her dangerously, just waiting to pop its cork and had come out in a massive blow. Months of turmoil eating away and she regretted it; she had overreacted and lost the plot and acted like a complete fool. She looked at her naked hand again and felt a new wave of tears come down her face.

What had she done?

She replayed his words over and over, 'If that comes off it stays off'

Did he mean it? was it over?

She knew it had been a knee-jerk reaction and she hadn't meant it. She just wanted to show him how hurt she was, how angry. It had been stupid. She knew though how stubborn he was and he didn't make threats, not even in the heat of the moment. They had only fought that way once before and he had come after her immediately.

He had not come after her this time. There was no sign of him.

Her phone remained silent in the bag beside her. She sat contemplating going back but knowing it would be pointless; he would be gone. He made it clear he was going, regardless of how she behaved; she felt ashamed but also justified. He had made her feel this way; normally attentive and welcoming, he had just cut her off, pushed her out in the cold and made her feel desperate and manic. She wanted to go back to this morning and start her day again but she knew she couldn't.

She didn't leave the cottage again for the rest of the day and he didn't call or appear. By evening she called Abby, barely able to conceal her tears and emotion on the phone. Abby cried too, blaming herself and the added pressure they had caused her brother.

She hadn't seen him either. Hadn't spoken to him, had been avoiding him after a massive row at the house and staying with Duncan. He had told her to butt out of his life. He had been livid with both her and her father and it had ended badly.

'He's been under a lot of pressure lately, so much more than normal. I've heard him on the phone and all the usual clammed up Rob signs are there. His heads in overdrive and he deals with it by closing down and distancing himself from everyone.' Abby explained to a tearful Rose.

'He can't just shut me out that way, I didn't know how to react; so I acted like a mental person.' Rose sighed heavily, toying with the cushion on her lap and stretching her legs out on the couch, nestling the phone into her ear more closely as though she was willing Abby nearer.

'That's the thing babe; Rob has never had to consider a girlfriend when he gets like this.... I mean Morag has never counted and normally she's a huge part of why he's gone into black out mode again. He's just used to dealing with things alone and on his terms, this is all new to him and he probably has no idea how he made you feel.'

'I don't know what to do, how to fix it.' She sighed heavily, Muffin trailing in to paw at the couch beside and whine to get up. She leaned down, scooping him onto her lap and stroked him absentmindedly.

'Honestly... When he's like this we just leave him alone. He comes out of it a lot quicker and happier that way.' Abby sighed too.

'The thing is.... I threw his ring at him and pretty much told him I didn't want to marry him, so I can hardly leave it alone.' Rose felt the tears brimming up again as she said it allowed for the second time. Her heart aching badly with regret.

'He's dealt with the crazy that is Morag for fifteen years, I'm sure you're a picnic compared to her. Give him breathing space; I don't doubt that he loves you babe, a lot more than you realise, and it won't be long before he comes looking to fix this mess.'

'So, I do nothing but wait?' She let her head drop back onto the couch arm and stared at the ceiling wistfully.

'Play it by ear... You know him in ways that I don't. If you feel you should call or text him then do it, or if you want to wait on him making the first move then let him. Rob's hard to predict at the best of times.'

What was simmering behind those steel eyes and sharp mind? How many things he was pushing around to fix and keep control of?

She suspected that he had been bottling up way more than the situation with Morag for a while and maybe it had just overflown with too many balls up in the air for him to handle. Abby had caught glimpses of the stress and strain in passing and figured it had all gotten on top of him. The situation with Morag tipping the normally balanced scale and Rose had just made it monumentally worse.

'I will leave him be to simmer, maybe by the time he comes home he won't be so pissed at my dramatic ring return.' Rose tried a smile and a hint of humour but it fell badly. Her heart wasn't ready to make jokes about her behaviour, as for right now she was pretty sure Rob and her were over… Again.

Abby told her not to worry, sure that when he calmed down he would come running with his tail between his legs, but Rose wasn't so sure. He was angry. Really angry. She had behaved like an insane witch. Throwing his mother's ring at his chest like that. Ending what they had on a whim like it was meaningless.

Why would he want to marry her now?

He was trying to get away from an irrational female holding his life captive and certainly wouldn't be looking to tie himself down to the exact same thing.

Chapter 35

The next two days literally dragged agonisingly by. He didn't try to contact her at all and she knew that he would have collected Morag and settled her at home as he had planned. She wondered what he had said to the other woman. If he had even bothered to keep trying to tell her that he had moved on and needed her to stop.

Did he really need to anymore?

It ate and gnawed away at her, tainting every moment of every hour, unsure what she even was to him now. If in his head, she had ended things for good.

Abby took her to the cinema on Saturday afternoon, to distract her and give them both some much-needed bonding time, seeing as lately they hadn't done much of it. Rob was giving both the cold shoulder it seemed and the girls left him out of conversation.

The film did nothing to lift either of their reflective moods, some romantic chick flick which was annoyingly engagement and drama based and full of family hilarity. Dinner at a cheap fast food place after was strained and they had to admit neither was in the mood to be sociable, both equally distracted by Rob and their own fights with him.

She dropped Abby at home later that night feeling the sinking ache at the absence of his car, the lack of contact. The dark lights of his rooms as she drove around the wide park to turn and leave; it was like he had just ceased to exist in her little world. His lack of presence was like a black hole in her heart consuming any light.

She pulled up his number a hundred times to phone him but could not bring herself to press call. She knew she should be the one to do it, after all, she was the one who had broken off their engagement in a flurry of female insanity. She just couldn't. He had his reasons to be sorry too, he had partial blame in this and the way he had pushed her out. Stubbornness setting in, Rose's worst flaw was this internal sense of injustice that made it impossible to be the one to reach out to him.

At night, she was restless in bed, sure every noise or creak was him driving up to the cottage, but it wasn't. She couldn't sleep. Crying sporadically and getting up a hundred times to get water or tissues, or to toss and turn. She must have readjusted her cushions a dozen times and even opened and shut her window and curtains a dozen more. Poor Muffin had even vacated the bed and gone to sleep on the couch away from her restlessness.

She left her bed when it was still dark, barely grazing morning, and built a fire in the lounge. Taking her mind off everything and hoping to warm the icy shivers that had been raking through her alone in the bed. The summer was ending and the colder nights moving in slowly; It just made her feel more depressed and alone. She just could not get him out of her head and it was slowly driving her into insanity.

Warmed by the flickering flames, she finally drifted to sleep on the couch. Finally finding some peace to her inner turmoil but dreaming restlessly, tossing and turning, yet again; only this time on a narrow couch and barely stayed still through into the early hours of the Sunday morning. Muffin had moved back to the bed in a bid to be free and he slept alone and in peace.

Getting up from another night without him made it feel even worse. Part of her always hoping he would appear; pulling her to him in the dark like he always did and wiping all of this away; but he never materialised.

He would be coming home today. Maybe he already was. It was early but he had not been sure if he would have an overnight arrival or early morning so he could literally come home at any time, if not already. Her heart sank when she checked her phone for the hundredth time and it still showed nothing from him.

At least with the distance between them, he had an excuse to stay away. Back home there was nothing to use as an excuse for his staying away, except that he didn't want to see her.

She tried not to watch the clock. Tried to go about the morning as she normally would. Feeding Muffin and taking him a walk; a long soak in a bubble bath and an age choosing something to wear before spending a crazy amount of time on her hair and makeup and even longer painting her nails.

Listlessly pacing from her work room a dozen times to fetch tea and notes, wearing her rugs threadbare with her manic prisoner like stalking around her floorspace. The walking around a sign of her inability to just settle, her mind elsewhere while her ears were still tuned into every noise outside, waiting endlessly for familiar tyres on gravel. She couldn't stand it anymore.

The clock had dragged slowly to noon and there was no way she could deny his return anymore. He would be back for sure; his flights always came in early morning and the drive home was less than an hour from the airfield.

He wasn't coming.

She couldn't stay here like this, torturing herself and she knew how stubborn he could be; they both could be. Maybe he was waiting for her to make the next move. He had said 'When she cooled down'

Maybe that's what he was doing right?

Torn with indecisiveness and struggling to decide.

Go or stay?

Fuck

Muffin gave her a quizzical look as she asked out loud. No answers in the little cute face, staring at her with hanging tongue and cocked head. It was almost as if he was saying 'Why are you still here?

She realised without deciding, her body was already moving around, collecting her bag and phone: her head taking a moment to catch up with the plan and her heart going into complete erratic overdrive, beating so hard her chest was heaving. Stubborn Rose was in full control again and she was pushing herself to go face the issue head on.

What was the worst he could do? Break up? She had already done that for the second time. If anyone had a reason to be insecure it sure wasn't her.

Could he refuse to see her?

Sitting here alone was worse, the agony of not knowing what was happening between them. At least knowing he had turned her away wasn't the same as endlessly waiting, second guessing if he would appear. She would go up and if he told her to leave then she would know exactly where they stood. Telling her to go away would be a clear message that he was done with her and their relationship.

Swallowing down fear and pride, she drove up the long sweeping drive to the familiar dark stone manor, towering above her. The plants and trees had started to darken in colour lately, giving the old building a more sinister vibe as autumn approached, more historical and foreboding.

Rob's car was parked neatly in its usual spot, shaded by a large tree near the house and the mere sight of it sent her heart plummeting, sure he was now home and hadn't been anywhere near her intentionally. Not that she could blame him, she had acted insane and she didn't deserve any other treatment.

Pulling up and parking beside the sleek black car, she lost her nerve almost instantly. The car was like a foreboding presence and knowing he was here had her feeling suddenly terrified. Nausea rising and a dizziness clouding her vision, anxiety biting at her insides. She rested her face on her steering wheel for a moment, trying to steady her breathing and calm her shaking hands, closing her eyes and steadying her shaking body to get a grip. She was aware of the hotness of her face, drowning out all noises as she listened to the blood rushing from her brain. She brought her arms up to cushion the sides of her face and wrap over her head, trying to dig down deep for some sense of bravado to get out the car in between deep slow breaths.

It wasn't needed. The click of her opening door startled her and the soft smooth voice that followed had her heart stop mid beat.

'Are you planning on sitting out here all day?'

She hesitated, looking sideways at his waist and torso but bit her lip, steeling her nerves and glanced up. He was agonisingly handsome, leaning down towards her, dressed in jeans and a t-shirt, looking effortless as he always did. He had his hands resting above her door frame and supporting his weight, making his shirt to pull up to expose a small inch of carved abdomen. A sight she had ached for, but now was being tortured by. His hair freshly cut and his face cleanly shaven, he smelled of that familiar seductive scent and his face as unreadable as always. Cold perfection, just like the first time she ever laid eyes on him.

'No, I was just……' Her voice trailed off quietly. Unable to meet those eyes she knew were trained on her. She fumbled, pulling out her keys and bag and moved to get out as he stepped out of the way. She wanted to stare at his face, breath him in and throw herself around him but her pride and uncertainty held her back. Instead, she silently straightened up, sensing him moving back out of her way further, closing her door and locking it; he was standing with crossed arms watching her. His nearness affecting her far more than she was letting on.

'Now the question is, are you here to see Abby? Or are you here to see me?' His face was giving nothing away and his tone was hardly friendly. His posture standoffish as she felt her voice breaking in an attempt to answer; she couldn't stand this anymore, or he way he was coolly looking at her. It was torture, the tension deafening. She turned to face him, twisting her keys anxiously in her fingers and could barely look into that gorgeous face, tense and close to tears as he angrily frowned at her. All signs of still being majorly pissed.

'Rob.?…' Her words were broken off by the familiar red car pulling in beside them, sending her stomach into a frenzied mess. Her voice hushed into silence at the appearance of the other woman's car.

Fucks sakes!

Morag parked up as they both watched, glancing back and trying to read his steady gaze as he watched the car manoeuvre slowly and carefully; watched his unmoveable form, but she got nothing. He didn't seem surprised to see the other woman either, she guessed it was why he was out here; waiting for Morag.

Wouldn't be for me, he never knew I was coming and didn't exactly ask me to come.

Rose's breathing was getting shallower and she was unsure how to behave. She had began picking at her nails absently, eyes no longer on him as it was almost unbearable to look at him this way. He was still focused on the approaching red head and his body language was sending off a very clear 'stay away from me' vibe.

Morag slid out of the car, her body clothed in a figure hugging grey tracksuit and long sleeves with a briefcase in one hand. The hint of dressings and bandages on her wrists and hands peeking from under the edges of her cuffs. Her red hair piled up on top of her head messily, her face free of all traces of makeup, giving her a youthful almost innocent look and for a moment Rose never recognised her. She looked like a young sweet girl, completely vulnerable and doe eyed. She could imagine that once upon a time this was the version Rob had loved, that innocent and almost Rose like version of the woman in front of them.

Rose turned her eyes to the gravel, kicking with the toe of her trainer at some loose moss, unable to look at the approaching woman anymore either and feeling wholly uncomfortable and majorly emotional. Rob greeted the new arrival with a smile, leaned in to kiss her on the cheek and sent another shooting pain through Rose's heart. She acted like she didn't see and instead plastered a friendly face on.

'Morag, you remember Rose? Abby's friend!' Rob raised an eyebrow at Rose with a hint of sarcasm in his tone, but he was masking it enough to appear friendly and normal.

If he was trying to punish her then it was working. Her heart pounding through her chest painfully, her eyes prickling with tears. She couldn't stand this anymore, the man she loved wasn't this cruel.

Morag nodded and gave her a small forced smile to which Rose feigned a smile in return.

'Nice to see you again Morag.' Awkwardness looming, the atmosphere strained and Rob seemed uncaring about it all. 'I really should go and see her, we had, errr, plans.' She lied hopelessly, almost tripping over her own words. Rob flashed her a sardonic tiny half smile and then turned away towards the other woman without a goodbye. Morag followed suit and immediately pulled him into a hushed conversation, making it obvious Rose was both unimportant and easily dismissed.

I hate you!

Turning away, Rose tried to steam away gracefully, trying to not stop and break into a flood of tears in front of them or let her heart fall right out of her body and shatter on the gravel. She didn't wait for an invite when she got to the large looming entrance, but pushed open the heavy wooden door, almost fleeing up the stairs to Abby's room; glad that it was unlocked and she had no need for her key. Knocking on Abby's door desperately when she reached it and pushing it open reluctantly, she found it empty.

Her heart was trying to leave her body by way of her chest, her lungs struggling to cope as the overwhelming frenzy of erratic emotions and war against tears enveloped her. She sank down on the bed trying to gain control, trying to cradle her face in her hands. She wanted to be sick, knowing now she shouldn't have come.

How could he be this way towards her? Was it really over? Did he really not want her anymore?

She should have realised that his silence had been a message that it was over, that she had blown it. Her behaviour and throwing back his mother's ring had sealed her fate and she had been too stupid to realise it. Rob wasn't some immature, erratic person who lost his temper and stamped his foot. Rob was someone who didn't have any space in his life for any more crazy needy women making life hell for him.

She couldn't let the tears start or they would never stop, but she couldn't stop them. Pacing, trying to get a hold of herself, she knew she needed to leave. Abby wasn't home, she had known that already as she was still staying with Duncan to avoid her brother and Rose had been too caught up in seeing him to think about that little fact. She couldn't stay here. She needed to leave, to breathe, to break down in private.

Standing up purposefully and pushing every screaming emotion down, she walked to the grand gilded mirror. Deep breaths, calming breaths. In through her nose and out through her mouth with hands trembling, she smoothed her hair and face. Pep talking the face in the reflection to appear relaxed; wiping her eyes and dabbing away the threatening tears, smoothing it all away.

Putting that rehearsed mask back on that she had spent weeks perfecting when he had devastated her life once before, straightening her body and breathing deeply.

She could do this! All she had to do was get up, walk purposefully down the stairs and out the front door and leave.

She could fall apart when she was driving down that god damn long ass tarmac, but right now she needed to save face. Keep some dignity. It was all she had left.

She took one last calming gulp of oxygen and made her way out of the door slowly, the hall seemed deserted and silent. No sign of either of them. She carefully picked her way down the stairs, afraid to make more noise than necessary, her eyes glancing around suspiciously in the eerily quiet and empty house as though even the staff were missing.

Were they still outside? Shit! What if they were?

She stopped, faltering on the stair and regaining some composure with the shake of her head. She would have to do this, have to put her chin up and just walk by. Get to her car. Smile, say goodbye and leave, feigning bravado for just a few moments longer.

'Undecided about whether you're coming or going?' His voice made her freeze, unable to look around. The same tone of heavy sarcasm and mild anger. 'Maybe should have told you she wasn't here.' She looked around at the direction of his voice, catching him lazily watching her from the kitchen door, his body leaning heavily against the frame.

What was he doing? Why was he making it like this?

She couldn't bare the cold and distant glare anymore, avoiding the way he was staring at her. Glancing around, looking for his new visitor nervously in case she was witnessing this horrid scene, she could feel her body beginning to tremble badly once more, he cut in again

'She didn't stay! Was passing by and popped in with this.' He held up a folder with the museum logo on the cover before sliding it back onto the table outside the kitchen door. Rose, still standing on the last step, staring his way now that he had drawn her vision with the file, was unsure what to say. Slightly relieved that Morag was gone.

For the first time in her life words would not come to her, he was making her crazy nervous and she couldn't think straight. Her clammy hands and mouth that had suddenly gone very dry were all making her even more anxious. Feeling that same prick of emotion in her eyes, she looked away, closing them to blink away any tears and took the last step onto the marble floor.

'If you're trying to hurt me... Punish me...It's working.' She finally whispered, unable to look his way for fear she would lose all control. There was silence after her words, she couldn't bare it, couldn't bare the huge vast emptiness between them and the signs he no longer wanted her. After a moment of pensive waiting she moved to leave, unable to look back as her emotions held on by a thread.

'That's it?' His voice was cutting and cold. 'Nothing else to say, Penelope¿ The use of that pet name was enough to break her, knowing he only used it when he was pissed or they were no longer together. A stupid reason to lose all resolve at saving face but she couldn't help it.

'Don't R... ' Her voice broke. The damn finally breaking under pressure and the torrent of emotion bursting forth, she sunk down onto the step helplessly, wrapping her arms around her face and sobbing uncontrollably. Losing all ability to fight it and letting her heartbreak pour out in a very dramatic fashion, like a child who was completely distraught.

She heard him swear before his footsteps hurriedly came towards her and his arms pulled her up unexpectedly to cradle against him. She was too angst to dissect what that meant or even push him off.

'Come on.' His voice was softer, that harsh tone gone against the side of her hair as he ushered her down the hall towards his room; thinking better of the closeness to the bed he pulled her into his office and sat her down in his leather chair gently, letting her go to walk away and return with a box of tissues. Rose continued to stare at her own lap, tears falling, unable to meet his eyes and tried to reel back in the flood water. She tried to calm her erratic breathing and took the tissues gratefully, wiping her face and blowing her nose to console herself back to a calmer state. He didn't say anything, just walked away from her to a nearby unit and back again immediately to the edge of the desk beside her seconds later.

'You forgot something last time you were here.' His voice was flat and unreadable, he slid something across the desk, the scraping noise bringing her eye up to meet the small black leather ring box that skidded to a halt right beside her. Rose glanced up at him in a moment of surprise, her eyes questioning but his expression was the same cool unreadable as always, reaching out for it she clicked it open, revealing his mother's silver ring and glanced up again in confusion.

'You're giving me this back?' She whispered, her voice shaking and swallowing hard. Her brain a frenzy of questions and frenzied emotions.

'Fights are part of the package Rose. Sometimes I'm an asshole and sometimes you're unbearable. I'm still pissed at you and I'm guessing the feeling is mutual but that doesn't mean I just walk away; you can't get rid of me that easily, whether we like each other right now or not. You don't give up at the first hurdle!' His voice was still harsh but the sarcasm gone, the slight tone of warmth in there somewhere.

Rose bit on her lip to stop the sudden surge of tears flowing from complete relief, closing the box again and pulling it into her lap possessively, she felt another tear escape, this time it was shame. He was keeping his distance, watching her with that unreadable coldness.

'You didn't call.' She brushed the moisture away. 'Didn't text.' Another fell just as quickly. 'I figured you were done.' She hated how feeble and quiet she sounded, her heart aching with the effort. She heard him sigh before he moved closer, pulling her chair round slowly as he leant over her, his face softening as he lifted her chin up to meet his eyes. Shaking his head, gently he brushed away a tear with his thumb, drawing her closer so they could lock eyes.

'I was being a man. It's what we do when we're pissed and trying to balance a lot of shit at once. We clam up…I'm used to dealing with things alone…We had a fight, Rose, that's all it was. I didn't want to talk to you until I calmed down, I knew I would say things I didn't mean and hurt you.' He slid down onto his knees, taking the box from her lap and retrieving her ring from inside before throwing the box back on the table carelessly, he lifted her hand sliding it back on her finger slowly; stopping to kiss the bruises from her overeager removal days before. That tiny tender act making her heart ache freshly as she gazed at him with wide eyes and a fluttering heartbeat.

'Thought you said once it came off it stayed off?' She was watching him now, her emotions calming slowly, his beautiful face, smooth and devoid of anger giving her peace. His eyes pale and soft as the storms moved away, while her manic emotions were being brought back under control, warmth began returning to his features completely.

'I lied.' He looked up, still holding her hand in his, a look on his face she couldn't read. He sighed again, shaking his head gently at her, a small smile breaking across his face. 'What am I going to do with you, Penny?'

She shrugged, still feeling fragile, looking up at him coquettishly and longing for him to touch her properly. To wipe away this excruciating tension between them and smooth over the last torn parts of her heart, convince her they really were okay. He gazed at her for a long moment.

'If you want a kiss you're going to need to come closer.' He smiled softly as though reading her mind; that familiar twinkle appearing in his eye once more and revealing the Rob she had been aching to see. She didn't need to be told twice, obediently she moved forward towards him.

He didn't hesitate, moving purposely at her, brushing noses gently, dragging out the agony and finding her lips in a slow confident movement, parting them easily. He sunk his mouth against hers. Softly at first, enjoying the touch of her against him once more, savouring the feeling of her breath against him after a weekend of hell and just breathing her in. Losing himself in the one place he had been longing to be. It was a kiss to wipe away the pain and anger, slow and tender, feelings of relief washing over both of them.

He didn't need to say anything more, the kiss said it all. As though they had been holding their breath, waiting to exhale, the surge of emotion and longing, forgiveness and relief all wrapped up in the tender moment; his hands finding her face to pull her closer. His mouth deepening the kiss, making it clear he was no longer mad at her, she was no longer mad at him and they were doing what they did best to fix all the hurt.

Sitting back on his haunches and gently smoothing back her hair in that familiar affectionate way, he smiled, bringing her eyes to meet his.

'Promise me baby… Promise me that no matter what we fight about, no matter how bad or how big it feels… That you will never doubt how much I love you or that I'm in this for the long haul… For the forever.' He kissed her gently on the forehead. 'I will always come back for you…Even if I need a few days to cool off from that infamous Munro temper… I'm sorry about the way I behaved…The things I said, I was being a dickhead.'

'I promise.' She reached out, kissing him again gently and was met with no rejection. Her heart filling with joy at the ability to just do this once more, to feel secure that they were still together and engaged. 'I'm sorry I threw your ring back at you… I'm sorry I acted like a crazy bitch.' She rested her forehead against his jaw, breathing in the smell of him as her nose grazed his throat, enjoying his arms around her and feeling like this is all she ever needed in the world to feel content.

'I deserved it.' He mumbled huskily.

'I know.' She smiled weakly at him, now eye level again as he frowned in mild mock outrage and scooped her out of the chair in an easy swipe, sending the items on his desk flying and the chair spinning uncontrollably. Rose squealed at the suddenness of it, caught up in a bundle high in his arms.

'I know how to make it up to you, though.' He kissed her firmly again on the mouth, moving her back to the desk and sliding her butt onto the smooth surface. Swiping the rest of the stuff from behind her off the edge with one arm, straight to the floor in a clattering mess. He didn't break free until he had pushed her down to lay across the smooth wooden expanse. 'I have thought of nothing else for days.'

'Really? Even while hating me?' Her voice was heavy with anticipation, breathless at his passionate kiss.

'There's nothing in the world like make up sex, all that pent-up anger and frustration. Even pissed I would never hate you baby, I couldn't stop thinking about you.' That dirty twinkle in his eye, all return of that boyish grin and relaxed face. 'Knowing just how fiery and passionate you are… I know you won't disappoint.'

He didn't give her a chance to reply, leaning down to capture her mouth, igniting that burning desire quickly, their hands clawing at each other's clothes in a frenzy that overtook almost instantaneously.

With her legs hanging off the desk freely so that the only place she had to put them was around his waist, he was all over her, kissing and nibbling and pulling her free of any garments covering her skin as she followed suit, yanking his t-shirt over his head and raking her nails over that expanse of chiselled torso and muscular shoulders.

It was with the same feverish urgency and wild passion of their reunion in Abby's bathroom. That surge of insane need to be joined with one another, naked and writhing, only this was more intense, more frenzied and full on. They weren't drunk this time, they were fuelled by days of anger and heartache and the craving need was overwhelming.

Rose was not normally one to move above a moaning and writhing when she climaxed but he had her calling out, groaning and panting in ecstasy. Unable to control her cries as the tidal wave of orgasmic ripples crashed over her. His own muffled moans lost in her neck in unison as they came crashing down, sated, on top of the desk after only minutes of hot, hard sex. It was definitely a keeper for the memory bank, not the longest session in which he had devoured her body but definitely the most primal and passionate to date.

Heavy breathing, with sweat droplets spritzed over their naked skin as they began to untangle limbs, still Rose lying flat on the hard desk-top. Rob gave a satisfied groan as he moved to get off her, bracing on his palms by her head and leaning in to give her a slow long and gentle kiss, his tongue brushing hers, yet not fuelling more lust, this was a 'thank you for making my day' kind of kiss.

He moved back, straightening his arms to let her up, her legs still around his waist as he suddenly froze. She felt him stiffen over her, the change of atmosphere and the small noise which escaped his throat had Rose lift her head and look up at him. Still leaning over her, she realised he was looking at the door and followed his gaze.

Her blood instantly running cold, her heart stopping and her legs losing all capability at staying around his waist, she inhaled sharply at the sight before her. Morag stood in the doorway, wild-eyed, mouth open, chest heaving. Like a woman on the verge of a massive break-down, she was holding some folders in her hands and as they slid to the floor she made an incomprehensible cry.

Rob turned back to Rose, a frown of regret instantly across his face and a murmured curse as he quickly released her, pulling her up to sit on the desk and pulling his clothes up quickly with one hand, the urgency of their need for each other meaning his jeans and boxers had stayed pretty much close to where they were meant to sit.

He pulled Rose up off the surface fully, helping her to her feet and standing in front of her so he was shielding her modesty and handing her, her clothes. His t-shirt was laying on the chair by Morag's side so was left alone for the time being as he proceeded to right himself. Rose hurriedly covered up, standing behind him facing away and pulling her dress over her nakedness, hastily kicking her lace panties under the desk. Her face was burning with the heat of complete mortification of the situation they had suddenly found themselves in.

Fuck, fuck, fuck

'Morag, come to the kitchen with me and we can talk.' Rob was speaking soothingly, but she was shaking her head, the tears falling freely.

'It was her?' Pointing past him as Rose turned towards them, pulling her shoes from under the desk and trying to calm her elevated pulse and shaking limbs. She couldn't look the red head in the eye.

'Her? All along? Your kid sister's mate? What is she even twenty yet?' Morag spat, her voice high pitched and cracking, the obvious extreme distress all over her.

Rob seemed lost for words for a moment, sighing and trying hard to think fast and make this less traumatic. Trying to manoeuvre her into the next room, trying to make her follow but her gaze was intent on Rose, standing openly looking at every inch of her. Hating her.

'Rose is twenty-seven, Morag. You knew there was someone, it's not like I haven't kept trying to tell you. Yes, it's been her all along.' He had given up trying to turn her and instead pulled the seat forward from the door frame, lifting his top and sliding her down on the chair with little resistance. Morag was too focused on open mouthed staring at Rose.

'I'm sorry that you saw that, that you walked in on us…' He pulled it on, covering his tanned torso; the spattering of hair across his body glistening a little with the exertion of what they had just done still.

Rose had nowhere to go. Trapped in the room with her only close exit being closed in by Morag sobbing in the chair he had pulled in front of it. Morag looked at him with accusation

'You bastard!' Morag sobbed once more, her voice had lost conviction and fire and she just sounded helpless and hopeless. Rob sighed and slid down to his knees in front of her, looking at Rose for some sort of help, but she just stood motionless like a deer in the headlights, unable to offer a single word of support. Wide-eyed and completely out of her depth. All she could muster was a slight shrug and shake of the head. She knew her face was probably blushed and hot and her hair wild, so she concentrated her efforts on trying to smooth away the remnants of their lovemaking from her appearance.

'Morag…I love her. This isn't some affair or casual thing.' He was trying so hard to be gentle, his voice low and calm, his eyes on the woman's face once more as she silently cried. 'I never wanted to hurt you but I can't go on living this way.' Morag turned towards him and stared. Tears falling. Face crumbling still but no verbal response.

Rose sunk down into his chair and tried to keep her vision on other things and not the intimate way they were closely facing one another. The mess on the floor of the stuff he had swiped off. His laptop teetering dangerously close to the far corner of the smooth surface and looking to tumble off at any second. The picture frame they had accidently broken laying in pieces under the edge of the desk near her lacy underwear. The fact her pink bra was hanging from the curtain pole over the window in a distasteful manner and not exactly something she wanted Morag to see, adding more insult to injury.

Rose couldn't really offer anything in way of useful dialogue. The woman was glaring at her now and then as she swung from Rob's face to Rose's, with so much hatred and confusion. Rose wanted the ground to open up and swallow her whole. Rob was trying to help, dabbing Morag's face with a tissue, uneasy at the lack of reaction and calm tearful posture. Even Rose knew this was out of character for Morag, this weird quiet response and lack of hysterics.

'How long?' She finally broke the silence and her calculated gaze landed once more on Rose's face. 'How long have you been screwing her?'

He looked startled by the question but didn't falter, didn't rephrase her question for her, knowing she was acting out of pain and hurt.

'On and off for a few months. After the charity dance, a week or so after.' He sounded remorseful, knowing that lying to her, hiding this from her in the beginning, had been wrong. Regretting it now that they were here and realising this admission only made things so much worse for her to swallow.

'Earlier? Acting like she was here to see Abby... Was that part of the charade for my benefit?' Morag sounded venomous, anger seeping through her shock and upset, her voice hitching slightly. Rose could see the woman's hands trembling in a mirror to her own.

'No.' He glanced back at Rose, seeing her tense awkwardness and throwing her a supportive look, a weak smile and a little look that was somehow apologetic. 'We were fighting, I was being an asshole.' Rose gave him a small smile back, warmed that even in this moment he would still look at her that way and still be saying sorry in his own way.

'But other times we saw her? That was pretence, right?' Morag snapped his attention back with more accusations, her tone haughtier with every word as though she was slowly building from desolate to fury.

'Not always, it was complicated and we broke up for a while... But there were times... Yes... That we acted like nothing was going on. I didn't want to hurt you more than I was Morag, you need to understand that all of it was for your benefit. To protect you.'

'How is lying to me and hiding the truth, protecting me? You have been sneaking around with her, letting me believe everything was fine.' The pain so much more to bear than she was capable of as she tried to process all the facts. Through the haze of the pills, they had been making her take, she was struggling so hard to piece things together while forcing down the unbearable betrayal.

'Morag... I have tried to tell you so many times I was seeing someone, I even told you I was in love with her. I told you when I brought you home again that I was serious about someone and tried to talk to you even then but you wouldn't listen. You go off on one and become delusional, denying it and then acting like it's not happening. We have been going around in circles for weeks with this. We weren't fine... Hiding my love life so as not to upset you isn't fine or normal Morag. We're friends, nothing more, it shouldn't have to be like this.' Rob was trying to reason with her, no longer drying her tears but instead his hand was covering hers on her knee. Giving her gentle comfort and despite knowing it was platonic for him, Rose had to look away as the tiny bite of jealousy hit her in the stomach.

Morag began to shake her head, pulling her hand from his and using both to push her hair back from her sodden face, a movement that made her seem less lucid so suddenly, more childlike.

'I can't listen to this bullshit. I can' think straight while you and you're bit on the side are staring at me like that.' She snapped at him, Rose could see him visually stiffen and sigh heavily. Guessing that his reaction was reversion of her attitude back to denial. He seemed at a loss for words, a hand coming to pinch the bridge of his nose as though he was dealing with a stressful client and taking a moment to think about what he wanted to say, Rose sunk in her seat a little more, just wishing she could leave the room.

Morag turned wild eyes back on her, as though trying to work something out and sizing her up. It sent a jot of fear through Rose's stomach and her skin tingled, immediately looking away from the hateful scowl yet feeling her eyes running all over her. Pausing her searching gaze on Rose, Morag sat upright in a bolt, straighter and somehow fiercer; her face paled further; gulping down hard, she lifted a shaking hand as though it was too fragile to move and pointed at Rose slowly.

'You gave her your mother's ring?' Accusingly spat, the shrill tone of building rage and heartbreak sliced the air as hints of hysterical Morag came into play. Rose recoiled, pulling her hand out of sight and mouthing a sorry as Rob glanced back at her briefly. Rose's nerves had become a jumbling mass of jelly.

'Morag! I'm sorry.' Rob put his hands on each side of her, trying to bring her focus to him. 'I should have told you… I didn't know how to do it when you got upset coming home… To make it easier… Rose and I… I asked her too… We are going to get married… I want a future with her, I know I should have told you sooner but I really didn't know how to do it.' He lifted one hand up towards her face smoothly, stroking her face gently, trying to make the news more bearable. Rose looked away, the feeling of discomfort and major jealousy raising inside this time. She knew she was being stupid.

He's trying to save a drowning soul from complete destruction. Not making a move on his ex.

'No...No. You're not!' Morag's voice became higher, louder as she slapped his hand away viciously.

'Morag. I'm sorry.' Rob sat back, putting his hands down on his knees, still staying near her but leaning back as though he was expecting an outburst.

'NO! It's not happening!' She snapped, this time her tone furious and loud. Wild eyes flying back and forth between Rose and Rob and looking more than a little manic.

'Nothing you say. Nothing you do can change how I feel about her. I can only tell you that I'm sorry.' Rob reached out to her again, trying to catch her hand as she began tugging at her hair, ripping at it cruelly as though trying to pull it out, her eyes swimming with fresh tears and her face twisting to control the onslaught of heartache.

She was manically shaking her head, pushing him away. Rising to her feet and grasping at her own arms, Trying to self-comfort. Trying not to lose all control. Rose watched in complete dismay as the woman unravelled before her eyes.

'Let me leave Rob! I need to leave... I'm trying to keep my shit together. Trying to show you I can keep my shit together, but you need to just get out of my way.' Her voice was shaking wildly, her body vibrating with the effort of clinging onto the last of her control and stopping herself from snapping into the hysterical woman of weeks ago in the hall.

Rob slid back, moving to his own feet so she could freely shove the chair away and turn to the open door. Morag stood shakily, her thin frame looking suddenly so fragile and small beside his muscular body that towered over her.

'You won't do this to me! You love me! I know you do! You just need to get over this... this thing... This affair. I forgive you. I do.' She was back to rambling, her voice up and down in both tone and volume as her brain scrambled through a million emotions.

'Morag listen to me...' Rob tried.

'NO... You listen to me! You take that whore and you screw her fucking brains out until you have had your fill. You get it out of your system. You hear me? Fuck her any which way you want, up the ass for all I care, but you do it and you forget it. You forget her and then you come back to me and we fix this. We go back to how we were.' Morag's voice was high pitched and screechy, her finger shaking as she waved it near his face, her eyes wild and unfocused as tears washed over her cheeks.

'Morag please!'

'You come to me with that fucking ring and you grovel for me, because you love and want only me. You'll realise you were wrong. You'll realise that you need me. You'll see, we're meant to be, you and I. I'll take you back and we will never speak of this again. Never speak of her again!' Her insane words were coming out like verbal diarrhoea as though she was trying to convince not only him but herself too. A sea of uncontrollable pain in that face and body and Rose could only stare with complete disbelief.

'Morag!' Rob was trying to keep his cool, straining against every part of his will not to snap at her because he could see how desperately she was trying to stay in control. Morag made a move to the door and he started after her, but she held up her hands hushing him, a dangerous look on her face. Her body violently shaking, her chest heaving and a return to that furious violent woman of Rose's memories.

'Stay away from me... You stay away. Until the scent of that whore is long gone from your body and your bed. While she is anywhere near you then you don't get to fucking touch me or breathe my air. I don't want to be tainted with that vulgar skank.'

Even Rose could tell Rob was holding back his anger with every ounce of effort he could muster, she could see it all over him and his tense and poised body. Holding back everything he wanted to say, like a coiled snake who could lash out at any moment. She knew without seeing them, his eyes would be almost black with darkness and fury. He looked dangerous in a way that suddenly gave Rose chills. Afraid of the change in him so suddenly and knowing this was not a good move for anybody in this room.

'Morag!' Rob had gritted his teeth, his voice strained and clutching to hold it. Losing a piece of his controlled temper, despite how hard he was fighting.

'She's my Fiancée! I won't be getting over her, getting her out of my bed or removing her from my life, now, in the near future, or ever. I won't be running to you either! I'm trying to do this the decent way and spare you, but I swear if you call her a whore one more time or insult her in any other way, I'll physically throw you out this house via the nearest window and I won't stop to open it first.' Rob's sinister tone and deadly serious glare gave Rose chills, she bit hard on her bottom lip, gulping down and transfixed on his face.

Morag gasped. Her face crumbling at the way he had spoken to her, the threat and his general behaviour towards her; Rose assumed this was all new. His looming height dwarfing Morag's tall slender frame, but the air between them crackled with raw energy and rage. Rose was shaking physically. Terrified. Her hands covering her mouth, her skin pale and clammy. Afraid of the developing scene, afraid of this man whom she did not recognise, afraid of this woman on the verge of snapping who had previously given reasons to fear her.

'You will leave her!' She commanded, finding her voice and trying to keep her glare steady on Rob's face, trying to intimidate him with hatred.

'Never!' The steel of his voice matched his body. Rose could not bear this any longer. She felt like she was going to pass out with the overwhelming anxiety and fear of this mounting tension between them.

'Morag?' She got up quickly. 'I think you should leave. Everyone needs to cool down and have a little breather before this turns really nasty.' Rose moved forward hesitantly, aware that Rob moved in front of her protectively, instantly shielding her from a direct attack from Morag whether it was her intention or not. Morag's eyes swung at the motion of what he was doing, putting himself in front of the woman she had every reason to despise right then and it only angered her further.

'You cannot fucking tell me what to do! This is neither your concern nor your house, and the relationship between me and him has fuck all to do with you.' She scowled at both of them, a sardonic grin appearing as she shook her head. Motioning up Rob's body which was now fully in front of Rose so she could only peek around him to see the other woman. Morag seemed to be laughing that he would choose to shield her over consoling Morag.

'This is her concern. Anything that concerns me, concerns her and this will be her home soon enough… Like I said already, she's agreed to marry me. She will be Mrs Munro! … Look Morag, she's right; this is only going to end up one way if we carry on, so how about you just get out!' Rob's voice was of the devil himself. Sinister and dark. There was an air of daring her to disobey him, he sounded dangerous and violent as he quietly brought his icy stare to Morag's face. It was such a strangely calm reply that Rose barely heard it. Her chest heaving as she stood wide-eyed and motionless, waiting for Morag to go or erupt.

Morag snorted and let out a truly manic, blood curling and simply eerie laugh that made her sound demented. Rose shrivelled back, afraid of the tension sizzling in the room, afraid of the raging anger within Morag's face when she stopped cackling and brought daggers back to Rob's face, her skin a shade of scarlet, a battle going on inside her. Morag glared with such hatred it could melt metal.

The whole room paused for what seemed an eternity, no one moving or speaking for long drawn out seconds in which Rose could hear every single beat of her heart, before Morag turned and stormed out without warning. Morag knew this battle was more than she could handle in her current state. Knowing this was a side to him which had never shown itself to her. Knowing when to go. So she had dropped her tail between her legs and retreated to lick her wounds. Rose sighed and realised suddenly how jellylike her legs were as her knees began to tremble. Reaching for the desk to steady herself as she exhaled.

When they heard the manor door slam ceremoniously, Rob sagged, letting out a massive sigh and cursing loudly. The terrifying persona dropping instantly, rubbing his head and making some unnatural 'argh' noises before turning and slamming a cupboard door with his flat palm and making Rose jump out of her skin.

He looked like a boxer ready to go ten rounds in that fleeting second and Rose was glad to see how quickly he brought some control back to his manner, he looked up at her apologetically and motioned her to come to him with a hand gesture. She didn't hesitate, running into his arms, feeling the security pull around her as he breathed into her hair and moulded their bodies into one perfectly.

'I'm sorry baby. Sorry for this whole shitty weekend and climatic scene.' He kissed her on the head, burying his fingers in her hair and pulling every inch of her tight against him more firmly as if somehow it wasn't enough.

'I wish we could just erase all of it. The last few days, the last few minutes.' Rose sighed against his hard chest, closing her eyes and just feeling him around her, her heart full to bursting with how good this always felt and just how safe she was right here.

She could feel the tension in him relaxing as he took comfort from her against him; breathing her in and using the feel of her to ground him. Rose had no idea how much she calmed him, how anytime he needed that surge of encouragement or confidence boost, or just needed to calm down, he would wrap himself around her and get lost in the smell of her. She was a drug like no other and he needed her more than air.

'It wasn't how I would have done it, but it's done. She knows what we are to one another and how serious it is, she knows who I am in love with. … I don't know what happens now, but I doubt she will be able to deny any of that little scene happened, even in her screwed up mind.' Rob's voice was husky now, tiredness setting in after a long as hell weekend and even longer nights.

'She saw us… All of that?' Rose cringed as she pulled back to meet his face, her mind racing with Morag's reactions over and over like it was stuck on repeat.

'I guess. I have no idea how long she was here but she would have at least heard us from the second she walked into the other room.' He looked over her shoulder at the desk and the scattered papers, stationary and stuff on the floor.

'That would have been horrible… For her I mean. Jesus Rob, I feel so awful.' Rose felt tears prick her eyes, trying hard not to feel empathy for Morag but failing. She couldn't imagine what finding Rob in a very compromising position mid orgasm with another woman would have done to her. She didn't ever want to feel that kind of pain or experience that trauma.

'I know I should be feeling really bad about that, but damn I'd do it again.' Rob smiled jokingly, trying to lighten the atmosphere and slid his arms around her waist possessively, turning her so he could snuggle his face into her neck and bringing her back to him from the chaos inside her mind. Reminding her that she would never find him with anyone else, or in anyone else's arms.

'She was really livid. She looked terrifying.' Rose shivered, unsure whether it was the memory of Morag's glare or the fact he was breathing against her neck so gently her skin was tingling. Her body was running cold now the exertion had worn off and adrenalin was dispersing.

'It's going to be okay baby. She can't come between us this time, I won't ever let that happen again. I promised you, remember?' He brought her back around, nose to nose with him, his arms latched around her loosely and stared deep into her chocolate brown eyes, a look of complete seriousness ingrained in the pale depths.

'I don't trust her… Something about the way she looked when she left.' Rose had to admit, she was more than a little afraid of the other woman and that look on her face would surely give Rose nightmares in bed later. Rob shook his head.

'Morag's only a danger to herself, and good at making my life a misery when all hell breaks loose...There's nothing she can do. Not really... Her anger will be aimed at me, but I'm not about to go back to sneaking around and hiding you. In time she will finally just have to accept this; accept us.' He paused thoughtfully. 'I'm just worried she does something dumb to herself, although after the scare cutting her arms gave her; I'm not so sure she would hurt herself that way anymore.'

Lifting her chin to him within the circle of his arms, she kissed him slowly, resting her forehead against his as he leaned down nearer her height.

'You don't think she will try and hurt herself this time?'

'That time, years ago... She was in a different place; mentally she was worse. I know it's hard to believe, but she has come on so much since then and moved on in small ways, with counselling and medication. That accident in the house, it scared her. I could see it in her face. She didn't want to die Rose.' Rob looked convinced, his grey eyes focused on Rose's face as though trying to imprint how she looked in that moment to memory. He seemed completely engrossed on her mouth, rather than the topic at hand. He nudged his groin into Rose with a hint of a wicked smile, leaning down to graze a kiss on her mouth but she pulled back.

'That was before all this!' Rose tried to bring his obviously wandering mind back to the conversation, only too aware of how many subtle signs he was giving off against her body, indicating that he was starting to think about sex once more; the days of not speaking making him more ravenous than normal. Rob had the ability to turn to sex at the oddest moments.

He shook his head, something in his eyes assuring her that he didn't think Morag had it in her anymore to try and take her life. She was stronger. She had more to live for despite all of this, more than she had back then. He sighed, seemingly getting the hint he wasn't about to get a replay on the desk and instead loosened his hold a little.

'When she sees that we're going ahead with the engagement party and the wedding, she will realise it's gone too far. That I'm serious. About us…About you! And she'll have to accept it. I don't know what that means for our friendship but I'm hoping she finally moves on and lets me have a life at last.'

Rose nodded quietly. Her fingers tracing his mouth lightly, watching him as she digested all of this for a few moments.

'Thought you were against engagement parties?' She smiled softly, seeing that warmth in his eyes fully returning to normal.

'Well. It's all been set up. Planned and paid for by my father, so would be a bit of an arsey thing not to go.' He grinned, the drama and tension abated.

'And her?' She queried with a frown.

'If she shows up, which I doubt she will, I'll make sure she can't ruin it. Won't ruin it. Hire security if I have too and let someone else deal with her for a change.'

'I think I may need a bodyguard after the way she looked at me.' She jested but the cold shiver running down her spine was a giveaway that she didn't actually mean it as a joke.

'You have one! Both by day and night.' He nudged her suggestively, kissing her forehead again, he pulled her away from him and scooped to start collecting the stuff on the floor and dumping it on his desk. 'Besides Muffin looks like he would be a ferocious protector.' He laughed as she bent down to help, he stretched out, leaning up and reaching out for her bra over the curtain pole and flung it over her shoulder with a grin and a shake of the head. A definite twinkle at the memory as he moved forward to the desk

'Rob?' Rose snagged her bra from his shoulder and tugged it towards her.

He looked up from picking the laptop up and sliding back to where it normally sat, fluidly moving around the room and returning some sense of calm to the mess.

'Hmmm?' He answered absentmindedly while straightening some stationary holders.

'You handled it really well, even if it didn't seem like you did.'

'Still feel like a class A asshole though baby. I know I can't keep running after her trying to fix her life anymore, she's not my problem. I don't want too!' He stopped to watch Rose pulling on her underwear with a disappointed frown and a cocked head as she manoeuvred her bra under her dress to get it on while staying modest.

'You're sure about the party? I mean we don't need to have it if you think its cruel? If she…' Rose carried on, ignoring the way he was watching her.

'No.' He straightened up to meet her face, catching her as she struggled to latch her clasp at the back, reaching instead and unzipping her dress so he could do it for her.

'No more allowances for her. No more handling everything with kid gloves. This…' he spun her when he had righted her bra and zipped her dress back up, pulling her hand and kissing her above her engagement ring. 'This is our life together. I need to stop making you put up with shit for her; she needs to realise that you're my priority now and that I'll not make any changes for her when it comes to us anymore. You're my life.'

Rose slid against him, her heart beating whole and steady. Pushing down the dread that had become a familiar ache in the back of her mind and losing herself into his strong arms while a deep pit of dread tried its hardest to push through.

Chapter 36

Abby was probably not the best person to unload her guilt over the scenario with Morag too. Currently bent double in severe hysterics and hyperventilating from lack of oxygen, she was begging Rose to tell her again in exactly what position Morag had caught them.

'Abby!' Rose was hauling at her, trying to gain some control. 'It's not funny!'

'It totally is! Tell me again was that before or after the 'Ooooh aah ahh ,YES' screams.' She mimicked a dramatic orgasm as Rose batted her again. Her own face flushed with embarrassment and trying hard not to giggle at Abby.

'Abby!' Rose had to fight to keep a straight face but the girls laugh was infectious. 'Stop it! If Rob hears you, he will pulverise you.'

'Before, during or after????' She was prodding at Rose suggestively. Relentlessly

'After! During? Maybe? Technically! I don't know how long she was there.' Swiping away her poking fingers and invasive eyebrow gestures, Rose tried to hush her once again.

'Oh, my god. That's class!' She was wiping her eyes and trying to hold her aching sides, her face several shades of pink and red from the amount of laughing and tears.

'This was not the reaction I expected, to be honest!' Rose sighed and slumped down on the bed.

'Well, obvious yuckiness aside, considering it's my brother, but I would have loved to be a fly on the wall for that little scenario.' Abby was still grinning, still giggling sporadically. As she finally slid down beside Rose on the bed, flopping down with exhaustion.

'You're sadistic, you know that?' Rose nudged her playfully.

'You're surprised? You're marrying my brother; we share genes. It should have been noticed before now that we're both not quite right in the 'whatsits'.' She made a mock circular motion at her temple and fell back on the bed, fatigued from her bouts of hysterical laughter. Rose pushed her legs away as they came to rest against her on the end of Abby's bed.

She had come up here to offload some tension while her betrothed was busy downstairs, lost in a million calls. She had stayed here the last few days, lost in the feeling of being back in his arms and his bed but the niggling anxiety had plagued her following Morag's departure. Abby's return had been a welcome relief.

'He hasn't heard from her Abby, not anything! Not a word.' She bit her lip anxiously, that knot in her stomach that had been growing the last few days was getting harder to ignore.

'Maybe she's finally done the world a favour and…'

'Abby!… For god's sake!' Rose chided a tad too harshly. 'He saw her car last night, on one of the back roads past town…She hasn't topped herself, okay? Besides, someone would have informed him if she had done anything to herself, he's her emergency contact. Rob doesn't think she will.' Rose raised a brow at Abby, a sign she wasn't impressed.

'Could be her ghost haunting the roads like a lonely…' The deepening frown and serious look paused her mid-horror tale and she smiled instead. 'Sorry. Bad taste!'

'Rob isn't saying much, closing down on me again I guess. He's tried to give her some breathing space. I know he's on edge. Unsure if this is it.?…If this silence is how it's going to be and she just fades away from his life or if this is the calm before the storm.' Rose sighed, completely out of her depth with this and trying not to over think how quiet he had been about it. He wasn't pushing her away this time but he wasn't exactly verbalising his own thoughts either.

'Except she works for him technically! The museum is only running because of him.' Abby rolled onto her stomach and began picking at imaginary fluff on the duvet alongside her. Rose fell back on the bed alongside her friend with a deflated exhale.

When did this get so uncomplicated and never ending?

'Rose, you need to get drunk and dance the night away and forget about her!' Abby pointed out, a chirpy tone and a serious expression.

'Ummm…I'm pretty sure all my troubles have started that way since the day I came here.'

'Perspective my love! Perspective!… Drunken behaviour bagged you the idiot downstairs on more than one occasion. I'm sure contrary to my sense of tastes, you're pretty overjoyed at that fact. Well, sounds like your happy with your lot sometimes, when you think the house is empty.' Abby grinned wickedly, catching Rose's eye with a wink.

'Oh my god Abby! Really?' Rose gushed, her face flaming almost instantly.

'What?' Abby held up her hands in childish defence. 'I'm not the one moaning and groaning down there, am I? Banging the headboard into next week. Must say though I am impressed with his stamina.' The giggling which followed was stifled by a swift whack over the head with the cushion Rose was holding.

'Jesus¡ Rose heaved, mortified at the thought of people hearing them, especially Abby!

'Maybe wanna tell Rob that sound proofing might be something he should look into. Or at least moving his room away from the kitchen and cosy, everything down there, echoes up here.'

'You do realise now I'm going to be constantly aware that everyone can hear us.' Rose groaned.

'SOUND PROOFING!!!' Abby said it slowly and deliberately at her friends blushing red face, raising brows and annunciating clearly.

'Sometimes, I feel more like your mother than your best friend, you know?' Rose was pressing her palms to her flaming cheeks, trying hard to cool her embarrassment.

'Technically in a few months, you will be.'.

Rose raised an eyebrow questioningly as Abby shrugged.

'Rob's more of a second dad than a brother. That makes you my step mother, sister in law, to be.'

'Maybe in your twisted world of whatsits.' Rose tapped at Abby's temples and crossed her eyes. 'If that's true, you shouldn't be asking your step mother, slash, sister in law, to be, if she was mid-orgasm when that woman barged in.' Rose chided playfully.

'Just like to know you're keeping the old man satisfied. And vice versa.' Abby grinned wickedly once more, that youthful devilish face of hers alive with naughtiness.

'Really!' Rose shook her head and blocked Abby from rolling into her for the second time, the girl was a wriggler.

'You know what they say?...Long happy marriages are the ones filled with fights and fucks. You two seem to have that down to a T.'

'You really are a tasteless tramp sometimes, with that mouth...How does Duncan put up with you?' Rose scrambled on top of her, to suffocate her with a pillow childishly.

'He's far worse than me, and he silences me with the ability to make me squeal.' Abby retorted boldly.

'Oh, my god! Abby?... Really? You're just after telling me I'm practically your mother and then you tell me that. You do realise I'm going to have to bleach my ears. Your brother is convinced you're still a virgin and sleep in Duncan's spare room down there!' Rose fell back onto the bed hopelessly, a little shocked to find her sweet innocent Abby was not so sweet and innocent after all.

'Really? Is he thick? I'm going out with a hot-blooded farm man. He herds cows who openly shag in fields on a daily basis, has probably delivered more calves than birthdays and he definitely knows about the birds and the bees. He may look quiet and gentle, like a manly muscular giant, but trust me, he's practically bent his bed frame with the pounding he gives me.' Abby chuckled, no hint of shame or embarrassment at her revelations at all.

'I'm traumatised!' Rose breathed slowly. Unable to really digest any of this conversation.

'Shut up, you wuss.' Abby leant up, kissing her on the cheek playfully. 'If everyone was as sweet and innocent as you Rose, the world would have no need for porn channels.'

'Where did this fowl potty mouth come from?' Rose blinked at her in complete awe.

'I think it's always been there, but my new family of future in laws are a bad influence on me... Farmers!' She shrugged unapologetically. 'Besides, don't look so shocked, my wavering nineteen fifties heroin.' She was standing in her room now, pulling out dresses to hold in front of the mirror, flattened to her body. 'You practically live with my brother! You're okay with his nympho ways and put it down to what? Being male?... Hate to tell you, it's more of a family trait than testosterone my lovely. And more than likely will pass it down to your sweet angelic cherubs.'

Rose could only shake her head. Amused and shocked but completely speechless. She had to agree, Rob was definitely very open about sex, highly sexed and shameless, much like his sister. Rose couldn't be shocked at how she was as she was a lot like him.

'What about this for the party?' Abby turned to her, holding up a slinky black dress with a high split to the thigh and low-cut bodice. A little more lady of the night than the sister of the groom.

'I think your brother could do with one less traumatic experience this week Ab's. Maybe the white or cream one. Less skin and more sweet little sister; at least pretend you're virginial still.' She pushed, trying to limit the hissy fit Rob would take if he saw her dressed like that.

'Fuck that! I have a boyfriend to keep on his toes. Gotta show him what he's clinging onto, keep him keen and jealous!' Abby wiggled her butt at Rose and continued to preen in the mirror with the scrap of fabric.

'Where ever do you get your romantic insight Ab's?' Rose slid off the bed, pulling out a less devastating dress and handed it to her. Removing the black one carefully from her grip and chucking it to the chair nearby in a slump.

'I learn from watching you two. A good example of how not to be!' She grinned wickedly. Rose shoved her from behind playfully with a smile and caught her eye in the reflection.

'Which one got a proposal first?' Rose stuck her tongue out.

'Look if you're happy with that old-fashioned ring on your finger, settling down to play lady of the manor, and popping out the next generation on Munro kids in succession, then that's fine. I'm more of a live young and go travelling around the world before I even contemplate marriage and babies.'

'You make me sound old you know.' Rose sighed and still watched her beautiful friend in the mirror, stroking her hair from behind in a maternal way.

'I'm warning you, I know him too well. Too much like my dad. He will keep you barefoot and pregnant until your womb drops out your ass!' Abby threw back with a raised brow and wide-eyed look that was a little too knowing.

'I'm pretty sure that's not where your womb is likely to drop out. It only disturbs me thinking that you and Duncan are doing something awfully wrong if that is your understanding of biology. Stuff I don't want to even contemplate, or know about.' Rose dodged the baby topic.

Abby wiggled her rear provocatively again with a devilish grin and bumped Rose backwards lightly. She caught her balance and moved back to perch on the edge of the bed once more, still watching her with the dress she was swishing around.

'My dad would have had fifteen kids if he could, you know? I think Rob will be the same.'

'I'm sure I would probably die if I tried to produce fifteen kids in succession, Abby. I also have some say over it.' Rose smiled seriously, smoothing out her own summer dress across her knees. Abby turned to her slowly and surely and looked her dead in the eye with a laugh.

'You have met my brother, haven't you?' Abby clocked her head to the side, smiling widely when Rose eye rolled. Suddenly looking thoughtful, Abby's face took on a more sombre look. 'You have?... You know?... Been careful right? Used contraception or condoms?'

'Yes.' Rose smiled surely, answering quickly, but then faltered. 'Most of the time.'

'Most of the time?' Abby blinked at her with a frown, worry overtaking that smile.

'I'm on the pill Ab's. Been on it for years. Sometimes I forget to take it occasionally, but I can assure you, everything's been regular as clockwork.'

'Sure?'

'Sure!' Rose mentally counted the weeks in the back of her mind, satisfied that she was only becoming paranoid because of Abby. She hadn't missed her monthlies and she wasn't due just yet.

'Okay. Just don't start becoming a baby factory too soon. We still have a lot of fun and parties to be had, before you settle down to be boring. Need my dancing partner for some time yet!' Abby grinned, swishing her hair over her shoulder as she returned to the mirror for more preening and ogling of dresses.

'I promise.' Rose had to admit that it was something which had never even crossed her mind seriously.

Kids! Yes... One day she wanted them.

Right now with Rob?... Maybe! It wouldn't be bad if it happened. She wouldn't be unhappy about it.

She brushed it away. Too soon and too serious. She still hadn't even married him yet.

Chapter 37

There had been a buzz about town for the last couple of days. Spending more time at the manor now than ever before, she got to see preparations start to formulate over their engagement party first hand. Imagining this must be how every event at the house started off and a little in awe of how much went on behind the scenes to the grand events.

A huge workforce of staff was called in to clean the large halls and downstairs' rooms adjoining thoroughly; every detail was meticulously seen too, even the corners. Large chandeliers were lowered, dusted and cleaned to sparkle for the approaching day. Curtains removed and professionally freshened up. Floors buffed and polished. A crew of ten or fifteen people, bustling around for hours on end attending to every small aspect of making the place sparkle.

Cases of glasses, crates of alcohol and endless boxes were carried in over a few days and disappeared under Alice's watchful eye to some secret storage place. Boxes of linens and place settings and beautiful table décor and candles. The stream of people who came and went with swatches and floral samples, cake samples, food samples, seemed overwhelmingly never ending and Rob, Abby and Alice, just took it all in their stride.

The event coordinator Deborah, Rob's very efficient assistant, appeared only once; talking to everyone as though commander and chief before sweeping off with Hamish Munro's folder of details in hand and setting things in place. Hamish had set the party in motion, but he left the minute details to the normally invisible employee, who was obviously used to this responsibility, judging by the speed in which tasks were dealt with and vans were arriving.

Rose couldn't help but feel the anticipation and excitement every time she walked into the big hall. The room being set out far in advance so preparations could be made, table decor calculated and buffet food chosen, generally how it would all look with one corner being completely set up to trial the finishing touches.

Abby was old hat at this kind of thing, wandering behind the stream of people with checklists and 'umming' and 'ahhing'. Nodding and signing sheets of paper, seemingly disinterested in most of it. Rose was overwhelmed with the vastness of it all and shuddered with fear every time Abby told her she would soon be wearing the crown as 'Hostess with the mostest', soon enough; Laird's wife took over all of this kind of thing apparently. Along with a ring came the title and upkeep of this house, overseeing the social aspect and generally becoming the master of the party bar, just as Rob's mother had been.

Rob, although still attentive to her, had withdrawn somewhat over the last couple of days. He was still dealing with work issues and she knew he was still on edge about the way things had ended with Morag. He was more aware of not shutting her out this time, really trying not to, and it was endearing to see him trying to get used to the new behaviour of sharing and letting her in. It couldn't be easy for him, having to be the one, who after so long of looking after this fragile woman was now the cause of her pain and distance.

He disappeared briefly when he had too, but mostly he had been working from his home office. He liked having Rose close by, easy to find her and strip her naked when the longing overtook him or he needed to relieve stress, and he had grown a huge attachment to Muffin, who sometimes stole the space between them in bed. Currently Muffin was in his office with him, using Rob's lap as a nap cushion. It wasn't the first time she had woken to find both gone in the early hours of the morning, seeing them in the distance outside. Rob jogging along the wood line with her little fur ball bouncing along beside him, tongue flapping free as he joyously kept pace with his new master.

Alice had taken a huge soft touch to Muffin, plying him with a never-ending trail of treats, homemade dog food and always a bone for him by the fire in the cosy room. Tommy had even made him an enclosure in the side garden, so he could be let out from the kitchen door to run wild, a new shiny kennel at the far end and of course lots of Tommy attention when he was out there too. He had become everyone's stand in child, to adore and spoil mercilessly. Today he was sporting a woolly jumper, made by one of the knitting group ladies as the weather was cooling and had another ten packed in a box in Rob's room from other equally generous needlers.

Her parents were arriving hours before the party and staying at her cottage. She had popped down from time to time to keep the place clean, light the odd fire and make sure it felt lived in. She missed it sometimes but the lure of Rob was more than the lure of the cottage and he needed to be there right now, near his office so he could working later into the night. Near family, while they expected him to get involved in the preparations and everything going on.

Rose was starting to feel more at home in the manor anyway, enjoying her time lounging with him in the cosy or sharing tasks in the kitchen when they were hungry. She had set up her art supplies in a small unused study downstairs; borrowing an old desk from one of the disused bedrooms and shelves from another. This house had so many rooms and halls littered about, she wondered if she would ever see them all and learn to navigate her way around. It seemed every time she went wandering she found another door she had never been behind before, a labyrinth of canvas covered rooms and nooks galore.

She discovered the manor had a cellar purely by accident, when Muffin managed to get himself down there and had been crying relentlessly. Hearing him, but not finding him, in a surge of panic before Alice appeared rosy-cheeked from washing floors elsewhere in the big house. She had listened for a second, before leading Rose down a small hall, concealed behind the kitchen via a door that looked like a wall panel and into a creaky stairway down to a floored and musty wine cellar. Stacks and stacks of wooden racks, mostly full of dusty bottles and a whole sectioned off area where the party supplies were being kept. Crates and barrels of various alcohol and of course a huge corner dedicated to the whiskies that the Munro named graced in its familiar packaging. Muffin was hiding behind a stack of sacks, shaking in fear and shivering from the cool temperature down here. Relieved to be rescued and pampers and cuddled by his heroin's.

There was only one more full day left before their party and Rose knew he still had not heard from Morag. The town was buzzing; elegant invites sent near and far and RSVP's received with barely any declined. Yet from her, complete radio silence.

Munro family. Turner family. A gazillion locals and those further afield that had connection with the Munros had all RSVP'd to accept. Local news reporters for small town papers and magazines had shamelessly asked for open invites and she knew a couple of photographers for the latter were to appear when the festivities began. Rob hadn't been kidding when he said this news would interest more than the local gossips. It seemed the entire north of Scotland and outer islands were buzzing about this event and many were travelling far to come. The Munro's were a known family and as lots of them lived further afield, then this was becoming the party everyone wanted to attend.

Rob had been quiet all day, coming and going, always stuck to his phone or closed in his office with a serious expression on his handsome face. Or walking in and out with his nose in papers and oblivious to the chaos around him as he passed from office to kitchen for coffee and back again.

She had barely seen much of him since breakfast this morning, she knew he had managed to salvage some sort of resolution to his construction issues and business seemed to be returning to normal. She had to get used to this side of life with him, knowing the house and all the expensive perks were all possible because he worked hard and long hours. Because he was a huge deal in the Munro Empire and over seen far more than she even knew about so his father could stay in retirement. Not that any of it really mattered; she would have followed him anywhere, even if he had been penniless and living in a shack. Rob was enough and all this just added to how much she loved him.

She opened the door to his office quietly, placing the tray of food and coffee on the side table and turned to leave him in peace. His focus was on his laptop and the landline fixed to his ear in mid conversation. He held up his hand to catch her attention and motioned for her to wait with a half-smile; Rose stood patiently, watching him type something while propping the phone to his ear, he said his goodbyes and dropped it back down, catching it easily and replacing it on the cradle.

'Come here baby.' He smiled lazily and stood up from his chair as she approached, guiding her to sit in the warm leather instead and planting a kiss on her as she slid past him obediently. He reached out across the smooth table in front of her, pulled over a pile of papers and a shiny dark folder, depositing them in view and sitting down on the edge of the table so he could look over her them too.

'We're moving!' He declared huskily, a smile still stuck on his face and a knowing look in his eye. Rose looked up in alarm, immediate protest forming on her lips as she caught the humour in his smile and glanced back down questioningly as he tapped the papers. Looking down she realised the first few were paint charts and furniture brochures and a layout of the manor plans.

'I'm confused.' She looked back and forth from him to the pile of papers. Rob slid out the dark glossy folder from the base of the pile; an architect's name and logo emblazoned in gold foil on one corner and flipped it open to reveal a spread of technical drawings and symbols, notes and details, that she didn't understand.

'It's a floor plan! Plans to turn three rooms into one master bedroom; one en-suite, one room a la Rose, and a new office for me.' He leaned further over her so he could flick to an exact page.

'Where?' She laughed quizzically, sure this was some abstract joke and already finding a million reasons she never wanted to leave this village or even this house.

'Upstairs. This end of the house. Somewhere I doubt you have ever ventured.' He shrugged, flicking over to another page of drawings and leaning in to plant a kiss on top of her head. Rose sighed a little with relief, knowing they weren't about to up sticks and move anywhere.

'And this is for us? Why?' She queried, still a little unsure.

'Because, my beautiful bride to be, as happy and cosy as we are down here every night, it wasn't really ever planned as a love nest. It was a bedroom of convenience so I could work and sleep without wandering far and disturbing Abby or my father, when he still lived in the house.' He was back looking at the plans and shuffling papers around to find her the designers view.

'And? What's wrong with it?' Rose smiled softly, a warmth flooding through her when she saw the hints of images with soft feminine decor and a blazing fireplace in among the sheets.

'Something you once said got me thinking.'

She laughed, confused, and trying to think back to tit bits of conversation in her mind from the past several months.

'I said I wanted to move into a bigger room?' Rose couldn't ever remember any conversations regarding the living or sleeping situations, as long as he was with her and snuggled close, she would live anywhere.

'Not exactly…You said you didn't really like being here without me. I figured that's partly because you don't feel like this could be your home. Is your home.' He was gazing at her now, watching as she slowly moved papers around on the desk, trying to take it all in and decipher what half of it meant.

'Rob. I'm still getting used to this place, it's like the never-ending story, always expanding everywhere I go. Labyrinth in the north!' She laughed as she again flipped a page, seeing more samples and colour schemes that mirrored her homely cottage perfectly.

'You're going to be living here as my wife. I don't want to bring my bride back from our honeymoon to try and fit into my life. I want this house and this life to be as much yours as it is mine.' He was fully staring at her now, watching her every move and waiting.

'So, a new bedroom, and what is room a la Rose?' She blinked up at him, catching his eye on her and the way he was smiling, sending shivers and warmth flooding through her once more with the sheer look of adoration.

'That would be Abby's title for it. You need room to work, paint and draw.' He shifted from the desk, pulling her hand and beckoning her to follow as he got up and hauled her with him possessively. Turning at the door to stroke her cheek with his thumb and trace a gentle kiss across her mouth teasingly. As always Rose's body reacted greedily and felt disappointed when he turned, taking her hand once more and leading her further into the house.

Leading her up the familiar stair, they turned left along the darker end of the house towards the less used rooms, which were mostly full of sheet-covered furniture and drawn drapes. He pulled open double doors at the very end of the long shadowy hall into a vast wide space of light and airiness which had her blinking her eyes to adjust.

Two matching huge windows were facing them and letting a huge amount of sunlight glare in at them, dazzling her vision with the sheer power of light. A huge stone fireplace was nestled against one wall to the right and someone had cleared and cleaned this space so it was completely bare of all furniture, coverings and dust. And of course, clear of any window coverings to protect her eyes.

'This would be the bedroom.' He walked in, turning her around in an arc, letting her see the huge size and space and giving her a moment to let it sink in, it really was a huge space with a tonne of potential. 'Over there some fitted wardrobes and units. Maybe room for a sitting area; you know, our own living room to cosy up in. Whatever you want!' He led her back out to the small hallway, to a door directly to the left of the space and effortlessly opened it. Another large room with equally large windows, again bright and spacious and completely blank, a cream canvas ready for a new purpose. This one was slightly less vast than the first and minus a fireplace. Rob let her go as he moved into the middle of the space, extending his arms and gesturing around him.

'This would be split into two. A large en-suite with a huge bath for two. Spacious shower, twin sinks and vanities... His and hers! Plenty room for some water sports.' He winked naughtily, leaning out to catch her hand, pulling her towards the centre of the room with a suggestive twinkle in his eye. As soon as he had her close he pulled her body to mould his and butted his groin into her with a wink, Rose sighed and shoved him off playfully. With another grin, he turned back to showing off the room to her.

'Would take in this space and one huge window here. The other window would be in your space with an internal hall running along over there, where the current entryway is, leading to your own little haven. Can only get to it from our bedroom that way, so no unwanted guests. Your own secret hideaway to work in peace and would keep noise to a minimum even when the house was full of people.' He looked thoughtful for a moment. 'Unless you wanted a bigger room? Then we have one across the hall, it's not as big as this one, but still pretty huge if it was only for you and no bathroom.' Rob regarded her as though waiting for an answer, and extended his hand out to her when she made a move towards him. She shook her head, kissing him gently on the mouth when she was back in his embrace.

'It sounds amazing.' her eyes were filling up with emotion, completely touched that he wanted to do this for them, for her.

'There's more.' He pulled her towards the far window, the one earmarked for her own private studio with a grin that was beaming, as though he was about to share the most wonderful secret. 'Look out over there.' Rob positioned her at the window in front of him and pointed out in front of her into the wilderness, her gaze following. The view across the fields was beautiful and amazing, the hills in the distance and the large forest to the right vaguely familiar.

'Once they sort out the north forest. Cut back some of the foliage and remove a couple of trees then you will have an uninterrupted view of the back side of the cottage right there, baby.' He pointed more directly at a tiny hint of her cottage peeking from behind a tree. Her hand drew to her throat, taking an emotional gasp and turning into him to throw her arms around him.

Such a thoughtful tiny detail. It meant so much more than he realised. Seeing that quaint dainty house even when she was not physically there would make life here perfect.

'Thank you, Rob it's perfect.' Her voice was soft with gratitude and happy tears as she nuzzled into him, looking around again to catch another glimpse of her tiny haven. It really would be the most perfect view.

'You will always have that place, Rose. I'll even sign a prenup making sure that no matter what, it stays yours and yours alone.' His deep voice and serious tone made her squeeze him tighter, her heart ready to burst with emotion. She shook her head, knowing that even if they ever parted, he would never take it from her. Her haven. Her heart. Rob knew how much she loved it.

'What about your office and the room downstairs?' She blinked up at him adoringly from her angle, unshed tears of happiness being swallowed down as she focused on the most gorgeous grey eyes in existence.

'I need to keep some sort of bachelor pad in this place, for nights you turf me out. I'd rather a bed than a couch to toss and turn the night away in.' He joked and kissed her quickly on the cheek.

'Shut up, you daftie.' She smiled, elbowing him lightly in the stomach as he laid his arms easily around her shoulders, her head nestling against him as she still stared at the beautiful view. This corner of the house was the one she could see when she stood tiptoe in her kitchen; so many months ago, that glimpse of the dark house and overgrown tree line. It warmed her knowing that from the cottage she would be able to see their own special part of the house and from here she could see her own special little hideaway.

'I'll move my office up across the hall. Keep it separate from our room so I don't wake you when I have to work late. The rooms down there will stay as bedroom and a small sitting room for guests, like your parents. I want to keep close enough that I can still crawl into bed and molest you should I need a break.' He chuckled, nuzzling into her neck from behind and sending sparks through her body.

'Still have your priorities then!' She giggled and then wriggled as his nuzzling became more of groping and nibbling and a hand tried to slide under her dress.

'Always, my number one priority is molesting you.' Rob spun her around so he could catch her front on, picking her up to pull her legs around his waist and carrying her out of the room that way. Sitting high on him, with his hands under her butt, and her hands on his shoulders. Rose laughed and leaned down to kiss him a little more passionately, feeling that inner surge of satisfaction when he had to quickly put her down; unable to control himself and pinning her to the wall for an erotic kiss that left both panting and his hands up her dress. Rob wickedly manoeuvred her for a breathless quickie right there, dress still on and underwear pulled aside, mumbling in her ear about 'christening their room'. He was good at long and slow love making, but equally good a five minute speed sessions when the passion overtook them.

Finally, looking more flushed and ruffled than before, they walked out of the room, still pawing and kissing one another.

Pulling her back to the hall outside the doors, he stood in the wide space and motioned around them with one hand, it was darkened from lack of windows and a little dim.

'The plans include this area too. Turning these rooms into one suite by bringing this area here to a close with an outer doorway. Once were safely tucked up in here we will have privacy, so you can wander about naked without worrying about anyone's eyes except mine.' He was looking at her in that devilish way again that brought a smile to her face. He had the knack for making her feel like the sexiest woman alive.

'You're sure you want to do this Rob? Its, so much work and upheaval.?. So much money!' Rose had to drag her eyes off of those wide, strong shoulders and inviting muscular body, still reeling from the passion of minutes ago and aching to be back in bed this very moment with him.

'Honey, you're marrying into a family that has no financial issues. You need to start getting used to the fact that money will never be a problem. Start abusing your right as my wife to max out my credit cards. Buy whatever you want... A new car. A million dresses...A room full of kinky underwear.' Again, with the glint in his eye and she knew it was not a joke, Rob was rather partial to her sexiest underwear and had made her keep it on a few times with lovemaking.

'Ummm, yeah, I don't think I could do that.' She laughed, feeling weird about talking money, even though it was inevitably part of a marriage. They had never broached the subject before now and she didn't really have any clue as to how rich the Munro's really were.

'Fine. I'll just give you a bank account and keep it topped up.' He shrugged as if that was the perfect solution and seemed to ignore Rose's 'I don't think so' laugh.

'Rob? Be serious...What could I possibly want? Or need? This house is paid for, full of food and people running after me. The cottage paid for too, so not even rent or a mortgage. I earn money, I'm financially stable, I may not be a rich Munro...'

'Yet!'

She laughed at him and his raised brow and carried on.

'Yet! But really, I am not some gold digging big spender. I'm happy with what I have and I don't need anything. Definitely not a new car!'

'I'm sure Abby will soon enough introduce you to her favourite designer dress boutiques and shoe shops, when she knows you have a sea of cash. She gets a limit on her spending every month.' He kissed her head and pulled her along the hall, back to the familiar balconied rooms where Abby normally dwelled and looked back at her with a steady gaze. 'Talking of dresses, at least let me pay for a new dress for tomorrow?'

'I have a dress!' Rose could only shake her head at him and smile.

'Shoes?' He raised his other brow.

'Already delivered!'

'Perfume?' He was frowning now, obviously getting exasperated at how completely self-reliant Rose was when it came to money.

'Bought weeks ago, on a trip with your darling sister.' Rose giggled at his slightly sour expression and reached out to smooth away his frown with her fingertips.

'There must be something I...?' He was exasperated now. She covered his lips with her fingertips

'I'm not with you for the presents and money Rob. I'm all good. Trust me.' She leaned up to kiss him on the cheek, resting back on her heels to smooth his open shirt collar and steal a grope at that hard six pack and muscled chest through his clothes.

'You're wounding my male ego here.' His eyes had darkened somewhat and she wasn't sure if it was annoyance or lust, he was focusing on her cleavage as her hands ran over his shoulders once more.

'If it matters that much, surprise me with something... Flowers! A bottle of bubbly before the party. I'm easy pleased. I just need you!' He pulled her onward a little but she stopped him before they reached the stair, turning to pull his loosened tie down towards her, biting her lips suggestively with a naughty look in her eye and husky tone. 'Or maybe just something you're really good at.' The grin on his face appeared instantly as he got the hint.

'I'll give you that a hundred times a day, if that's what you want.' Rob leaned in close to murmur the words, reaching down yet further to kiss her intensely and wrap his arms around her possessively. Rose succumbed to another passionate kiss, tongues meeting and hands exploring her ass.

'Oh, give over and get a room.' Abby's voice cut in as she trailed up the stair, dragging her college bag behind her. the bump, bump, as it hit the stairs behind her.

'I was in the process of doing that?' Rob grinned at his baby sister, batting her head with his palm as she passed close by.

'Finally!... Did she like the plans?' She cocked her head, stopping to regard them both.

'She!' Is right here Ab's, and can answer for herself.' Rose butted in, still wrapped in Rob's embrace and snuggling into him.

'Great, well?' Abby enquired impatiently.

'Yes. I love the plans and ideas. I'm really happy and I think it's going to be fabulous living on the same floor as you.' Rose grinned at her and laughed at Abby's eye roll.

'Did you inform my dearest brother that we require sound proofing?' Abby threw a cheeky smile as she passed them on the floor and walked off into her room nearby. Rose shook her head at the retreating figure and saw Rob frowning after her questioningly.

'Your sister claims that everyone can hear us when we.... You know...' She nudged him suggestively and watched that serious face break into a smile and wicked look.

'Can't argue with that.' He laughed, his cheeky grin an almost identical match for his siblings and no hint of the embarrassment Rose had felt when Abby had informed her the first time. Not that she expected Rob to feel ashamed about it, he didn't care.

'You two are far more alike than I care to admit.' She raised her own brow at him.

'It's hardly a surprise!' He winked at her.

'Yes, I know, because as she keeps telling me, you're from the same gene pool.'

'Well, it's no coincidence that your best friend is the sister of your betrothed. You must have a serious attachment to our gene pool.' He moved in to nuzzle her once more.

'I must!' She smiled, letting him trace small kisses across her neck before he spun her around to face the hall below them. The balcony in front of her and the great sheer drop in her vision.

'This my love, is going to be all yours... Bedroom first, but then everything you see, all those doors and rooms tucked away. I want you to do whatever you need to make this place as much you as it is Munro.' He sounded completely serious.

'Rob, I can't. It's not right. This house, it's beautiful as it is.'

'It's dated and not been touched since my mother was alive, most of the rooms haven't seen any refurbishment since Abby was born. I've done the odd thing here and there, like the snug by the kitchen, the office, and guest room. I want you to make this our home Rose; the way I feel when I walk into the cottage and I feel you in every detail. Every cosy simple touch that screams Rose. I love being there because it's so you and I want that for here too.'

'What about your dad?' Rose gaped at him in wide eyed disbelief. Unsure what to feel at his request.

'He agrees. He even said that one day he might consider moving back to his old room, if the house was no longer a shrine to my mother's tastes. She wouldn't want us to live in the past and hold her memory in this way.' Rob was focused on the hall below, no hint of jest at all, just dead pan seriousness.

'Really?' Rose couldn't comprehend taking over this huge house and changing it that way.

'We all need this Rose...I'm sure my bank manager won't agree, but I think it's time to start over fresh.'

'Ruin your house with my love of fluffy cushions and floral prints.' She laughed, cuddling back against him and trying not to feel fear at what he was asking.

'Breathe some life and love back into these halls. Make it a place we want our kids to grow up. I'm tired of this museum. Fill some of these rooms again, more staff... More noise.' He sighed and rested his face against her cheek, both of them gazing across the space.

'More parties!' Echoed Abby's voice from somewhere nearby.

'Less alcohol for Abby.' Rose chimed in with a grin.

'I don't know. There're some advantages to her passing out stone cold drunk.' Rob stifled an ouch as Rose elbowed him in the stomach. Still never admitting to Abby that their makeup sex had started in her bathroom, feet from her unconscious body, and as she was in ear shot. Rose wasn't about to tell her now.

'Whatever!' Abby muttered cluelessly and joined them on the balcony, overlooking the hall floor and its endless bright marble surface and dated furniture.

'Get rid of some of the ancient antique crap that makes this place feel like a Jane Austen set.' She pouted and pointed out a wooden side table with ornate legs that Alice had arranged a huge flower bouquet on.

'I'm pretty sure the antique 'stuff' are probably Munro heirlooms, and very expensive.' Rose informed her with a maternal frown. Abby shrugged.

'It can all go into storage or be sold.' Rob cut in. 'Unless there's anything you want to be left here or like. We're not an overly sentimental family when it comes to furniture. Start from scratch if you want.' He sighed over her head this time, resting his chin on her.

'You're both serious, aren't you?' She pulled her head free, looked up at him, craning her neck in bewilderment.

'Deadly!... It's time Rose. A new chapter. No more grieving and living in the past. My mother would want the next lady of the house to put some life and smiles back into this house. She would have loved you, everything about you and what you have brought to my life. She would agree with me on this.' Rob smiled softly at her and gave her a squeeze, Abby nodding in agreement with a wistful look in her eye at the mention of her mother.

Rose stared back down at the vast floor again; the height quite impressive, taking note of the task before her. The huge task weighing down suddenly as she realised the amount of time and work it could potentially take.

'It could take forever to change this entire house.' She said aloud to no one in particular.

'Well, you are going to be stuck here married to 'that' for an eternity.' Abby pointed out, thrusting a thumb at Rob. 'Need to have something to stave off the boredom of domestic bliss.' She smiled and dodged Rob's swing at her head.

'Hey' Rob cut in. 'There's a lot to be said for domestic bliss missy.' He chided, trying for a second grab at her but she moved further away with a giggle. Rose tried to wriggle out of the way, expecting a childish sparring to begin but Rob pulled her closer and wouldn't let her go with his strong arm around her waist.

'On tap sex!' Abby shrugged. 'That's the only perk I can think of.' She had walked back to the balcony, further along so she was out of Rob's reach and looking back down at the floor below.

'But you wouldn't know about any of that, though, would you?...Being a sweet innocent untouched child!' Rob grimaced and threw her a shady look that had no hint of humour, a definite rocky path for Abby to be treading along. Rose cut in as she saw the tilt of Abby's head and the mouth pursing with a sarcastic response that would most likely make Rob self-implode.

'Nope, she wouldn't! Needs to just shut up and go play with her toys...Don't you Abs?' Rose shooed her away with hand gestures and warning looks.

'Yes of course. The Barbie's and such!' Abby rolled her eyes and headed back off towards her room, knowing when a fight was brewing and for once doing as Rose was pleading with her eyes for her to do. Last thing she needed was Rob going into big brother mode over sex and strangling Duncan to death.

Rose stifled a laugh as she caught the terrifyingly protective look on Rob's face as he watched his sister walk off and close her door.

'You don't think she's let that boy get to third base, do you?' He asked a tad aggressively, a frown taking over his face and jaw tightening. Looking away, eyes wide in alarm, Rose just shrugged.

'Who can tell? Abby's not naive or dumb when it comes to boys.' Rose hoped he wouldn't keep pushing, she didn't want to lie to him but at the same time, she didn't want to grass on Abby. He pondered the thought silently, staring back at Abby's door and muttered something about needing a stern word and a man to man with that boy, almost under his breath. His grip on Rose a little tighter than before.

'Is this what you're going to be like?' She turned, pressing her back against the balcony, pulling him closer so their bodies pressed together

'When?' He swung his eyes back to her.

'When you have little girls of your own running around and they get their first boyfriends?' She giggled, instinctively reaching up to smooth that furrow of his brow away.

'Worse! Because they will most likely look a lot more like you and that will just make me crazy bad when it comes to guys trying it on.' That furrow only deepened with a hint of fierceness.

'I may have to make sure we only have sons then.' Rose couldn't help but giggle at him and his over protective ways.

'That could work!' He grinned, breaking that scary look and normal calm and gorgeous Rob features returning. Lifting her under the butt to meet his mouth, he began kissing her again.

'Want to get a head start on perfecting our baby making skills... You know, perfection takes practice.'

Chapter 38

Her parents arrived early the next day, bubbling with excitement as she settled them into the cottage and almost being squeezed to death with overzealous hugs and kisses.

Her room was looking a lot barer since she had packed up a lot of personal things and moved them to the manor. Rob had encouraged her to start transitioning her things up there, to slowly get used to the idea the cottage was no longer her main home and that his was. It had felt weird at first, moving her things to his, putting some of her clothes hanging in the space he had cleared for her in his wardrobe. The addition of a few trinkets and pictures on his shelves had made her realise how right he was about the room; it was undeniably male. Dark wood and cool blue tones, masculine, modern furniture and a wall of technology. She couldn't just add to the room her soft girly things and make it look more unisex. Her things just stood out even more harshly against the male décor and the space more of a squeeze now two people cohabited. With only a handful of her clothes from here, his wardrobe already looked maxed out. She hadn't even shown him the space her shoes needed as most were hidden under her bed at the cottage and would most likely have given him heart failure.

Her mother held her captive for more than an hour, she wanted details and stories, to bask in the nearness of the beautiful ring and hear all the wonders of the party planned for tonight. She had missed her. Rose's brothers would unfortunately not be attending, not that she had thought they would. One lived in New Zealand for a start and could travel for a wedding but not for a party. The other was in the forces; an RAF officer and had not been able to get any leave on such short notice, but she had spoken to both on skype; promises made to make sure they both got here for the wedding and Rose knew they would come, she wanted them to meet Rob properly and not via internet calls.

She drove back to the house with her dress and shoes firmly zipped inside a clothes protector, her bags of more items and makeup safely stowed on her passenger seat as she made the short journey which was now almost second nature.

Rob met her inside as he was heading out to meet a client and told her to take everything upstairs.

'Put your stuff in my mother's old room baby, our room of choice for tonight, for old times sakes.' Rob winked and pecked her on the cheek as he relieved her of her cases.

'Hmmmm... Sounds good to me.' She smiled coquettishly at him and led the way to the stairs.

'Nice big tub in there for some clean fun later, if you're game?'

Rose immediately smiled at his obvious intentions, heat creeping up her cheeks and a quick glance back at that wicked look.

'I don't think clean is the right word for what you have planned.' She giggled and climbed the stairs, dodging staff with feather dusters and canvas sheets.

'Me? I'm an innocent boy with no filthy intentions at all.' Rob mock gasped and winked at her. 'Besides, up here, away from the rest of the house... Good for sneaking off mid party and requires no sound proofing.' Rose could only grin and kerb the urge to roll her eyes at him.

He kissed her goodbye when he dropped her bags in the bedroom and promised to be back soon, leaving with a light smack on her butt which made her yelp. He had already been up at some point, his clothes and shoes were draped casually over the plush comforter, some aftershave and male products on the vanity, cufflinks and his bow tie neatly beside them.

Rose added her clothes to the bed, unzipping the bag and hanging up the pale gold coloured gown. Its lace sleeves and fitted bodice completely see through, figure hugging and floor length with an open back coming to a V at the base of her back. She pulled out the satin camisole dress that went underneath. Strappy and cut in the back to match the lace with small clips that would conceal the join of the two dresses, keeping them in place as one. She had found it in a vintage boutique with Abby and fallen in love, long before she knew she would be having an engagement party and it somehow felt right. She had found pale gold satin heels with diamante straps, crossed delicately over her toes and ankles, to go with it more recently on an internet scourge for the perfect pair.

It was too early to start getting ready but Abby had arranged for a hairdresser to come by soon and get them looking fabulous. Rose had turned down the offer of a makeup artist, feeling that her own skills with her own makeup would make her feel less showy and dolled up, nervous that tonight was not just about enjoying herself but really about being introduced to the public as the future lady Munro. Having people taking their pictures and asking them questions so people could nosey and read all about the romantic fairy-tale story. She supposed to outsiders looking in, it was pretty spectacular.

Handsome rich Laird who inherited his title early on. Love at first sight with some big city dwelling artist, pulled to the cottage of her dead aunt. It had it all. Romance. Money. A dramatic love story and damaged woman clawing them apart, if only they knew the turmoil behind closed doors. She couldn't blame them really, she would have read about it too if it hadn't been her life.

Rose pushed Morag out of her mind's eye as the thought crept in again, as it had done many times over the last few days and swallowed down the surge of trepidation once more. Morag added the drama to their love story, and lately the lack of it had been unnerving both of them. No one knew where or what Morag was doing but she couldn't stay hidden for much longer.

* * *

The hours went by so quickly, Rose felt like she could barely catch her breath. Her long soak in the beautiful tub had been drawn out with Rob's return, joining her and making it less of a clean soak than she had intended. They had left the floor drenched and soapy and ended up trailing water and suds across the threshold into the open room and the bedroom rug. He really was incorrigible. Her moans and cries muffled purposely, aware that Abby's room was closer up here and she could not get the words 'sound proofing' out of her mind.

Locking Muffin in the bedroom after walking and feeding him and making sure he had everything he needed had taken only minutes. Calls to her parents to arrange the finer meeting details for later that night and seating plans. She had eaten a light meal to carry her through to the evening buffet while Rob was taking a last-minute conference call downstairs and Rose just felt like the day was spinning away too fast.

The hairdresser had insisted on using one of the large empty rooms downstairs to fix the girls hair in stylish up do's; Rose opting for an elegant knot, low down at the back of her head with her hair curled prior so it looked less neat and smooth. Some loose tendrils curled lightly and hanging free and it was all held securely with a vintage clasp Abby had found at a junk shop the week before. Rose's make up was in keeping with the romantic vintage style and her reflection in the mirror calmed some of her nerves, even without her outfit on, she looked beautiful.

She pulled on her dress in front of the bedroom mirror as Rob came in, already in his tuxedo and bow tie and looking devilishly handsome, like a sexy James bond in a modern remake of Octopussy. She smiled appreciatively at him in the mirror, catching his eye and the way his eyes skimmed her body with unconcealed lust.

'You look stunning baby. Most gorgeous woman I have ever laid eyes on.' Rob came up behind her, zipping up her dress the last of the way and ran fingertips across her exposed skin above the low back.

Rose's body tingled in response, closing her eyes to enjoy the feel of his hands on her.

'Guess I look like I go with you then, you look incredibly hot.' She giggled and opened her eyes, once again locking gaze on his reflection and the smile beaming back at her.

'Have a standard to upkeep.' He laughed and slid something out of his inner jacket pocket, holding out a small silver wrapped box in front of her with a smile and a nudge.

'You did say if it mattered that much!' His voice tickled her neck, her skin coming alive at the proximity of him and excitement at the appearance of the gift, sending her stomach into butterflies.

'Rob! I told you... No gifts.' She laughed, turning and kissing him before wiping her subtle shade of lipstick from his mouth with her fingertips, finally taking the box from his hand. She moved past him to the nearby table and laid it down so she could use both hands to open the latch and open it carefully. Removing the lid, then the expensive paper and revealing a flat smaller velvet box encased inside the larger one, she glanced up at him in anticipation, feeling like pretty woman and unable to stop smiling.

He was watching her carefully, eagerly, awaiting her reaction and saying nothing at all. She withdrew the smaller box, pushing everything else aside and clicked it open to reveal a beautiful set of earrings and necklace in the same vintage style and stones as her engagement ring. An obvious antique and stunningly delicate and beautiful. She gasped and traced the pieces with her manicured finger, admiring the detailed cut and almost perfect colour match of the stones to her ring.

'Oh my god Rob, it's breathtakingly beautiful.' She exhaled, letting him take the box and remove the necklace, turning her back to the mirror so he could close it around her neck and let it nestle against her clavicle. Rose could only gawp at it in the mirror, completely in awe of such beauty and overcome with emotion.

'Beautiful jewellery for a beautiful bride to be.' He whispered, kissing her below the ear and moving off to retrieve the earrings. She turned back, taking the earrings, which were more like delicate short studs and put them carefully in her ears as her eyes filled with moisture, unable to stop looking at them in the mirror.

'You like?' He watched her, a smile creeping over his face at her obvious reaction. She was admiring them, touching them gently. He could tell without even asking, the blush of happiness on her cheeks, the gratitude in her eyes and the smile covering her face.

'Yes. There so beautiful and elegant. Perfect... So unique, and a perfect match for my ring... Where ever did you get them?' She turned to him with a dazzling grin before returning to admire them lovingly.

'Believe it or not, I came upon them by chance. When I headed out this morning to pick up a necklace at Brookstone's, the antique place, I had already chosen for you. This had just been brought in, sold on from an estate that had no surviving inheritors left. I saw it and immediately knew it was meant for you.' Rob was back behind her, hands on her shoulders and jaw against her head.

'That's kind of sad.' She glanced down forlornly, playing with the delicate pendant on her chest and angled it up to look at it closely.

'That's what happens when you don't fall in love and have any children to leave it all too.' He answered, watching her and once again letting his eyes skim the length of her appreciatively.

'Not much chance of it ending up back in that situation anytime soon then.' Rose smiled up at his reflection once more, catching the way he was looking at her and blushing furiously. Despite the intimate ways she knew him, sometimes it still made her act like a flustered teen when she caught open desire on that far too perfect face.

'Something to treasure and pass down to a daughter for a change.' He winked.

'Daughter?' She laughed playfully and frowned his way.

'Ok, girlfriend of one of our many sons.' He corrected, remembering a previous conversation about only having sons and brushed back a strand of her hair across her neck tenderly.

'Start our own tradition, passing on our own little piece of beauty.' Rose gazed at the necklace once more, warmed by the sentiment of that thought.

'Exactly.' Rob patted her butt. 'Ready to make a grand entrance?' He turned her slowly to him.

'No. But I'm sure you will look after me.' She slipped her arm into his strong familiar muscular one, feeling him tighten against her hand protectively.

'Always baby, always!'

* * *

It was even more overwhelming than she could have prepared for; Grand entrance was an understatement. The halls and grounds were already heaving with people when they finally emerged, early arrivals and local reporters milling around inside with glasses of free champagne being sipped down. The mood already electric with excitement and happy anticipation as they descended arm in arm. Flashes were already starting to go off by the edge of the stair and shouts of turn this way and people shouting out both of their names in a flurry of activity. Rose was overwhelmed, but followed Rob's lead, letting him guide and shield her and tried not to look like a petrified bunny in the headlights.

They obliged, smiling and murmuring to one another about 'goldfish in a bowl' and 'don't forget to give them your best side,' amid giggles and secret hand squeezes. There was a lot of back slapping and congratulations as they reached floor level, from people they both knew and didn't. Swarming in masses of reporters and locals. It was impossible for Rose to keep track. Between meeting a sea of people whose names ended in Munro, people who seemed to have some connection or acquaintance and a lot of familiar faces which had scrubbed up to a high standard. Some of her own distant family members and vaguely familiar folks that she was sure were relations on both sides.

Her parents were barely able to get a moment with her before more people cut in. If it was not for Rob's steadying arm across her back, his calm easy manner and ease of dealing with this craziness, she would have curled into a ball, overwhelmed and terrified. His warmth and presence, a constant calming influence and the way he shielded her with his body when people got too close around them. Her protector and carer, she couldn't love who he was any more than she did in that moment.

Her face began to ache from smiling, her skin tender from the endless sea of people kissing her on the cheek and when they were finally swept through into the huge ballroom, her eyes glittered with raw emotion at the beauty of the place and the overall emotion of the evening so far.

Taking in the room for the first time, fully prepared and set up, she could barely catch her breath. The muted golds and creams, rustic heather, moss and white floral arrangements on candle lit tables. Moss and willow vines, wrapped around the bases of candles and glass lanterns. Even the huge velvet drapes had been replaced with fairy light-studded, floaty white voiles, going from hugely high ceiling to floor in pools of soft fabric. Tall floral arrangements lined the corners on gold pedestals, each with a nestling of twinkling lights. Lit candles in crevices and corners and the huge fireplace filled with a spectacular array of them, all flickering gently among more floral arrangements. Tables all layered in smooth cream linens, lace and satin runners in complementing shades. The settings were all laid out elegantly and effortlessly with an orchestra playing soft music in one corner on the podium that seemed to move anytime this room had a function. Subtle classical music and she noted they all had on pale gold bow ties and matching waistcoats under dinner jackets.

Past the elaborate buffet spread at the far end of the huge dancefloor was another smaller podium, one table heavy laden with gifts and cards, a white post box for cards that people were merrily sliding white envelopes into and a stunning four tier cake. All cream and gold with floral details sweeping up across the layers in a spiral with a small bridal couple made of expensive china stood on top. Delicately hand painted and obviously very old. Rose moved forward out of Rob's grasp as he was pulled aside into a group to converse, coming to stand before the cake in awe.

'We do things in style.' Abby grinned. following her new sister in laws gaze. 'It's from our parent's wedding cake.'

'It's beautiful Ab's. The whole room is breath taking; I just can't find the words.' Rose felt the emotion crack in her throat and her eyes filled up. She dabbed at the corner of her lashes with a tissue and smiled at Abby.

'Should be for what it cost your husband to be.' Abby winked, throwing him a dazzling smile as he moved towards them now and shrugged it off.

'Husband?' Rose pressed questioningly. 'I thought your father was throwing about cheques for this.' She smiled up at him as he slid arms around her from behind and took a look at the cake himself.

'He was, but the old man has no sense of style. I needed to up the game and make sure our first function reflected my beautiful bride. Needed an injection of class.' Rob cut in smoothly and kissed her on the back of the head.

'It's all so beautiful Rob.' She meant it as she leant around to kiss him softly, giggling in surprise as he moved in like lightening for a deeper, harder kiss. Picking her up and pulling her feet off the ground, bringing her up to his height for a toe curling snog that make her feet curl back. A nearby cheer and clap of hands reminded them of their public status and he slid her down, smoothing out her dress for her and skimming her body sneakily with a twinkle in his eye. She laughed, never ceasing to find amusement in his ability to turn everything to sex.

'Never as beautiful as you.' He whispered sexily in her ear as he slid her arm into his and led her back into the throng of arrivals coming into the grand room.

* * *

The party soon took on a less formal feeling. The sea of well-wishers, extended family and friends, finally giving them some breathing space to dance and enjoy the party.

Damien appeared mid dancefloor throng and attempted to swing Rose away from dancing in front of Rob, throwing him a wide grin and a cheeky wink as he hustled her off comically. Rob caught her arm protectively, waving a mock fist under his chin which resulted in Damien grabbing him in a male hug, shaking hands and slapping each other on the back amid shouts over the loud music and the sounds of 'congrats bro' waving Rose's way. Leaning in quickly, Damien planted a kiss on the cheek of Rose and dodged Rob's swipe at his head with a laugh. Damien soon moved off to throw some moves at a nearby blonde in a purple dress, much to Rob's relief.

Rob pulled Rose back into him for a slower dance, resting her easily in his arms as the tempo slowed and couples filled the floor, his face against her temple. Softly embraced in his safe haven, feeling light headed and surreal, Rose couldn't help but think back to the last time they had danced on this floor together and how different it had been. She looked up at him adoringly and smiled at the memory, so much happier to be out in the open and most definitely wrapped in his loving embrace for all to see. For the first moment in her life since falling under the spell of Rob Munro, she felt completely still inside. Her mind focusing on nothing other than the feel of him against her, the familiar scent and the security of his hold and all thoughts of that troublesome red head fluttering away on the notes of the melody around them.

* * *

She was aware all night of the sea of smiling faces that kept tabs on them. People could not help but smile at the couple; the weirdness of human nature to want to stare at a couple in love and grin and feel warm and gooey inside. To hold their loved one's hands and squeeze as they reminisced what their first years together were like when young and full of lust. It was uncomfortable at first, but as the night wore on and drink infused her blood, her inhibitions faded away.

She found it easier to ignore the creepy staring and focus on having a good time as alcohol started to tilt her world, making everything a bit more sway and a lot less formal. Her vocabulary a bit on the sloppy side, Rob who never seemed to care about eyes on them, as he ran hands over his fiancée or pulled her in for passionate kisses on the dance floor, seemed to be handling his alcohol better than her. He still seemed in control, lucid and bright-eyed, despite seeing him empty several glasses and shifting to bottles of beer. The man could put it away like a typical Scot and he was coercing Rose to keep up with him with constant refills of her glass.

Rose's mother danced with Abby and Rose until her poor legs ached for a break and left them to it. Her father finding some male bonding time amid a sea of equally black bow tied males, including Rob and Hamish. Several of the faces around them seemed familiar, recognising a couple of Rob's cousins and school friends, it wasn't hard to find plenty of dancing partners while Rob was pulled into male bonding time or Abby was wrapped around Duncan.

The food was amazing, canopies divine; a spread fit for a king and although Rose tried not to make a pig of herself, found she was drawn to eat every twenty minutes. Unable to stop taste testing it all; between savoury and sweet foods, she literally never stopped grazing at the table. The upside was the alcohol levels in her blood were soaked up a bit, making her slur less noticeable when she swayed from conversation to conversation and she was most definitely full before long, with Rob in awe of how much she could actually put away in her small frame. Not that he couldn't eat, Rob was worse than Rose and seemed to have a bottomless pit of a stomach to match his ability to drink the bar dry.

Abby caused a minor scene when dirty dancing with Duncan on the floor and Rose had to intervene, stopping Rob dragging them apart. Pulling him away quickly and calming him on the side lines with fast words and sweet talk. He was not an easy guy to smooth over. Rose was about the only person in existence who had ever been able to tame him at all when fury descended and even she had to admit, when drunk he was near impossible to distract. He was not impressed with Abby as it was; the daring black dress that didn't leave much to the imagination was bad enough, but practically having sex on the dancefloor with risky dance moves and over the top snogging and groping was a push too far. Rob liked Duncan normally but whenever alcohol, baby sisters and sexy moves were involved, trouble always brewed. Hamish luckily had not even seen anything otherwise Rose would have been pulling two Munro men off to the side lines to remind them of milling reporters.

Rose eventually pulled him along the hall for a breather to calm him down, finding the close proximity of his gyrating sister and her boyfriend only keeping him simmering on the edge of fury. Finding one of the nearby rooms vacant that had been set up for stragglers needing a seat away from the party, Rose dragged him in with all her powers of persuasion. He slid down into a chair obediently as she stood over him and glared like a petulant child, every muscle in his body was tense and ready for action.

'Rob she's growing up. She's almost twenty!' Rose soothed, trying to smooth that frown away from his forehead and just meeting another glare. He was agitated and resisting Rose's hands on him, getting up to instead reluctantly pace back and forth. More evident he was far drunker than he looked, and far less in control.

'I know okay!... It's just... She's my baby sister and she will always be a little kid to me!' He turned to Rose, raising palms and almost growling as he thought about the scene again.

'I'm sure my brothers say the same thing.' She interjected. 'Imagine what they would say if they saw half the things we got up too.' She smiled softly, trying to make him stand still and let her touch him. His behaviour was petulant and a tiny bit irresistible to her in that moment, she couldn't help the smile creeping across her face.

'That's different! That's you and me...That's... argh!' He sat down frustrated and dropped his head into his palms, his elbows on his knees and his tuxedo jacket straining across his shoulders when sitting that way.

'That's what?' Rose nudged him with her knee playfully.

'My intentions are pure. There's a ring on your finger! I never ever laid hands on you without knowing I would end up with you... That you were going to be mine, always.' Rob sat up and looked her dead in the eye, that serious tone and angry furrow still evident.

'He might put one on hers before long.' She realised she had said the wrong thing as his eyes darkened and in a flash, he was back on his feet.

'I may wring his neck before he gets a chance.' His voice aggressive as he ran his hands through his hair distractedly and moved to start pacing again. She pushed him back down to sit instead and he didn't resist her this time.

'Why¿ She was laughing now. 'He loves her. She loves him. If anything, I'd say it's your sister that manhandles that boy, not vice versa. She has your hot blood. The poor guy just gets dragged along regardless.' Rose smoothed her fingers through his hair, taming some of the spiking going on that he had caused when running his own through it. His instant glare made her laugh and she slid down beside him, kissing him gently on the lips, hoping to smooth over his ruffled feathers. His face serious but he kissed her back.

'Is that what I do to you?' He looked at her a little more gently this time, his expression softening to one of questioning and a little frown of worry.

'Ummm. No… I'm a big girl. You may have some persuasive skills Mr Munro but I'm not someone who is easily dragged along! Trust me, anytime you lay hands on me, the feeling is mutual.' She assured him with another kiss, a finger trailing over his jawline and tracing his bottom lip. His face relaxed a little, the talk of sex bringing that twinkle back into his eye and making him forget why they had even come out here in the first place. Like an eternal dog on heat, she laughed and nudged him playfully.

'We could go upstairs for a little while. Take my mind off of it.' He winked and she knew it was only half in jest, his eyes were already roaming over her dress checking for ways to get her out of it.

'We could, but I think you may ruin my hair. And there are still reporters looming around taking pictures.' She sighed and waved towards the door they had come through airily.

'There are ways round that.' He was leaning in closer, finding her mouth, his hand sliding to her neck and pulling her to him seductively. She could taste the alcohol on his breath and it made her stir unexpectedly. Bringing back memories of bathroom floors and drunken reunions.

Who am I kidding? I can never resist him.

'Your bathroom is closer.' She breathed. It was all the permission he needed before he was up on his feet, pulling her along almost instantly by the wrist, sneaking past some people milling in the hall, he ducked her in another door. Heading a route she had never known, further into the depths of the narrow halls of the house, away from eyes and people and into areas where no lights had even been put on. Pulling her into a darkened room, shadows and sheeted furniture everywhere, he clicked open an internal door and slid her inside with a gentle hand and followed her in, closing it behind them. It was a bathroom she had never laid eyes on before.

'I figured we could christen somewhere new.' He grinned, lifting her up to slide her butt onto the vanity carefully, his hands already sliding up her naked smooth legs, bringing her dress to her thighs and putting himself between her knees. Her skin tingled and sizzled under his touch, immediately feeling that familiar aching warmth down deep inside. That longing they never seemed to quench for long. He moved in to kiss her, one hand gently cupping her throat, his other sliding into places that made her moan.

* * *

It wasn't long before he was pushing against her, inside her. Her back cold and pressed against the large mirror with her legs wrapped snugly around him. His hands holding his weight and hers against the wall as she clung to him; her dress up around her waist and his trousers around his ankles. She had pulled off his bow tie and her lipstick kisses were scattered over his naked chest where his unbuttoned shirt sat open. They were trying to stay quiet, but the moaning and gasping echoing around them was lost to their ears. Lost in pleasure and only aware of what they were doing to each other as they climaxed together in a flurry of heavy breathing and burning skin, collapsing in a sated heap on the vanity.

Satisfied and exhausted from the fast-paced passion which had overtaken them, he stood, holding her up for a few seconds to catch their breaths and cool the heat on exposed skin. Her hair was still very much intact. She giggled as he finally leant off her, able to let his legs take his weight again and release her onto the vanity with a lingering kiss.

'Our own engagement party, Rob!' She smiled accusingly. 'You are the worst!'

'Told you…I'm the victim… This is all you.' He grinned, pulling up his clothes and freeing his shirt so he could button it up again and tuck it in. She was looking around for her satin thong and trying to twist her dress back around, while sliding off of the high unit. He helped her down and held them up with a smile

'You should stay commando baby, it's god damn sexy as hell.' He winked her way, sliding alongside her to use the mirror while he fixed his bow tie back into neat perfection.

'Ummm, No! If I go out there panty less then you would be like a horny schoolboy all night, trying to get me back in here.' Rose raised a brow at him and started smoothing out her dress with little success.

'I can't argue with that, it's making me horny even thinking about it.'

He was putting his jacket back on as she smoothed out her hair and sighed at her lipstick mess, her cheeks rosy and her face glowing under her sheer makeup. That was not so easy to fix without her bag, so she had to try and wipe away the smudges and smears and pat her face with tissues and calm the tell-tale blush on her skin.

'You really are a terrible influence on me! Look at me… I look like I've just run a mile.' She sighed and gave up trying to rectify her reflection.

'You look as perfect as always, a little rosy cheeked but I like it. Tells me I'm doing something right baby.' He winked and kissed her on the cheek, cupping her butt as he moved past her.

Soon they were smoothed out and fully dressed, stopping to press her against the wall for a passionate kiss, he led her back out of the room in the same sneaky manner they entered. Holding her hand, they easily slid into the hall among the crowd of people, feigned innocence on both of their faces. No one seemed to have noticed their absence or the slightly satisfied, relaxed manner, in which they both looked now. Or the obvious glow and high colour on her cheeks that she had been unable to conceal.

The party was again in full swing, some loud thumping tune supplied by the appearance of the DJ, hidden behind some curtained booth. The orchestra was now free to get drunk and be merry and enjoy the rest of the night.

Rob swung her around to dance, that look on his face of sheer satisfaction and a wink at what they had just done. She shook her head knowing he was the worst influence on her she had ever known, she had never been this way with anyone else. She had never even thought she had it in her before she had met him. Swinging her back against him and around in time to the beat, she closed her eyes and got lost in the music.

* * *

The party fizzled out slowly.

She couldn't remember much of the end of the night, after being plied with enough alcohol to sink a ship. Rob filling her glass anytime it emptied, telling her to let go because he was there to take care of her. There had been shots on the bar, a drinking competition and memories of Rob bending her backwards over a table, to a chorus of chants, egging on, and propping a lime in her cleavage that he had happily retrieved with his teeth. She assumed there had been tequila. Lots and lots of tequila.

Her head ached and her body was in agony.

Opening a sleepy eye in the semi-dull room around her, she could see Rob's naked body flat out across the bed on his stomach, a sheet skirting across his ass and only just concealing it. She was in the same state. The bedding was strewn wildly across the floor and only one single sheet half covering them, half sliding to the floor. Even the cushions were about three feet from the bed and spread in a wild mess. Discarded carelessly.

Their clothes were literally spread across the room, his bow tie hanging on the chandelier, his shirt hooked up on a picture frame on the far wall. The dressing table across from her had been disturbed quite dramatically, the surface items mostly on the floor and the few still on the surface were laid on their sides.

She had a brief memory of being propped nakedly on there at some point, the familiar frenzy of sex on cold shiny surfaces, a hazy memory. Her dress was hanging carelessly from the open bathroom door and she could see Rob's trousers in a crumpled heap just inside.

What the hell had they done?

It looked as though they had been making a porn film, trying out every surface and corner of the room and throwing their clothes around for effect. There was an empty bottle of champagne and glasses sat by the window. The curtains hanging funnily and she realised the curtain pole had been hauled off the wall at one side. Dangling dubiously and barely holding on.

What the actual hell?

She had practically no memory of many of the events that had taken place in this room or even half the party and she wasn't sure she wanted to remember, judging by the tenderness of every inch of her skin and battered body. Light marks dusting the surface of her thighs and butt, they looked like finger prints. Rob's back was marked with red claw marks and something resembling a bite on the back of his shoulder.

Jesus!

He moaned in his sleep and shifted lazily, his breathing changing as he opened his eyes and groaned again. Pulling his hands up to shield his face from the tiny rays of light coming through the heavy curtained windows. Rose was now sitting up slowly, to avoid making her thumping head worse, taking in the absolute chaos of the room around them. Aware that the nearby armchair was laid on its back on the floor and her satin thong was nestling therein quite comfortably.

'Rob?' She nudged him absently, still trying to make sense of the room. 'Rob?' She nudged again, a little more insistently. 'We definitely came in here alone, right?'

He moved and lifted his head, looking around before slumping back down and groaning once more.

'Yes. As far as I can remember, although that's not much. Why? His voice was hoarse and lazy, he sounded like he had been yelling all night and he was in as much of a state as Rose.

'It's just the room looks a little... Crime scene massacre.' She grimaced as her blurry eyes got a little clearer and she could see just how much of a mess there really was. Rob turned onto his back and looked around slowly, no sign of surprise on his face.

'That's what happens when I fill you up with tequila.' He winked, making a moaning sound as he moved up the bed and tried to find a cushion to prop himself up. 'You got a bit wild baby.'

Rose looked at him dubiously, not sure if he was joking.

'You don't remember do you?' The smile moving across his face told her he wasn't.

'I thought you said you didn't remember much either?' She blinked at him, moving her body so very slowly and snuggling closer to him in an attempt to bypass the queasiness and even more pounding in her head.

'I remember enough to know we were alone and that you were like a crazed nymphomaniac on speed.' Rob grinned this time, lost in the memory apparently. She tried to feign a smile, feeling strangely mortified instead.

'Was I that bad?'

'It depends on what you term 'Bad' as?...In my opinion, you were that good!'

Rose sucker punched him softly, turning back beside him, her body reminding her of its fragility almost instantly and making her wince.

'Stop looking at me like that.' She could feel his eyes on her face. The grin giving away exactly what he was remembering.

'Hard not too...If I thought I loved you before, last night only made me even more mad for you!' He smacked her butt lightly and nudged her suggestively.

'It's not funny.' She laughed, cringing as he stroked her back, her skin and its tenderness obvious.

'I think we should add tequila to the mix more often, Our honeymoon drink of choice. But I may need a week to recover when we get home.' Rob slid down the bed again, obviously finding sitting up making his own headache worse too. She looked at him suspiciously over her shoulder.

'You? Need to recover? I really must have put you through your paces!' She laughed as he came to spoon her from behind, plumping cushions under his head so he could get as close as humanly possible.

'And then some.' He sighed, sliding up a tad to meet the side her face and planting a kiss on her nose from his awkward angle before settling down. 'I was kind of scared! Especially when you pushed me against the wall, dragged your nails down my chest and bit me mid-session. I think I have bite and nail marks in places I can't even see. I'm pretty sure there was borderline domestic abuse in there too.'

'Shut up.'

'Don't worry. I think I was just as bad. Judging by the marks and sexy glow on your skin. I think we were equally matched in fierceness.' He returned to laying behind her, stroking fingertips down her exposed thigh soothingly, one of the few places her skin didn't hurt.

'Promise me we shall never utter a word of this again.' She pushed back against him, her tone serious with a hint of a smile.

'I don't think that's going to be possible. I want to reminisce at every opportunity, and I think most of the house heard us last night and may have questions. Concerns for your safety… Maybe mine!'

'Rob?' She groaned, feeling the heat creep up her neck in shame and wondering how on earth she would ever face anyone in this village again.

'Yes, baby?' He breathed against the back of her neck.

'I need aspirin!… Water!… A week of sleep!' Rose sighed heavily.

'Is that all?'

'And we definitely need sound proofing!'

Chapter 39

The house was almost free of traces of the party, the formally dressed cleaning staff moving from room to room on the ground floor, removing remnants of the celebration and spray killing the lingering smells with strong cleaners. Rob and Rose stayed in bed till noon before finally, starving, dragged themselves to the kitchen. Both suffering from the hangovers from hell as though their bodies were in after effects of some sort of forgotten beating.

A few Munro's had wandered aimlessly around, smiling and thanking them for a fantastic night as they had come downstairs. Equally rough looking and a little lack lustre. Rob informed her a few had stayed in the guest rooms and probably more than he even remembered allowing as they watched a strange, red dressed, blonde girl, doing the walk of shame out the front door as they got to the kitchen. Everyone was suffering. No one flashing any winks or smiles at the pairs noise last night. She guessed they had not been the only noisy ones and was more than a little relieved.

Hamish Munro's sporran was hanging in the centre of the hallway about twelve feet above the floor on a mounted stag's head. Somehow a symbol of the night everyone had taken part in. Things had gotten crazy and it seemed everyone was in the same state. Even Alice, nowhere to be seen at the late hour, Muffin sleeping by the cooker with a fresh bone under his nose and no one familiar, that wasn't hired to be up at this time, was milling around.

Looking at Muffin guiltily, Rose realised she must have let him out of there room on returning in the early hours. Maybe that had been a good thing considering what they had got up to. He would have been traumatised if he had been locked in a bedroom with Rob and her and whatever acrobatics they had been trying out.

Rob made her scrambled eggs and toast in the kitchen, he was looking better than her already and they ate in the cosy room, spread out lazily, watching Jeremy Kyle. Laughing and cringing at the storylines and the state of the guests.

Finally settling into easy silence in front of an old movie. A passion they both shared in their down time, both too worse for the wear to even want to talk anymore and feeling like a day of TV and sleep was on the cards. Muffin was now curled under Rob's arm on the couch.

Traitor!

He was fast taking his cuddles and lap time with Rob nowadays and Rose had to practically bribe him for attention when she wanted it, Muffin truly adoring his new pack leader.

Her parents were staying in the cottage tonight. A text confirming, they were in a similar sorry state and that they would be leaving early and would see her next time. No need to drag anyone from their recovery to say goodbyes.

Abby would be dead for the rest of the day, hiding out in bed. Rose inwardly hoped she had the sense to sneak Duncan out a window and not bring him through the house now Rob was up. She knew her only too well, and knew in Rob's irritable hungover mood, he would literally knock the young man out.

Rose must have dozed off in front of the TV. The calm quiet cosiness of lying there doing what domestic couples did, watching rubbish daytime television and pigging out on snacks in sweat pants and t-shirts.

Rose awoke, his body shifting under her where she had been curled up against him, an arm laid around her. Rob was throwing his phone across at the table agitated, his face a thundering sight of tension.

'What's wrong?' She yawned and stretched sleepily, leaning off him to sit up and face him while straightening out limbs and easing away her stiffness, rubbing her eyes with the back of her fist.

'A million and one missed calls and ten voicemails.' He gritted his teeth, still staring ahead past her at the television set. Her heart sank, she knew only too well but she had to ask anyway.

'Morag?'

'Who else? She finally breaks the silence!' He huffed. The laugh was not one of happiness and he seemed bristly and agitated. Something cold in his demeanour, almost aggressive; she had not seen him this way since the day Morag had walked in on them and felt her heart sink and the return of that knot of anxiety low in her stomach almost instantaneously.

'What did she say?' She probed dubiously.

He scooped up his phone, punching the screen with his thumb harshly and handed it to her to listen. Too angry to summarise, his expression telling her that he was simmering on rage and trying not to let Rose see it.

His voicemail recording told her he had ten messages. To listen to number one press star, so she did. The screechy, slurring, angry voice, pouring abuse and insults into his phone made her feel sick to her stomach. Angry, cruel words. How much she hated him and his whore. The descriptive way she described her anguish knowing he was there celebrating their impending marriage, then sobbing, pleading for him to leave Rose and come back to her and then more angry abuse.

How could he do this to her? How could he be so cruel? Did he not love her anymore? How could they so publicly humiliate her? It went on and on and on. She couldn't listen anymore so ended the call and slid his phone back down softly, her nerves completely frayed and tears threatening to creep up from the pit of her body.

'She even describes your dress! She was here. She saw us!' He snapped, moving out of Rose's reach and leaning forward to lean his elbows on his knees and run a hand through his hair, his shoulders bunched up and taut.

'When? What? Last night?' Rose's head was too fuzzy for this, the wave of nausea no longer down to alcohol consumption.

'Yeah. The third of fourth voicemail. She says something about you lording over the manor in your showy gold dress...She must have come here last night.' Rob flopped back again, against the couch, reaching out to scoop her hand into his and entwine their fingers protectively. Rose felt the ice grip inside her. That old feeling of foreboding and fear sweeping up faintly. It had been giving her a break of late but now it was back like a familiar old friend that you no longer wanted to hang around.

'What does this mean Rob?' Her voice wobbled slightly. He shook his head, his jaw set firmly and clenching. Accentuating its squareness and looking more aggressive.

'I need to go end this crap! Enough is enough Rose. No more being nice and keeping my cool. I've had enough. She's not part of the picture. This is not her life to fuck with!' He snapped again, then frowned her way with an apologetic look, pushing his face forward to lightly kiss her on the forehead.

'She's not well Rob.' Rose tried, she had no idea why she was defending her but if it calmed his temper then she would.

'It doesn't matter anymore baby...This time with you. The last couple weeks without her hanging over my life, made me realise how done with this shit I am. I'm happy. Happier than I ever thought I could be and I want you to be happy, when she appears again it just ruins everything between us.'

'I am happy Rob.' Rose reached out to smooth away his frown instinctively, he caught her fingers mid-air and held them against his chest instead.

'Come on Rose? This crap doesn't mean anything to you? It's hanging over us, always in the back of my mind. It's the only thing we've ever fought over. Almost ended us. I'm sick to death of it all and I'm always worried in case she shows up here when your home alone. I even changed the locks when you started staying here so she couldn't just walk in on us again.' He let go of her and moved forward again, restless and unable to settle, he leaned back on his knees and sighed.

'I thought you said she was only a danger to herself?' Rose queried nervously.

'Abby told me she slapped you in the face that day! That was before she knew about us...Before you were her biggest threat. I don't want to take any chances with her volatile outbursts, if she laid another hand on you Rose, I wouldn't be responsible for my actions. If she kicks off, her anger will be aimed at you and I may not be around to intervene. I would literally rip her fucking head off if she touched you.'

'What are we going to do?' Rose tried to ignore the mounting anger coming off him in waves, curling up on the couch and pulling a cushion to her lap for comfort.

'I'm going to speak to my solicitor and try a new approach. Show her I'm not messing about anymore. Hit her with a restraining order and deal only via him... Any correspondence! I don't know how else to tell her I'm serious about this, to tell her to stay away.'

The sickening tightness in Rose's stomach hit hard. She knew this was a bad idea and he wasn't thinking straight because he was pissed off, she knew when he was mad he acted out impulsively and seemed to disconnect feelings and compassion. Her gut was screaming that what he was doing was the worst possible course of action where the other woman was concerned. She knew he would regret it when he calmed down too.

'I don't know. Maybe you need to see her again?...Talk to her?' She tried to sway him gently, reaching out and wrapping herself around him from behind, resting her cheek on his back and listening to the hammering of his heartbeat.

'No! It does nothing... It changes nothing!...I don't have anything more to say to her. She can't keep on insulting you, leaving me messages about you and not expect me to react this way.'

'You're angry Rob. Tired and hungover. You're not thinking straight! Sleep on it. Think it over. Don't do anything rash. It may just make this worse.'

He was leaning forward further, his forearms on his knees as he glowered at his phone on the table, shaking his head, his body felt poised and ready to jump up and Rose knew she was barely keeping his temper under control.

'No. Not this time. I'll change our numbers. Get the drive gated so no one can enter without buzzing the house first. A video cam, maybe even a gatehouse and constant security guard. Close her out. Warn her off. It always starts with calls and threats Rose. I need to think about you now, about looking after you. I can't leave on business knowing she can show up throwing shift around and attacking you.' He darted to his feet, pacing the floor in agitation, his temper hitching and voice teetering on a more aggressive tone.

'Rob, your scaring me.' Rose recoiled back to her previous curled position on the couch and watched him warily.

'You didn't listen to all ten messages Rose.' He stalked towards her, scooping to plant a quick kiss on her forehead before grabbing his phone from the table purposely.

'I need to go make some calls. There may be a need for some security in the short term until I put things in place. I don't want you to be scared.' He walked off through the kitchen and disappeared without another word or a backward glance, that stony set to his face that screamed stubborn Munro mode and she knew it was best to leave him alone. She had gotten to know how better to deal with him like this and Abby was right, space to blow it out and work through it was the best thing for him. He sometimes just needed alone time.

How could she not be scared? Look how he was reacting!

She wondered what else had been in those messages to make him behave this way, her mind churning with anxiety.

* * *

He stayed out of sight for hours, locked away making calls and doing what he did when he was overwhelmed emotionally. He shut everyone out. She heard him in passing when she retrieved some items from the bedroom, sounding serious and business like, but not clear enough to make out any of the words, so she left him alone, sensing that it would be best.

Rose tried to catch up on sleep and daytime TV, she helped Alice bake some cakes and meandered the house for a bit, getting to grips with the layout of the rooms upstairs and where her new bedrooms were going to be.

A van showed up around dinner with two men in black clothes, some obscure logo on their t-shirts and Rob took them off, walking down the drive. His arms animated as he pointed out some points of interest to them, one of them taking notes on a clipboard. Another car showed up later in the evening. A man in a tan suit and briefcase, being guided into Rob's office via the hall door he rarely used as he left the men in black to continue surveying the grounds without him. It was obvious these men were security companies to make the Manor a fortress.

Rose felt uneasy, a sickening dread developing at just how far he was taking this. She wanted to ask him exactly what had been said in the remaining voicemails but fear halted her.

Had she made threats towards him? Towards Abby? Towards Rose?

She knew if she had threatened Rob he wouldn't be handling it this way. He could handle himself, especially when it came to Morag. This had hit a raw nerve. It had to be one of either his sister or her. Most likely her... After all, she stood in the way of Morag's happiness and was the only threat in her delusional path to happy ever after with Rob.

Rob caught her in passing, another couple of new faces in scruffy clothes in tow.

'Hey baby, sorry I have barely seen you all day, might be busy until bed.' He leaned in, kissing her chastely, despite the hovering men behind him. Rose eyed them up and came back to his face questioningly.

'Will you tell me what's going on then?' She pushed with a lowered voice.

'Later. For now, just promise me you will stay in the manor and not go anywhere for today.' He looked serious.

'What? Why?' Rose wasn't about to be put on house arrest without explanation, but he just frowned her question away. Kissing her on her mouth to silence her.

'Later.... I'll see you in bed. Love you.' Throwing her another quick kiss, he left before she could get him to elaborate further. A look of serious storms brewing in those steel grey eyes and furrowed brow that just gave her more reason to worry.

* * *

She was in bed lying awake, back in their familiar room beside his office when he came home, staring into the darkness at the ceiling. She had wanted the familiarity and cosiness of this room, instead of his mother's suite upstairs. The closeness to the drive to hear him return so she would be able to anticipate his coming to bed and be awake for him, so she could talk about this whole crazy day and his over the top security measures.

She listened to him undress and felt the relief as he slid into bed beside her. Pulling her close the way he always did, even that gentle familiar motion bringing her a little peace.

'I'm awake.' She whispered, sensing the tension running through him and nestling into his arms with a sense of relief. All day her anxiety levels had been through the roof and she just needed him to make her feel better.

'Sorry baby. I'm too hungover and too tired to do anything more than lay here with you.' His voice was low and husky in the darkness, his chin brushing her shoulder from behind as he got comfortable around her. She turned in his arms to meet his face in the darkness, letting out a small laugh, momentarily breaking the tension.

'I was not asking for that!' She smiled, feeling his breath tickling her lips, close enough to touch.

'Can never tell with you.' He grinned, laying lips against hers and smiling back, she could feel the movement against her mouth, almost seductively.

'You're mixing us up again.'

Tracing her facial features gently with his fingertips, he was silent a moment, breathing against her face as they lay nose to nose, unusually quiet for him.

'You couldn't sleep?' He asked quietly, fingers now tracing her arm. She shook her head, sliding her hands up his chest and across his shoulders, further around him until she had her palms on either side of his strong neck. She needed him to be connected to her right now, to push away the weird emotions of the day and just be with him. His distance all day had affected her more than she cared to admit.

'All this... It's making me worry.' She sighed lightly, feeling his mouth move to hers and softly graze her lips affectionately. A chaste and gentle kiss.

'There's nothing to worry about. I'm making sure of that and taking care of it.' Rob's arms moved around her body and pulled her to mould into his snuggly, all muscle to curves and a perfect fit.

'It seems a bit extreme. All those security men and fence erectors. Who was the guy in the suit?'

'I'm being cautious. He's a security advisor for the camera's I want. All these years leaving this place so accessible was stupid, it's about time I realised how dumb that was and get the place locked up tight.' His voice cleared a little, pushing tiredness back and sounding more awake.

'She's not going to show up with a gun and take me out, Rob!' Rose tried for humour but it felt flat between them.

'It's not just her. It's the realisation Rose that anyone can just drive up to the house. Walk in and... ' Rob hesitated, falling silent and making Rose's heart beat elevate, worried about what he wasn't saying.

'It's how it's always been.' The manor had always been the hub of the community and its doors open to anyone who needed to see the Munro's.

'Times change. It's not the same world out there and we're not exactly low profile. Especially now after that party. We have money and titles, no matter how obsolete they actually are. There's always that chance that someone would mean harm to any one of us.' Rob had loosened his grip on her, was being evasive and plumping his cushion a little aggressively. She could read him, he was getting agitated as she was hitting a raw nerve.

'But this isn't about that, though, is it? What did she say Rob?'

He fell into uneasy silence, confirming her doubts and making her queasy with nerves. He was obviously fighting with himself internally as to whether he should answer her, the silence drawing out far too long.

'What did she say?' Rose repeated more insistently his time, catching his chin in her fingertips and tugging it down to meet her. She had pulled herself up now, leaning over him and trying to see his face in the dark. She was not going to let up easily and he could see that.

Rob shifted, pulling away and sliding out of bed. Stalking to the bathroom and flicking on the light as he leant against the wall beside it. Gently illuminated the room enough to see her face and showing her just how tense he really was, his muscles straining. For once he still had boxers on instead of his usual strip to skin approach in bed and a darkness in his look she wasn't accustomed too

'She said she would make you disappear, so we could be together. That if I wouldn't get rid of you then she would.' The dead pan tone and flat expression confirmed that he had believed every word of Morag's threats and was why today he had gone into protective overdrive.

Rose frowned, that feeling of nausea climbing to her throat and almost strangling her.

'And you believed her? You think she will try?' Her voice wavered, her hands beginning to tremble as she sat up in bed, pulling the sheets up over her bust.

'I'm not waiting to find out…If anything happened to you…' He broke off, his voice losing strength and the look of sheer despair on his face, it almost made her break. She reached out for him, wanting both to comfort him and be comforted by him; he followed her outstretched hands obediently and slid back onto the bed, cradling her.

'She was manic. Most likely drunk. You know she says this crazy kind of stuff.' Rose sounded more convincing than she felt, trying to explain this away, more for her own peace of mind than his. She didn't want to believe that Morag could pose any real threat in this way.

'She's never made threats before.' He sounded flat and tired and his tone did nothing to alleviate her growing fear. Rose fell silent, her thoughts racing, her heartbeat elevated.

'You're making me scared Rob. This isn't you.'

'I'm sorry baby…I'm tired, I'm hungover and I'm stressed. Ignore me. I'll never let her hurt you, there's nothing to be scared of…Just do me a favour. Stay here. Don't go out. Stay in the manor until I sort the security, for my own peace of mind. Let me talk to my lawyer and see my friend at the station. Let me be over cautious Rose. Let me make sure that threats, empty or not, can't be carried out okay?' He pulled her in tight against his chest and buried his face in the top of her hair, inhaling slowly and holding her that way for a moment. 'I love you so much.' He kissed her head and then pushed her back gently so they both laid down on the bed again, wrapped together.

'I promise, for the time being.' She breathed against his neck, trying to close her eyes and block out the anxious thoughts racing through her brain.

'I couldn't function, you know? If anything happened to you…If I lost you…I couldn't be like my dad and just go on with life.' Rob's voice broke, he buried his face in her hair before sliding down to cradle his cheek against her bust instead, his arms sliding around her waist, the way a child looking for comfort would. Rose's arms automatically moved around his head, holding him tight, feeling his arms crushing around her possessively. 'I would serve time in jail for what I would do to her.'

'Nothing will happen… I know you won't let it.' She soothed. Rob reached up, hungrily searching for her mouth and pulling her down below him. The need to be surrounded by her, to escape the emotions coursing through both, overtaking him and he no longer wanted to talk about this. He wanted to be lost in the feel of her, imprint her touch, taste and smell in his mind for an eternity.

Sliding off her nightdress and trailing kisses down her abdomen slowly, Rob manoeuvred her body and Rose was only too happy to succumb to him. This wasn't about passion and fulfilling a sexual need, it was about comfort and the need to be lost in the moment, shutting out everything else, stop his overactive brain and exhaust his body into oblivion. It was about losing himself and letting her be the only focus.

He moved over her, feeling her legs move apart to accommodate his own, his surge of heat and hormones never failing him. She moaned as his hand moved down, searching her out, arching her back at his touch and exposing her naked body. This is what they both needed and it lasted unquenchable hours into the early morning light.

Chapter 40

She had only been cooped up in the manor for a couple of days and already she felt like she was going stir crazy. A serious bout of cabin fever as Rob came and went. He had business to deal with and overseeing the work which had started on the grounds; there were contractors, vans and strange men milling around, trimming back foliage and trees in various areas around the gardens. From the windows, she could see an army of men erecting wrought iron fences; diggers and excavators in the far distance down the side of the house, before the forest treeline, and a van with security cameras and scrolling script printed on the side.

Men were trailing wire and boxes around in plastic wrap and placing them evenly along the fence line every twenty metres and workmen to start the renovations upstairs had also arrived, making lots of noise and mess and banging about over her head. The hum of power tools and sawing for hours on end was slowly sending her out of her mind. The never-ending trail of people, mess and chaos, as they carried things up and down. Half the house was covered in plastic to protect the walkway they had created and every inch felt invaded by strangers and noise. Alice was having a breakdown with all of it.

Rose was tense and headachy. Unable to work surrounded by all this chaos and never-ending trundling of strangers in her personal space. Muffin had had to be confined to the cosy room indefinitely and was currently howling his little lungs out in protest, but letting him loose would be disastrous with all these trampling feet and open doors.

Alice was fretting and moaning about it all and wandering about like a headless chicken, nagging her poor husband to death, sweeping up and hoovering aimlessly. Hamish was staying well clear of all the changes and had barely been seen since the party while Abby was completely AWOL.

It was okay for Rob, he got to leave and go to his office in the nearby city to escape it all. Even Abby had deserted her, unable to cope with the huge invasion and packed a bag. She had skipped out, completely unaware of the reasons behind the security with a kiss and a wave, before getting into Duncan's beat up jeep and disappearing in the midst of the machines.

There were three huge round men, all dressed in black, continuously trailing around like they belonged in a 'Men in black' or an 'MI5' movie. Checking in with her every time she looked even close to venturing near the door and it was driving her insane. It would have been amusing, their radios crackling and obvious mouthpieces, like cheesy commandos, or police wannabes, had it not been so damn frustrating for her.

The house had run out of rooms to explore and even starting lists for her own plans on decor had been abandoned quickly. She could not think straight with all the noise, could not find a single place that was not affected in some way by either tools, sheets, men, or all of them.

She called Rob for the fifth time, agitated and on the verge of a tantrum, complaining about the lock down he had her under and how much she needed to go get some quiet in her own cottage and work.

'I'm going out.' Rose didn't even give him a chance to say hello this time.

'Baby, you're not going anywhere today. We talked about this.' Rob was keeping his tone friendly, that hint of stubborn peeking out, but he knew better than to give her attitude today. Five previous calls had taught him to handle her with kid gloves while he wanted her to do as she was told.

'You can't keep me prisoner in this house!.... Especially when you're not even home to keep me company.' She started to feel emotional, tears welling up in frustration and stopping temper from moving in. 'We didn't talk about it... You made me promise and then seduced me.' She sniffed dejectedly.

'Rose.' Rob sighed down the phone, having a stressful day himself and having to try and placate her on top of it all was taking its toll.

'Don't Rose me! Like you're my father and I'm some petulant child, you have no idea how crazy I am going here with all this upheaval. I need to work Rob.' She snapped at him, temper flaring and then quickly abating as she returned to tearfulness.

Rob sighed heavily again, a slight edge this time, to his voice.

'I know this isn't ideal, but it's temporary... I love you, I just need you to have some faith in me for a few days and do as I ask.' His voice faded a little as he moved the phone from his ear, voices in the background taking his attention for a moment.

'I'm going out.' She yelled at him this time, feeling angry that he was distracted and even angrier that he was pretty much grounding her without conversation, just 'NO'.

'Rose, you agreed to stay put for a few days until I got the place secure, we're just talking around in circles.' Coming head on with his tightening voice and contained anger, sparks simmering between them. Rose was pacing around, her mobile stuck fast to her head and gripping it with ferocity. Banging in the rooms behind her were grating on her nerves and as she tripped over yet another cable she snapped again.

'You made me agree when naked and being distracted, that was hardly fair and now you're treating me like I get no say.'

'I'm not doing this to keep you prisoner, I'm doing it to keep you safe.'

'It feels like the same thing right now.' She was being childish, frustration oozing from every pore.

'Baby, why are you being difficult?' His voice was strained, a tiny tinge of pleading, all anger fading away and turning to indulgent sighing.

'You said all of this was for your own peace of mind, right? That you're being over cautious. That tells me that you don't think it's probable that she really is a threat, so then why can I not just go to the cottage for a few hours?'

He was silent for a moment His brain turning over, trying to think out a plan of strategy or an argument that would appease her.

'Look, fine.' He sighed heavily for the tenth time. 'But if you go then you take one of the security guards with you and you don't leave his side.' Another voice on Rob's end was informing him of a meeting that he was apparently late for.

'Not a chance!' How could Rose relax with some stranger sat there, aware of his presence, this large black clothed, steroid freak, she barely knew. Some looming man filling up her sitting room.

'Look he can drive down behind you and sit in the garden for all I care. Just have him with you.' Rob was moving around, probably getting his papers together to leave and trying to not rush her off the phone.

'No!' Rose snapped, folding her arm across her chest and putting her foot down literally.

'For the love of god Rose. You do realise I am in the middle of a meeting and standing outside a conference room squabbling with my girlfriend over house arrest.' Despite his obvious agitation, he was still trying hard to be gentle and probably clenching his teeth to hold his temper.

'Then let me go and I will leave you alone.' She replied sassily, smiling to herself as she could sense his resolve weakening.

'OKAY, look… I want you to stay put when you get down there. No little trips to town or walking Muffin. Stay inside and don't go anywhere until I come home and lock the doors. I'll come for you when I'm done here and drive you back myself.' He sounded defeated, unable to deny her anything that she really wanted and knowing this could go on all day if he didn't give in.

'You love me.' Rose felt victorious, a smile spreading across her face.

'That is the only reason I have not strangled you so far!' He was quick to reply.

'You wouldn't, you would miss me far too much!' She felt happier and lighter; her earlier tantrum subsiding.

'I mean it Rose. I'm not playing… For me… Please just don't go anywhere else for today.' The pleading tone of seriousness in his voice made her take note, she felt a little guilty for being mad at him when really, the root of this was his need to protect her because he loved her. She couldn't be mad at him for that.

'I won't. I need to work on these commissions, I just need some peace and quiet and I will be an extra good girl.' She beamed, twirling in the room and almost falling over that darn cable for a second time, kicking it away sharply.

'Well, the cottage has plenty of that I guess. So, we are sorted? No more crazy calls to give me a hard time over having you locked up like Rapunzel?'

'I promise!'

'Just be careful baby. Be alert. For me. Just humour me!'

They finally said their goodbyes and Rose hung up feeling pensive. She shook her head, feeling irritated at how much he was taking this to heart, how much he had let Morag mess with his head. This was not like him at all.

Rationally what could the woman possibly do?

Morag didn't even know where she lived right?

* * *

The cottage was a welcome relief. Her eyes had taken in the road on the drive down suspiciously, aware of the paranoia inside her from the recent events. No matter how many times he had told her it was just caution, it didn't help. He had wound her up into a twisted tight ball, afraid of her own shadow, despite Rose trying to tell him how ridiculous he was being and it annoyed her. She needed to get a grip. She just knew she couldn't stand another second walking around those rooms like that, she needed to just carry on. They had plans and a life to get on with and she needed to stop letting her imagination run wild.

What could Morag possibly do? She wasn't that out of whack with reality that she would be so stupid as to come after Rose.

She sunk into the couch, stretching out with relief; the calm and peaceful quiet surrounding her, badly needed like a moment of pause inside a crazy whirlwind lately.

Muffin was running wildly back and for like he was possessed, sniffing out all the familiar scents and rolling and rubbing himself on all the furnishings. He had missed this place too and was more than happy to be back here, away from restrictions and strangers once more.

Rose wasn't ready to work, she needed some breathing space to unwind, some chill out time to soothe her frazzled nerves and sore head and just to enjoy the solitude after the last few days. Knowing Rob would be hours and she had as much time as she needed, his meetings were back to back as he was finally getting the french contract back on track. She had no reason to hurry and no intention to do so either, her day was pretty much her own. She opted first for a bubble bath in her old familiar tub; the call of its white shiny ceramic as alluring as a siren right now.

God, I missed this place.

She threw Muffin a juicy bone from the fridge, her parents had left behind, some left over take away food and snacks were a welcome treat with a note listing the use by dates for Rose. They assumed she still spent a lot of time down here, unaware that she had pretty much moved into the manor on a permanent basis.

As she left the bath running, she moved to her old room, the fresh scent of already washed bedding filling her senses as she entered... Typical of her mother. The place was spick and span, sparkling clean. She had guessed her mother had nursed her hangover the way she knew best, with a mop in hand. Her dad most likely on the couch for the duration, acting like he had a serious bout of man flu. She smiled affectionately at the image the smell had conjured up in her mind.

Tipping out a can of food for Muffin, so he would leave her in peace, she headed through, stripping off quickly and slid into the hot water. Easing away her tensions and listening to the familiar sounds of the house, the creaks and groans, the birds outside and the distant sounds of machinery digging up the manor tree lines.

He really was taking this a little too far. Turning their home into a scene from the bodyguard. She couldn't blame him though. Maybe he was right, maybe it was time they thought about making it more secure. The house was obviously full of valuable things and the family were known to be wealthy. It had been unprotected for too long and they had been lucky to date. Counting on the fact they knew the small community and locals and trusted that no one would dare break in or steal from the manor.

Times were changing and maybe having it updated inside and out in readiness for any future children wasn't a bad thing. She would feel better knowing her children would be safely tucked inside high fences and state of the art security in future years to come. Rose relaxed a little in the hot soapy bubbles, the quietness giving her mind time to rationalise and put all of this into perspective. She had missed this, missed her own space to take a bath or just vegetate while surrounded by girly things.

* * *

Trailing from a lazy relaxing bath, wrapped in a fluffy dressing robe, Rose submerged herself in her illustrations without bothering to stop and dress or even brush her hair. Her own cosy room with art on the walls and her supplies lined up neatly, easy to reach and see.

Rob was right about one thing; the new rooms and space he was creating for them would be well loved, like having the cottage inside the manor. A place to pad around half dressed, a paintbrush in her hair, bare feet and chilled. Music playing softly in the background as she worked. Surrounded by their own little world, freshly created just for the two of them. She was looking forward to its completion more every day and the excitement growing.

They had poured through charts in bed the night before, choosing colours and wallpapers and some of the fitted furnishings in readiness and she had to admit, it was something she was really looking forward too. The interior designer had already begun mood boards and layout plans, the work moving along swiftly, seeing as there was not too much that was structural. Rob had impeccable taste, but he was giving her a free rein to make it any way she wanted, knowing it mattered more to her to have the homely part of the house than it did to him. Their little love nest, her own breathing space, a place she felt like she belonged rather than just hanging out at his house.

She could hear Muffin scraping at the back door, whining to get out. His can of food from earlier obviously wanting to make an exit and soon. It had grown darker and Rob would be along soon so she didn't have time to walk him. Well, she had promised she wouldn't. Opening the back door into his little enclosed garden she left it swinging in the cool air and headed back in to pull some clothes from her half empty wardrobe. Thinking she should move more of her clothes and start going through the shoes under her bed once the house calmed down a little.

Rob had been at her to officially move in with him, meaning to finally take every last piece of her up to the house once and for all and she had been dragging it out. She was sure that she wanted too, but unable to let go of this place so easily. Somehow having the excuses to come get things as she needed them, leaving her an opening to come back and forth had made it more bearable. Not that she needed excuses, she knew he wouldn't have issue with her coming here anytime she wanted, to chill out or work. She just wasn't ready to let it go, she had not really felt like it was time to say goodbye to the cottage just yet.

It was although she sensed him approaching, and as headlights pulled into the car park, shining through her small windows, she pulled on her jeans quickly. She was done for the day anyway. The last hour of painting was spent absently fussing and going over minute details that didn't really need touch ups. A sign she needed a break and a fresh start tomorrow. Right now, she wanted nothing more than to go home with him for dinner and some much-needed Rob time, alone in whatever bed they were using tonight.

He knocked the door before walking in, meeting her in the hall as she slid on her shoes; she reached up to receive his kiss as he asked if she was ready.

'I just need to go call Muffin in, he's out back doing his business.' She wandered through the lounge, pushing a bag towards him that contained more of her clothes and he lifted it dutifully with a smile.

Going to the back door and calling her little dogs name, she waited patiently, the darkness moving in fast and began to get irritated with his lack of response or appearance.

'Muffin? Here boy!' she made kissing noises and clapped her hands; her usual call to return to her. There was silence and she strained her eyes to look into the dim garden, cursing that he may have found an escape route and had made use of it. He was occasionally a disobedient boy when he found something to be getting into.

Rob called her from the front door, asking if she was coming and she called back to wait a minute. He was standing waiting, having already put the bag in the car, his engine still running and wondering what the holdup was.

'Muffin!!!' Rose was losing her temper and moving out into the garden impatiently, her eyes taking a moment to adjust to the near darkness. She caught a glimpse of his light furry butt beside the kennel and shook her head in annoyance at him.

'I swear if you're trying to dig your way-out Mr, I'll have serious words with you.' Getting closer she realised something was wrong, the way he was lying on his side motionless and had not peeked back at her at all, even though he had been caught red handed

'Muffin baby?' She said more gently, a knot of fear rising in her stomach as she shuffled closer to him, sending panic rising to her throat; a sense of fear riding up instinctively.

Saying his name softly again, her voice shaking, she moved forward cautiously. He was laid out panting heavily, his small tongue flopped out onto the damp grass salivating profusely, his eyes wide and glazed over. Unresponsive to her, even in the semi-dark, she could tell something was seriously not right, sheer panic overtaking her.

'ROB! ROB!' Rose began yelling hysterically, crouching down, afraid to touch her little fluffy bundle but visually searching for signs of injury. Frantically roaming his lifeless little body with her eyes and then fingertips for signs of cuts or blood, her hands shaking wildly and her heart bursting through her chest. Tears were streaming down her face as she tried to get him to sit up, begging him to be okay and talking to him through a flurry of sobs. Rose was pleading for him to raise his tiny head, her nose almost touching the tiny dark brown nose as he just lay motionless with glazed fixed eyes on nothing and no change to his rapid breathing.

Rob's footsteps moved fast across the grass towards her as Muffin's tiny body started to convulse, a deep gurgling from his throat, sending her into instant panic and hysteria. Unable to react, frozen in fear but clutching at Rob's arm as he slid down beside them, grabbing the tiny fur ball in his hands and tipping him up so his nose and face pointed towards the ground.

A surge of yellow vomit poured out, mixed with undigested food and grass, the gurgling and twitching subsiding after a few moments. Rose began crying loudly, her hands over her face repeating 'Oh my god, Oh my god' as her heart wrenched into a million pieces and she completely fell to bits. Rob jumped to his feet, looking around for signs of what he'd eaten as the small animal convulsed again with more vomit pouring from his mouth, through half open teeth.

Rob turned quickly, motioning Rose to follow and pulling his jacket off so he could wrap the dog gently inside and keep him warm. Leading the way back through the cottage, trying to get Rose to come with him and calm down, all she could do was grip onto the hem of his shirt, like a lost child, unable to function on any level, blinded by tears and murmuring incoherently through sobs about her 'baby.'

* * *

The drive to the emergency vet felt endless, she sat cradling him, crying and sobbing and holding his limp body wrapped up like a newborn baby. He was cold and non-responsive and had long closed his eyes on the journey. She was repeatedly telling him he was a good boy, to not be scared, while tears streamed down her face and she kept looking to Rob for reassurance.

Muffin felt cold and alien to her, his normally hyperactive little self like a wet rag on her lap. Rose's tears were blurring her vision so she could barely see, her nose running and her speech almost unintelligible as Rob tried to talk to her. All she could do was tell Muffin over and over that he was going to be okay.

Rob was on his mobile, driving at speed and getting directions from the vet about where to go, not caring if he got a fine for being on his phone and too rushed to stick it to his blue tooth. He looked like a man on a mission, furrowed brow, serious tone and driving like Schumacher, with all concentration on the road and the voice on the other end of his phone.

It was late but the Vet was still open and awaiting their arrival, Rob kept leaning forward in his seat, looking to the side and round for openings and exits as he followed directions to a place he had never been, fixated on getting them there as soon as earthly possible.

Muffin's little eyes were streaming fluid and kept opening and closing, losing the fight he had left and making Rose even more hysterical in the process. She tried not to shake him, to stop herself freaking out, but her panic was taking control. She had never been more petrified in her life and had no sense of control or ability to navigate how to deal with this, he was like her child and she was completely overwhelmed with terror at losing him.

Rob was calm and quiet, always the man of control in a crisis and being her rock right now with his steady cool presence and calm head. Turning the car smoothly into roads and corners, glancing in his mirrors repetitively, he kept leaning over and feeling the small animals throat, holding his fingers to his nose to check he was breathing before shifting gear and speeding up. Every so often he would squeeze Rose's knee to tell her he was right there with her and would do anything to get Muffin help, he was the only reason she hadn't completely gone over the edge.

Rob had to restrain Rose when the vet took Muffin through to the surgery, crying and trying to cling on, not really thinking about what she was doing. Lost in hysteria and clinging to her precious fur baby, afraid it would be the last time she saw him breathing and knowing he would be scared without her by his side.

'Rose?... Rose! Look at me. You need to let them do their job. He's in the best place. Trust me baby, let him go.' Rob was grabbing her flailing arms, trying to turn her to face him and trying to wipe the wetness from her face, pained by the puffy red eyes, tear streaked face and look of despair he could see there. Rose didn't respond, just collapsed against him and let out a new tidal wave of sobs, his hand cradling her head against his chest protectively. He moved her to the waiting room and sat her down on his lap, pulling her up easily and sweeping her into a hold like a child, smoothing her hair until she began to calm again and the wracking sobs became more of a simmering bout of sniffing.

An hour passed and she sat looking numbly at the door, held against him, her breathing steady and quiet, but silently watching; blankly waiting and finally completely calm from sheer emotional numbness. She had cried herself into silence until no more tears could fall.

Rob tried to get her to drink coffee while watching that white door leading to the treatment room, endlessly holding her breath and pushing away his offerings of cups or snacks. Chewing the edge of her nails and tapping her foot listlessly against his leg, she felt like the waiting was going to make her insane. Rob didn't stop her, just held her close and stroked her hair, knowing the agony of the endless waiting was torture for her and just trying to be what she needed in that moment.

Finally, the vet appeared and she jumped up, racing towards him at speed and almost taking down the magazine rack stood in the way. Rob was barely able to keep up with her as the man raised his hands, obviously used to distraught owners. Bringing calm and quiet with a gesture and a sympathetic smile.

'He's stable and sedated.' The man said softly, Rob coming up to slide his arms around her shoulders behind her.

'Any idea what's wrong with him?' Rob's deep voice over her head was calming her manic panic, unable to form questions of her own and searching the man's face for any clue to an answer.

'There's a chance he has ingested something highly toxic, either a plant or something left in your garden. The way you said he threw up in the garden has probably purged his system of whatever it was quickly. Most likely saving his life. He's sedated and medicated and we need to await blood results to be sure of what he has poisoned himself with before we can truly treat him, for now we are treating him with standard meds and saline and will have to keep him in to be watched.' The man's no-nonsense attitude and serious tone had Rose numbly nodding, unable to think straight and still letting Rob take the lead.

'He's in the best place, I trust that you will do what you can for him and keep us updated.' Rob pulled Rose closer as though looking for any sort of response, all she could do was stare wide eyed around her, trying to take in the fact that her baby was going to be here without her and scared.

'We will call if there is any change and you can come in after noon tomorrow to see him. We will have the bloods sent out first thing, but they take a day or two to come back.'

'I want to see him, now.' Rose broke in, her voice weak and cracking with the effort, fresh tears filling her eyes.

'He's asleep for now....' The vet started but Rob moved Rose aside and stepped in.

'Look, she won't rest at all if she can't see him, just a few seconds, just to see he's breathing and give her some peace of mind.' Rob was in business tone and although friendly there was a forceful underlying tone.

'Okay, a few seconds.' The vet relented, knowing a stubborn man in his face when he met one.

The vet led them through to a little room with cages built into the walls from floor to ceiling. Muffin was lying motionless inside a shiny steel cage, a furry blanket below his fragile little body and a lighter one keeping him warm. One of his tiny little legs was poking out above the cover, shaved and a drip taped in place, keeping him hydrated. His poor little face was sodden from runny eyes and nose and his white muzzle stained yellow and brown. He was breathing softly and slowly, sound asleep and looking more peaceful than before; more alive. There was a shallow dish of water nearby and puppy mats lining the floor of the cage around him but he just looked so helpless and small.

She heard the vet telling Rob they had pumped his stomach to be sure whatever he had ingested was completely gone and felt a fresh wave of tears. Touching his little face through the bars, the urge to pick him up and kiss his little velvet muzzle overwhelming her. She whispered to him through the bars.

'Good boy. I love you puppy, I'll come back tomorrow. Don't be scared baby, you be a brave little boy for Mummy.' Tears wet her cheeks as Rob finally managed to drag her away from the bars. Saying something to the vet and literally walking her out of the building in a firm embrace and giving her no chance to fight him on it. She could barely function, her brain unable to formulate anything but extreme grief.

She stopped in the car park, suddenly aware of rising nausea, a product of her hysterical crying and emotional torture. All coming bubbling to a head in a dramatic way. She threw up in the bushes with Rob cradling her against him and holding back her hair. Softly saying things to try and soothe her but she pulled away angrily, pushing his arms off her and stomping away from him to pace erratically.

'She did this!' She screamed pointing back at the medical building accusingly. 'She poisoned him!' Her voice was hitched and tears were once again flowing freely.

Rob's face tightened, a frown appearing and he softly shook his head at her, reaching out for her but she waved his hands away as he got closer.

'Rose. I don't think this was deliberate.' Rob followed her across the car park trying still to get hold of her once again, endlessly patient with her outburst.

'Yes, it was! She did this to him!... She did!... ' She broke down again as he came to her side, sliding arms around her, she pushed him off, not wanting to be consoled. A fresh wave of rage and hatred that she had never felt for that woman before, almost consuming her.

'You said it yourself. She made threats. She wanted me gone!' She blurted out.

'Rose, you're upset. You're not thinking straight...' No matter how much she paced away from him, he was still following her, still trying to pull her into his embrace.

'Don't you dare use my own words against me!' Rose turned on him, yelling, unable to control it while he was trying to figure out how to respond to her like this. 'He's innocent! He would never hurt a fly... He's just a tiny little animal who never bothers anyone.' Rose cried out, sobbing; self-pity wracking her as she paced around the car park once more, unable to stand still as adrenalin coursed through her blood and her body shook with the after effects of shock. 'She's trying to get to me! To hurt me... She can't take you away, so she's taking something else I love!' She stamped around, kicking rocks away on the gravel surface.

'Rose,...?' Rob was looking for the right words, trying not to make her worse. 'I think this is just what it is... An accident... The weather lately has been damp and colder, stuff grows in the garden when it's like that. Fungus and plants that are toxic. I think he just ate something he shouldn't have.'

'You're building Fort Knox up at the house and I'm over reacting because someone poisoned my dog?' She was livid, the tears still falling, her nose running as she rounded on him accusingly, meeting him and pulling herself up to try and match his height. She was in full on battle mode now and wiped her tears with her sleeve.

'You're right! This is on me... All this paranoia and overreaction. I've filled your head with this crap, made you think she's out to harm you. That's my fault Rose. I jumped ahead and never thought things through, it was a knee-jerk reaction and I see now it's complete nonsense. Morag wouldn't poison Muffin, she wouldn't come after you in that way and she sure as hell isn't stupid enough to jeopardise her career and her life in this way.' Rob raised his palms defensively, giving up on following her and instead taking a calmer approach.

'No, she would just smash up your house and slice her own arms open¡ Rose spat back at him, throwing her hands up.

'Rose you need to calm down. Think rationally about this.'

'Why can't you see it?' She cried in exasperation, pushing him in the stomach as though trying to make him see sense, completely over wrought with emotional frustration. Rob, realising he was only making her worse, pushing her further into a fight, changed tactic. Lifting defensive palms again and slowly moving towards her as softly as he could, soothing voice and soft words.

'I believe that you think she did this baby, I just want to take you home right now.' Rob was now level with her, a hand sliding over her shoulder carefully, she fought him off again, only this time with less fight and he sensed she was wavering. Her energy finally spent.

'She did this Rob.' She announced hopelessly, resigned to more quiet tears as exhaustion overwhelmed her.

'Blood tests will tell us for sure Rose, there's no point speculating anymore until we know for sure, okay? Let me take you home. You need to sleep and I want to look after you.' Rob slid his arms about her shoulders finally, meeting no resistance and instead she slumped against his body, allowing him to do whatever he wanted.

She nodded numbly, unable to yell anymore, unable to fight, just exhausted and broken, longing to pick up her little fur ball and rub that tiny nose on her face. He manoeuvred her slowly, hugging her close and leading her to the car, treating her with kid gloves and buckling her into her seat. Kissing her temple gently as he clipped her into her seat and driving them home in utter silence.

* * *

She laid in bed watching every hour on the clock, Rob was lying beside her in the dark, his arm across her, but he knew she needed to be left alone with her thoughts. He hadn't slept either, just laid watching her, being there. Equally worried about the small animal and missing his tiny presence between them on the bed, missing his soft furry muzzle resting on his inner arm where he had grown accustomed to it every night.

When the vet rang next morning, she practically yanked his phone out of his hand, devouring every detail and questioning the receptionist with the skill of the Gestapo.

Muffin had woken from sedation in the night, drank some water, responded well and was looking brighter this morning. He was still very sick, but they would have to wait on blood tests to know for sure the extent of what was going on in his little body. All signs looked good for the time being and the vet said she could come and see him around noon if she wanted. They wanted him to stay until the blood work came in, meaning up to forty-eight hours of separation for Rose.

After repeating everything word for word, she avoided conversation with Rob, knowing only too well she would just argue with him over Morag's involvement. She was sure this was down to that scrawny bitch whether he believed it or not.

He tried to coax her to eat breakfast after almost dragging her in the shower and washing her hair for her. She was lifeless, emotionally exhausted and physically tired from lack of sleep. He knew better than to try and push her, leaving her to wrestle with her own inner turmoil as he soaped her down and rinsed her in the clean white cubicle. He made no sexual advances, sensing it was not going to help, but instead held her, kissing her closed eyes when she broke down in relief, holding her tight and murmuring that he loved her when she wrapped herself in him.

* * *

He took her to the clinic a little after noon and left her to sit with Muffin for a little while as he sat with the receptionist, filling out papers and settling the bill so far.

Rose stroked Muffins face through the open cage door, felt his gentle licks and kisses on her face and cried when he warmly nuzzled his little head against her mouth. Whining softly for her to take him out and attempting to get up even though he was still too weakened.

Just seeing him a little more like his normal self, lifted her heart a tiny bit and brought some peace back to her scattered brain. She wanted him home but the fear that poison could still wrack his tiny frame until they were sure of what it was, held her back. She wanted them to make sure there was no lasting damage and that her little fur baby was going to completely recover. She wanted to murder that bitch for this and nothing anyone could say would convince her that Morag wasn't involved.

On the drive home, Rob informed her he had called off the security staff and downgraded the speed of the fencing and cameras on the manor grounds.

'Why?' She turned to him with a furrowed brow and snippy tone, incensed that he was back tracking on his decisions.

'Because I was being stupid baby. I see that now. Over cautious and I was making you insecure and paranoid and right now we need some calm around the house for a few days.' He was driving them down a country lane slowly, the sun shining despite the mood in the atmosphere around Rose.

'You're wrong. I think she's entirely capable of carrying out her threats. I think you should still go ahead and finish!' She turned away from him to look out the window at the passing scenery, annoyed that this was still an issue between them. Pissed that he could really side with Morag on this.

'Rose… I will finish the house, I just don't think there is any urgent need. It's making things crazy.' He reached out and stroked her cheek, ignoring her shrugging him off with annoyance, her moods had been all over the place for the last twenty-four hours and he wasn't taking it personally.

'No Rob, it's her that's crazy and I know for a fact she hurt my baby!' She gritted her teeth, still focused on the view and trying to not raise her voice in temper, she had no energy for another argument today.

'You don't know that. You suspect… There is no proof. There's no reason for her to hurt Muffin. I don't even think she's aware of where you stay or that you even have a dog.'

'Everyone know us, Rob. Everyone greets Muffin wherever I go; you would have to be dead not to know who I am in this village or who he is to me. My living at the cottage is common knowledge, especially since I became the future Mrs Munro. It wouldn't be hard to find out, to come there in the cloak of darkness and hide out or leave something for him to find in the garden.' She spun on him, eyes narrowed and tone tight. She couldn't believe that he couldn't see this.

'I really don't think she did this, I know her. I'm sorry that I let things get out of hand and made you believe she could do something like this, but Rose… Baby… I swear I don't think she's capable of poisoning an innocent dog.' He squeezed her hand, sure that he was right and convinced he was giving some rest to her suspicions. She listened silently, her eyes watching the scenery once more, knowing arguing was futile and her mind stubbornly set that he was wrong.

Chapter 41

Rose had him drop her at the cottage when they got back into town. She couldn't face the noise of the men upstairs crashing around, pulling down walls and causing chaos in their new living area. She wanted quiet, time to lay down and sleep and some space to pull herself together. She knew her head was too full of suspicion over Morag's involvement and didn't want to cause any more arguments; she knew she had been unfair on him, distant and self-absorbed and told him that she would come home tonight if he just let her have some head space.

He kissed her warmly, understanding that need to deal with something alone, assuring her that she was to call anytime she wanted him to come and he would. That if she wanted to stay here tonight he would too. She felt grateful, tearfully held him close as he stroked her hair gently.

'I'm sorry I'm being this way.' She rested her face against his chest, his hand stroking her back tenderly.

'There is nothing to be sorry for. You're upset and tired. Take all the time you need.' He kissed her on top of the head gently.

'Stop being so understanding. I know I'm being awful.' She raised her chin to look at him, those perfect stormy grey eyes, warm and inviting, even though she was being hell on earth.

'No more awful than I can be baby. Just try and relax. Go to bed and enjoy the quiet. I have work stuff to take care of, but I will only be a phone call away. I'll drop anything and come over if you need me.'

'I love you so much.' Her voice was fierce and raw, the doubts of insecurity gnawing at her because she felt like she was pushing him away.

'I know you do, but I love you more.' He pinched her cheek and rested his arms about her shoulders, smiling down at her adoringly.

'I bet you don't.' Rose broke into a smile, despite her aching heart, his face close and comforting and his ability to just always make her feel so safe and secure, overwhelming her.

'I am pretty sure I could prove it.' His eyes had started twinkling suggestively and she buried her face against him with a giggle, loving his ability to always involve sex.

'You don't need to prove it, I already believe you.' She held him close, breathing in his familiar smell that was only him, before turning her chin up towards his face once more with a twinkle in her own eye. 'Maybe you could, though, later, when I come home?'

'Anytime.' He laughed now, kissing her on the forehead lightly and ruffling her hair. 'Just call me and I'll come straight back, I promise.'

'I just need some time, a little nap and quiet. I just need to pull myself together in normal surroundings, away from all those strangers and chaotic mess. I need to absorb everything and pack up some of Muffins things for him coming home when he's well. It will make me feel better.'

'They won't be around for long, things will be more normal soon baby. Just think of our new little love nest. That's what's keeping me going. And a special place to keep Muffin out of harm's way.'

'He would like that, his own cosy corner, instead of sleeping in bed with us.' She smiled, her heart lifting at the mention of her little fuzzy faced cutie pie, talking this way was healing her heart and giving her hope that he would be coming home soon.

'I agree with that. Too many males in our bed currently and I'm not one for sharing.' He kissed her again, lingering a moment, his hand on her throat softly, holding her face in place so he could gaze at her before moving up to release her.

He gave her a light hug by the door and she watched him drive away smoothly. A sense of loneliness and a moment of doubt, wondering if she should wave him to stop and stay with her after all. She stopped herself, pushing it down. She needed some quiet and space if she was going to pull herself together and she had to do it alone. Had to stop raking her head over and over, mentally torturing herself, sure that Morag was involved and letting it pull them apart.

The sight of Muffin's little chew toy under the chair made her cry, wandering the rooms, pulling out all his little treasures and bones that he loved to push under the furniture. She piled them all into a box, finding his spare fluffy bed and packing it up with them. When he came home she wanted him settled and safe in her room, surrounded by familiar things, smothered with love. She packed all his cans of food from the cupboard, his treats and spare chews. Somehow it made her feel better, more positive, that packing his little things for his return was reminding her that he was really going to be okay. She didn't want him at this cottage anymore; the safety and security was tarnished here. She wanted him to never set foot here again, away from the watchful eye of Alice and Tommy in the manor gardens.

Maybe it was time for her to finally remove all traces of their time here together, pack up anything she wanted and close this place up. Let her parents use it as a place to stay when they visited.

All the charm and stability ruined, it felt as though it was dirty; that somehow believing that woman had walked over her grounds, laying a trap for her little dog had marred the very core of this place and it was no longer her beloved cottage.

She was tired, over emotional and not thinking straight. Rob was right. But for now, standing there in the room, she just wanted to pack it all up and say goodbye and never come here again.

Her mind made up, she found boxes and bags in the outhouse and laid them on the lounge floor. She knew she would be hopeless at organising everything without some sleep and headed through to her bedroom to take a nap first. A surge of heat and happiness at the familiar sight which held so many memories for her and Rob, making her feel a little less desolate.

Moving across the padded comforter and curling up in the plush cushions, allowing her mind to wander across every cherished moment, every memory, times he had made love to her in this bed. Sad that they would probably never venture down here again and if they did it would be brief and sporadic. She no longer needed or wanted this space around her.

Focusing on his voice inside her head, she closed her eyes. His face in her mind's eye making her calm, he made her feel like everything was going to be okay and even though she had chosen to be here alone, she suddenly missed him more than ever.

She cast her mind back to the first time she saw him, the first moments and angry encounter. The way he had yanked open her car door aggressively, but not to yell, to ask if she was okay because he thought she had been injured by the near miss of his car. Those cool grey eyes and tanned handsome face, mere inches away; she had been too angry to really notice just how gorgeous a specimen he really was in those fiery few minutes. She recalled how her heart had pounded from her chest and it only made her want to bash him in his stupid head, an instant reaction that she never understood until much later; the sparks between them.

Her mind wandered forward to the first kiss in this very cottage, that brief unexpected grazing of his lips against hers, so natural and automatic and now something he had done a million times in exactly the same way. Still, each time making her breathless and light headed as though she was born to be kissed by him.

The first time he carried her to this bed, the anticipation, the fear and the overwhelming desire for him. He still made her feel like every time, as though it was the first time over and over; never tiring of her body and never ceasing to evoke that same passion from her. She loved him more than she could bear.

The ups and downs of their rollercoaster relationship, when her world was falling apart and Morag controlled everything they did. The makeup and the break ups, she cringed at the memory of throwing his ring back at him stupidly, she groaned as she remembered it clearly. All of it was behind them, ready to face a new chapter, a new life.

A marriage.

She had never imagined that the day she arrived here so long ago, seeing that chipped overgrown mess and wondering what she had done, that she would fall head over heels in love with someone like him. She didn't deserve him. His patience, his strong protective instincts and generous heart. His hard, hot body, carved and toned, strong and male. His flawless chiselled face and dark looks. The ability to change his eyes depending on his mood. She would never tire of those eyes and their ever-changing depths. That face, that mouth. His ability to spin her upside down with a touch, bring her to the verge of complete meltdown, aching for his body to join with hers. He could do it all with just a look when it suited him and he knew just how to play her in every way, instinctively tuned to her wavelength.

He had come into her life, turning it all upside down from day one, changing everything for the better, even when things didn't seem that way. And she knew that no matter what, she would follow him to the ends of the earth. She would do anything to protect what they had. She wouldn't let that woman come between them anymore, she wouldn't let that woman hurt her family, her dog or her relationship. She would fight claw and tooth to make sure that from this moment on this was not just on Rob; it was not just his duty to protect her but it was hers too. To protect him and their life together as much as he did; a partnership.

It made her more determined to end this chapter under this roof. To finally dedicate the entirety of her time to the manor; no more running down here, no more using it as a hideout. She would need to deal with the chaos at the house, knowing it wouldn't be forever. It would be worth it all to finally have somewhere they could call theirs and theirs alone. To be able to close the door and hole up in the privacy and solitude of the haven he was creating for her. To be with him every moment from now until death, to be content with a whole future ahead of them and everything that held.

She finally drifted off to sleep, lost in the thoughts and whirlwind of emotions stirred up by this long epic journey to this moment. The friends she had made, the life she had carved out here and the happiness it all brought her in the end, despite the turmoil. All of it had made her stronger.

Lost in the darkness of a comforting slumber, finally taking her exhausted mind to a deep dark place to relax and unwind, much needed zoning out time to reset her switch and set her mangled thoughts adrift.

Undisturbed she slept soundly for hours.

* * *

It was darker than she expected when she awoke, aware that she must have been asleep for a long while. Checking her phone, she saw a text from Rob asking if she was awake?... Assuming she would still be asleep he had left her alone, knowing how exhausted she had been. She texted him back.

'**I just woke up, slept for hours. I just need some time to pack up the rest of my stuff here. I miss you and I feel better. I love you. Xxx**'

He responded immediately.

'**Want me to come help you? I miss you too baby. Can't wait to see you xxx**'

Rose smiled at his fast response, feeling his presence around her.

'**I won't be much longer, I need to do this alone. xx**'

Rose wanted to say goodbye to her little home finally, time to look around one last time and fully separate herself from this place. She wanted to walk away tonight with no reason to keep coming down here.

'**I'll come when you're ready, just text me. I'm cooking us dinner, running us a bubble bath and then we're going to bed to**

watch a marathon of old movies in my mum's old room. We can spread out and snuggle up with popcorn when you're home. I aim to make you feel a hundred times better before you fall asleep, baby. Xx'

She could not think of anything more that she wanted to do, he knew exactly how to look after her. He had moved most of their things to that room now over the last couple of days, giving them more space until the suite was ready to be moved into. A room more suited to her feminine needs and a place ready for Muffin to come home too that was a lot more comfortable than his cramped bedroom by his office. He made her feel warm and loved, always attentive to her needs, always striving to make her happy. It just made her love him even more as they said their brief goodbyes.

She had more stuff crammed into this little house than she expected, having to light the fire and turn on the lights due to the growing cold in the air and earlier darkness. Winter was coming in from the hills and warning them that summer was leaving. She knew from past experiences that winter this far north could be brutal, and in a way, she was glad she would be warm and cosy in the walls of the manor with its modern heated floors and central heating. It wasn't as late as it seemed, it was just the signs of the seasons changing and the darkness falling in earlier every evening and making it feel far later.

She packed up her entire workroom, stripped her shelves bare, desk cleared of everything and walls lacking any sign of her ever being there. Later she would turn this back into a guest room for her parents to use as they pleased. Another task for another day. Sure it would have more purpose when her family used it for visits.

It hadn't taken long to extract herself from the rest of the rooms, no real method or neatness to filling the bags and boxes. She just wanted it done and had practically swiped it all in haphazardly. Her bedroom was far easier, most of her things were already in Rob's bedroom, just a handful of clothes and toiletries, a tonne of shoes and the odd personal trinket and treasure. The other rooms were not much worse. She wanted to leave the place still homely and habitable for when her parents or brothers came up north to visit; she didn't have a need for much, just all her pictures and nick knacks. She knew starting over in the new suite being built she didn't need to bring very much. Rob had made it clear he expected her to use the accounts he had set up, spend his money and start picking whatever she wanted for the house, a new start for them both.

She dumped the bags and boxes near the front door in the hall, stacking them up against the wall and sent him a message asking him to come down in about ten minutes. She wanted the time to wander the rooms once more. Check everything was off and see it alone for one last time in case she got upset; she didn't want him to see her sad about leaving. She was ending it the way she had started, solo. She did not know when her family would have need of it again and wanted to treat this like it would be a long while.

'**Okay baby I'll head up to you in ten xx Love you, Penny.**'

She read the message with a heart-warming grin on her face and slid the phone into her bag, leaving it by the door with the mountain of stuff she had accumulated since coming here. Unlatching the front door in anticipation for him, turning off most of the lights, the only glow from the fire in the living room as she walked around. Taking one last look.

Moving to the lounge she chose to sit on the couch and watch the last glowing embers thoughtfully while they started to die out. It would heat this room for a while yet after she was gone and slowly go out. It felt symbolic. Like she would be leaving a small warmth behind long after she had gone. Staring into the depth of the fiery orange and yellow coals, the odd flicker of a flame fighting to remain alive, she heard a small sudden noise from the rear of the house. Pausing to listen carefully, her heart elevating slightly as she cocked her head and strained to hear it.

The wind was getting up and a tree branch gently tapped the back window, giving her a fright but then laughing at her own stupidity. He would be here soon, she had nothing to fear from the wind.

She got up, moving to the kitchen, wanting one last check of the back door to make sure she had locked it. The lock sometimes stuck and had easily opened many a time when she was sure she had done it in the past. She had a chain she could slide on, to make sure it would stay locked.

The light switch had always been in a stupid place over by the far side of the room, so entering the kitchen it was in inevitable darkness as she walked into the small neat space in the moonlight.

She walked in boldly, suddenly her skin prickling from sixth sense as she paused, her blood ran instantly cold. Her body stopped, her gaze frozen on the door in disbelief as it stood freely open, a gap of several inches as it swung gently in the darkness. There was a slight breeze coming in to swirl around her eerily, making her skin tingle with goose bumps as the blood drained away to be replaced with sheer terror. Her breath halted and her heart skipped a beat; the sudden feeling of warmth behind her as someone stood breathing in the shadows.

She was too afraid to turn. The icy cold slide of fear starting at her toes like a tidal wave as it moved up, enveloping her body. Her eyes started stinging with moisture and emotion. She tried to take a steadying breath, glancing around for something to protect herself, without making it obvious that she knew she was not alone, but could see nothing within reach. Feeling the movement before it reached her, she jumped away, spinning, fierce glints of eyes and teeth as the figure came at her, trying to claw at her face as she screamed out in fear, lashing out defensively.

Adrenaline kicked in and Rose fought back impulsively as the hot body surrounded her violently, with teeth clenched and a determination to get out of this unscathed, knowing Rob was on his way and he would be here soon enough. She just had to hold her off until then, knowing fine well by the snarling abuse and clawing hands that her attacker was Morag.

The grabbing fingers and slapping hands were surrounding her head and face, caught up in her own struggle to hold her away, hitting her back. Rose was already breathless, already acting without thought, but just sheer impulse and panic, her own sense of survival kicking into gear. They bumped and rolled into the units and shelves, grappling at one another, grabbing on and trying to get the better of the other and ending up on the floor, surrounded by falling crockery and smashing dishes.

Morag was stronger than she looked, her hands tangling in Rose's hair and yanking her head back painfully. A slap collided with Rose's face, burning and stinging as claws grabbed at her mouth and tried to gauge at her eyes. Grunting and crying out, Rose's clothes and skin was grabbed and yanked mercilessly, nails torn across her exposed flesh. Her fists managed to collide with firm bone several times, grunts following and dragging Morag to the ground in a heap to try and get the better of her.

Rose was trying to break free into a forward run as she scrambled to get up, but the woman grabbed her from behind with deathly speed, sending the pair of them crashing forward, head first into the closed cupboards.

Rose took a massive whack to the top of her forehead, seeing stars momentarily and sliding down, losing her faculties and sense of reality almost instantly. The other woman was dragging her lifeless body over towards the centre of the floor, flipping her onto her back, climbing on top of her and pulling at her shoulders, trying to get her hands around Rose's throat. Fighting back with heavy limbs and nothing but darkness around her, Rose was flailing her arms, trying to shield her neck and face, trying to hit out. She was desperately trying to protect herself from this crazed attack while Morag was trying to claw at her still; frustrated with the battle and screaming in her face that Rob was hers.

Rose, despite her dazed brain, was managing to still hold her own. To shield the onslaught of nails and fists with the might from nowhere, she managed to throw her off. Thrusting her with her body and every ounce of strength she could muster, back against the far side with a dramatic crashing noise. Clambering to her feet and sliding her arms across the bunkers, trying to pull her weight up and looking for anything to grab in defence. Rose's hands caught on smooth objects, knocking things out of reach desperately. Her hands scrambling in fear but unable to really grasp anything of value that may help her.

Morag was back against her, arms around her neck, trying to choke her, trying to pull her down. They stumbled, tripping over discarded items in the dark and Rose was thrown to the corner, hitting her back hard on one of the door handles and knocking the wind out of her. She slid down unable to breathe, unable to control the jelly-ness of her body as she hit the floor. Morag was clambering around on her knees, looking for her, unable to see her in the shadow of where she had fallen and giving Rose a moment to gather her scrambled senses. Rose struggling to catch her breath, her ribs crushed and painful, the burning panic as she fought to breathe and was overwhelmed with nausea.

Morag was illuminated on the floor by the soft moonlight coming from behind clouds, like a creature crouching down on all fours, wild-eyed and sobbing, she used the light to lurch forward, grabbing something from the counter and was by Rose in seconds, holding the long kitchen knife out towards her from her crouched position threateningly. Rose recoiled in fear.

'You couldn't just leave him alone, could you?' Morag hissed, her breath heaving dramatically. 'He wasn't yours to take… He was mine!'

Rose dragged oxygen into her lungs trying to find her voice, her body shaking violently and her eyes glued to the sharp metal, glinting in the light mere inches from her throat.

'Morag please… I didn't take him… He chose to come to me.' Rose's voice was shaking, breathless and low, she was terrified at seeing nothing but hatred in Morag's eyes and unsure if Rob would even get here in time anymore.

'No … NO…You seduced him… You wrapped him up and made it impossible to leave you… I know your type! … What did you do Rose?' The strangled voice and hitching hysteria in Morag accelerated Rose's heartbeat, boosting her adrenaline. 'Flutter your lashes and give him perverted sex that he couldn't refuse, do things for him that no decent woman would do?'

'Morag, I swear… Please don't do this, it's not that way. He loves me. I love him.' Rose was gasping through tears, unable to conceal her fear, curling up small and trying to keep the point of that blade away from her neck.

'What do you think I'm going to do Rose? …. Hurt you?' Morag bursts into an insane laugh 'Maybe I will… Maybe I should… I should kill you for what you have done to me… You need to leave…Go far, far, away and let me have what is rightfully mine.' She swung the knife around carelessly, the heavy weight making it look unstable in her hand, her own eyes streaming scornful tears.

'This is my home Morag…' Rose pleaded desperately, but it only fuelled Morag's manic anger.

'No, it's fucking not! It's my home… It's Rob's home… You're an outsider… An intruder that doesn't belong here in my village… If you leave I can have my life back!' She spat cruelly, shuffling closer so that the knife inched nearer Rose's face. Morag was kneeling taller than her and looking menacing.

'He doesn't want you Morag.' Rose was finding her inner strength, that inner stubborn and fiery part of her, unable to back down even though sense told her to be submissive. She had let this woman rule her life for too long and was choosing the worst possible time to rile her.

'He does… Rob just sometimes gets distracted…I know there have been others… You're not the first whore he took to bed… Like the rest, he will end it with you and come back to me, like he always does.'

'Then why are you here? If you are so convinced that he will leave me and come back to you, then why do you even need to do this?' Rose snapped, anger replacing fear and pig-headed rage at how much the woman ruined everything, kicking in to push logic aside.

'Shut up… Shut up!' Morag clawed at her head a moment, trying to clear her racing thoughts, looking deranged and uncontrolled. Rose could see the mental turmoil reflected in her face. 'He gave you his mother's ring… You're a clever little witch, aren't you? Wonder how you swung that one?' She jabbed at the air again with the sharp tool, turning it so the light reflected across it's width in a terrifying way before bringing her focus back to Rose.

'He loves me Morag… Really loves me… He doesn't love you.' Rose lifted her chin defiantly, refusing to be a victim even if this was to be her last moment in life.

'What the fuck would you know …. You have no idea about the love we share. If you did you wouldn't be hanging on like some sad desperate puppy with your fucking doe eyes. Can you not see how pathetic you are?'

Rose held her tongue, wondering if Morag was really talking about Rose at all. Her clearly unstable state hinted that she was talking about herself and delusional about it.

'If I left he would come after me Morag, and you know it.' Rose knew this for certain and knowing he was coming soon to save her had strengthened her resolve to keep her talking. 'He's on his way, he will see what you are doing and he will hate you for it. You have no idea what this will do to your relationship with him. He will never forgive this.'

'No… He fucking won't…He will understand…He always understands!' She jabbed the knife in the air menacingly and once again rubbed her face as though trying to get control. She was all over the place, her voice and tone up and down, her moods shifting from sorry to cruel and then anger and back to sadness.

The flash of headlights through the cottage indicated Rob had arrived, relief swept through Rose's body as she cried out for him, not caring if Morag tried to silence her. Breathlessly at first, but then screaming on him frantically, bringing her hands up defensively as Morag lurched at her, attempting to quiet her by holding the knife to her throat and gripping her by the hair. Rose tried to push her hand away, trembling at the realisation of what Morag intended to do to her. Rose again cried out, determined to alert him.

Rob would be in the house by now, he had to be, he had to know that she was here. Feeling the grip tighten harder and finally causing her to hush. That sharp point pressing into her skin, biting at her neck with its coldness and causing her heart to stop in her chest.

Rob heard the cries from the door and burst through. Searching in the darkness and coming to a halt at the kitchen door, the moonlight showing him enough to stop him in his tracks. His powerful form taking up the doorframe but Morag had a tight grip on Rose. Still heaped on the floor, unable to move with the crouching form of Morag leaning over her, backing her into the corner. The woman was clutching at Rose's shoulder now with one hand and the other holding the point of a large knife at Rose's neck. Morag turned her face towards him, eyes flashing like a demon.

'Morag?' Rob's hands went up, palms forward defensively, his face changing from sheer despair to that instant mask of coolness that appeared when he was in crisis clean up mode. 'Just put down the knife.'

'Go away Rob. Go away!' She screamed at him and Rose shuddered as the knife moved further up her neck scraping her flesh like a burning poker. She closed her eyes tight for a moment, afraid that it would descend into her throat and squirming back to try and put distance between her and it. Rob moved back, still holding his hands up as though trying to show her he would make no sudden movements, his eyes never leaving Rose.

'You don't want to do this Morag! You don't want to throw away your life by doing something you would never be able to live with.' His voice was unsteady, despite his calm demeanour. Rose could barely make out his face but she could tell he was trying to keep his head together and to her, he sounded afraid.

'You think this is what I wanted?' She screamed at him. 'That this is what I planned?' Morag was sobbing through her anger, her voice crackling and her body vibrating.

'Just put it down and we can talk. Please. I'm begging you.' He was desperately trying to make out Rose's face in the dark, his eyes barely able to see anything more than their outlines and forms and the shining metal of the blade at her throat.

'I came here to talk… To her! ' She motioned with the knife at Rose, moving it away from her neck and waving it in the air like a pointer. A tiny wave of relief ran through Rose's body as she tried to edge away, but the grip on her shoulder tightened. Hauling her back to Morag's side brutally and making it clear she wasn't done with her yet.

'Why? It's me who you should be angry with.'

'I wanted to see her… Tell her to leave you alone! … You were not listening to me, Rob. I didn't plan this. Any of this! I was hurt… I was angry with you… I just needed to see her…Warn her off…' The woman let out another sob and rubbed her sleeve across her face childishly, sniffing hard.

'Morag, please. Just let her go. Look at me. Talk to me. We can fix this together, you don't need to involve her.' Rob edged forward slowly, his voice softening as he tried to get through Morag's hazy clouded logic.

'LIAR!' She spat angrily and pushed him to move back again, afraid that angering her would mean she turned back on Rose, now she had the knife turned at him.

'Rose isn't the person you want to hurt. It's me you're angry with. Me that you should be pointing that at.' His voice was shaking, his emotions on the brink of collapse as nerves and the sheer impact of this scene hit him. Morag let go of Rose's shoulder, rubbing her eyes dramatically with the freed hand.

Rose, seeing her moment, pulled away, crawling along the cupboards at speed against the units out of reach of her grip, the sharp point still stuck in mid-air between her and him. Blocking her escape so all she could do was sit out of reach, poised and ready to run as soon as she got a chance. Morag seemed oblivious to Rose's almost escape, so focused on Rob and glaring at him with a broken heart.

'You know what I got this morning Rob¿ Morag laughed through tears and gritted teeth. She sounded so detached from the various versions of Morag that she didn't seem real at all. 'A fucking letter!…Informing me that you're taking steps to get out a restraining order against me… Warning me off… Telling me to stay away from you.' She broke down crying again, clutching at her hair. 'After everything, we have been through together… Fifteen years, Rob! Every god damn thing I have been through and the one person I trust most, cuts me loose. Warns me away?…WHY???' She screeched at him.

'I'm sorry Morag. It was wrong. It was stupid. I just wanted you to understand that I wanted it all to stop, that things couldn't keep going on this way. I was tired of this never-ending cycle we go through.' He sounded genuine, reaching out with his hand as though gesturing her to come to him, looking inviting. His voice was steady but betraying the panic and emotion in the undertones and the way his gaze kept flicking to where Rose crouched, checking her every second to see she was okay. He was trying to placate Morag and get his girl the hell away from her. 'It all got out of hand, you were behaving erratically. Making threats. I didn't know how else to handle you anymore.'

'You are stupid!' She spat viciously. 'You had everything I could offer. All of me! You just pushed it away again and again and for what? For that!' She pointed the blade at Rose again, causing her to lift her hands instinctively and Rob impulsively moved forward and then back again when Morag spun her head to face him with a sneer.

Rose's own face wet with tears, a hot thick liquid had made its way down her skin on the left side, her eye stinging with its invasion and making everything blurry on that side.

'Morag, please. If you're using her to hurt me, then I'm right here. You hurting her is the same as sticking that knife right here.' He thumped his hand on his chest over his heart. 'So why not just do it? If I'm the one you want to punish then leave her alone and turn that blade on me.'

Rose shook her head, unable to formulate any words, panic searing her heart. Her head shaking involuntarily.

No Rob, please.

But Morag just cried out

'NOOOOOO!… I love you!… I don't want to hurt you… I want you to do to her what you did to me. I want you to come back to me and forget you ever met her.' She was shaking wildly, the knife swaying once more and her body giving up on her, sliding down from kneeling to sagging.

'I never wanted to hurt you Morag. I didn't choose to fall in love. It just happened.' Rob moved closer, gently stepping, small easy movements but she felt his closeness and panicked. Screaming out and grabbing for Rose again, managing to catch the fabric of her hooded top and yanking her a tiny bit closer. Rob froze, sliding back calmly, keeping her eyes on him.

'You think I just woke up one day and wanted to throw you aside. You were my friend, someone I cared about. I knew you needed me. I just couldn't do it anymore...I was weak and I let you down.' He soothed, his manner calm and genuine.

'I need you more than she ever could!' Morag reverted to quiet tears, hands shaking once more and the knife drooping before her.

'Maybe that's true Morag... Maybe you're right... But it's not about her needing me. It's about ME needing her.' He was gaining control of his voice, the fear being replaced with strength and conviction, a new tactic as he saw her resolve beginning to crumble. 'And if you do something to take her from me, I'll never recover. I'll never come back to you Morag. Even if she was gone. Even if she chose to leave me. I would never forgive you... I would blame you for an eternity and hate you for it.'

Morag's hand began to shake, the knife waving in the air between the two women.

'Why couldn't you just love me enough?' Her tone was lowering, her screams now soft sobs as reality seemed to come back to her and his words had started to filter through.

'I tried Morag, I tried to be who you needed. I tried to love you the way you wanted all these years. But I couldn't. I tried to help you instead, but all I did was keep you like this.'

She shook her head at him, watching him from her slumped shape on the floor and crying dejectedly. Rose held her breathe, seeing the woman losing her violent rage and becoming more submissive.

'If I had let you move on. If I had made a clean break and allowed you to accept we were over Morag, I don't think we would be here now.' Rob shrugged, moving into the room a little, very slowly and carefully.

'You're wrong.' The fight was draining from the woman and Rose feeling braver was trying to edge forward towards Rob as he motioned her with a nod. The knife held loosely just out of reach from either of them but not being held aloft anymore.

'I'm not wrong Morag, if I hadn't kept picking up the pieces, kept coming back into your life over and over. Torturing you and stopping you from ever moving on, then where would you be now?'

'You just needed time to forgive me. We were good together and I ruined it all with lies.' Her gaze on the floor was now at her own feet, silently sobbing.

'Morag the reason you felt you had to lie about the baby, was that even then, you knew I didn't love you that way. You knew I would do the right thing by you. Ask you to marry me, even though deep down you had known for a long time I no longer looked at you like that. I was stuck in a relationship with you because of guilt and for one drunken night, a sense of duty.' Rob extended a hand in Rose's direction, urging her to keep moving towards him and trying to get close enough to intervene if Morag saw her.

'Stop it' Morag was silently crying, her shoulders lifting with every shuddering breath and looking completely spent.

'I wasn't what you needed. I just stood in the way of letting you see what you needed. Stood in the way of you going out and finding your own life. I was the problem!'

The woman cried out in anguish, tears falling fast and thick, shaking her head but unable to argue. Rose paused mid crawl, fear biting down once more and afraid to move another inch. Rob paused too, eyes widening and waiting to see what would happen, taking another sliding step closer.

'You're always what I need. I don't know how to go on without you!' Morag sobbed loudly, still her eyes on the floor.

'I don't want to be in your life anymore Morag. I want a life of my own. A life with Rose… I'm sorry, but that's how it is, all of this has just proven how toxic I am in your life.'

There was a pained stretched silence. Morag motionless, letting his words filter through her foggy brain as she sat silently staring. The tears falling fast down her cheeks and dripping onto her shirt. The knife fell from her fingers silently, clanging to the ground as she broke down, giving into the overwhelming pain with a release of sound that closely resembled a wail.

'I never wanted to hurt her.' She cried, falling down onto the floor face first, her hands following to the ground as she curled up into a ball and wept desperately.

Rose grabbed the cold sharp weapon from the floor where it had fallen and moved forward like lightning into his outstretched arms. She threw it away from them into the lounge to the side of him and burst into tears. It slid loudly under the couch out of sight as he pulled her against him breathlessly, turning her away from Morag's crumpled body and shielding her. Crushing her against him with a force that almost winded her, he pulled her back, his hands searching her body and face for wounds, his face searching hers, asking if she was hurt.

Forehead to forehead, as he inhaled loudly, the sweeping sound of relief that he had her in his arms and she could feel his body trembling now, his breathing shallow. His shoulders heaving as he tried to regain control. She had never seen him so scared, kissing her firmly and pulling her towards him in another bear hug as though she might disappear at any second and again returning to checking her over for signs of injury almost frantically.

Rose felt her knees go weak and the blood draining entirely from inside her. The acute relief at being safe, suddenly sweeping over her.

He kept pulling her away, desperate to keep assuring himself that she was okay and scanning her body again and again, sure there was a concealed injury that he was missing, returning her to his chest every few seconds, needing to hold her close and protect her. She could see his face clearer now, the moonlight shining from the window to the side of them, directly on his tense features, his eyes full of tears and emotion and his hands shaking.

'It's going to be okay baby, I've got you. I'm here now .... It's over.' He murmured, soothing words, for both their benefit, soft and hoarse, almost a whisper. Stroking her face and arms, kissing her forehead and calming both of them. He pushed her behind him protectively, turning and looking down at the woman on the floor who was now a sodden mass of pathetic weeping, completely oblivious to anything around her. Rob Pulled out his phone and pressing 111, he handed it to Rose to take; she just stood mutely trying to reel in her mind, automatically putting it to her ear but she was not really listening. Shock taking over in place of adrenaline.

Rob moved forward slowly, stepping over the frail and pathetic heap on the tiles where Morag sobbed manically; no longer a threat to anyone. Lost in her own pain and reality, that everything around her had finally crumbled to ashes. He flicked the light switch on. illuminating the mess of the kitchen, the broken torn up dishes and pans and scattering of utensils. The chaos of having everything in sight thrashed around by hands clutching in the darkness. It looked like there had been a tornado of destruction and it brought physical pain to Rose's heart to see it all now. Turning to the knife block, Rob picked up the whole thing and moved it up high to the overhead units, where Morag could never reach them. He took the ones from the dish rack and placed them up beside them, clearing the kitchen of anything Morag could use to repeat the attack.

It was obvious she was spent and wouldn't have the ability, but it was making Rob feel calmer; having a focus. Stopping to rub his hands across his face and through his hair and pull himself together, inhaling deeply again, taking steadying breaths and regaining calm control. Turning, he looked at Rose in the light of the electric bulb, his face crumbling instantly as he saw her for the first time in proper light. He crossed the room in quick strides and pulled her face close to his. Rose was still numbly holding his phone to her ear, oblivious of anyone on the other end.

'Shit baby.' He pulled up his t-shirt, holding the soft fabric to her face and pressing it against the blood trickling down, it was almost at her cheek now. She could feel its warm descent. His eyes tracing her swollen bruised lips, bruised face and tear stained cheeks. Cursing under his breath repeatedly, eyes filled with a look of anguish and anger tearing him apart. He was struggling to keep control, the urge to turn on Morag evident in the tense set of his jaw and deep angry frown.

'I'm okay.... It's worse than it looks.' Rose cleared her throat, her voice was weak and trembling and barely audible but Rob pulled her back into his arms.

Rob could hear the voice coming from the phone, asking her which service and realised she was oblivious to anything right now, shock setting in. He took it from her, looking down at the pitiful sight on the floor cruelly, lost in its own mind and heartbreak. He felt nothing but hatred for her now, all sense of empathy had died the second she had done the one thing that would forever make him hate her. She had dared to hurt his Rose.

He asked for police and ambulance.

Chapter 42

Rose stood overlooking the fields and the forest below the window, the back of the cottage shining in the early light. She no longer cringed at the sight of the tiny building nestled among the trees and foliage. The feelings of anxiety and panic had subsided finally and of late the nightmares had faded away into peaceful slumber again most nights. That night had affected her more than she could ever have guessed and the weeks following in a torrent of anxiety and emotion, afraid to leave Rob's side, afraid to be alone. She had been jumpy and paranoid, an emotional wreck who could barely sleep and convinced attackers were always lurking in the shadows waiting for her.

The counsellor had assured her that it was normal, she had been through something traumatic and it had affected her on many levels. Rob had squeezed her hand through every session, unable to even be alone to talk to a therapist and needing him more than ever to make her feel safe.

Rob was strong and patient, ever understanding of what she was going through. Holding her close whenever he saw her waver, always gentle with her, despite her moods and erratic tears. Taking as much time away from work as he could to calm her frayed nerves, reassure her and help her slowly settle back into a life and routine. He had been on edge too, for weeks, unable to rest easy without her by his side and always checking in on her almost obsessively. He had taken her on every business trip that he could, she had finally had her weekend in the French villa and it had done them a power of good. He would brush away shadows in the corners for her, leaving lights on at night even when he was laid by her side, always there, close enough to protect her, should she falter.

She had not stepped foot in that cottage again for months, letting him take control of its maintenance and clean up. The first time she had tried, an overwhelming wave of nausea had overtaken her; a severe panic attack. She had felt as though she was being strangled, her heart crashing and clawing to get out. Her vision had begun to blacken and he had picked her up, taken her outside into the air, helped her bend down to catch her breath and push the panic back down again.

She had been stubborn, despite that episode, steeled in her decision that she wouldn't let Morag do this to her. Persistent and walking down there with Muffin and Rob a few times and always the same feelings arose within her. She had finally been able to open that door and walk in without falling apart when her emotional scars had begun to heal. Able to look around and feel a tinge of that affection for the place returning, slowly. Spending longer moments at every visit and frequently wandering down there with Rob, knowing how important it was that she overcame her fear of being there.

Rob had gone straight back into overdrive, securing the manor for her, making all the changes he had planned and then some, just so she could sleep easier at night within the manor walls. Not that it had been necessary anymore; Morag was gone. But he needed to feel like he was doing more to protect her; it was as much for his healing as hers. She had been thankful of the fortress he built around them, it had in a way, eased her into recovery quicker. The security of living within safe walls and fences, camera's and intercoms that made access to her near impossible, unless they were invited.

Morag was far away now; she had been committed to a long term psychiatric ward after the court case, pending assessments and treatments and deferring jail time. The judge, seeing a woman with deep emotional issues and a traumatic history thanks to her solicitor who had painted a heart-breaking picture, took pity on her.

Morag had a long history of mental illness, inherited from a mother who had been inflicted with the same pain and suffering. She had committed suicide when Morag was only seven years old and had been the one to find her, blue and contorted on the bathroom floor, foaming at the mouth from the cocktail of drugs she had ingested; a sight no little girl should ever have to endure. Morag had then been left alone after that, to an abusive alcoholic father who mentally, sexually and physically abused her. Always silent about what he was doing, afraid it would make it worse, she had given birth to a premature stillborn at the age of fourteen alone in the woods. It had rendered her unable to conceive children, a fact even Rob seemed shocked to hear in that echoing courtroom, knowing that the lie about a baby, years before, had run far deeper. The solicitor had gone on to explain that after giving birth to a still born, premature, she had hidden the body by burying it in the hills surrounding her family home.

Her father had finally been jailed years later when, still abusing her, when she had found the courage to speak out. With the support of a man she had fallen in love with, Rob Munro, he had given her the courage and strength to finally to end the agony with his support. Rose had looked up at him at that point, his face still and deadpan while he listened to the story being laid out and her heart swelled at what she was learning, who the man she was marrying had been, even from an early age, and understood more than ever why he had tried to hide their relationship at first.

Morag had attempted suicide in her early twenties, Rose knowing that this had been when Rob had broken things off with her which had resulted in a long hospital stay and continuous mental health support since. She had been diagnosed with an array of mental health issues, most of which required medication that made her feel groggy and unable to carry on with a normal life. Affecting everything she did and she often made the bad decision to stop her treatments in a bid to feel more lucid. Her only constant support had been her friend Mr Munro. The nearing of his wedding to the victim, Miss Turner, causing her a complete breakdown and anguish at the loss of the only stable thing in her life. She had lost control of her faculties, pushed by heartbreak and anguish and had not meant for things to get out of control in that way.

It had given Rose more insight, pity and sorrow for her, than she had ever thought she could feel. Looking at her pale dishevelled frame across the silent room, she had seen only despair. A woman locked inside her own head, her own prison cell of agony and torture. She had felt pained at the hopelessness in her eyes and that deep understanding of why Rob had always felt compelled to try and save her. She looked like a wounded unloved animal that so desperately just wanted to find someone to love and take care of her. But Rose could never forgive her for hurting Muffin.

Rob sat motionless, barely taking his eyes from Morag throughout the defence speech. Unreadable, no sign of anything except indifference. Morag had made the one mistake that she could not take back. She had harmed Rose and lost every last ounce of feeling he ever had for her, she had made him sever compassion and he was watching her as though he didn't know her at all. He was only here to make sure she was punished for it; he didn't feel empathy or sorrow for her anymore.

The judge had not sent her to jail for the crimes of which she had been found guilty. Aggravated Assault, taking a hostage, Unlawful use of a weapon. Attempted murder of Muffin. The police had piled a list of charges against her that mostly sounded ridiculous, but instead, she had been sent for evaluation and help and was going to be where she needed to be. It was far, far away. Chosen by her defence in a bid to separate her from the people and surroundings that were fuelling her ongoing misery, the judge had agreed.

Rose had felt nothing but heartbreak for her as she had watched her lifeless cold face in the courtroom when the judge made his speech, the way her eyes lingered on Rob as she was being taken away by uniformed men. Devoid of any signs of life and just broken. Rob had turned to Rose, away from her gaze and slid his arm around her, pulling her temple against his mouth and kissing her lingeringly.

A last message, or an act of cruelty?

Maybe relief that she would finally be gone. Rose had watched the woman go, that look haunting her for days after, seeing her in her mind's eye and remembering nothing but the look of complete devastation.

In her absence, Morag had instructed her own solicitor to sell her house and car and she had them inform Rob that he no longer had to worry about her. That she was sorry for everything she had done and knew she would never be a part of his life or future ever again. Rob shrugged the man away, told him he did not want to hear it and tried to shuffle Rose quickly out of the court room, a protective arm around her, but he held out a letter to Rose as they did so.

To Rose, it was an apology letter that Rose never read, never opened and never kept. Rose had burned it in the fire of their bedroom when they had gotten home, Rob standing silently by with no resistance.

Rob had received a long thin envelope on legal stationary weeks after the trial, word from her lawyer that she intended to make a life away from here when she was finally well enough to be released and handed in her resignation at the museum, not that it had been needed. He had already relinquished her duties to a new museum curator who was turning the old building into a much more attractive place to visit. Rob was still donating money as he got things underway and things were looking promising for the old relic.

Morag was finally choosing to walk out of his life. Letting him go. Letting them move on with theirs to finally be able to focus on just them. To put all the endless mess, heartache, drama, and confusion to bed, finally.

The manor was finally complete. She knew Rob had pressed the contractors to work fast and he had her mind occupied with fabric swatches, paint charts and trips to an endless array of home decor boutiques for weeks in a bid to help her. They made a start on other parts of the house too, bringing some cosy and modern touches to its vast emptiness. Keeping her busy, motivated and distracted. It had helped. The focus on something other than her over active imagination and paranoia was a welcome relief and she could go hours without dwelling on any of it.

Muffin had recovered fully, no long-term damage and was soon running about wildly like his old little self. Helping to heal her heart. Rose had been right, something Rob never stopped apologising for and glad that Muffin had pulled through. The court case had revealed how the other woman had left poisoned meat in the garden in a bid to hurt the little animal and get at Rose. A sadistic move to inflict the same pain on her that Morag felt she was going through herself and a bid to try and scare her to leave the village. Premeditated and just a shocking reality of how far down that road of mental illness Morag had slipped. Rob had looked ashen in court for the first time, shaking his head in bewilderment and staring at her with eyes that seared. He didn't know who she was anymore; he had been in minor shock at the admission and it had only pushed him further into his hatred for her.

Rose took a sabbatical from her work, but finally a few weeks ago she had picked up a paintbrush and began to work her magic on watercolour paper. The peace of mind and tranquillity returning enough to let her enjoy the process once again. Her mind was happy to settle on the task in hand once more and her agent had been thrilled. Always encouraging and ever understanding. She was healing, she was finally back to being more like the Rose they all missed.

* * *

She smoothed her hand over her satin dress and the warmness of her stomach, feeling that usual surge of satisfaction and happiness as she admired the scene before her. She loved standing here looking at this view when the world was just waking up. It brought her so much peace and tranquillity now. Something that this place had been lacking lately.

Hearing Rob's voice from the doorway, she turned to smile at him fondly. He too was already dressed, knowing they had a lot to do before the ceremony and was best to get themselves organised first. His pale grey suit bringing out the soft grey in his eyes today; his eyes mostly stayed this soft light colour nowadays, a sign that he was more relaxed and very happy; except when they fought. Sometimes she felt like she started small squabbles just to see that darkening storm once more. Fascinated by it.

He was looking at her the same way he always did, that unreadable expression that made it that no one ever knew what he was thinking. But she knew. Unlike the days when she could never read him, she had finally mastered the inner workings of his head. He was thinking about getting her naked again and dragging her back into the bathtub like he had earlier this morning. He was as looking as devastatingly handsome as ever, moving towards her as he tapped his watch, gesturing that they needed to go. His hands slid around her waist and rested across the gentle curve of her abdomen. Smoothing down the same part of her dress she had previously touched.

'You look beautiful.' He nuzzled in against her, his face coming to the side of hers.

'You look handsome.' She replied, sliding her own hands over his and squirming a tiny little bit closer to him. She felt his mouth on her neck, his hand moving up to brush her hair aside and give him full access and began to laugh gently at his obvious amore.

'Rob? if you start this again, we will never leave this room.' She moved him back, allowing her space to turn and reached up to his mouth, accepting a slow tender kiss.

'I'm pretty sure you wouldn't mind.' He had that familiar twinkle in his eye; Rose gently pushed his stomach playfully, aware that he was right and slid past him to walk past her desk and head to the door.

Her latest artwork was propped ceremoniously in view, she glanced at it, a warm feeling filling her with pride. It was the first of her illustrations that would be used in a book of stories written by Hamish Munro. He had surprised them all with a declaration some months ago he wanted to write, leave a legacy for his grandchildren. But he didn't want to write just anything. He wanted to tell stories of the 'Princess of the North' who had travelled far and wide to break an evil curse, battled a serpent-like dragon and saved the sleepy castle from a crumbling spell. Awakening the hero from a horrible love potion to set him free. His humour always present and the irony not lost on them all. It had not surprised Rob that Rose's painting of her 'Princess' had a halo of long dark brown hair and flowing gold gowns. Her steed a pink unicorn with a little white fluffball as her sidekick!

Hamish now resided back in the manor and a part of their busy life. A welcome presence every day, he was always around to help run things and take some of the manor duties off of Rose's shoulders. He helped with the mundane, such as keeping the grounds organised and helped Rob when the business was causing him stress. Hamish had found new life once more and was loving being part of a busy family again. Just the addition of Rose and Muffin to this house had seen a transformation already, more staff, small changes to the house, more events at the weekends in the ballroom that brought the community here once more and he was lapping it all up and loving being the chairman of many community clubs. Rob glanced at her piece on the table, smiling and straightening it gently, proud of his wife and proud of his father.

Taking one last look around her bright studio, she closed the door behind him as he walked out, moving along the narrow hall into their bedroom. The soft, modern room, cosy and homely, where they spent a lot of their time nowadays, locked away together in the solace. Muffin was curled asleep on one of the long comfy couches in the sitting area, to the far side away from the bed, nestled in front of the low burning gas fire, set in the massive brick hearth which was warming the room to the perfect temperature. Cold days had begun to move away again but the air still held a tinge of frost and they kept this fire on most of the time to give the rooms a homely feel.

They finally descended the main stairs, taking in the chaos of the people running around, staff awaiting orders. The caterer was looking about ready to throttle her hired waiters for the day and a young girl approached Rose with a floral display, asking where it was to be placed in the main entrance. Rob left her to go perform her duties as 'Lady of the Manor'. The house buzzing was with excitement and it didn't take Rose long to tend to the questions and needs of the never-ending stream of people moving through the hall to the ball room and back. Basking in their congratulations and small hugs, she had begun to get used to this, the demands and the responsibilities. Being treated like a celebrity by everyone, lately, she could take it in her stride.

Rob disappeared into his office, pulling out his speech and sorting through some final business papers in the few minutes of calm before the storm. It wouldn't be long before they had to be at the church and already this morning it had been jam packed with things needing to be done. The hours ticking away.

Rose tended to Abby amid a group of hairdressers, giggling girls and makeup artists and helped her get ready. Alice was mid-meltdown over the chaos and mucky feet on the marble floor and was running around with a dust buster trying to keep it all clean and sparkly. Barking orders at her new apprentice housekeepers and ordering them to smooth down their uniforms and aprons. Tommy brought round the car as Rob ordered and people were milling around with final touches and last-minute orders.

The house was always brimming nowadays, the new house keepers under Alice's fretful command were being barked at and ordered to stop getting under her feet now, the air of panic at the approaching hour and there was a sense of urgency and simmering chaos in the air.

Rose felt calm in the middle of the tornado, cloaked in a bubble of happiness that was drowning out the noise to a bearable hum. Looking around now at the pulsing atmosphere and the eager faces, she felt the excitement rise. It was going to be an amazing day.

* * *

The church was stunningly beautiful, soft piano music drifting towards them as small flower girls littered the aisle with petals and confetti. Rose felt emotion tug at her throat, watching them as tears filled her eyes. Rob's hand in hers tightened, showing he felt the same way and she squeezed it back. Catching his eye to smile wholeheartedly.

Hamish appeared at the door, handsome in his kilt, sliding his hand into the awaiting crook of the blushing brides awaiting arm and began to bring her forward. Tears evident on both of their faces. He leant down to kiss her cheek before he led the way more purposely, muttering words about her beauty into the hushed room and elegant aisle. The sweep of her gown as they began to ascend was heard in the complete silence as she moved into the room, a breath-taking sight. The hushed tones of the small gathering inside the crammed room began as she walked in, held securely in Hamish's strong arm and compliments could be heard being uttered all around. She truly looked stunning.

Soft music began to sway over them from a speaker in the far corner, only adding to the beautiful atmosphere and the romance of this very moment, Rose held her breath, her throat aching with emotion. It was magical.

There were more people outside who could not fit in, straining heads in the open doors to see and once again hushed silence as she moved in time to the beautiful soft music.

Abby looked stunningly beautiful. The ivory dress accentuating her peachy blushed skin and green glittering eyes, swept up hair in her long lace veil made her look so young and innocent, so ethereal. Everyone looking at her was mesmerised to how beautiful a bride she made and Duncan could barely conceal his emotion as he stood at the altar.

Rob leant in, his arm around Rose's waist and kissed her lightly on the back of her exposed shoulder, both of them warmed by the memory of their own wedding several weeks before. The memory of its perfection still bringing goosebumps to her skin as Abby's father walked her towards the man who would now be her partner and protector in life. Rose felt a huge surge of deepest pride and emotion, almost the feeling one would have for a sister getting married. Abby and Duncan looked perfect together.

Duncan was overcome with emotion completely when she reached him, unable to tear his gaze from his blushing bride and stop the tears forming. His normally soft face a little rosy and unsure, fear that he would wake up and find all of this was nothing more than a dream. He looked tall and handsome, his large upper form skimmed in tailored black and sporting a traditional kilt with his family tartan. The room hushed, listening intently to the beautiful words through their vows and the magic of the ceremony.

* * *

The hall was alive and bustling with the guests chattering animatedly, the meal had been served and cutlery and chinking glasses filled the air with a messy kind of harmony. A hum of conversation and low music in the air. Rose couldn't help but glance towards the newlyweds along the table, their love for each other obvious as Duncan tried to feed Abby some of his food in a hopeless romantic way. Unaware of the eyes on them and warm smiles they were receiving.

Rose arched her back lightly, feeling that familiar strain and lower pain and sighing loudly as she tried to release the pressure a little. Rob's hand immediately went to her back and he smoothed it down instinctively, massaging it lightly, finding the source of her discomfort with practised hands.

'You okay? Do you need to go lay down?' The concern in his voice made her love him even more than she already did.

'I'm fine. Just stiff from sitting here.' She smiled at him, relaxing forward in the chair as he rubbed out the knots in her lower back.

'We could go for a walk in the garden. Let you stretch out and get some air.' He was frowning at her, always overly concerned with her welfare and it only made her smile.

'Honestly I'm fine… I'll just be glad when this is no longer in my way.' She pointed down at the bulging belly below her, feeling that surge of protective instinct and running her hand over the bump affectionately. His hand moved up to caress it too, stopping with a smile at the familiar flicker and lurch under the skin of a kick. His eyes full of pride and warm emotion.

'She's going to be like her mother.' He raised his eyebrows, smiling widely. 'Already a kicker.'

'More like her fiery aunt Abby!' Rose laughed. 'Seriously Rob, I'm okay.' She reached up, running finger tips across his face and trying to smooth away that concerned frown. 'She's not due for a few weeks yet silly.'

He had been treating her with kid gloves lately, even more so since she had taken that pregnancy test that morning. Her 'sickness bug' lingering for way longer than most bugs lasted. Feeling tired and emotional for days on end and reacting irrationally over the smallest tiny things. They had put it down to the emotional strain she had still been feeling at first, but the sudden need to start eating weird food concoctions had started Alice raising the suspicion. Particularly the morning she had almost run to the fridge in desperation for pickled onion juice.

They had sat tensely in the bathroom, waiting on that stick to change colour, neither talking, sitting facing each other, him on the bath edge and her on the toilet seat. Their wedding up in the air and mid-planned at that time, unsure if she was going to need a bigger dress. Unsure if they needed to move the dates forward or back, neither sure they were even ready for this little surprise. When Rob turned it over, grabbing at the box to check the result chart on the back, he broke into a huge grin, all doubts and uncertainty erased in one final sweeping realisation he was about to become a father. Scooping her up and swinging her around the bathroom, which of course had resulted in her sudden need to throw up. Rose had been reeling in shock and it had taken her far longer than him to come to terms with it.

Here they were now. Weeks of hormonal tears, tantrums, smiles and crazy cravings, that had him out at two am in the morning fetching her food sporadically. Proudly obvious, happily married and almost nearing the arrival of their unexpected baby. Their surprise little miracle. Rose could not have planned this life but she couldn't have asked for it to be any more perfect.

When the staff were moving tables and clearing the dancefloor, her parents appeared, the same clucking and fluffing around her that Rob annoyingly displayed.

Did she need a seat? A walk? A cushion? Did she make sure not to eat any of the seafood at dinner? Or the peanuts? Did she want to take a nap or put her feet up? Her mother could come sit with her. Rob could give her a message if her back was sore. Her dad could fetch her some fruit juice. Or a footstool.

For the love of god!

They were driving her slowly mad, but she knew they all meant well and the irritation had long subsided, replaced with heavy sighs. Complacent with this temporary reality, she would have to get used to this now.

Her parents were in the planning stage of selling their house to move here. The cottage a good place to settle in while they looked for a home of their own in the surrounding land, one with room for many grandchildren. They had already been working on Rob, convincing him that siblings should be born close in age and all in a row; obviously the more the merrier so when they grew up Rose and he could have an early retirement, still young enough to enjoy life. It had made her grimace when she had seen him agreeing and cast him a warning look and a haughty glare.

Let her get through this one pregnancy first and at least try her hand at motherhood before planning on knocking her right back up.

Her parents wanted to be close. They wanted to see the children grow up. They wanted to help and have a part in the lives of the future mini Munro's.

Rob pulled her close for the first slow dance after Abby and Duncan graced the floor. A romantic melody the new couple had chosen, locked eye to eye, arms entwined and lost only in the closeness of each other. Rose slid easily into Rob's strong arms, a practised motion, as natural as breathing, her head leaning against his shoulder and sighing contentedly. Turning her belly slightly to the side so she could lean into him.

'I love you Mr Munro.' She sighed happily and almost sunk her full weight into him.

'I love you more, Mrs Munro.' He kissed her on top of her head tenderly.

'Doubtful!… I know I have been a hormonal maniac lately.'

Rob lifted her chin with his finger and moved down to gently kiss her mouth tenderly, that ever surge of heat between them threatening to raise up even here on the dancefloor even when surrounded by family and friends.

'It's kept thinks interesting, kept me on my feet and never bored honey.'

Rose reached up, kissing him again, this time with more purpose, his first grazing of lips had ignited her fire and she wanted more satisfaction than just affectionate kisses. She kissed him seductively and he responded willingly, a soft moan escaping from her throat as she moved against him a little more intently. He pulled away, his eyes beginning to twinkle with amusement, clouding his own desire and smiling widely at her.

'Surely not Rose?' He frowned good humouredly and brought his nose down to meet hers, laughing softly at her eternally high libido lately.

'I can't help it.' She laughed. 'It's the hormones!' She shrugged and allowed her hand to smooth over that perfect six pack and up to those hard pecks a little more longingly.

'Woman! Lately, you have been insatiable. Even I'm struggling to keep up and that's really saying something!'

'Have I worn you out?' She looked mockingly concerned and just continued to let her hand wander over him.

'Nah, I'm made of sterner stuff than that.' He grinned once again, dropping a kiss on her lips. This time, she moved up to him, making it more passionate, insistent that she wanted more than just loving caresses.

'I should hope so.' She whispered, nudging him suggestively, her eyes pleading like a child.

'It's my sister's wedding!' Rob laughed again and shook his head softly, she could already tell she was winning, his arms moving around her firmly and eyes changing to more solid grey.

'Never stopped us before.' She grinned back. Both fully aware of sneaking off at their own wedding to fornicate in his old office wildly and loudly several weeks back. Like hunger starved maniacs after a bout of her inability to do anything but sleep or lay down in bed for weeks. Her morning sickness finally subsiding for the big day.

He looked around, trying to see how easy their exit would be amid a room of people who were way too interested in them.

'You're going to be the death of me.' He only half meant it and was already in the process of hatching an escape plan. Equally burning for her now and equally unable to push down the amount of lust burning through his blood, she ignited this response in him way too easily.

'Is that a yes?' She bit her lip seductively, raising an eyebrow as she watched his face cave. She knew that he would never turn her down, she had way more will power than him when it came to hot wild sex.

'Start a marriage as you mean to go on.' He winked, sliding her hand into his and turning from the floor. 'Maybe you should feign some sort of pregnant swoon, make it easier to get out unsuspiciously.' He glanced at her, looking her over speculatively.

'Why can't we just sneak away, like we always do?' Rose pouted. He glanced down again, this time at her round belly and raised obvious eyebrows.

'Not quite as nimble and easy to push into dark corners lately my love.' He grinned cheekily.

'Hey!' She mock slapped his arm. 'What are you saying? That I'm fat?' Rose frowned at him with a fierce look, not serious but not entirely joking either.

'Whoa! Don't put words in my mouth. Not fat baby. Never! Just fragile and keeping our baby warm, and not so quick at exits anymore when we want to go be naughty in dark rooms.'

Rose had to agree, it was hard not to waddle lately, she felt like her lower body was one huge round beach ball. She could barely see her toes anymore when she looked down and graceful manoeuvring was near impossible.

He led her across the hall, making small apologies to well-wishers, excusing his wife.

She needed to lay down, ahh yes, the baby was making her tired. Yup not long now to go. Yes, very excited about its arrival. Nope, no names picked yet.

Rose kept her mouth shut, sure she would give the game away or break into giggles at least, impatient and squeezing his hand to tell him to hurry up. The sea of people who always greeted the couple nowadays, the tidal wave of congratulations and warm hugs, only made Rose more frantic and horny. Pulling at him restlessly as the minutes wore on.

He was really trying to get them out of there but the place was mobbed and they still held celebrity status for these people. He cast her an apologetic look and finally managed to slide her into a locked room, far enough away from the party not to be heard and amazingly unseen.

'Finally!' She laughed, feeling his hands go to her hips and his mouth finding her easily, hitting her with a passionate kiss.

'Rose?'

'Hmmmm?' She was kissing his neck, pulling off his tie and unbuttoning his shirt absentmindedly. Impatient to feel him against her.

'Maybe I should leave this on.' He pointed down at his colourful kilt and sporran and she laughed.

'Maybe…Laird Munro. You should shut up and stop making me wait!'

How could he argue with that?

The End

Acknowledgements

There are so many people I could thank and list for the creation of this book, so many people I feel I really should thank, who have in some small ways contributed to my journey in writing a novel ready for print. But in doing so, I feel I would be dampening down my appreciation for the ones who really went above and beyond for me when I first set to task the first publishing of my very first book. So yes, I want to thank all of you who are in my life, who know who they are, for the patience and encouragement for without every one of you, this wouldn't have been such a seamless journey. However, I know that every one of you will understand my reasons for naming only a few.

So not to put more importance on one person than another, I will list them in the order in which they joined my writing journey.

To Ross, the long suffering other half of me, your patience, eye rolls and support started me off. From letting me write undisturbed for days on end, to enduring a messy house and microwave dinners, and no end to the lack of clean socks. To telling me you were proud and buying me a pc so I could write away from my desk! And No, you will still never get to read it, so eyes off!

To Jacqui Brough, my little blog bestie, who encouraged me from the moments of query when I raised interest in going back to writing, now that I was an adult with so much time to spare. You were the first to know my intentions, the first to read my raw chapters, as I fired them out, and encouraged me every single step of the way. You fell so hopelessly in love with my story that you gave me the confidence to keep going. You're my funny girl, my crazy nuts sister from another mother. Let's elope!

To Shirin Coglon and Grace Bell, my editors and chiefs, my crazy and strict mentors. You don't let me away with anything and you certainly do not let me away with bad writing. You have been my friends for years but my second hands for months, without your guidance and help I would still be looking at that manuscript and trying to figure out what to do with it. Your presence daily keeps me sane, your calming when I'm a whizzing out of control bag of impatience and you know how to offer critic with a grin. You're my shadows for life so get used to it, as I'm sewing us all together.

To my sister Melissa Marshall, the photographer extraordinaire, even though we didn't find the right time to shoot a cover with your skills, I see it being in our futures. You were one of my first fans, before you read a word and you are my eternal Beta Reader. You keep me inspired and you give me good gossip for future scenes!! Ha ha beware! You're the lovely girl who will forever push me to keep going, whether you realise it or not. One day we shall share a title, your pictures and my words and it will be perfection.

To my writing twin, Elle Harvey, for the never ending long chats, brainstorming and smiles. The endless bags of cakes and tea and the patience of a saint. We shared a journey into writing and even though we chose our own path in the books we have produced, it was that journey together which honed our skills and set us up as book buddies for life. You are the Yin to my Yang! We shall make that book tour to New York and share a pew one day.

To Jessica Meeks, my graphic designer and long-term friend. You made my book as beautiful as anyone could, your skills have always been second to none and I trust you with every design task I could ever dream up. You are the patient long suffering and smiling friend every girl like me needs. You are the secret weapon in my bag of tricks and may you long grace my life with your skills and smiles!

I cannot go on without a thank you to my parents Jim and Sylvia Marshall, for my first computer at seventeen and the encouragement to write, for understanding that staying up till 5 am pounding a keyboard was normal for a nocturnal creative and for never reading anything I wrote for fear of getting put on the naughty step. Please do not read this one either, I may never be able to look you in the eye again. Ha ha

There are more of you who have contributed in some way, to all of you - I thank you immensely, everyone made this book possible, everyone gave me a little bit more courage to pursue this and everyone made me push myself a little bit more.

Leanne xxx
(aka Lenny, Lee, Liana, Annie!)

For my team, we made it together and we finally did it! We're like the A team, only cuter and far more glamorous and our love of slippers beats black transit vans any day! Here's to the next one!

xxxxx

About the Author

L.T. Marshall was born and raised in Scotland, although moving around to various parts from the age of nine meant she was raised partly in the central belt, but considers the highlands her true home. She currently lives with her Fiancée and two children in the central belt, near Glasgow.

She has always been a creative soul, between drawing, painting, writing, and crafting. Her interests are varied and often non-related, she relishes variety and fun. She wrote her first novels in her very young teens but did not really pursue a serious career in writing until much later in life. She still runs a creative business named 'Liana Marcel' which developed a personality of its own online and continues to receive followers who purchase her hand crafted makes.

To find out more about Leanne please follow her on her social media, she can be found on Facebook, Twitter, Pinterest, Youtube and much more. She openly encourages reader interaction.

25165044R00306

Printed in Great Britain
by Amazon